# SLIGHTLY TEMPTED

Center Point
Large Print

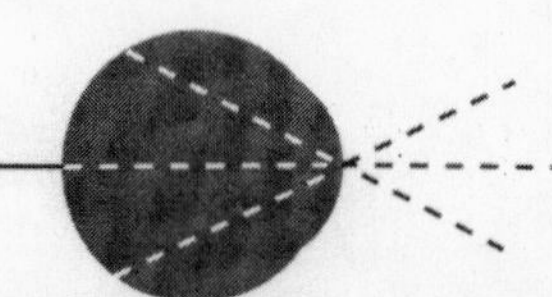

# Mary Balogh

# Slightly Tempted

Center Point Publishing
Thorndike, Maine

This Center Point Large Print edition
is published in the year 2004 by arrangement with
The Bantam Dell Publishing Group,
a division of Random House, Inc.



The text of this Large Print edition is unabridged. In other aspects, this book may vary from the original edition. Printed in Thailand. Set in 16-point Times New Roman type by Bill Coskrey and Gary Socquet.

ISBN 1-58547-425-8

Library of Congress Cataloging-in-Publication Data

Balogh, Mary.
Slightly tempted / Mary Balogh.--Center Point large print ed.
p. cm.
ISBN 1-58547-425-8 (lib. bdg. : alk. paper)
1. Great Britain--Fiction. 2. Nobility--Fiction. 3. Large type books. I. Title.

PR6052.A465S567 2004
823'.914--dc22

2003026082

# Chapter I

It still felt somewhat strange to be part of a gathering of the crème de la crème of English society again and to hear the English language spoken by virtually everyone. Not that the English were the only nationality present, it was true. There were also Dutch, Belgians, and Germans, among others. But the British predominated.

Gervase Ashford, Earl of Rosthorn, was standing just inside the ballroom doors at the house Viscount Cameron had leased on the Rue Ducale in Brussels, looking about him with considerable interest. He was searching for familiar faces. He had seen several since his recent arrival from Austria, but he expected to see more here. The vast majority of both ladies and gentlemen looked exceedingly young to him, though. He felt strangely ancient at thirty.

Most of those young gentlemen, and a few older ones too, wore military dress uniforms—some blue or green, but most scarlet and resplendent with rich facings and multitudes of gold lace braiding. Like peacocks, they outshone the ladies in their pastel-shaded, softly flowing, high-waisted gowns. But the ladies looked delicate and very feminine in contrast.

"One feels at a distinct disadvantage dressed even in one's very best civilian clothes, does one not?" the Honorable John Waldane said ruefully into Gervase's left ear—the buzz of a hundred voices or more all raised to be heard above the rest of the hubbub plus the sounds of the orchestra tuning their instruments more than occupied his right.

"If one came here with the intention of impressing the ladies, yes, I suppose so," Gervase admitted with a chuckle. "If one came to be an invisible observer, no."

At the moment he preferred to be as unobtrusive as possible. He still felt a little self-conscious around British people, wondering how much they remembered from nine years ago, and wondering too just how much there *was* for them to remember. Although there had been a few rather public scenes, he was not sure how much of that whole sordid business had become public knowledge. Waldane, who had been one of Gervase's acquaintances at the time and who had hailed him with the greatest amiability when they ran into each other two days ago, had made no reference to it. But, of course, the reputation Gervase had earned since then was undeniably notorious to anyone who had spent time on the Continent.

"Old Boney will probably be captured any day now and dragged back to Elba and kept in irons for the rest of his life if any of his guards have a brain in their heads," Waldane said. "These officers will no longer have an excuse to play at such gallantry or to dazzle the ladies with such a gorgeous display."

"Jealous?" Gervase chuckled again.

"Mortally." Waldane, slightly more portly than he had been nine years ago when Gervase last saw him, and balding at the crown of his thinning fair hair, laughed ruefully. "There are some ladies one might enjoy impressing."

“Are there?” Gervase raised his quizzing glass the better to see to the far side of the crowded ballroom. He recognized Lord Fitzroy Somerset, the Duke of Wellington’s military secretary, in conversation with Lady Mebs, and Sir Charles Stuart, British ambassador to the Hague. But his attention moved obligingly onto the young ladies, none of whom he could be expected to recognize—or feel any particular interest in if he did. His tastes did not run to the very young. “By Jove, you are right.”

His glass had paused on one member of Sir Charles’s group, who was even then turning half away from its other members in order to greet the approach of two young officers of the Life Guards, gorgeous in dazzling white net pantaloons, scarlet coats, blue facings, and gold lace—and dancing shoes instead of their cavalry boots.

She was a very young lady indeed—not long out of the schoolroom if his guess was correct. He would not perhaps have noticed her if Waldane had not set him to the task. But, having looked, he was forced to admit that sometimes one could draw sheer pleasure from simply gazing at extraordinary beauty.

He was gazing at it now.

She was really quite outstandingly lovely, the more so perhaps because the simplicity of her white gown was in marked contrast to the bold richness of the uniforms worn by the two officers. It was a short-sleeved, low-bosomed, high-waisted gown of lace over satin—but Gervase was not interested in the gown. His practiced eye noted that the body beneath it was slender and long-legged, coltish yet undeniably feminine. Her neck, long and swanlike, held her head at a proud angle. And proud she had every right to be. Her dark hair, piled elegantly and threaded with jewels that might well be diamonds, gleamed under the light of a thousand candles in the chandeliers overhead. Her face—oval, dark-eyed, and straight-nosed—was classical perfection. Its beauty was nothing short of dazzling when she smiled, as she did in response to a remark made by the officer on her right, raising a lacy white fan to her chin as she did so.

It seemed to Gervase that he might well never have seen a lovelier woman—if she could be called a woman. She was little more than a girl really—but as breathtakingly lovely as a perfect rosebud that has not yet burst into full bloom.

Fortunately, perhaps, for the young lady in question and any parents or chaperons who were hovering in her vicinity, he preferred mature blooms to tender buds—they were more amenable to being seduced. He had looked his fill and was prepared to move his glass onward.

"*That* one would be well worth impressing," John Waldane said, noting his friend's pursed lips and the direction of his gaze. "But alas, Rosthorn, she has eyes for no man unless his broad shoulders are encased in a scarlet coat." He sighed forlornly and theatrically.

"And unless he is not a day older than two and twenty," Gervase agreed, noting the youth of the two Guards officers. He must indeed be getting old, he thought, when even military officers were beginning to look like schoolboys playing at war.

"You do not know who she is?" Waldane asked as Gervase turned away, intending to remove to the card room.

"Should I?" he asked in reply. "She is someone important, I presume?"

"One might say so," his friend told him. "She is staying with the Earl and Countess of Caddick on the Rue de Bellevue, since their daughter, Lady Rosamond Havelock, is her particular friend, though her brother is here too. He is attached to the embassy at The Hague in some capacity but is currently in Brussels with Sir Charles Stuart."

"And?" Gervase prompted, making a circular motion with his hand as if to hurry his friend along.

"One of the officers talking to her—the taller, golden-haired one on her right—is Viscount Gordon," Waldane said. "Captain Lord Gordon, Caddick's son and heir. The only son in fact. Hence the military commission in the Life Guards, I suppose—all glory and gold lace but absolutely no danger. They will prance around on horseback on the parade ground, looking magnificent and sending all the ladies into a collective swoon, but they would swoon as a body themselves if this threat of war against Boney were to prove more a reality than an exciting game."

"They may surprise us yet if given the chance for glory," Gervase said more fairly. He took one step toward the ballroom doors. Obviously Waldane, mistaking his interest in the dark-haired girl for something more personal than it was, wanted him to beg for her identity.

"She is Lady Morgan Bedwyn," his friend said.

Gervase paused and looked back at him, his eyebrows raised. *"Bedwyn?"*

"The youngest of the family," Waldane said. "Fresh from the schoolroom, newly presented at court, the richest prize on the marriage mart if she has not already been snatched off it by Gordon. I understand that an announcement is expected any day. You had better keep your distance, Rosthorn, even if the wolf *did* remain behind in England when she came here." He slapped a friendly hand on Gervase's shoulder and grinned.

*The wolf.* Wulfric Bedwyn, Duke of Bewcastle. Although he had not seen the man for nine years and had not particularly thought about him in four or five, nevertheless Gervase could feel all the cold fury of an old hatred as he was reminded of him now. It was to Bewcastle he owed the strangeness of these English faces and these English voices, and his own self-consciousness in being among them—*his own people.* It was to Bewcastle he owed the fact that he had not been in England—*his own country, his father's country*—since he was one and twenty. Instead he had wandered the Continent, not really belonging in France despite his French mother because he was English by birth and the heir to a British earldom, and not safe in many other European countries under French occupation for the same reason.

It was because of Bewcastle—whose friendship he had once cultivated—that his whole life had been turned upside down and permanently changed for the worse. Exile really had seemed almost worse than death for the first year or so—that and the terrible humiliation and his impotence to convince anyone that he had been wrongfully treated. He had consoled himself eventually by becoming exactly what he was expected to be—a rake who cared for nothing and no one except himself and the gratification of his own desires, whether sexual or otherwise. He had certainly allowed Bewcastle to win in more ways than one.

Ah, yes, he realized in that flashing moment while he still looked over his shoulder at Waldane, the hatred, the burning desire to do Bewcastle harm in return, had not faded in nine years. It had only been pushed beneath the surface of his consciousness.

And now he was in the same building—the same *room*—as Bewcastle's sister. It was almost too good to be true.

Gervase looked across the ballroom once more. She had one gloved hand upon the sleeve of the golden-haired officer—Captain Lord Gordon—and was proceeding with him onto the dance floor, where the lines were forming for the opening set of country dances.

*Lady Morgan Bedwyn.*

Yes, he could well believe it. She carried herself with all the proud bearing, even arrogance, of a born aristocrat.

He could make mischief if he chose, Gervase thought, his eyes narrowing on her. The temptation was almost overwhelming.

As she took her place in the long line of ladies, and Captain Lord Gordon—a handsome young stripling—went to stand opposite in the line of gentlemen, her full smiling attention was on him. And he was very eligible—the son and heir of an earl. Indeed, she was thought to be all but betrothed to him.

The thought of causing mischief grew even more appealing.

She was doubtless an innocent, despite the arrogance. She had probably been hedged about with governesses until the very moment of her presentation and with chaperons ever since then. He, on the other hand, was anything but innocent. It was true that, despite his reputation, he had only ever turned his seductive charms on women who could match him in experience and, usually, in years too. But if he chose to turn those charms on a young innocent, he might perhaps succeed in turning her attention away from a scarlet coat.

*If he chose.*

How could he not so choose?

As the music began, he felt the very definite stirrings of a slight temptation. Though truth to tell, it was not so slight either.

Lady Morgan Bedwyn performed the steps of the dance with precision and grace. She was small-breasted, Gervase could see, and willowy slender, neither of which physical attributes normally aroused him sexually. He was not aroused now, of course, merely appreciative of her perfect beauty.

And yes—quite powerfully tempted to make trouble for her.

"Are you for the card room, Rosthorn?" John Waldane asked.

"Perhaps later," Gervase said without withdrawing

his attention from the dancers, whose feet were thudding rhythmically on the wooden floor. "I must go in search of Lady Cameron and ask her to present me to Lady Morgan Bedwyn at the end of the set."

"Oh, I say!" His friend reached for his snuff box. "You devil you, Rosthorn! Bewcastle would challenge you to a duel even for raising your eyes to his sister."

"Bewcastle, as I remember it, does not deal in duels," Gervase said disdainfully, his nostrils flaring at the remembered insult. "Besides, I *am* Rosthorn. It is quite unexceptionable to request an introduction to the girl, Waldane. Or even to invite her to dance with me. I am not planning to invite her to *elope* with me, you know."

Though there was a wicked sense of satisfaction in imagining how Bewcastle would react if he *did* run off with the girl. Did he dare contemplate such a thing?

"Five pounds on it that she will insist upon dancing every set with a scarlet uniform and will grant you no more than the time of day," John Waldane said, chuckling once more.

"Only five?" Gervase clucked his tongue. "You wound me, Waldane. Make it ten, or one hundred if you wish. You will, of course, lose."

He could not take his eyes off the girl. She was Bewcastle's *sister,* someone close to him, someone dear to him. Someone through whom Bewcastle's pride and consequence, even if not his heart, could be hurt. It was doubtful that the man had a heart—any more than he himself had, Gervase thought cynically.

It was strange how fate sometimes turned in one's favor—though it was about time. Belgium was as close as Gervase had come to returning home even though his father had been dead for longer than a year and his mother had long been urging him to come home to Windrush Grange in Kent to take up his inheritance and his duties and responsibilities as the new Earl of Rosthorn. He had been in Vienna when Napoléon Bonaparte escaped from Elba in March. Now, two months later, he had taken the tentative step of moving to Brussels in Belgium, where the British and their allies were beginning to gather in some force for the expected showdown with Bonaparte. Many of the British who had sons in the military had brought their wives and daughters and other family members with them. A large number of other Britons had come flocking there too simply because Brussels during this spring of 1815 was the social place to be.

And that number included Lady Morgan Bedwyn, sister of the Duke of Bewcastle.

Ah yes, he was very much more than *slightly* tempted.

Fate had dealt him a potentially winning hand at last.

LADY MORGAN BEDWYN was ever so slightly bored and more than slightly disappointed. She had hated the whole idea of a come-out Season and had fought Wulfric—the Duke of Bewcastle, her eldest brother and head of the family—on the issue for a whole year or more before she turned eighteen. She did not want to giggle and simper behind a fan and become a commodity at the great marriage mart, she had protested, being looked over and bid upon by all the callow, pimply male youth with which London was sure to abound—just as if there were nothing else in life but marriage and nothing else to *her* except looks and lineage.

But of course Wulfric had insisted—quietly and inexorably without ever raising anything louder than his eyebrows. But Wulf's eyebrows—and his quizzing glass—were at least twice as formidable as the combined voices of a whole regiment roaring out its battle cry. And of course her aunt Rochester, that veritable old dragon, had taken her firmly under her wing when she arrived in London and had soon had her decked out in the obligatory uniform of a young lady making her come-out. In other words, everything was white and delicate and made Morgan look half her age—*not* a desirable thing when one was just eighteen. And then Freyja—her elder sister, Lady Freyja Moore, Marchioness of Hallmere—had arrived in London with her husband the marquess to sponsor Morgan's presentation to the queen and her come-out ball and first few official appearances in society.

Finally the whole tedious come-out business had been an accomplished fact. Morgan had hated almost every moment of it. She had felt like a *thing*—a very exclusive, precious thing, it was true, but still an object more than a person.

She was glad afterward, though, that it had happened. For despite her reluctance to endure a London Season, she *did* possess a restless, adventurous soul and a lively, intelligent mind that needed constant stimulation. And suddenly, both adventure and food for the mind had presented themselves when Napoléon Bonaparte had escaped from his prison on the island of Elba and returned to France. London drawing rooms had buzzed with the news and with speculation of what it would all mean. Surely the French people would reject him. But they had not done so. Soon London had been buzzing even louder with war talk. Was it possible that the Allies, so cozily ensconced in Vienna while engaged in peace talks, were going to have to fight one more great battle against Bonaparte?

It quickly became apparent that the answer was yes—and that the battleground would be Belgium. No less a personage than the Duke of Wellington went there in April—to Brussels to be more precise—and other important personages from all over Europe had gone to join him there.

Morgan had found the whole business fascinating from the first moment, and—since she was a Bedwyn and the Bedwyns notoriously flouted convention and never dreamed that certain topics were not suitable for a lady's ears—she discussed the situation and the possibilities endlessly with the rest of her family.

And then she had been given the chance to go to Brussels in person.

The armies had begun to prepare for war, and some of the British regiments and a large number of their officers were in London. The latter began to appear at public functions in their uniforms—and one of them had begun to pay determined court to Morgan. She had found it mildly diverting to consort with the handsome, golden-haired, uniformed Captain Lord Gordon, son and heir of the Earl of Caddick—to go driving with him, to sit with him and his parents and sister in their box at the opera, to dance with him at balls and other assemblies. She had developed a friendship with Lady Rosamond Havelock, his sister.

And then Captain Lord Gordon had received word that he was to go to Belgium with his regiment, and the Caddicks, including Rosamond, had decided to go after him to Brussels. Dozens, maybe hundreds of other members of the fashionable world were going there too. It would be a great lark, Rosamond had said when Morgan had been invited to join the Caddicks, under the chaperonage of the countess.

Everyone had thought, of course, that there was a serious courtship developing between Morgan and Captain Gordon. Although he had seemed to think so too, as had Rosamond and the Havelocks, Morgan had been far from ready to make any decision that would bind her for life. But she had desperately wanted to go to Brussels, to be close to the developing crisis and the building action, and so she had pleaded with Wulf to allow her to go.

She had expected it all to be a grand political and intellectual exercise, the conversation wherever she went serious and stimulating. What a foolish expectation!

In fact, being in Brussels was hardly any different than being in London had been—the days and nights were filled with one frivolity after another. She almost wished that Wulfric had refused his permission for her to come with the Caddicks. It was all a little disappointing.

Of course, there were advantages to being in Brussels. There was a wonderful sense of freedom, for one thing. There was no Wulfric to watch her every move, quizzing glass in hand, and no Aunt Rochester to *frown* at her every move, lorgnette in hand. There was only Alleyne, the brother closest to her in age, who was here with the embassy under Sir Charles Stuart. But though he had promised Wulf to keep a brotherly eye on her, he really had been doing no more than that so far. It was more like half an eye, in fact.

Lady Caddick was an indulgent chaperon. She was also a rather silly woman. Lord Caddick lacked all character—or, if he had one, Morgan had not yet detected it. She liked Rosamond, but even she liked to talk of little more than beaux and bonnets and balls. Captain Lord Gordon and the other officers with whom they were acquainted liked to bolster their masculinity by telling the ladies not to worry their pretty heads about any topic that Morgan was inclined to find interesting.

It was all somewhat provoking to a young lady who had grown up with Bedwyns and had foolishly expected that other men would be like her brothers and other women like Freyja.

The opening set of country dances at Viscount Cameron's ball was almost at an end. Morgan enjoyed dancing with Captain Lord Gordon because he really did look very handsome and dashing in his uniform and he danced well. When she had first met him she had thought that she might fall in love with him. But now that she was better acquainted with him she was having some serious doubts about him. He had told her earlier in the set, when the figures threw them together for more than just a few seconds, that he felt very strongly about his role as an officer in the fight against tyranny. He was quite prepared, he had added, to die for his country if he must—and for his mother and his sister and . . . Well, he did not yet have the right to add another name, he had concluded with a smoldering look at her.

It had seemed a little theatrical to Morgan. And more than a little alarming. The Caddicks and many other people, she had realized, assumed that by accepting their invitation she had also acquiesced in a future betrothal to their son. And yet their stated reason for inviting her had been that Rosamond would be in need of female company.

"I was hoping," he said now as the music ended, "that the orchestra would simply forget to stop playing, Lady Morgan. I was hoping we could go on dancing all night long."

"How foolish!" she said, unfurling her fan and plying it slowly to cool her flushed cheeks. "There are other ladies awaiting their turn to dance with you, Captain."

"There is," he said, offering his arm to escort her back to his mother's side, "only one lady worth dancing with—but I may not, alas, dance two sets in a row with her."

Could it be true, she wondered, that he was nothing more than a foolish, posturing young man? But he was also a man facing war and possible death. She must remember that—it would be unfair not to. A man could be forgiven a certain measure of sentimentality under such circumstances—as long as he did not overdo it. She smiled at him but spoke firmly.

"No, you may not," she said. "I wish to dance with other partners."

Lieutenant Hunt-Mathers was one of the group around Lady Caddick and Rosamond. He was awaiting his set of dances with Morgan, which came next. He was neither as tall nor as handsome nor as dashing as Lord Gordon, but he was a well-bred, amiable young man and Morgan liked him even if he did have a tendency toward insipidity. She turned her smile on him, removing her hand from Lord Gordon's sleeve as she did so.

But before she could enter into any sort of conversation, she became aware that Lady Cameron was addressing Lady Caddick and asking permission to present the gentleman with her to Lady Morgan Bedwyn. Permission was granted, and Morgan turned her attention politely their way.

"Lady Morgan," Viscountess Cameron said, smiling graciously at her young guest, "the Earl of Rosthorn has requested an introduction to you."

Morgan looked assessingly at the earl. He was not an officer. He was dressed elegantly in gray silk knee breeches and silver embroidered waistcoat with a black, form-fitting evening coat and white linen and lace. Neither was he a particularly young man. He was tall and well formed and handsome enough, though, Morgan conceded as she curtsied and noticed that he had lazy gray eyes, which appeared to be looking back into hers with a certain amusement.

She saw nothing in the Earl of Rosthorn to arouse great interest, though. He was just one of dozens of gentlemen who had effected an introduction to her since her presentation. She was aware that she was considered beautiful, though in her own estimation she was too dark and too thin. More to the point, she knew that as the daughter of a duke with a very large fortune of her own she was attractive to single gentlemen of all ages and ranks. She was, after all, a commodity on the marriage mart even if she was now in Belgium rather than London and even if the perception *was* that she was almost betrothed to Lord Gordon. She responded politely to this newest introduction and asked him how he did, but she dismissed him in her mind as a gentleman who could be of no personal significance to her. And she regarded him with the cool arrogance that usually discouraged attentions she did not welcome. She *hoped* he would read her expression accurately and not ask to dance with her.

It alarmed her sometimes to realize how jaded she was at the age of eighteen.

"I am doing very well, I thank you," he said in a voice that somehow matched his eyes—both lazy and faintly amused, "and am all the better for having been introduced to the loveliest lady in the room."

The silly flattery was spoken as if he laughed at himself for saying it.

Morgan did not dignify his words with any response. She wafted her fan before her face and looked into his eyes, her eyebrows slightly raised, her expression openly haughty. It was an expression at which all the Bedwyns excelled. Did he really think her *that* silly and brainless? Did he expect her to simper and blush with pleasure at such foolishness? But why would he not think and expect just that? Most other gentlemen did and thereby displayed how brainless *they* were.

The humor only deepened in his eyes, and she realized that he must have accurately read her thoughts. Good! But his next words dismayed her.

"Dare I hope," he asked, "that you still have a free set sometime this evening and that you are willing to dance it with me?"

Botheration! she thought as her fan stilled for a moment and she searched about in her mind for a polite way to refuse him—she disdained to simply lie and tell him that she had promised every dance of the evening.

Someone else did that for her.

"Oh, I say!" Captain Lord Gordon said in the languid drawl he sometimes affected when talking to someone he considered his inferior. "Every dance of the evening in this corner of the room has been promised, my fine fellow."

Morgan's eyes widened in outrage. How dare he! But before she could have the satisfaction of framing a suitably biting retort to depress such pretension, the Earl of Rosthorn turned the captain's way, a quizzing glass materializing in his hand and raised to one eye, and regarded him with disinterest.

"Accept my congratulations, Captain," he said. "But I feel constrained to disabuse you of a misapprehension you appear to be under. It was not you I was asking to dance."

Morgan only just stopped herself from crowing with delight. What a perfectly delicious set-down! Suddenly she was regarding the earl in a totally different light. A man of such quick wit and assurance of manner was a man after her own heart. He reminded her of her brothers.

"Thank you, Lord Rosthorn," she said as if nothing had occurred between his asking and her answering. "Perhaps the set after this next?"

Immaculately dressed and well groomed as he was, she thought, there was something faintly disreputable about his appearance, though she would not have been able to put into words what it was. Perhaps it was just that he was considerably older than she and must therefore know more of the world and its ways. Not that she would ever admit to any naïveté. There was something nonchalant, something ever so slightly dangerous, about him.

"It will be an honor I shall anticipate with the greatest pleasure for the next half hour," the earl said.

It must be his lazy eyes, she decided—and his lazy voice. But no, there was something else about his voice that explained more clearly the impression of slight danger she was getting. He spoke with a French accent.

Morgan fanned her face slowly and watched him as he turned and walked away.

"The fellow is fortunate that there are ladies present," Lord Gordon was saying to his circle of cronies, his voice shaking with anger. "It would have given me great satisfaction to slap a glove in his face."

Morgan ignored him.

"My dear Lady Morgan," Lady Caddick said when the earl was out of earshot, "the mysterious Earl of Rosthorn must be very taken with you to have made the effort to be introduced to you."

"*Mysterious,* Mama?" Rosamond asked.

"Oh, yes, he is quite the mystery," Lady Caddick said. "He succeeded to his father's title and fortune a year or so ago, but no one had seen him for years before that or has seen him during the year since—except now here in Brussels. It is rumored that he has been hiding out on the Continent gathering intelligence for the British government."

"He is a *spy?*" Rosamond gazed after him in wide-eyed rapture.

"There may very well be some truth in the claim," her mother said. "It would certainly explain his appearance here in Brussels when intelligence concerning the French must be greatly in demand."

Morgan's interest was further piqued. A dangerous man indeed! But the sets were forming for the next dance and the orchestra was poised to play again. Lieutenant Hunt-Mathers stepped up to her, made her a stiff military bow, and extended one arm.

# CHAPTER II

GERVASE SPENT THE NEXT HALF HOUR IN THE CARD room, strolling among the tables watching the games and exchanging nods and pleasantries with a few acquaintances. He kept one ear tuned to the music.

Lady Morgan Bedwyn was every bit as lovely from close to as she had seemed from across the ballroom. Her creamy complexion was flawless, her eyes large and brown and generously fringed with dark lashes. He had been considerably amused by her reaction to his deliberately lavish compliments. She had stared him down like a jaded dowager. She was not, it seemed, the silly girl he had expected her to be.

That blank, haughty stare must be a Bedwyn gift. Bewcastle had been a master of it. Gervase had been at the receiving end of it the very last time he saw the man. The expression on Lady Morgan Bedwyn's face suggested pride, conceit, vanity, arrogance—all those related aspects of character that hardened his resolve.

Finally the music came to an end, to be replaced by a louder buzz of conversation from the direction of the ballroom. It was time to go and claim his partner. Bewcastle's *sister*.

The noise and gaiety in the ballroom seemed to belie the fact that they were all here—especially the officers—because a war was imminent. But perhaps it was the very possibility of such a catastrophe that set everyone to enjoying the moment to its fullest. The moment was perhaps all many of them would ever have.

He located his partner in the crowd and made his way toward her. He acknowledged Lady Caddick, her chaperon, with an inclination of his head and bowed to her charge.

"Lady Morgan," he said, "this is my set, I believe?"

She nodded her head regally. She and the golden-haired young lady with her were surrounded by young officers, all of whom looked at him with thinly veiled hostility.

"It is a waltz," the other young lady said. "Do you know the steps, Lord Rosthorn?"

"I do indeed," he assured her. "I recently spent a few months in Vienna. The waltz is all the rage there."

"Rosamond!" Lady Caddick said quellingly, perhaps because the girl had spoken to him without first being formally presented to him. But the older lady's tall hair plumes dipped graciously in his direction. "You may waltz with Lady Morgan, Lord Rosthorn. She has been given the nod of approval by the patronesses of Almack's."

He held out one arm to Lady Morgan, and she placed her hand lightly on his sleeve—a slender, long-fingered hand encased in a white glove.

"The nod of approval of the patronesses of Almack's," he said, raising his eyebrows as he led her away. "It is of some . . . significance?"

"It is all utterly tedious," she said with a look that reminded him again of a jaded dowager. "A lady is not permitted to waltz in a London ballroom until she has been granted their permission."

"Indeed?" he said. "Pray why?"

"Many people do not approve of the waltz," she said. "It is considered fast."

"Fast?" he asked, bending his head closer to hers.

"As in improper," she said disdainfully.

He grinned. "Ah, I see," he said. And he did too. Good old England. It had not changed. It was as prudish as ever.

"I had danced it a thousand times at home with my dancing master and my brothers," she told him. "But I was not allowed to dance it at my own come-out ball!"

"Just as if you were a child!" he said, looking shocked.

"Precisely!" But she looked suspiciously into his eyes as they took their places on the dance floor and waited for the music to begin.

Lord, but she was a beauty!

"Are you a British spy?" she asked him.

He raised his eyebrows at this abrupt change of subject.

"There is a rumor to that effect," she said. "You have been gone from England for a long time. It is thought that perhaps you have been engaged in intelligence missions for the British government."

"Alas, I'm afraid I am nothing so romantic," he said. "I have been away from England for nine years because I was banished from there—by my father."

"Indeed?" she said.

"It concerned a woman," he said with a smile, "and the theft of a priceless jewel."

"Which you stole?"

"Which I did *not* steal," he said. "But do not all accused and convicted thieves say the same thing?"

She regarded him for a moment from beneath arched eyebrows. "I am sorry you are not a spy," she said. "Though I daresay you would have been unwilling to answer any of my questions about the military situation anyway." She turned her head toward the orchestra dais—the music was beginning at last.

He set his right hand behind her waist—it was so slender that he might almost have spanned it with his two hands—and took her right hand in his left. Her free hand came to rest on his shoulder.

She was very young. And exquisitely lovely.

And Bewcastle's sister.

Dancing was one thing at which he excelled. He had always loved the elegant figures of the minuet and the quadrille, the vigorous intricacies of country dances—and the sheer erotic thrill of the waltz. Perhaps the British were wise to protect their very young from its seductive pull.

He led her off into the dance, waltzing and twirling with small, careful steps while he tested her knowledge of the dance and her ability to follow a lead. She had been well taught. But she possessed something more than just precision and accuracy. He could feel it even during that first minute, when they danced as sedately as everyone else around them.

She showed no further inclination to converse, and he felt none. She smelled of some soft, floral soap or cologne—violets, perhaps? She felt very youthful, very slender, in his arms. She was light and warm and pliant, and he could feel her slippers moving across the floor only inches from his own shoes.

"Is this how the English waltz?" he asked her.

"Yes." She looked up at him. "Is it not how everyone waltzes?"

"Shall I show you how it is done in Vienna, *chérie?*" he asked her.

Her eyes widened, though whether in response to the question or to his use of the French endearment she did not say.

He twirled her with longer strides and a wider swing about a corner, and she followed him. He even elicited a sparkling little smile from her.

The waltz had never been intended to be a plodding, mechanical affair, everyone twirling slowly and in perfect time with one another. He danced it now as it was surely meant to be danced, his eyes and his mind focused upon his partner, his ears bringing in the music and pouring its melody and its rhythm into every cell of his body, his feet converting that rhythm into movement.

It was a sensual dance, intended to focus a man's attention on his partner and hers on him. It was meant to make them think of another kind of dance, one more intimate still.

No wonder the British had misgivings about the waltz.

He whirled her about until the light from the candles became one swirling band of brightness overhead, and wound her skillfully in and out of the more slowly circling couples, noting with satisfaction that she stayed with him every step of the way, that she showed not a moment's fear of missing a step or colliding with a fellow dancer or losing her balance. The bright uniforms of the officers, the paler pastel ball gowns of the ladies, all merged into a swooping melody of color.

By the time the first waltz of the set came to an end she was bright-eyed and slightly flushed and a little breathless. And even lovelier than before.

"Oh," she exclaimed, "I like how it is done in Vienna!"

He dipped his head closer to hers. "Would the patronesses of Almack's approve, do you suppose?"

"Absolutely not," she said, and then laughed.

The music began again. But it was a slower, more lilting tune this time.

He waltzed her through the crowds as before, weaving in and out, varying the length of his steps, taking several smaller ones, and then moving into wide, sweeping swirls that forced an arch to her back and her neck. He felt the music with his body, moved with it, challenged it, took liberties with it, felt the magic of it. And she moved unerringly with him, her eyes on his much of the time. He held her fractionally closer than the regulation hold, though they touched nowhere except where regulations allowed.

She sighed aloud as the music drew to a close again.

"I did not know the waltz could be so—" she said, but one circling hand, which she had lifted from his shoulder, suggested that she could not think of a suitable word with which to complete the sentence.

"Romantic?" he suggested. He moved his lips closer to her ear. "Erotic?"

"Enjoyable," she said, and then she frowned and looked at him with a return of her earlier hauteur. "That was not a very proper choice of word! And why have you called me *chérie?*"

"I have spent nine years on the Continent," he said, "speaking French most of the time. And my mother is French."

"Would you call me *dear* or *sweetheart,* then, if you had spent those years in England?" she asked. "Or if your mother were English?"

"Probably not." He smiled into her eyes. "I would have lived all my life with English sensibilities and English inhibitions. How dull that would have been. I am thankful my mother is French, *chérie.*"

"You must not call me that," she said. "I have not permitted it. I *am* English, you see, with all of an Englishwoman's sensibilities and inhibitions—and dullness."

She was, he thought, every inch Bewcastle's sister. Except that he had spotted the rebel beneath the aristocrat, the butterfly eager to fly free of its cocoon. And the woman behind the youthful exterior who was surely capable of hot passion.

"I do not believe you for a moment," he told her softly, smiling into her eyes. "But if I may not call you *chérie,* what else is there? What sort of a name is Morgan for a lady?"

"It was my mother's choice," she said. "We all have unusual names, my sister and my brothers. But mine is not so very strange. Have you not heard of the Morgan of Arthurian legend? She was a woman."

"And an enchantress," he said. "You are aptly named after all, then."

"Nonsense," she said briskly. "Besides, I am not Morgan to you, am I, Lord Rosthorn? I am *Lady* Morgan."

The music began again for the last waltz of the set as his smile turned to laughter.

"Ah," she said, brightening, "a lively tune again. Dancing can often be very tedious, Lord Rosthorn, would you not agree?"

"As danced the English way, I would have to agree with you," he said. "But the Viennese way is more . . . er, interesting, would you not agree?"

"When you paused, you intended that I think of that other word, did you not?" she said. "I believe, Lord Rosthorn, you are flirting quite outrageously with me. But beware—I am not as gullible as I may look. Yes, let us waltz the Viennese way since it is more *interesting*." She smiled at him.

All of the sunlight and all of the warmth of a summer day were in that smile, and he realized that she was playing him at his own game—or what she thought was his game. She was far more interesting than he had expected. She might even prove a worthy foe.

He hoped so.

"You have talked me into it, *chérie,*" he told her, sweeping her into the dance, holding her smiling eyes with his own. "We will perform that *erotic* dance."

Her cheeks flushed. But she would not look away

from him, he noticed. He smiled slowly back at her.

ALMOST ALL THE BRITISH visitors to Brussels had driven out to the village of Schendelbeke and across the temporary bridge over the River Dender to where, on the riverbank near Grammont, the Duke of Wellington reviewed the British cavalry. The Prussian field marshal von Blücher was there too.

It was a picturesque setting for such a spectacle. And pure spectacle it was too. First the cavalry stood still for inspection, and Morgan, sitting in an open barouche with Rosamond and the Earl and Countess of Caddick, would have sworn that neither the thousands of men nor the thousands of horses beneath them moved a single muscle. Then Lord Uxbridge, their commander, marched the cavalry past the duke, and it seemed that they moved so perfectly in time with one another that the whole force was a single unit.

"How could any normal woman not be in love with every single one of the officers?" Rosamond asked with a laugh, though she whispered the question so that her mama would not hear. Morgan sometimes found her friend just a little silly in her enthusiasms, but really she had a point on this occasion. Morgan would not have missed the outing for anything in the world. She would probably be paying insipid afternoon calls with Aunt Rochester now if she were still in London. On the other hand, when she had tried a short while ago to draw the Earl of Caddick into a discussion on whether the necessity for military discipline ought to outweigh the human right to individuality, she had drawn blank stares from the ladies and a mere grunt from the earl.

The Life Guards were part of the review and were turned out in all their scarlet, immaculate splendor. They were mounted on magnificent and perfectly trained horses—the best in all Europe, according to Captain Lord Gordon. He was among them now. So were many other young officers who were part of their usual group of friends.

If ever matters did come to the point at which the British cavalry was forced to gallop into battle, Rosamond predicted aloud, the French cavalry would surely venture one look at them and take to their heels in sheer panic. The French infantry would be too terrified even to flee. Not that matters ever *would* get to that point, of course.

Morgan was not so sure on either count. Alleyne had warned her just the day before that the situation was beginning to look rather grim and that it was altogether probable that the Caddicks would decide to return home to England soon. And surely, she thought, years of warfare should have taught everyone in Europe that it would be foolish indeed to underestimate Napoléon Bonaparte and the French soldiers who had always fought for him with such unflagging bravery. Many of the British, of course, were unwilling to admit that anyone was capable of bravery except an Englishman.

She kept her thoughts to herself.

After the review was over, Captain Lord Gordon and several of the other officers rode up to the barouche to pay their respects to the earl and countess and to chat with the young ladies. Morgan was very aware that this afternoon's visual spectacle was no circus show. It was the reality of real men preparing for war—for killing and being killed. She twirled her parasol above her head and gazed at them each in turn. It was hard to picture all this male vitality in so desperate a struggle.

"The Duke of Wellington is anxiously awaiting the arrival of more foreign troops," Lord Gordon was explaining to her, having maneuvered his horse right alongside the door next to which Morgan sat. "And it is said he is terrified lest the rest of the seasoned troops who fought with him in the Peninsula not arrive back from America soon enough to push the French back should they be foolish enough to attack us here. But it is clear to see that our cavalry alone is strong enough and ferocious enough right now to complete the task with ease."

There was a cheer from his grinning fellow officers.

"Would you not agree, Lady Morgan, after having watched the review?" he asked.

Morgan knew very well—surely everyone must—that it was always the infantry that won or lost a battle.

"You certainly looked very formidable indeed," she told him.

"And the Life Guards in particular?" he asked her. "Everyone knows that we are the cream of the crop, so to speak, that all the Englishmen of highest rank choose the Guards—if their families can afford it—and that we have all the best horses. Have you noticed how the rest of the cavalry and all the infantry and artillery regiments look up to us with envy and awe? Especially the green jackets?"

His companions cheered and laughed again, and Lady Caddick smiled complacently. Rosamond was engaged in a private conversation with Major Franks, who had ridden around to her side of the carriage.

Morgan wished they did not all seem so disconcertingly like a group of schoolboys predicting a win at cricket over a rival school. She could not help wondering a little uneasily how such unseasoned troops would perform under fire. Most of the green jackets Lord Gordon had referred to were riflemen, and most had fought in the Peninsula and were seasoned, battle-hardened troops. Many of them were somewhat shabby in appearance, but Morgan had noticed that other soldiers spoke of them with considerable respect.

"The Life Guards did look particularly magnificent," she agreed.

He smiled warmly at her. "You must not fear, Lady Morgan," he said. "For one thing, no Frenchman in his right mind is going to fight for Bonaparte again if it can possibly be avoided. For another, Brussels is surrounded by our own Allied troops in an impenetrable fortress of protection. And for another, if all else fails, the Life Guards certainly will not. You are quite safe from harm."

There was another good-natured cheer.

"I do not feel threatened," she assured him.

"We would not keep you here in Brussels if there were any danger, I do assure you, Lady Morgan," Lady Caddick told her, "and as I assured the duke, your brother, before we came here."

"In a way," Lord Gordon said with boyish eagerness, his whole attention still on Morgan, "I am sorry that Bonaparte never *will* get close to the doorstep of Brussels. I would love nothing better than a battle to show him a thing or two about the English cavalry in general and the English Life Guards in particular. If Wellington had had us with him in Spain, I daresay it would not have taken him so long to push the French back into France."

"Perhaps not," Morgan said. "But you are here now."

She was feeling decidedly indignant. Until just last year, her brother Aidan had been a cavalry officer. He had battled his way across Portugal and Spain and into France, fighting the Peninsular Wars with Wellington's forces every slow step of the way. She had never heard him claim that his regiment—or even the cavalry alone—had won the war. He always spoke with respect of all the military forces—cavalry, infantry, artillery, British, and allied—who had fought. He even spoke with respect of the French. But then, of course, Aidan was older and more experienced.

Her thoughts were diverted at that point when her eyes alighted on the figure of the Earl of Rosthorn, who was riding a short distance away with a gentleman Morgan did not know. She recognized the earl immediately. She had not seen him since the evening of the Cameron ball, but she had not forgotten their waltz—or their conversation. Although honesty forced her to admit that she had enjoyed herself at the time, she remembered with disapproval. He had treated her with a familiarity she resented—he had persisted in calling her *chérie* even when she had commanded him not to. And he had quite deliberately set out to shock her, telling her about the causes of his banishment from England, and using that word—*erotic*—to describe their dance. He had used it twice. And he had held her just a little too close while waltzing with her and had even moved his head a little closer once or twice to speak softly in her ear. He was, of course, a rake, and he had used his charms on her as if he thought she were a green girl and therefore quite unable to discover what he was about.

She had made up her mind after the ball that if he approached her ever again, she would give him the cut direct. She was not going to dance to anyone's tune. She was a Bedwyn, after all.

The earl had seen her. His eyes met and held hers, an expression on his face that was not quite a smile—it was half mocking, half amused. It lit his lazy eyes and tugged at the corners of his mouth. Morgan disdained to be the first to look away. She raised her eyebrows in what she hoped was a fair imitation of Wulfric when he wished to depress pretension and turn the recipient into an icicle. And then Lord Rosthorn was guiding his horse in the direction of their barouche, winding in and out of the press of other carriages and riders.

Botheration!

The group of officers parted to let him through, a few of them looking somewhat surprised.

"Ah, Lady Caddick, ma'am," he said, taking his eyes off Morgan at the last possible moment and touching the brim of his hat courteously to the countess. "I was hoping to encounter you here. How do you do?"

"Lord Rosthorn," Lady Caddick said, all amiability. "Have you been enjoying the review? I was never better entertained or more proud in my life. Are you acquainted with Caddick?"

The gentlemen, who apparently were indeed acquainted, exchanged affable nods, and Lord Rosthorn addressed the remainder of his remarks to Lady Caddick herself, while the rest of the group paused politely and looked on.

Morgan was more than a little irritated. She was longing to give him a withering set-down on some pretext.

"I am planning a picnic in the Forest of Soignés," Lord Rosthorn said, "and am in the process of considering my guest list."

"A *picnic!*" Rosamond exclaimed, looking away from Major Franks and darting a bright look at Morgan.

"A picnic by moonlight," Lord Rosthorn added, smiling warmly at Rosamond before returning his attention to her mother. "It would give me the greatest pleasure, ma'am, if you and Lord Caddick would agree to be among my guests and to bring your daughter and Lady Morgan Bedwyn too."

Rosamond clasped her hands to her bosom.

"And your son as well," Lord Rosthorn added, "and any other officer of the Life Guards you would wish included in the invitation."

"That is extremely civil of you, Lord Rosthorn," Lady Caddick said. "We would be delighted to attend, would we not, Caddick?"

Lord Caddick grunted.

"Splendid!" the earl replied. "I shall do myself the honor of calling upon you in Brussels as soon as I can give you more specific details, then, ma'am."

He did not linger. He turned his horse and maneuvered it through the crowd again to rejoin his friend a short distance away. But before doing so he looked fully at Morgan, made her a polite bow, and favored her with that half-smile again, as if they shared some amusing secret. She half expected him to call her *chérie*.

"Well!" she said crossly to no one in particular.

She felt considerably ruffled. How dared he? He had not addressed a single word to her. He had scarcely even looked at her once he was close. And yet she had been given the distinct impression that they were all invited to his picnic because of her.

What was he up to?

She would dearly have loved the opportunity to consider his invitation, twirling her parasol nonchalantly as she did so, and then to refuse it quite publicly and distinctly without offering any excuse. Simply no. Instead, she had had to sit in silence and listen, like a child whose wishes are not consulted.

It would serve him right if he really was planning his picnic for her sake and she failed to attend.

His French accent had been quite noticeable throughout the short conversation. But he was British, was he not? Did he expect her to find his accent irresistible just because French—or English spoken with a

French accent—was said to be the language of love? A rake might at least be more subtle in his approach.

Of course, she thought, pitting her wits against those of a rake would surely enliven her days somewhat—her days really had become rather tedious. And the idea of a picnic by moonlight in the Forest of Soignés had definite appeal.

"Who does that fellow think he is?" Lord Gordon asked, his voice irritated, one of his hands tapping out a rapid tattoo on the door of the barouche. "He expects us all to be impressed by his title though he has not set foot in England for years but has instead been moving around the Continent acquiring an unsavory reputation. I can believe it too. He muscled his way in at the Cameron ball two evenings ago and took the first waltz with Lady Morgan, which *I* had determined should be mine."

"I had promised the set to no one, Captain," Morgan reminded him sharply while Rosamond turned to talk excitedly to Major Franks and the other officers buzzed among themselves and Lady Caddick was making some remark to her husband. "It would have been improper to dance with you again so soon after the opening set. The Earl of Rosthorn was properly presented to me and asked formally for a set of dances, a request that I granted."

"I beg your pardon," he said hastily. "It is just that I find the fellow impudent and would not have him force his attentions on you if you are unwilling. Perhaps you are not."

"If I were unwilling," she said, "I would give him the

cut direct, especially if he were indeed impudent. But I cannot construe a properly made introduction at a ball as *forcing* attention upon anyone. And today he made his invitation very properly—and very generally—to your mama."

"I beg your pardon," he said again stiffly.

It was the closest she had come to quarreling openly with him. But really, Morgan thought, he could be very tiresome. And possessiveness was something she would tolerate in no man who was not her husband—or even in her husband, she decided, amending her thought.

But now look what he had provoked her into, she thought, turning her eyes on the departing figure of Lord Rosthorn. Here she was defending the man when she was feeling more than a little annoyed with him.

What *was* he up to?

## CHAPTER III

PREPARATIONS FOR WAR PROCEEDED APACE IN Belgium. Every day brought fresh troops and supplies and artillery—though never enough for the Duke of Wellington, it was said. But not many people believed there was any danger to Brussels itself. Very few returned to the safety of the British Isles. Most threw themselves with ever greater enthusiasm into the entertainments offered daily for their amusement, determined to stay close to husbands and brothers and sons and lovers for as long as they were able.

The evening picnic in the Forest of Soignés to be hosted by the Earl of Rosthorn proved more popular than any other entertainment so far. Of the dozens of invitations sent out, only three refusals came back.

It had, of course, been an idea conceived entirely on the spur of the moment, Gervase admitted to himself after talking with Lady Caddick at the military review, which he had attended with the express purpose of encountering Lady Morgan Bedwyn again. Waldane had laughed at him and told him a little maliciously that he would be the envy of every hostess in Brussels—provided the party did not get rained upon. But Gervase had not cared. He had hired an agency, turned over every detail of the preparations to its expert care, even the compiling of the guest list—he had simply instructed them to invite everyone who was anyone—and carried on with his days as if he were to be no more than a guest himself.

By the time the appointed day dawned, all the preparations had been taken care of and his only concern was the weather. But after a morning of intermittent showers and a cloudy afternoon, the sky had cleared by teatime and the sun shone from then until it set. The moon was up even before full darkness descended, and darkness itself brought millions of stars twinkling overhead. It was also a warm and windless night.

Now, Gervase thought as he surveyed the site, commended the head of the agency, who was present to act as usher and to oversee the catering and all other details of the proceedings in person, and awaited the arrival of the first guest, he had better hope that Lady Morgan

Bedwyn would not find some excuse to stay away.

She had bristled with almost visible annoyance at the review, when he had virtually ignored her after looking his fill and had addressed himself—with perfect correctness—to her chaperon.

And she was a very proud, haughty young lady. She might well decide to punish him by remaining at home with a headache or some other mild indisposition.

But he would wager upon her being too proud to make a false excuse and too bold not to face his challenge head-on. She must have *recognized* the challenge. She was not, he had been delighted to discover, a foolish young lady.

Even so, he conceded, this was a colossally expensive gamble.

The envy of every hostess in Brussels, for the love of God!

MORGAN, WEARING A PALE green evening gown that had seemed to her to somehow suit the occasion, was sitting in the open barouche beside Rosamond, their backs to the horses, while Lord and Lady Caddick sat facing them. The evening could not possibly have been lovelier for such an event if they had had the ordering of it, Morgan thought, lifting her face to the sky, which was quite visible through the high branches of the trees.

The picnic was to be a large and lavish entertainment, she had learned since the Earl of Rosthorn had extended his verbal invitation beside the Dender. Everyone she knew had been invited. Even Alleyne was coming. So were a large number of the officers of her acquaintance—including, of course, Captain Lord Gordon.

She almost had not come herself. She had even considered the message she would send along with the Caddicks—she would insist upon their going, of course. She would have them inform the Earl of Rosthorn that she preferred to remain at home with a good book this evening since she had been out every night for a week and was a little weary of being entertained. But Lady Caddick would never pass along such a message, of course. She would doubtless tell him that Morgan had a headache or some such lowering thing.

Besides, she scorned the whole idea of avoiding him. It would be far better, she had decided, to go and confront him and make him understand that *if* this picnic had been arranged with her in mind, then he had made a massive error in judgment. She would show him that she found his rakish attentions a colossal bore.

She had never before had a rake to contend with. Wulfric would have had to raise only half an eyebrow in London to frighten away any who had even *contemplated* dallying with her. And Aunt Rochester had hovered like a large, gorgeously plumed bird of prey.

There was, Morgan admitted to herself, a certain exhilaration in the prospect of matching wits with a practiced rake.

"The air is warm now," Lady Caddick remarked, "but one wonders if it will not cool off later. Perhaps we ought to have brought the carriage, Caddick."

Lord Caddick grunted, and Morgan and Rosamond exchanged smiles. They both preferred the barouche.

What happened at an evening picnic? It was a question Rosamond had asked repeatedly during the past few days. Would it be similar to an afternoon picnic? Would they sit around on blankets, eating chicken legs and lobster patties and sipping wine? Would there be strolls in the forest afterward? But would it not be too dark among the trees? Perhaps, she had suggested, the darkness would provide an excuse to get lost for a few minutes with the gentleman of one's choice.

If that happened with her, Morgan thought dryly, the gentleman would almost undoubtedly be Captain Lord Gordon. Or the Earl of Rosthorn . . . Now that might present an interesting challenge, at least.

The Forest of Soignés was like a great cathedral, she decided, breathing in the verdant fragrance of it while the carriage moved onward and thinking of incense. There was very little undergrowth. To either side of the road the beechwood trees soared overhead on smooth, massive, silvery trunks, like mighty marble columns. Their branches fanned out far overhead like an intricately fretted ceiling. The forest inspired awe, as a Gothic cathedral might. One felt in the very midst of something powerful, something mysterious, something beyond the mundane here and now, something that lifted one's spirit to another plane.

Suddenly Morgan's fingers itched to paint it all—the forest and the spirit within it. Suddenly her life during the past few months seemed very trivial. She missed the countryside about Lindsey Hall and the frequent hours of solitude she valued so much.

"I wonder," Rosamond said, also gazing upward, "if there will be enough moonlight visible through the branches to enable us to see what we eat? Perhaps the forest was not the best choice of site for a picnic after all."

But no doubt the Earl of Rosthorn would have thought about that potential problem and found a solution—or at least whoever he had hired to arrange the picnic would have done. Morgan doubted he had lifted a finger in preparation himself. And she was quite right about the one thing, of course. As the barouche approached the appointed picnic site, they could see lanterns—hundreds of them in every color of the rainbow—strung among the branches of the trees.

Suddenly the forest had a different type of enchantment—a man-made one, more human, more intimate, more romantic. It was just as appealing in its own way as the natural beauty Morgan had just been lost in.

"It is magical," Rosamond said, her eyes shining. "Like Vauxhall Gardens."

Small tables had been arranged among the trees, each laid with a crisp white cloth and set formally with fine china and crystal and silver. Each had a small colored lamp glowing at its center.

But the splendor was not just visual.

"Listen!" Morgan held up one hand. As the carriage drew to a halt and the rumbling of its wheels and the clopping of the horses' hooves died away, they could hear music. It was being provided by a small orchestra seated on a wooden dais farther back from the road among the trees. A larger wooden floor had been laid below the dais.

"There is to be *dancing!*" Rosamond exclaimed,

squeezing Morgan's arm tightly.

Whoever had planned this for him, Morgan thought, had obviously done an expert job. This picnic, she guessed, would be talked about for days, even weeks to come.

Other carriages were approaching along the road they had just traveled, their lamps ablaze to illumine the way ahead. But numerous guests had already arrived. Among them were several scarlet-coated officers.

"This," Rosamond declared with conviction, "is going to be the very best entertainment of the Season so far."

As the coachman set down the steps and opened the door of the barouche, Morgan could see that the Earl of Rosthorn was detaching himself from a group of guests and coming their way. He was looking very splendid clad all in pale silver and white. He was dressed formally in knee breeches and white stockings, she could see. It was a fashion that suited him—his legs were long and muscular and well shaped. He was smiling that rather lazy smile of his and looking really very handsome.

Morgan set her hand in his after he had helped Lady Caddick down.

"This is like something out of a pastoral idyll, Lord Rosthorn," she said. "It is very well done. I must commend you."

His eyes laughed at her as he handed her down.

"Then my labors have not been in vain," he said. He gazed deep into her eyes before turning to Rosamond.

Ah, she thought, she had not been mistaken, then. *Of*

*course* she had not been mistaken.

"We are quite determined to enjoy ourselves more tonight than at any other entertainment of the Season, my lord," Rosamond was telling him. "Are we not, Morgan?"

"I shall do my best to see to it that you do," Lord Rosthorn told her. But it was at Morgan he looked as he spoke.

He waved away a very superior-looking servant when the man would have ushered them to a table, offered an arm to Lady Caddick, and escorted the four of them in person to a table close to the orchestra and the wooden dancing platform. From there they would have a clear view of the whole picnic area, which was like a large, pillared ballroom with a green leafy ceiling, slightly uneven floor, and fresh air to breathe in with the smells of forest and earth. And colored lamps to add an aura of romantic enchantment to the whole.

He bowed to them but did not linger. A waiter was hurrying toward their table, a wine bottle wrapped in a crisp white cloth in his hands.

For the next hour or so Morgan sat there with her party. After everyone had arrived and been seated, they were all served with a cold supper of fine and sumptuous foods while listening to the orchestra play and a tenor sing. The beauty of the singer's voice quite brought tears to Morgan's eyes. Afterward they were visited at their table by several young officers, and Lord Caddick excused himself to join a group of his male acquaintances beneath a beech tree a short distance away.

Captain Lord Gordon and Major Franks invited Morgan and Rosamond to stroll about the picnic area with them in order to converse with mutual acquaintances, and Lady Caddick, in response to an anxious glance from her daughter, nodded her gracious consent.

The orchestra was taking a break. The dancing would begin when they returned, Lord Gordon predicted to Morgan. He thought the wooden dancing floor a somewhat sorry substitute for a polished ballroom floor in an elegant home, and the orchestra not as fine as some he had heard in Brussels, but he hoped Lady Morgan was enjoying herself anyway.

"Enormously," she assured him. "The enchantment of the trees and the light and color from all the lamps more than compensate, surely, for a wooden dancing platform that has had to be laid over the uneven forest floor and an orchestra that must contend with less than ideal acoustics."

"Oh, but of course, absolutely," he agreed. "I could not agree with you more, Lady Morgan. I was just afraid it might not be to your taste. It is indeed a splendid entertainment."

And here she was again, she thought, being provoked into defending the Earl of Rosthorn's entertainment. In fact, though, despite the novelty of a moonlight picnic, the evening was settling into being much like almost every other evening since her presentation. But at least they were outdoors amid truly lovely surroundings. A part of her inward being detached itself from her social self, which smiled and conversed as good manners dictated—and watched as if from the tranquil, silent heart of the forest itself.

*If only* she were sitting here painting instead of socializing.

The Earl of Rosthorn was standing at their table when they returned, conversing with Lady Caddick. He turned to smile at Morgan.

"Ah, here you are," he said. "I hope the supper was to your taste?"

"Yes, I thank you," she assured him. She noticed how his pale clothes contrasted with the bright colors of the uniforms worn by many of his guests and thought that in some indefinable way he looked far more sheerly masculine than even the best of the officers.

"Perhaps, Lady Morgan," he said, "you would care for a stroll in my company?"

Just her. Not Rosamond too.

"You may go, Lady Morgan," Lady Caddick said graciously. "But remain within sight."

Lord Gordon cleared his throat as if to protest, but if he had intended to deter her, his gesture had just the opposite effect, of course. Besides, Morgan was curious to know how the earl would proceed. She was almost certain that he had done all this for her. Did he *really* believe that she would fall, all big eyes and heaving bosom, for such a lavish display of apparent devotion?

"Thank you," she said, favoring him with one of her haughtiest glances as she took his offered arm. "I should like that."

It was a hard, well-muscled arm. He was almost a full head taller than she, she noticed, though she was tall herself. He was taller than Lord Gordon. He was looking down at her with the now-familiar mocking smile—as if he *knew* that she recognized his game but believed he could win it anyway.

"It must have been quite a challenge," she said, "to plan a picnic by moonlight."

"I daresay it was," he agreed, "for Monsieur Pepin of the Pepin agency. But you would have to ask him if you wish to be sure. He *did* try to involve me with one or two of his more tricky decisions, but I reminded him that I was paying him a rather handsome fee to take all such tedious burdens upon his own shoulders. Did I do right? *Was* he reliable? One of his questions—momentous to his mind, I suppose—was whether to have tables brought out here or to have blankets spread on the ground."

His eyes now were positively laughing at her.

"Tables and chairs are more comfortable than blankets," she said. "And they looked very picturesque when we arrived, formally set as they were."

"I would have been crushed," he said, laying his free hand over his heart, "if you had spoken in favor of blankets."

Despite herself she smiled.

"And another question," he told her, "was whether to allow the moonlight and starlight to filter through the shades of the forest—assuming it would not be a cloudy night—while only the tables bore lamps, or whether there should be lanterns hung in the trees and so interfere with the beauties of nature. I am afraid I do not have the philosophical mind to deal with such thorny issues. I made it very clear at that point that I was *not* to be consulted again except with the direst emergency—like the moon moving to a different galaxy or an army of foresters moving into the forest to chop down the trees. *Did* Monsieur Pepin make the right choice, do you suppose?"

"Lanterns like these, strung just so, enhance the beauty of nature for such an occasion," she said. "They do not spoil it."

"I would have been devastated," he told her, "had you said otherwise."

She laughed outright.

How could one take such blatant, theatrical flirtation seriously? She was not meant to, she guessed. She also guessed that the Earl of Rosthorn was somewhat cleverer than she had expected. He had realized, of course, that she would know what he was up to and so was making no attempt to hide his motives. He was deliberately making her laugh and enjoy herself instead.

Well, she *was* enjoying herself too—this was better than boredom. But he had better not believe that she would be softened into compliance with his plans for her—whatever they might be.

They had been strolling about the picnic area, well within sight of Lady Caddick and anyone else who cared to check up on her movements—Alleyne, for instance, who was there. By now most of the guests were on their feet and mingling with one another. Laughter and animated conversation proclaimed the fact that Lord Rosthorn's picnic was a resounding success.

Morgan expected that he would return her to Lady Caddick's table after a decent while—and bide his time until the dancing began. But the earl was in no hurry to relinquish her company. He kept her hand tucked into the crook of his arm while he began circulating among his guests, exchanging brief greetings with most, stopping for a lengthier exchange with a few.

Morgan was acquainted with almost everyone and so was quite at her ease. But she noticed that he had her arm rather firmly pressed to his side so that she could not slide it free even if she had wanted to without drawing attention to what she did. He had every intention of keeping her with him—almost as if she were the hostess of the evening, or the guest of honor. Almost as if they were an established couple. It really was not quite proper for him to single her out thus for such prolonged and marked attention. She wondered if they would be spoken of tomorrow as an item—Lady Morgan Bedwyn, who was almost betrothed to Captain Lord Gordon, and the mysterious, rakish Earl of Rosthorn. It took so little to become the object of speculation and unsavory gossip—as of course he must be well aware.

But it amused her to play his game for a while at least. Only Lady Caddick and Rosamond and the officers awaited her once she was returned to her table.

She had expected something a little more . . . dangerous, perhaps, but the evening was not yet over.

Even as she thought it, he bent his head closer to hers and spoke for her ears only.

"The noise of conversation and the press of the crowd

are considerable, are they not?" he said, touching his fingers to the back of her hand on his arm. "Perhaps I ought to have exerted myself sufficiently to instruct the agency not to invite everyone *and* his dog. It would be very pleasant, would it not, to find more space and more room in which to breathe and feel at least the illusion of greater solitude?"

"I believe, Lord Rosthorn," she said, slanting him a sidelong glance, "it is said quite correctly that there is safety in numbers."

He recoiled as if in deep shock. "You thought I was suggesting something improper?" he asked her. "You have wounded my gentlemanly sensibilities. I merely intended to show you what Monsieur Pepin showed *me* shortly before the arrival of my guests. It is a remarkably clever something. Do allow me to show you. You will not even for a single moment step beyond the eagle scrutiny of your chaperon."

Lady Caddick, Morgan saw at a glance, was in the midst of a crowd of officers, who were all apparently playing merry court to her daughter. It seemed altogether probable that the lady had forgotten Morgan's very existence.

"Very well," she said. "Show me."

It had appeared to her until then that the lanterns had been strung in a rough circle about the picnic area. But in a few places, she could see when Lord Rosthorn pointed them out, winding avenues tangent to the circle had been created with more lanterns—places to stroll among the trees without being plunged into total darkness and without risk of becoming lost. Each lighted avenue eventually wound its way back to the main picnic area.

"Is this not brilliant?" he asked, a mocking gleam in his eyes. "I *almost* wish that I had taken an active role in the planning of this party so that I could claim credit for it—semiprivate avenues for those who wish to be semiprivate together."

Morgan paused when he would have led her into one such avenue.

"Brilliant indeed," she agreed. "But I do not need to go any farther. I can see very well from here how cleverly it has all been designed."

He laughed softly.

"You fear I seek to abduct you, *chérie?*" he asked her. "In full sight of a veritable horde of my own guests? At all points this central area is visible from the avenues, which are not, of course, real avenues but only winding paths through the trees. And you see? Already, even before the dancing begins, other couples have discovered these quieter walks for themselves. Allow me to show you."

His French accent had become more pronounced. And he had called her *chérie* again. He was, she realized, moving on to the next, more dangerous stage of his game. She wondered briefly why he had chosen her. Because she was very, very wealthy, perhaps? Rakes were not notorious for exerting their charms on the very young without some such motive, were they?

"But you already have," she assured him, gazing up at him with deliberately large, innocent eyes.

"Ah," he said, "you fear that I am a big, bad wolf. My

apologies, Lady Morgan Bedwyn. I would not press my attentions upon a young lady who is afraid of me."

Well, that did it, of course. Even though she knew very well that she was being jerked like a puppet on a string, she reacted as he expected her to react. She bristled.

*"Afraid?"* Her fingers found the fan that was dangling from one wrist, grasped and opened it, and fanned her face vigorously with it. "Afraid of *you,* Lord Rosthorn? Perhaps you do not understand what it means to be a Bedwyn. We fear no one, I assure you. Lead the way."

He grinned at her and she read appreciation in his eyes as they stepped into one of the lantern-lined avenues and were immediately caught up in the illusion of privacy and seclusion.

"Finally," he said, "I begin to enjoy the evening in precisely the way I imagined doing from the start."

"With me?" She fanned her face again and looked up at him, her expression haughty, even scornful. "You imagined enjoying it *with me?*"

"With you, *chérie,*" he said, his voice low.

"*All* this was for me?" she asked him. "This whole evening?"

"I thought it might amuse you," he said.

She stopped walking and closed and dropped her fan to dangle from her wrist again.

"Why on earth?" she asked him.

"Why did I believe it would amuse you?" he asked. "Because you are young, *chérie,* and the very young enjoy picnics and moonlight and music. Is it not so?"

"I meant," she said coldly, "why me, Lord Rosthorn? Why do something as lavishly extravagant as this for me when I am a total stranger to you? It was grossly presumptuous of you!"

"Ah, *mais non,*" he said, "not quite a stranger. We have been properly presented. We have waltzed together."

"But something as elaborate as this on the strength of an introduction and one dance?" she said, waving one arm imperiously in the direction of the picnic area. "I believe, Lord Rosthorn, you have singled me out for dalliance. I *believe* your intentions are not honorable."

"Honorable." He laughed softly. "I am not about to drop to one knee and beg you to become my countess, if that is what you mean, *chérie*." The swaying light of a lantern caught the laughter in his eyes. "But it seemed to me at the Cameron ball that I recognized in you a kindred spirit, one that chafes against the stuffiness of society's confines and longs for freedom and adventure. Was I wrong?"

"And any longing for freedom and adventure that I feel must necessarily lead me into dalliance with *you,* Lord Rosthorn?" she asked him scornfully. "You presume too much."

"Do I?" He tipped his head to one side and observed her closely.

"What did you plan?" she demanded. "You have gone to extraordinary lengths to get me here. Now what are you planning to do with me? Steal a kiss? *Seduce* me?" She raised her eyebrows. Perversely, she realized that she was enjoying herself enormously. Two could play this game.

*"Seduce?"* He slapped a hand to his heart and looked mortally shocked. "Would I bring these hordes of people out here, *chérie,* including a whole regiment of military gentlemen, I daresay, if my intention was to ravish you almost publicly? I might end my picnic in spectacular fashion by being hanged from one of these trees—or run through by a dozen swords."

"But you cannot deny that you planned to steal a kiss?" she asked.

He leaned a little closer to her.

"I would quarrel with your use of the past tense," he told her.

Being the youngest of the Bedwyns—by far the youngest and female to boot—had always set her at an enormous disadvantage during any family altercation. But if she had learned one tactic well it was that the best defense was frequently offense. And surprise.

"I suggest, then, Lord Rosthorn," she said crisply, "that we step out of this avenue, which according to your own admission is visible from every part of the picnic area, and into the forest itself. Or do you wish to be seen to kiss me—or to attempt to do so?"

He pursed his lips and his eyes danced with merriment. He made her a courtly bow and offered his arm.

"I wish to see the contrast between the night forest and the picnic area, of course," she told him as he turned them away from the avenue marked out by lanterns. "Between nature in its raw state and nature with man's interaction."

"Ah," he said, "so this is merely a nature walk, is it?"

"I may," she said with careful disdain, "allow you to kiss me before we return, Lord Rosthorn, or I may not. If I do, it will not be a stolen kiss but one that I grant—or withhold."

He threw back his head and laughed outright.

"You are not afraid that I will then steal a second and a third, *chérie?*" he asked her.

"No." Already light and sound had receded sufficiently that she could focus upon the forest. She stopped walking and looked up. "I will not allow you to. I probably will not allow even one."

"Perhaps no one has mentioned my reputation to you," he said, stopping too and releasing her arm in order to lean back nonchalantly against a tree trunk. He crossed his arms over his chest. "Perhaps I am dangerous, *chérie*. Perhaps you *should* be afraid of me."

"How foolishly you speak," she told him. "If you meant me any real harm, you would keep very quiet about your unsavory past and hope that I had not heard of it elsewhere." Though she had to admit to herself that standing as he was and *where* he was—in the dark forest with no one else close by except her—he really did look very dangerous indeed.

He chuckled.

"What is to be tonight's particular topic of nature study?" he asked her, his voice lazy and teasing.

Actually, it really was lovely to be away from the crowds and the worst of the noise. The night sky was still bright with starlight and scored with the high branches of the trees. She would punish him by pretending that there was no danger at all, that she had invited him out here simply for companionship.

"Have you ever considered," she asked him, "how fortunate we are to have been gifted with so many contrasts?" She turned around in a complete circle and then closed her eyes and breathed in deeply so that she would not ignore the smells.

"Male and female?" he said. "Near and far? Up and down?"

She turned her head to look at him with interest though of course she could no longer see him clearly at all. If she had asked that question of Rosamond or Captain Gordon or a dozen other of her acquaintances, she would have drawn nothing but blank stares.

"Light and shade, sound and silence, company and solitude," she said.

"Sacred and profane, large and small, war and peace," he added. "Beauty and ugliness."

"Oh, no," she protested. "There is no contrast there. Everything that is ugly to us is doubtless beautiful to someone or something else. The slimiest slug is probably beautiful to another slug. A storm, which brings rain and chill to someone intent upon a pleasure outing, is beautiful to a farmer who has been anxiously watching his parched crops."

"And what looks large or small to us will look quite different from the perspective of an elephant or an ant," he added. "Opposites are merely two sides of the same coin—one cannot exist without the other."

"Precisely." She stepped closer to him. "So contrasts are inextricably linked. They are only a way for us to process information, to understand, to appreciate. Past and future, for example. There are no such things really, are there? There is only now. But if there were not those contrasting perceptions, we would not be able to organize our lives or our thoughts. We would be overwhelmed by everything happening at once and a thousand decisions having to be made all at the same moment."

"We would be dying as we were born." He chuckled suddenly. "*This* is why we stepped into the forest?"

"Dalliance was your idea," she reminded him. "Mine was to escape the tedium of a grand squeeze of a social event for a short while."

"I am slain," he said, slapping one hand over his heart again. "All this was arranged for your delight, *ma chère,* and it is *tedious?*"

"Not at all." She stepped a little closer again. "It is magical, a feast for the senses. But it is only now, when I can also be aware of the darkness and silence and peace of the forest that I can fully appreciate the lights and the gaiety and the laughter. Having a picnic here, Lord Rosthorn, was an inspired idea, and I thank you for it." She smiled very brightly and very deliberately at him.

Her eyes had grown accustomed to the darkness. He was smiling lazily back at her.

"You *are* an enchantress," he said. "You have turned the tables on me, have you not, Lady Morgan Bedwyn? You have played me at my own game and talked philosophy at me when I would have been talking dalliance. You have even provoked me into talking philosophy back at you. But I am not so easily diverted from my baser instincts. I really must steal a kiss from you. And since you have bravely claimed that I will not be allowed to steal a second or a third, I had better make the most of the initial theft."

For the first time she felt a little frisson of fear. Though perhaps *fear* was not quite the word since she did not believe he would really grab her and seduce her against her will. They were also still close enough to the picnic area that screams would surely bring other people running.

What she felt was a quickening of her breath and a weakening of her knees and a realization that she had stepped far too close to him for comfort. And an understanding that it was not, of course, fear that she felt at all.

It was desire.

She *wanted* him to kiss her.

Consequently, she almost took a step back. She almost turned and hurried away. For she had played with fire and was likely to get burned after all. More, she was close to showing him how easily she could be dallied with, how easy a prey she was to a practiced rake.

Annoyance came to her rescue—as well as her Bedwyn pride. How ridiculous! He was but an idle rake when all was said and done.

She took another step forward and tipped back her head.

"Oh, you will steal nothing," she said, her tone cool, her voice admirably steady. "I came out here fully intending to be kissed. You have not been clever at all, Lord Rosthorn, only mildly diverting. Kiss me."

For a few moments he did not move. He lounged against the tree, his arms still crossed, and regarded her with obvious amusement. She raised her eyebrows and gazed back. And then he uncrossed his arms, pushed himself away from the tree, and cupped her face in his hands.

She expected something aggressive, something fierce, something forceful and masterly. Something, quite frankly, that would be earth-shattering. But his lips, when they touched hers, were warm, soft, slightly parted, and feather-light. If for the first moment she was disappointed, however, she soon changed her mind. While her lips remained still, his moved. He brushed them softly over her own, licked them lightly with his tongue, nipped gently on the lower one with his teeth, and then curled his tongue behind her lips to stroke over the moist, sensitive flesh within. The warmth of his breath caressed her cheek.

The effects of the kiss, she discovered, were not confined to the area of her lips. The whole cavity of her mouth ached, and then her throat and her breasts and her abdomen and her inner thighs. By the time he lifted his head away, she understood how even a single kiss could be a dangerous thing. She could feel his body heat from her eyebrows to her toes. She was shockingly aware of his maleness.

He dropped his hands to his sides.

"Very nice, *chérie,*" he said. "Very nice indeed. One could only wish that Belgian forests came equipped with mattresses and that chaperons—even ones as lax as yours appears to be—came with no sense of time at all. But we must, alas, be returning to my guests and the safety of numbers."

He offered her his arm with a courtly bow.

And so, Morgan thought, giving him a hard look before taking his arm, he had perhaps won this round of hostilities after all. For of course, he had not kissed her properly, not as one imagined a rake would kiss, not—surely—as he had intended to kiss her.

He had toyed with her instead.

He was a wily foe. She wondered if he would now have tired of the game and would be content to forget her existence after this evening while he went in pursuit of other prey.

Wulfric and Aunt Rochester would have an apoplexy apiece if they could see her now, she thought suddenly. And with good reason. She had taken on the challenge of outfoxing an experienced rake who for some unknown reason had marked her as his newest victim. And she was really not sure which of them had won.

Perhaps it was a stalemate.

# Chapter IV

A significant number of his guests noted their return to the main picnic area, Gervase observed, and the direction from which he had come. The same people would have noted his circulating among them earlier with the same lady. They would remember how long he had been with her at an entertainment where even husbands and wives were not expected to remain in each other's company for long.

By tomorrow—or even later this evening—they would have remarked on their observations to others who had perhaps not noticed. He and Lady Morgan Bedwyn would be an item within a very short while, he did not doubt.

As he had planned.

The trouble was that he found himself rather liking her. She was not by any means a simpering chit. And she had backbone. She had played him very well at his own game, and he still had not decided if she had won or not. He had, of course, intended to kiss her far more lasciviously than he had.

He had decided instead to throw her off balance.

But here she was walking at his side, looking cool and ever so slightly bored and oozing aristocratic hauteur from every pore. He might have resented her cool demeanor if he had not been almost sure that he *had* ruffled her somewhat.

"Alas," he said with a great sigh, "there is one duty I could not avoid no matter how hard I attempted to run and hide from Monsieur Pepin. I must announce the beginning of the dancing, and I must lead off the first set with the lady of my choice—or the first lady who will consent to dance it with me. And let me see now—I ought to know since Pepin showed me the program and suggested that I commit it to memory. Yes, yes, the first set is to be a waltz. You must dance it with me, *chérie*. You really must. You waltz well, and I can be sure of not shaming myself before all my guests by treading on your toes. *Will* you dance it with me?"

He looked at her with a mocking smile and was gratified to see her lips twitch.

"Oh, very well," she said with every evidence of disdain.

It was interesting that she had accepted. Very interesting indeed—though she was very careful not to show that she was *eager* to waltz with him, of course. She was such a worthy foe. He was sorry that hatred had led him to her and that hatred kept him in pursuit of her. But it was an irresistibly pleasurable thought that word of this evening and her indiscretion in spending so much time in his company would almost without a doubt reach Bewcastle in England.

He led her toward the wooden dancing floor. He handed her up onto it, joined her there, and addressed himself to his guests in the expectant hush that fell. The dancing would begin, he announced. The first set was to be a waltz. He invited them to take their partners and join him and *his* partner. Then, without waiting for the floor to fill with prospective dancers, he nodded toward the leader of the orchestra.

The music began immediately, and Gervase set a hand behind Lady Morgan's waist, took her right hand in his, and moved her into the steps of the waltz.

And so they danced virtually alone for the first minute or two, until other couples had gathered around them and joined in. For that minute or two they were exposed to public view again as they danced that most intimate of all dances. He smiled down at her and—instead of looking either shocked or embarrassed, as well she might—she looked boldly back, her perfect eyebrows arched high over her perfect eyes.

He concentrated his attention on the waltz and despite himself got caught up in the exhilaration of it while he smiled into her eyes and wove her in and out of the other dancing couples. The outdoors was a perfect setting for the waltz, he thought. They seemed part of the forest, he and his youthful partner, part of the night, part of the very dance of life itself. She tipped back her head to look up at the stars wheeling above the swirling branches, and laughed.

"Ah, *chérie,*" he said, his voice low, "we move together in perfect harmony, you and I . . . on the dance floor."

"You are a master of the speaking pause, are you not?" she said haughtily, her smile vanishing.

He laughed softly.

The pursuit, he thought, was going to take longer than he had expected. But he was not sorry. He was going to enjoy it every step of the way.

He had no chance to return her in person to her chaperon's table when the dance ended. A gentleman took her hand and tucked it firmly beneath his arm almost before her feet had stopped moving.

"*Thank* you, Rosthorn," he said with stiff courtesy. "I will take Lady Morgan back to Lady Caddick's side."

Lord Alleyne Bedwyn looked much like his eldest brother, especially now, when he was clearly annoyed. Gervase had no previous acquaintance with him, but he had seen him a couple of times about Brussels and had greeted him on his arrival this evening.

Gervase bowed to Lady Morgan and smiled before she was whisked away.

Ah, this was promising, he thought as he looked after them with narrowed eyes. If Bedwyn had noticed and been offended by what he saw, then others would have noticed too.

How fortunate for him that she had such a sorry creature for a chaperon.

"WELL, MORG," ALLEYNE said after he had walked her firmly into one of the avenues and they were no longer being jostled by the crowds, "you have been having a grand time of it tonight."

"I imagine," she said, "that everyone is green with envy at not having been the first to think of a moonlit picnic in the Forest of Soignés."

"I daresay," he agreed. "But you know very well what I am talking about. You have not gone falling in love with Rosthorn by any chance, have you? I thought you had more sense."

"Fallen in love with . . . Are you *mad?*" she asked him. "I do not fall in love with every gentleman who deigns to pay me some attention."

"I am glad to hear it," he said dryly. "But I certainly don't know where Lady Caddick's sense can be, allowing you to walk about with him after supper as if you were an old married couple and then disappear into one of these avenues for so long that I was about to come after you, and *then* letting you jump up onto that floor and waltz with him when you were the only two there. You will be fortunate if you are not the subject of some pretty nasty gossip tomorrow. You will be even more fortunate if it does not reach Wulf's ears. I thought she was a responsible chaperon. So, apparently, did Wulf if he allowed you to come here under her care."

"She has done nothing irresponsible," Morgan said crossly. "Neither have I. It is quite unexceptionable to stroll with a gentleman with whom one has an acquaintance. Even Aunt Rochester would not argue with that. And I have been granted permission to waltz. Lady Caddick did not know Lord Rosthorn intended to begin dancing before other couples joined us. Neither did I."

"Cut line, Morg," he said. "You know very well that Aunt Rochester would have been breathing fire and brimstone tonight even before you stepped off into one of these avenues and disappeared from sight. And while she was doing that, Wulf would have been dripping icicles. You would have been home in bed by now, and Rosthorn would have been chiseling ice chips out of his liver."

"Well, they are not here," she told him, "and no one appointed *you* my guardian, Alleyne. Do you not have anything better to do with your evening than watch me enjoy myself? There must be a dozen ladies and more falling all over their feet in their eagerness to dance with you."

Even Morgan would concede that her brother was devastatingly handsome, with his dark good looks and slim figure, even if he *had* been afflicted with the prominent Bedwyn nose. She was, in fact, the only one among them who had escaped it.

"I promised Wulf I would keep a brotherly eye on you," he said, "and it is beginning to look, Morg, as if I had better make that *two* eyes. Rosthorn clearly has designs on you."

"Nonsense!" she said. "We have merely enjoyed each other's company for a short while this evening. And he *is* a gentleman."

"Well, there you are wrong," he said, pokering up and looking disconcertingly like Wulfric for a moment. "In all but birth, that is. The man has a decidedly shady reputation, Morg. He has been on the prowl on the Continent for years, not always in the best company, and rumor has it that he left England under some cloud in the first place."

Morgan held her peace.

"Wulf would *not* consider Rosthorn eligible, you may be sure," he said.

"Eligible?" she said haughtily. "Must every man have marriage on his mind when he invites a lady to stroll with him, then?"

"He had better not have anything else on it," he said fiercely. "Not when the lady is my sister. I thought you were in love with Gordon."

"He grows tedious," she told him. "He is handsome enough to turn any girl's head, but he boasts and he postures. I keep trying to make allowances for his youth, but then I remember that he is four years older than *I* am."

He chuckled and looked his old self again.

"I know I can trust you, Morg," he said, squeezing her hand to his side. "We Bedwyns may be ramshackle, but we do know what is what. But you *are* an innocent, you know, even if you hate to hear it, and sometimes innocence can be a dashed dangerous thing. Promise me you will be careful around Rosthorn? I'll have a word with him if you wish."

"If you do," she said, bristling fiercely, "I'll borrow one of Freyja's famous left hooks and rearrange your nose, Alleyne. Of course I'll be careful. Not that there is any need. Lady Caddick is a perfectly adequate chaperon, and I have a brain in my head."

He laughed and cuffed her jaw lightly with his closed fist.

"I think I'll keep my nose as it is, then, if it is all the same to you," he said. "Shall I take you back to Lady Caddick? I daresay Gordon is panting for a dance with you."

She nodded and wondered what he would say—and do—if she told him this whole entertainment had been conceived and organized for her benefit. And that she had gone quite deliberately into the forest with Lord Rosthorn and allowed him to kiss her there—even though she had known very well that he had nothing but dalliance on his mind.

Alleyne would conjure up his very own fireworks display to rival the one in Vauxhall Gardens. He would probably take the Earl of Rosthorn apart limb from limb and lay out the pieces across the forest floor.

And what would *Wulfric* say and do? The idea really did not bear thinking of.

But she was not going to start feeling guilty. No harm had been done. Quite the contrary. A wily, practiced rake had thought to toy with her, and she had turned his weapons against him and come away from the experience quite unscathed. She was rather proud of herself.

Perhaps the Earl of Rosthorn, who really was a quite despicable man, would think twice before wasting his time and money on a young, green girl again.

Green girl! Ha! Gracious heaven, she was Lady Morgan Bedwyn.

SEVERAL DAYS PASSED before Gervase talked with Lady Morgan Bedwyn again. He saw her at the Salle du Grand Concert on the Rue Ducale one evening—the famous soprano, Madame Catalini, sang there and the Duke of Wellington was in attendance—but he did not approach her since she was in the very midst of an entourage that included her brother.

There was indeed gossip and speculation about them in the drawing rooms of Brussels, enough that several people would surely include word of it in letters home to England and it would become the *on dit* there too. The lady concerned was, after all, Lady Morgan Bedwyn, sister of the Duke of Bewcastle.

His scheme was working very nicely indeed. And he was not at all concerned that matters were proceeding slowly. He was in no hurry.

One morning when he was out riding and was cantering along the Allée Verte—a wide grassy avenue beyond the city walls, lined on both sides with straight rows of lime trees, a canal flowing beyond them on one side—he spotted Lady Morgan approaching, also on horseback, with Lady Rosamond Havelock. He was himself alone, having just parted from John Waldane and a few other of their acquaintances.

She was looking very fetching indeed in a bright royal blue riding habit with a jaunty little feathered hat to match. She rode sidesaddle but with such grace and assurance that she might well have been born in the saddle. A discreet distance behind the ladies rode a couple of burly grooms.

Gervase touched the brim of his hat and bowed from the saddle. Lady Morgan inclined her head graciously in return—she was playing the grand lady this morning, perhaps in response to the gossip that was still focused on them. She might have ridden on past without a word if Lady Rosamond had not spoken up.

"Good morning, Lord Rosthorn," she called cheerfully. "Is it not a lovely day?"

"After two days of rain it does feel remarkably pleasant to be outdoors again," he agreed.

"How fortunate," she said as the three horses came to a stop and the grooms halted where they were, "that you chose just the evening you did for your picnic. The weather has been quite unsettled since then."

"I trust," he said, "the entertainment was to your liking?"

"It was *wonderful!*" she assured him with all the unalloyed enthusiasm of a very young lady. "We enjoyed every single moment, did we not, Morgan?"

But that young lady, he saw when he turned his eyes on her, was looking gravely at him.

"Do you hear any news of the French, Lord Rosthorn?" she asked. "It is said that they are indeed on their way here."

"But you heard what Ambrose and Major Franks and Lieutenant Hunt-Mathers said last evening, Morgan," Lady Rosamond protested before Gervase had a chance to answer. "They told us we were not to worry our heads about the French. They will never get past our defenses to come anywhere near Brussels. Ah, here come Captain Quigley and Lieutenant Meredith," she cried as two Guards' officers rode up to join them. "They will give *their* opinion. Are we in danger of invasion by the French, Captain Quigley?"

The captain looked suitably shocked. "In danger, Lady Rosamond?" he said. "When the Guards are here to protect you? Old Boney will not be allowed to set one toe over the border into Belgium without having it shot off, you may rest assured."

"You must not worry your pretty head over such matters, Lady Rosamond," the lieutenant added. "Or over the safety of your brother or any other officer of your acquaintance. Boney would not dare attack us with the tattered remnants of his ragtag army. More's the pity."

They turned their horses in order to ride with the ladies. But Lady Morgan had scarcely glanced at them. She had kept her eyes on Gervase, a slight frown creasing her brow.

"May I be permitted to ride a short way with you?" he suggested, and she nodded, though somewhat absent-mindedly, it seemed to him.

They rode side by side, a little apart from Lady Rosamond and the officers, who were all talking rather loudly and laughing heartily. The two grooms, Gervase noticed when he glanced back, were proceeding along in their wake.

"I find it frustrating, even insulting," Lady Morgan said, "to be told twenty times each day not to worry my *pretty* head about such matters though they clearly concern me and all my countrymen and certain military acquaintances of mine in particular."

"It is in the nature of a gentleman," he explained, "to wish to protect ladies from harm and even from anxiety."

"It really is going to happen, then, is it not?" she said. "There really is going to be war again."

"Undoubtedly," he said, deciding instantly upon the sort of honesty with which he would reply if it were a man who had asked. "Any faint hope that the French will simply refuse to rally around their fallen emperor has been dashed. The French army is said to be very large indeed and very formidable. All of Bonaparte's most famous marshals have come dashing to his side, doubtless in the hope that he will restore all their lost prestige and glory. Yes, at least one more pitched battle seems inevitable. One must simply hope that *one* battle will suffice. If Bonaparte is the victor, there is no predicting the future."

"But what has happened was thoroughly predictable," she told him. "I said so from the start. People call Napoléon Bonaparte *Old Boney* and then make the assumption that a man with such a nickname must be a buffoon. But in order to have had the success he has enjoyed over the years he must be a man of genius and great charisma, must he not?"

"The coming battle will be a deadly one," he said, "and its outcome is far from certain, else Wellington would not be so openly worried about it. But I firmly believe there is no imminent danger to Brussels. The borders are strongly defended. If there were any real threat, most of the British visitors and all the ladies would by now be on their way home."

"Lord Caddick wishes us to go without further delay," she said, "and my brother Alleyne came yesterday to find out why we were not already on our way. But Lady Caddick refuses to leave until it becomes impossible to stay. She insists upon remaining close to Lord Gordon, and I can only applaud her resolve. There is so little that women are allowed to do, Lord Rosthorn. At least we can stand by our men."

"And Lord Gordon is the one by whom you will stand?" he asked her.

She leveled a straight look at him.

"That is an impertinent question, Lord Rosthorn," she said.

He smiled at her.

But she was not bent upon quarreling with him, it seemed.

"It is not Brussels and my own safety that worry me," she said. "I suppose that when the time comes I will be hurried away to safety long before there is any real danger to my person. But the men of the armies cannot be whisked away, can they? They must remain and fight. And die."

"Not all soldiers die in battle," he said gently. "Consider all the veterans in Brussels. They fought in numerous ferocious battles in the Peninsula—and many of them in India before that—and have lived to tell the tale."

"My brother Aidan among them," she said. "He did not relinquish his commission until after the Battle of Toulouse last year. But consider, Lord Rosthorn, all the countless thousands of veterans who are *not* in Brussels because they *are* dead—my sister-in-law Eve's brother, for example."

Her friend was laughing gaily with the officers, but Lady Morgan seemed not to notice them.

"Perhaps Bonaparte *will* be stopped at the border," she said, "but he will not simply turn meekly and go back home, will he?"

"It would seem very unlikely," he agreed.

"What exactly will he do, then?" She gave him a very direct look again.

"As a matter of pride," he said, "he will have to attempt to force a way through to Brussels itself. The Duke of Wellington's armies will not make it easy for him—or even possible, it is to be hoped. But he will, of course, try. If I were in his shoes, I would attack at the weakest point of defense, which is, perhaps, at the juncture between Wellington's defending forces and those of Field Marshal von Blücher. If he can bludgeon his way through at that point and turn their flanks and cut their communications with each other, he will stand a good chance indeed of winning the victory."

It was not the sort of gloomy prediction he would normally make to a woman, especially to a very young and delicately nurtured lady. But she was not as other ladies were—he was increasingly aware of that.

"Thank you," she said gravely. "Thank you for not making disparaging references to my pretty head, Lord Rosthorn, and for answering my questions without softening your replies. Sometimes I think the officers of my acquaintance are like toy soldiers playing at war games. But I suppose that is unfair. They merely make light of reality in the presence of ladies because they think us too delicate to face the truth. I daresay they talk more sense among themselves."

A loud burst of laughter from Lady Rosamond's group illustrated her concern.

"They will acquit themselves well if they are called upon to fight," he said.

"If?"

"When," he conceded.

She looked grim and pale about the lips.

"For years," she said, "when I was growing up I used to worry and worry about Aidan. War seemed so pointless to me. Why should the brother I adored be away from me and the rest of his family for so long when we needed and wanted him? Why should his life be in danger every single day? Why should I live in constant dread of seeing someone in military uniform ride up to the doors of Lindsey Hall, bringing word of his death in battle? I still think war pointless. Do you not, Lord Rosthorn?"

"Of course," he said. "But inevitable nonetheless. It is human nature, unfortunately, to fight. There will always be wars."

"It is in *men's* nature," she said. "Women do not fight wars. If women ruled their countries, there would be a great deal more common sense in our dealings with one another."

He smiled.

"You find that idea amusing, Lord Rosthorn?" she asked sharply.

"Only because I believe," he said, "that women are sensible enough to stay out of politics. They have better things to do with their time."

"Like stitching at their embroidery, I suppose," she said, "and drinking tea with their neighbors."

"And nurturing their children," he said. "And keeping their menfolk in line. And making sure that the world does not neglect the beauty of art and music and poetry."

"I wonder," she said, "if we are not thereby damned with faint praise, as the saying goes."

But the officers were taking their leave of Lady Rosamond and were turning to include Lady Morgan in their farewells and to assure themselves that she was indeed to attend a certain regimental dinner that evening.

Gervase took his leave at the same time, receiving an amiable nod of farewell from Lady Morgan as he did so.

Ah, he thought, as he rode away, resuming the direction he had been taking when he met the ladies, that had gone very differently from any of the flirtatious encounters he had imagined. It was a little disconcerting to discover that the lady had a mind and that she liked to use it. But if she chose to treat him in something of the nature of a friend, then so be it.

He had never been one to look a gift horse in the mouth.

ON THE MORNING OF June 13 Lord Alleyne Bedwyn called at the house on the Rue de Bellevue and spoke privately with the Earl of Caddick before being admitted to the ladies' presence in the morning room. They were all at home, it being a drizzly sort of day that had not yet cleared out enough to allow for a ride or even a visit to the shops.

"The Kieg-Densons, acquaintances of Sir Charles Stuart, are leaving Brussels at first light tomorrow, ma'am," Alleyne explained to Lady Caddick after greetings had been exchanged. "They have a daughter of their own and a governess whom they credit with a great deal of fortitude and good sense. They have agreed to allow my sister to travel with them as far as London. And Lady Rosamond too if it should be your wish."

Morgan stiffened, and Rosamond stared with wide-eyed dismay at her mother.

Lady Caddick fanned her face and looked troubled.

"I do not know, Lord Alleyne," she said. "It is uncommonly civil of the Kieg-Densons to make such an offer, but I cannot help thinking that Rosamond's place is with her mama and papa. And I cannot like the idea of abandoning Gordon in his hour of need. Besides, I cannot believe the situation is so desperate. Lord Uxbridge or the Duke of Wellington himself would have given the word if they considered that we were in any grave danger here."

"I can understand and sympathize with your sentiments, ma'am," Alleyne said. "I shall explain to Mrs. Kieg-Denson, then, that only Morgan will be traveling with them. You must direct your maid to pack your trunks without delay, Morg."

But before she could open her mouth to utter an indignant enough retort, Lady Caddick spoke for her.

"I cannot like it, Lord Alleyne," she said. "Lady Morgan was entrusted to my care by the Duke of Bewcastle himself. I do not have the authority to pass off that responsibility to someone else."

"I will take the authority upon myself, ma'am," Alleyne said. "And Lord Caddick agrees with me that Brussels has become a potentially dangerous place to be—especially for ladies."

He did not explain his remark. He did not need to. Morgan knew as well as anyone—though no one had ever put it into words for her—what could happen to the women of a fallen city when the conquering army was let loose in it. Was the danger really so great, then?

But even now her fears were not focused upon herself. Somehow it seemed cowardly to leave. And though she was not in love with Captain Lord Gordon or any of the other officers of her acquaintance, nevertheless she knew them and cared what happened to them. She felt sick at the thought of being sent away.

"I am not going, Alleyne," she said.

He lofted one eyebrow as he looked at her. But he spoke to Lady Caddick.

"May I speak with my sister alone, ma'am?" he asked.

Lady Caddick got obligingly to her feet. "I need you in my room, Rosamond," she said.

Rosamond made a face at Morgan as she followed her mother obediently from the room. Morgan also stood and went to look out the window. The rain had stopped, she could see. The pavement and road were beginning to dry.

"I am not going, Alleyne," she repeated. She could be very stubborn when she set her mind to it, as all her family knew.

He heaved an audible sigh.

"Shall we talk plainly, Morg?" he said, strolling in her direction. "I will not have my sister put at risk of being ravished by a French soldier. Is that plain enough for you? It is pretty safe to say that Wulf would not have it either."

"When the danger is that close," she said, "I will leave. I will be forced to. Lord Caddick will insist upon it, and Lady Caddick will understand that she must put Rosamond and me before her concern for Lord Gordon. I will wait until that moment, Alleyne. I will trust them to make the right decision. I was sent here in their care, after all. No." She held up a staying hand when he would have spoken. "Don't play elder brother, Alleyne. Just be my *brother*. I cannot leave now. I *cannot*."

To her chagrin she could hear that her voice was shaking.

"Because of Gordon, I suppose," he said, and raked one hand through his dark hair. "Is there an understanding between the two of you after all, then, Morg? Is that it? I hope it is not a secret betrothal. Wulf would have his head."

"There is not even an understanding," Morgan said. "But please, Alleyne, don't try to insist that I leave tomorrow morning. The Duke of Richmond's ball is set for the evening after tomorrow, and those plans would not still be proceeding if there were any imminent danger, would they? The Duke of Wellington is expected to appear there. Let us wait until the ball is over and then decide what is best to do."

"By that time," he said, "the Kieg-Densons will be long gone."

"But there will be other people leaving," she said. "There will be others with whom I can go if it becomes necessary for me to go at all. *Please,* Alleyne?"

She blinked her eyes furiously. She had never been either a weeper or a pleader, but she was close to being both at this moment. She simply could not leave Brussels. Not now. There might be a huge battle and she would not even know of it in London for days and days. The officers of her acquaintance might be killed and she would not know of it—but she would imagine the worst every minute of every hour of every day.

Alleyne made an exasperated sound.

"Morg," he said, "you are the youngest of us, the one all of us most adore. Why could you not also be the only biddable one among us? Very well, then. We will see what happens by the morning after the Duke of Richmond's ball. I hope I don't regret this for the rest of my life. It goes very much against my better judgment."

She hurried toward him, clasped her arms about his neck, and kissed him on the cheek.

"Thank you," she said.

"At least," he said, "Gordon is someone eligible, Morg. Wulf must approve or he would not have consented to let you come here with the Caddicks. You are sure you do not have an understanding with him?"

"I am sure," she said. But if he chose not to believe what she had said on the evening of the picnic about Lord Gordon's being tedious, she would not disabuse him. She *had* to stay just a little while longer.

"It might be just as well if you did," he told her. "There were tongues wagging after that picnic in the Forest of Soignés, as I am sure you are well aware. You allowed Rosthorn to hang on your sleeve for far too long. He has not made a nuisance of himself since?"

"Not at all," she said. "I have scarcely seen him."

That was not strictly true. She remembered riding with him for a while along the Allée Verte a few days before. But his manner had not been in any way flirtatious or his words loverlike. He had not once called her *chérie* or looked at her with those lazy eyes and that half-teasing, half-mocking smile. Instead, he had been good enough to treat her as a person rather than as a silly, delicate girl. She was *so* tired of being treated that way. He was the only man in Brussels—with the exception of Alleyne—who had been willing to admit the truth of the military situation to her.

"That is good to hear," Alleyne said. "We had better hope none of that gossip gets back to Wulf. The rain has stopped, I see. Do you want to run and fetch your bonnet and come walking in the park with me? I cannot help feeling I have neglected you since we came here."

"I suppose," she said before leaving the room, "it is because you are a working man at last, Alleyne, and have better things to do than run after a sister all day."

"I always did, Morg." He chuckled.

ON JUNE 14 NEWS ARRIVED that the French army was concentrated about Mauberge and that they had even crossed the frontier into Belgium. It was a mere showy flexing of muscles, according to general opinion in Brussels. There were over one hundred thousand Prussian troops guarding every road between Ardennes and Charleroi, and an only slightly smaller force of British and Allied soldiers guarding every road between Mons and the North Sea. There was no way for the French to get past.

But on June 15 there was a grand review of the troops quartered in Brussels on the Allée Verte, while crowds of onlookers watched, perhaps with a little more anxiety and slightly less gaiety than they had displayed at similar reviews in previous weeks.

And late that same afternoon, though few people heard of it, news reached the Prince of Orange and the Duke of Wellington that a Prussian brigade had been attacked close to Charleroi and that Thuin had been captured. Later in the day Wellington issued orders for the Second and Fifth Divisions to gather at Ath in readiness to proceed into action as soon as the word was given.

But for those British visitors who were staying in the city, there was still no extraordinary sense of urgency. It was generally known that the Duke of Richmond's ball was to proceed as planned and that most of the officers stationed in or near the city intended to be there. Word still had it that Wellington himself was to be a guest. A group of sergeants and privates of the Forty-second Royal Highlanders and the Ninety-second Foot were to entertain the guests with reels and strathspeys to bagpipe music. It was to be a grand affair indeed.

Fortunately, perhaps, for Morgan, Alleyne had been sent unexpectedly to Antwerp on embassy business and was not expected to return until the next day. She simply *had* to attend the ball. There was a sense of urgency, even a sense of history focused upon the occasion. Everyone knew it was going to be the last chance any of them would have to make merry together.

It was possible, of course, that the gathering of the troops was all so much maneuvering and that within a day or two they would be back in Brussels and Napoléon Bonaparte would be back in France and life would proceed as usual again.

It was more probable, though, that this was no false

alarm but that the armies were amassing for what would prove to be a deadly battle.

## CHAPTER V

UNDER THE CIRCUMSTANCES IT MIGHT HAVE BEEN expected that very few guests would attend the Duke of Richmond's ball on the evening of June 15, but in fact, it turned out to be the grandest squeeze Brussels had seen since the British had started streaming across the English Channel in large numbers more than a month before. Surprising too, perhaps, was the fact that officers of all regiments stationed in and about the city turned out in large numbers. Clad in the bright splendor of their dress uniforms with silk stockings and dancing shoes instead of their boots, they looked as if marching into battle were the farthest thing from their minds.

The ladies sparkled as if there were nothing more important in life than dancing and no place more desirable in which to do it than the Richmond ballroom.

But appearances could be deceptive. Gervase, having paid his respects to the duke and duchess, sought out a group of his male acquaintances and found that they were deep in conversation over the military situation. There was no doubt in any of their minds that by morning the whole army would be marching in the direction of the frontier. The only uncertainty was whether there was likely to be a pitched battle somewhere or whether the strong defenses of the Allies would deter Napoléon Bonaparte and persuade him to retreat. The consensus was that there would be no French retreat and that there would indeed be a battle.

The sounds of animated conversation and laughter rose even above the lively music the orchestra was playing. The rhythmic tread of dozens of feet performing the steps of a country dance underlay the hubbub.

Gervase caught sight of Lady Morgan Bedwyn, flushed and smiling brightly, vividly lovely in a white gown that shimmered in the candlelight. She was dancing with Gordon and seemingly had eyes for no one but him.

Gervase had not expected to see her. A number of British families, especially those with children and young female members, had left for the greater safety of Antwerp or for home itself during the past couple of days. He would have expected Caddick to have more sense than to remain when there were two young ladies in his household as well as his wife, though of course there *was* young Gordon to make them all reluctant to leave. Lady Morgan had probably felt that reluctance too. It was a wonder, though, that her brother who was attached to the embassy had not insisted that she leave.

There was something brittle, almost desperate, about her smile.

He had not spoken with her since that day when they had met on the Allée Verte and ridden together for a while. But he had thought about her a great deal. She had all the almost-unconscious arrogance of the Bedwyns, but she was also intelligent, forthright, and honest—all qualities that he admired. She was also attractive as well as classically beautiful. Despite the untutored way she had kissed him in the Forest of Soignés, she had stirred his blood.

Truth to tell, he was beginning to feel *guilty*. His hatred of Bewcastle and his desire somehow to make him suffer had not been one whit assuaged by the way he had singled out Lady Morgan Bedwyn for dalliance and gossip. But he did feel that perhaps his actions had been small-minded and he had begun to regret them. The best he could do tonight, he decided, was stay away from her.

MORGAN HAD NOT REALIZED until this evening that she would be able to smile and make merry and dance and converse and laugh in the face of such a looming catastrophe. She would have thought such behavior inappropriate, disrespectful, unfeeling, impossible. Yet she was quite incapable of behaving any other way. And if it was any consolation to her, everyone else was doing the same—Rosamond, the officers of their acquaintance, *everyone*.

It was the merriest ball she had attended all Season.

It was also the saddest. Somewhere deep down she was aware of the terrible fragility, the tragically ephemeral nature, of human life.

She danced the opening set with Captain Lord Gordon. She stood at his side later while the bagpipes droned and the Scottish dancers dazzled and awed the gathering with the energy and intricate footwork of their reels and with the imposing visual spectacle they presented with their swaying kilts and tartans. She waltzed with Lord Gordon at midnight, just as the Duke of Wellington was arriving, looking as cheerful and as festive as all the other guests. But by that time rumor had already made the rounds of the ballroom that the Prince of Orange, also a guest, had received a dispatch during supper informing him that Charleroi had fallen.

Charleroi was twenty miles inside the Belgian border.

Morgan's smile had not faltered. Neither had anyone else's.

She felt a strange, almost desperate tenderness for the captain—perhaps because everyone expected that they would make a match of it and he was always so eagerly attentive while she had felt nothing for him since their arrival in Brussels but a mild irritation—and sometimes not even so very mild. Tomorrow he would be going into deadly danger. Tomorrow he might be going to his death.

"I daresay, Lady Morgan," he said cheerfully as they waltzed, "we will have an early start of it tomorrow. But I am glad of that. I am glad Old Boney has dared to come and that we will have our chance to crush him once and for all on the battlefield. We will be heroes tomorrow or the next day or whenever the battle finally comes. I will make you proud of me."

Behind his boastful words, she thought, there must be a terrible fear.

"Your mama and papa and all who know you are already enormously proud of you," she said. "I am sure they do not need you to prove your courage in battle. Perhaps a battle may yet be averted." She did not believe it for a moment.

"Pardon me for having even mentioned such a topic," he said, twirling her with small steps and cautious precision. "I should not worry your pretty little head with such talk."

She tried to ignore the flaring of irritation she always felt when she heard those words. She smiled at him and focused her attention on him. If he needed her company and her admiration tonight, then she would not deny him. There was so *little* women could do.

They had reached the doorway of the ballroom, and he stopped dancing suddenly, caught her impulsively by the hand, and hurried her through it. Crowds milled about outside, but he glanced hastily in both directions and hurried her along a corridor to their right, past open doors leading into busy salons and card rooms, and along to the end, where he drew her into the shadowed privacy afforded by an open door.

"Lady Morgan," he said earnestly, "tomorrow I will be gone to join my regiment. I beg that you will grant me the favor of one kiss before I leave."

She might perhaps have drawn the line at that since she had no wish to be kissed by Captain Lord Gordon, but he did not wait for an answer. He drew her almost roughly into his arms, lowered his head, and kissed her hard. His lips pressed urgently, closed and hot and dry, against her own, bruising the flesh inside against her teeth.

Such behavior would normally have drawn a blistering set-down and a ringing slap across the cheek from Morgan. But not tonight. Tonight, at this moment, she was on the verge of tears, all her gaiety dissipated. She grasped the stiff fabric of his coat at the point where the sleeves met the shoulders and kissed him back with all the tenderness she felt for all the men who might die tomorrow or the next day in the stupid, deadly male game of war.

She was terribly aware of his warmth, his aliveness, his eager youth.

"Lady Morgan," he said with hot intensity when he released her mouth, "permit me, I beg you, to have the honor of fighting for *you* when the battle comes, to know that you wait for me, that you care for me."

He was asking for some promise, for something that of course she could not give. But how could she say a firm no, silly as his words would have sounded to her under ordinary circumstances? These circumstances were by no means ordinary.

"Of course I care," she told him, gazing earnestly at him. "Oh, of course I do."

"Permit me to know," he begged her, grasping her right hand with both his own and pressing it to his heart, "that you will grieve for me if I die, that you will mourn me and wear black for me for the rest of your life, that there will never be another man for you. Permit me to know this."

"Of course I would grieve," she said, beginning to feel uncomfortable. "But please do not talk of dying."

He drew her to him again, his arms even more fierce this time. But before he could lower his head to hers, someone grasped the handle of the door from the other side and pulled it closed. Their private little nook was private no longer. He released his hold on her.

"We must return to the ballroom," she said. "Your mama will be wondering where I am."

He drew her arm through his, set his free hand over hers, and squeezed it hard.

"Thank you," he told her as he led her back to the ballroom. "You have made me the happiest of men, Lady Morgan."

He believed, she thought, shocked and dismayed, that they now had an understanding, that they were just one step away from a betrothal. But she would not—*could* not—disabuse him. There would be time enough to do that when he came back from battle.

*If* he came back.

The noise in the ballroom, though as loud as before, had a different quality to it even though they had been gone for only a few minutes. There were already noticeably fewer uniforms present. Most of the officers who remained were not dancing, though the orchestra was still playing the set of waltzes. They were either in serious-looking groups or were taking their leave of family and friends.

"We have been ordered to leave now, without delay," Major Franks explained, catching Lord Gordon by the sleeve. He smiled and inclined his head to Morgan. "Nothing to worry your pretty head about, my lady. We will be back to waltz with the ladies again within the week."

Morgan heard a ringing sound that could not be coming from the orchestra or anywhere outside her own head. The air she inhaled felt suddenly cold in her nostrils. But she pulled herself together with a determined effort. This was not the time to indulge in her first ever fit of the vapors. She had wanted to come to Brussels, to be a part of history, to be in the thick of the action. She had wanted to know all about it firsthand.

Now that knowledge was almost overwhelming. She wondered if future generations would learn about the Richmond ball and wonder how military men and their women and families could have danced and made merry on the eve of such disaster.

"You must go to your mama immediately," she said briskly to Lord Gordon, noting the chalklike paleness of his face.

AMAZINGLY, THE BALL continued despite the fact that the Duke of Wellington did not stay long and had apparently admitted that they were off to war the next day, and despite the fact that the officers began to slip away to rejoin their regiments until very few remained.

Gervase saw Lady Morgan Bedwyn off on her own at one side of the ballroom, not dancing and not with her chaperon either. She was fanning her face and looking almost as pale as her gown. Her earlier smile and sparkle had deserted her. After a moment's hesitation he made his way toward her and offered her his arm without a word.

"Oh, Lord Rosthorn," she said after looking up at him with blank eyes for a moment. She tucked one slim hand through his arm. "I thought Lady Caddick and Rosamond would need to be alone together for a little while. They are in a great deal of distress."

"Permit me to escort you to the refreshment room and procure you a glass of something to drink," he suggested.

"Lemonade would be good," she said. "No, water. Water would be better."

He could smell violets again. Her hair was dotted with pearls. Small pearls had been sewn into the fabric of her gown, about the low neckline and at the hems of her short sleeves and skirt. She looked exquisitely lovely—and uncharacteristically fragile.

"Will they all be killed, do you suppose?" she asked.

"No," he said gently.

"It was a foolish question," she said. "Some of them will be killed. *Many* of them."

"Yes."

"I suppose my brother Aidan was called to battle like this a dozen times or more," she said. "I am glad now that I was never there, though being at home in ignorance and imagining the worst can be almost as bad. I thought I wanted to be here for this, even *needed* to be here. It promises to be a truly historic event, does it not? If Napoléon Bonaparte wins the battle, his comeback will be spoken of with awe for generations to come. If he loses, the Duke of Wellington's fame may well live through the ages."

He wove a careful path around other guests and led her to the refreshment room, where he fetched her a large glass of water. There were a number of other guests there, all men, gathered together in urgent conversational groups. He took her through into a small anteroom, where a few tables had been set up with chairs ranged around them. There was no one else in there, and of course it was improper to have her alone thus, without her chaperon's knowledge and consent. But propriety—or its absence—was the furthest thing from his mind tonight. She needed sympathetic company, he thought. She looked badly shaken. He seated her at a table, set the glass before her, and took the chair opposite hers.

"And does Captain Lord Gordon mean as much to you as Lord Aidan Bedwyn, your brother?" he asked.

She looked directly at him but did not admonish him for impertinence as she had on a previous occasion.

"He is a young man with vitality and dreams and hopes," she said, her dark eyes luminous. "He is dear to his family—and to himself. And yet he is caught up in this madness that humanity seems prey to. He kissed me before he left and begged me to wait for him and to grieve for him if he dies."

"Ah," he said. He wondered if she would awake tomorrow to the embarrassing memory of having confided something so intimate to a gentleman who was little more than a stranger to her. But then it was unlikely she would sleep tonight.

"How could I possibly have said no?" she asked him. "It would have been selfish, mean, cruel."

"Did you *wish* to say no?" he asked her. He had often wondered if she felt an affection for the boy. He was unworthy of her—a conceited young stripling who showed no sign of growing up into a mature man.

"Such questions ought not to be either asked or answered on a night like this," she said. "Emotion rules tonight. But the choice of a spouse is a serious business, is it not?"

"Is it?" he asked softly. It was something he had not thought about, for years, at least.

"Marriage is for life," she said. "I have always been determined not to choose hastily and not to allow my hand to be forced. It is very easy to fall in love, I believe. It is a highly emotional state. I am not so sure it is as easy to *love*."

"Love does not involve the emotions, then?" he asked her with a smile.

"It is not *ruled* by them," she told him. "Love is liking and companionship and respect and trust. Love does not dominate or try to possess. Love thrives only in a commitment to pure, mutual freedom. That is why marriage is so tricky. There are the marriage ceremony and the marriage vows and the necessity for fidelity—all of them suggestive of restraints, even imprisonment. Men talk of life sentences and leg shackles in connection with marriage, do they not? But marriage ought to be just the opposite—two people agreeing to set each other free."

"Many married gentlemen with their mistresses and married ladies with their cicisbeos would applaud your opinion, *chérie,*" he said.

But she looked at him gravely. "You have not understood," she said. "Anyone who does not intend to keep sacred vows should not make them. Married couples should set each other free to live and learn and find personal fulfillment. They are not two sides of a coin or two halves of a soul. They are two precious individual souls who have joined their freedoms to make something more glorious, more challenging, of their lives."

He was not sure whether to think her foolishly idealistic or wisely mystical. But he *was* fascinated by her. He had not expected that they would have a conversation like this tonight of all nights.

"You wish to love the man you will marry in this grand way, then, *chérie?*" he asked her.

"Yes." She looked directly at him again. "I do not need to marry for money or position, Lord Rosthorn, or even for security. I would rather wait another five or ten years—or even forever—than marry the wrong man. Though I would hope the wait is not forever."

Would the typical very young lady make much of a distinction between being in love and loving? he wondered. Would many ladies of any age state categorically that love and possessiveness could not exist together? He had not even made that leap of understanding himself. She was right, though, was she not? Would there be so many unhappy marriages if there *were* no such distinctions?

"It is a tradition with my family," she explained, "that love be the guiding force of our marriages. Our men are not expected to employ mistresses after they are wed." Her direct gaze did not waver. "They are expected to love their wives and remain true to them. The expectation applies to Bedwyn women too."

He smiled. "And are any of your brothers and sisters married?" he asked. She had mentioned a sister-in-law once, he seemed to recall.

"Three," she said.

"The Duke of Bewcastle is one of them?" he asked. He had not heard of Bewcastle's marrying. But how would he have heard it? He was not up-to-date on all British news and gossip despite these weeks he had spent in Brussels becoming reacquainted with several old friends and acquaintances.

"No." She shook her head. "Aidan is married and so are Rannulf and Freyja—all last year."

"And they were all love matches?" he asked.

"They are now," she said with conviction. "Rannulf and Judith have a new son."

Had Bewcastle loved Marianne? Gervase wondered suddenly. Had he been prepared to love her all his life? To remain faithful to her? He doubted it. It had always seemed to him that Bewcastle was incapable of love.

"And you do not love young Gordon as you would wish to love a husband?" he asked her. "And yet you did not say no to him tonight?"

"I did not quite say yes either," she told him, "but I doubt he noticed. I will have to say a firm no when he returns."

"He will be disappointed," he said.

"He would be more so," she told him, "if I married him. I do not believe I would be an easy woman to live with, Lord Rosthorn, even if I loved with all my heart. Captain Gordon does not love me. He loves the *idea* of me—a duke's daughter who has just made her come-out and is very wealthy. There is nothing else."

She was doing herself a gross injustice, he thought. But she looked up at him suddenly, her eyes stricken.

"He may die," she said. "How *stupid* all this is, Lord

Rosthorn. Stupid and deadly serious. How could I have sent him away with the truth ringing in his ears? I allowed him to believe that I feel as he does, that I will wait for him, grieve for him for the rest of my life if he does not return. And perhaps I will too. Who knows?"

Her eyes filled with sudden tears.

He reached across the table and set one hand over hers. She turned her own beneath it and clasped his hand tightly while she dashed at her tears with her free hand.

"I do not want this to be happening," she said fiercely. "Any of it. Can no one understand that war solves nothing? There will always be war, *always* in the name of freedom and peace. How can there be freedom when men die senselessly? How can there be peace when men have to fight to attain it? Humanity will always run in pursuit of those two desirable states and never ever find them." She looked at him with flushed cheeks and passionate gaze.

Two couples entered the room, took one look at them—and at their clasped hands—and backed out with muffled apologies. Lady Morgan appeared not even to notice.

"I daresay," he said, "Caddick will take you away from Brussels in the morning. Within a week or so you will be back in England with your family and life will seem less tumultuous again."

"It will not," she said. "Please do not patronize me, Lord Rosthorn—not you of all people. I would rather stay here. I would rather *know*. I would rather suffer with everyone else. But even if the Earl of Caddick does not insist that we all leave, Alleyne will. He has been in Antwerp, but he will return tomorrow. He told me before he left that he would insist I leave then if the situation had not improved. It has worsened." She sighed. "What will *you* do, Lord Rosthorn?"

"Stay here," he said. "I am not a military man, but perhaps there will be some way in which I can make myself useful."

"That is what I would like to do," she said. "I would like to make myself useful. You cannot imagine how helpless one feels as a woman in a situation like this—or in a thousand other circumstances, for that matter. But I daresay I will be leaving here tomorrow."

"I am on the Rue de Brabant," he said, and he gave her the house name. "If by any chance you have need of me, will you send for me?"

She half smiled at him.

"Because I am too weak to manage on my own? But it is a kind offer and I thank you for it." She looked down at their clasped hands, seemed to notice the connection for the first time, and slid her hand away to rest in her lap. "I believe I have been prattling. I tend to do that when I feel passionately about an issue. I feel passionate about war. It would seem strange, then, would it not, that I felt constrained to come here to Brussels even though my brother did not wish to give his consent? We ought not to be here alone, ought we? But nothing is as it should be tonight. Will you escort me back to Lady Caddick?"

He stood and offered his arm.

"The wars will be over," he said, "at least for a while.

And your dream of love will surely come true in time, *chérie*. You will be happy again."

She laughed softly. "Is that a promise, Lord Rosthorn?"

"Ah, but dreams cannot be captured with promises," he said. "Like water, they elude our grasp. But water is the staff of life. I *believe* your dream will come true if only because you will not compromise on it and let it go too lightly."

She laughed again. "I have not even asked you about your dreams," she said. "How unmannerly of me!"

"I am far too old for them," he said as he led her back into the ballroom, sparsely populated now.

It was perfectly true. He had dreamed powerful dreams as a very young man, and he had fully expected that most of them would come to fulfillment. But his youth had come to a premature end nine years ago. He had lived firmly within the realm of reality since then.

"But you must have dreams," she told him, "or life loses its focus, its passion, its very meaning."

Was *that* what had happened to his life? he wondered.

Lady Caddick was on her feet, watching their approach with an air of distraction.

"Ah, there you are, Lady Morgan," she said. "We are ready to go home."

Lady Rosamond Havelock at her side looked as if she had been weeping. She cast herself into Lady Morgan's arms, and they hugged each other tightly.

# Chapter VI

On the morning after the Duke of Richmond's ball, there was a general exodus from Brussels to Antwerp of those foreigners not connected with the military. By midday the roads were clogged with them and with their carriages and horses and baggage carts.

The Caddicks and Morgan were not among them. Rosamond had awoken with one of her infrequent but crippling migraine headaches. It was indeed more than a headache—it half blinded her, caused nausea and numbness down her left side, and made light and even the slightest sound or movement quite intolerable to her. Despite all the danger of remaining in Brussels and despite the urgings of her husband, who had never suffered from migraines as she herself had and therefore could not imagine how totally incapacitating they were, Lady Caddick remained adamant. Rosamond must remain where she was—quietly shut up in her bedchamber—until the worst of the indisposition was over. Sometimes these bouts lasted for three, four, even five days.

Lord Caddick offered to find someone willing to chaperon Morgan and take her to safety, but she assured him that Alleyne would be back from Antwerp soon and would make suitable arrangements for her himself.

Common sense told her that she should go as soon as possible, even if doing so meant traveling with near strangers. But it was hard to behave with common sense under such dire circumstances. The fact was that she could not bear to leave. She had acquaintances and even a few friends among the officers of the Life Guards and their wives. Most of the latter were remaining. Why not she, then? How could she leave and not know what happened to any of those acquaintances?

She had spoken the truth to Lord Caddick. Even so, she hoped that Alleyne would not return from Antwerp in time to send her on her way today. Perhaps by tomorrow there would be more news from the front. Perhaps the hostilities would all be over by then and she would not need to leave at all.

Alleyne had still not come by midday.

During the afternoon, restless and wanting to leave the house as quiet as possible for poor Rosamond, Morgan obtained permission from Lady Caddick to visit Mrs. Clark, wife of Major Clark of the Life Guards. She lived just a ten-minute walk away, and Morgan promised to take her maid with her. It was while she was taking tea with Mrs. Clark that she heard what at first she took for distant thunder. But Mrs. Clark smiled rather tensely when Morgan expressed the hope that there would be no torrential rain to increase the discomforts of the troops.

"That is the sound of heavy guns," she explained.

Morgan could feel the blood drain out of her head.

"They are far away," Mrs. Clark told her. "It is more a feeling, a vibration, than a sound, is it not? And who is to know where exactly it is coming from or who is involved in the action? Or indeed whether they are our guns or those of the French?"

Morgan half expected that Alleyne would come for her before it was time to leave. But she walked home with only her maid for company.

Alleyne had not called at the Rue de Bellevue. He did not call there for the rest of the day.

During the night they were kept awake for a long time—and Rosamond's sufferings were considerably increased—by the almost-incessant rumbling of wheels on the street, combined with the clopping of horses' hooves and the occasional shouting of men's voices.

They were not to be alarmed, Lord Caddick called from the corridor outside the bedchambers. The commotion was merely that of a long train of artillery passing through Brussels on its way to the front.

*Not be alarmed?* Morgan, who was standing at her window, a shawl about her shoulders, shivered.

Where was Alleyne? she wondered.

*Where were the officers she knew?*

By the following day it was too late to leave Brussels even though Rosamond emerged from her room looking like a heavy-eyed ghost to assure her mama and papa that the migraine attack was not as severe as some others she had suffered and that she was ready to travel at a moment's notice.

Early in the morning a troop of Belgian cavalry had ridden through Brussels from the direction of the front—Morgan had been awoken yet again by the noise—shouting to everyone they passed and to the sleepers inside the houses that all was lost and a crushing defeat had been suffered. But they had not stayed to answer anyone's questions.

They left panic in their wake.

Almost all the remaining visitors and many of the permanent residents were hastening to leave the city into which ravening French soldiers might be pouring at any moment. At the Caddick household all trunks and bags were packed and all was ready for departure after an early breakfast.

But there was an unexpected complication. When Lord Caddick sent for the carriage and horses and the baggage coach to be brought up to the front door, he was informed that everything on wheels had been requisitioned by the army for the conveyance of supplies to the front. No matter how much the earl ranted and raved and threatened and cajoled and was prepared to bribe, it quickly became apparent that indeed there was no conveyance to be had. There was no way of leaving Brussels that day unless they were prepared to go on foot, taking with them only what they could carry in their hands and on their backs.

That, of course, as Lady Caddick pointed out in a voice that expressed more outrage than fright, was out of the question.

And so they were trapped in Brussels.

Morgan, although she felt undeniably afraid, was glad.

Rosamond staggered back to bed.

IT BEGAN TO RAIN DURING the afternoon. There was a dreadful thunderstorm through the night—a real one this time—and the rain was torrential for hours on end.

It was impossible to know exactly where the armies were or what the meaning of yesterday's distant guns was. But as Morgan lay curled up in bed, resisting the urge to cover her head with the blankets and try to block out the sound, she found that it was not difficult to imagine the misery of thousands of men trying to find shelter and rest where there was none to be had.

At least, Lord Caddick announced cheerfully at breakfast, the rain would have made travel and easy maneuvering impossible. The roads would be quite impassable. There could be no possibility of a battle today.

Besides, Lady Caddick added, it was Sunday.

Morgan was worried about Alleyne. She was also concerned about Rosamond, who was still suffering miserably with her migraine attack. Lady Caddick was almost beside herself with distress, partly over her daughter's indisposition, partly over the threat to her own safety, but mainly over the uncertainty of Lord Gordon's fate. Lord Caddick ventured out to find what news was available, though there seemed to be far more rumor making the rounds than hard fact.

The rain had finally stopped, and Morgan, obtaining permission from a distracted countess again, took her maid and went to Mrs. Clark's house once more. The wives of the regiment's officers often gathered there, she had discovered, and on the whole they tended to be far more sensible than most other people, much less given to panic and belief in every sensational story that presented itself in place of reliable news. They were all gathered together on this particular morning. Morgan was relieved to find that they received her warmly as if she were one of them, not as an unwelcome intruder.

Shortly after midday the guns of the heavy artillery began firing again. They were closer than they had been the day before yesterday. It was impossible, after the first startled moment, to mistake their constant pounding for thunder.

The ladies spent a couple of hours sorting the medicines and other supplies they had gathered during the past day and a half, and rolling bandages. They talked quietly and even laughed as they worked, but Morgan, who joined in as busily as anyone else, could feel the tension and the taut fear that pulsed beneath the cheerfulness as they all tried to ignore the significance of what they did.

How difficult it must be, she thought, to be a wife who followed the drum year after year.

They were interrupted partway through the afternoon by a commotion on the street outside. Several of them crowded to the windows while Mrs. Clark and Morgan rushed outdoors. Foam-flecked horses galloped past, bearing cavalry with drawn swords. They were coming from the direction of the Namur Gates at the southern end of the city—from the direction of the battle.

"They are Hanoverians," Mrs. Clark said. "Not the Life Guards."

If they were galloping through other streets in as large numbers as they were doing in this one, Morgan thought, there must surely be a whole regiment of them. They were yelling in German, a language she did not speak. But there were plenty of people on the street willing to interpret.

"All is lost!" one man shouted.

"The French are on their heels," someone else reported.

Panic seized many of the other spectators. But Mrs. Clark took Morgan firmly by the arm and led her back inside the house. She shut the door behind them.

"The wounded will be arriving soon," she told the other ladies. "If the report is correct, the battle is lost and the French will be here soon too. But they will have wounded as well. We can either cower here and panic, or we can go out there and do what we can to help those who will need our help, regardless of the color of their uniform or what side they fought on."

Morgan looked at her with renewed respect and admiration and drew a deep, steadying breath. She had not been so far from panic herself just a few minutes before, she admitted to herself.

"I would rather go out there," she said.

Mrs. Clark swung toward her.

"But *you* really ought not, Lady Morgan," she said. "You should return to the Rue de Bellevue. The Countess of Caddick will be worried about you. What we are about to do is dangerous. More than that, it will be horrifying and distasteful. The sights will not be pretty."

"I do not expect them to be," Morgan said. "And I am not a hothouse plant merely because I am the daughter of a duke and unmarried. I will do my part. Please don't argue with me. I believe you are going to need every pair of hands available within a short time. As for Lady Caddick, she has Rosamond to tend and Captain Gordon to worry about. She knows I am with you."

Mrs. Clark did not waste more time on words. She simply nodded briskly and reached out one hand to squeeze Morgan's.

"We will go as far as the Namur Gates, then," she said.

IT WAS THERE THAT Lord Alleyne Bedwyn found Morgan an hour or so later. Not that he was searching for her. He had imagined her far away from Brussels by now. All the way back from Antwerp he had looked for her among the crowds of people moving in the opposite direction. But he had not worried when he did not see her. She was probably on a ship bound for England by now, he had convinced himself.

He had reported to Sir Charles Stuart without even thinking to call first at the house on the Rue de Bellevue that the Earl of Caddick had rented. He was now on his way south with a message for the Duke of Wellington. He had volunteered for the task. It might be a dangerous mission, Sir Charles had warned him, if the sounds of heavy artillery were any indication of the ferocity of the battle that was raging. But Alleyne had a hankering to see for himself what was going on. Besides, his elder brother, Aidan, had fought throughout the Peninsular Wars. Was *he* to shy away from merely delivering a letter to the battlefront?

Wounded from the past few days were beginning to straggle into Brussels on foot, some with bandaged heads or arms in slings, most without any covering for their bloody wounds beyond some torn and grubby rags. Alleyne looked with sympathy at the men as he approached the Namur Gates on his way south, and with admiration at the group of ladies who had already set up a makeshift bandaging station there.

One of the wounded was explaining to the lady who was holding a glass of water to his lips that today's fighting—a desperate and deadly battle—was taking place just south of the Forest of Soignés, not far from the village of Waterloo.

The lady was Morgan.

Alleyne swung down from the saddle at the same moment as she set down the glass and looked up and spotted him. She came rushing into his arms.

*"Alleyne!"* she cried. "Wherever have you been? I was worried about you."

He held her by the shoulders and shook her none too gently.

"What the devil are *you* doing here?" he asked her. "Why are you not in Antwerp by now, or on your way to England?"

"You told me you would come for me the morning after the Richmond ball," she reminded him.

"Devil take it, Morg," he said, exasperated, "I was delayed in Antwerp. Never tell me you did not have the sense to leave with the Caddicks. I'll have a word or two—"

"They are still here too," she said. "You do not imagine they would leave without me, do you? Lady Caddick takes her responsibility toward me very seriously." She explained to him the series of events that had kept them in Brussels.

"Devil take it," he said again. "I am going to have to get you out of here myself, Morg. We will be on our way as soon as I have completed this little bit of embassy business."

"I am needed here," she protested. "I am going to *be* needed for some time to come. I will do my part, Alleyne, even if I cannot actually fight the French as Aidan did. You must not worry about me."

He grasped her shoulders more tightly. "Wulf will have my head," he said, "and I can hardly blame him. I'll be back before nightfall. Then I'll be taking you away from here."

"Alleyne." She cupped his elbows with her hands. "Where are you going? Why are you here at these particular gates?"

"I have a message to deliver to the front," he told her.

Her eyes widened.

"Don't worry." He grinned at her. "I am not riding into battle, Morg. There will be no heroics for me. I'll be quite safe."

"Take care, then." She took a deep, slow breath. "Alleyne, if you should happen to hear word of the Life Guards . . ." She did not complete the thought. She did not need to. He pulled her into his arms for a quick, rough hug.

"I'll see what I can find out," he promised before releasing her and swinging back up into the saddle.

Through the gates behind her two cartloads of wounded were rumbling. There was the sudden stench of blood in the air, stronger than before.

She turned away, distracted, without saying farewell, and he rode off south through the gates.

Morgan, he thought. The youngest of them. All grown up and behaving with foolish courage, doing what would send most ladies twice her age into fits of the vapors. Actually he might have expected it of her, though. As much as Freyja—perhaps even more so—she despised the current image of the perfect lady as a wilting violet. He strongly suspected that it was the approach of hostilities that had drawn her to Brussels even more than Gordon. Gordon, in his estimation, was something of a popinjay.

He was damned proud of Morgan, out on the streets as she was tending the wounded instead of cowering inside the house on the Rue de Bellevue. But for all that, he had a quarrel with the Countess of Caddick, who had been entrusted with her care.

Wulf would have his head for not having sent her home long ago.

IT WAS A FEW HOURS after that when Gervase found Morgan in the same place. By that time a steady trickle of wounded had arrived, some of them severely injured. There were surgeons on the spot, doing what they could to deal with the worst of the wounds, plying their dreadful trade in makeshift tents. There were many women there too, cleansing wounds, bandaging the less serious ones, offering water and whatever comfort they could to the others.

It had been clear to Gervase as soon as he heard the

guns that within a few hours the press of wounded would present the city with a huge problem, quite beyond the power of the volunteers gathered at the gates to deal with. What was needed was some organization—a list of houses and their occupants both able and willing to accommodate the wounded, a way of directing wounded, surgeons, and nurses to those houses, and a way of supplying them with all that would be needed.

There were doubtless numerous other people setting about such organization, he thought. But there was no way of coordinating the efforts of them all. He could only do his part. He gathered together as many willing acquaintances as he could find, and together they did what they could, knocking on house doors up one side of each street and down the other, calling on apothecaries and grocers and anyone else who could possibly sell them supplies for a thousand wounded and more, and making endless lists.

Finally they were ready to approach the Namur Gates and set up a station whose purpose would be to direct bearers of the wounded to homes where they would find clean beds and food and water and a roof over their heads, and where they would be tended by kindhearted nurses and physicians.

There were all too few of those last two, of course, but one could only do one's best.

One very young lady was bent over what appeared to be a pile of bloody rags on the ground, Gervase noticed. The pile of rags turned out to be a young private covered with mud and blood, his right leg blown away from the knee down. Her hair was bound up in a blood- and dirt-smeared kerchief. Her muslin dress was creased and dirty and liberally streaked with blood. She was murmuring soft words to the lad as she cleaned his face with a wet cloth. He was in line—a long line—for a surgeon's care.

And then she stood up and passed the back of her wrist over her eyes in a weary gesture.

Good Lord! He suddenly stood rooted to the spot. She was Lady Morgan Bedwyn.

He hurried toward her and cupped one of her elbows with his hand.

"You are still in Brussels?" he asked unnecessarily.

For a moment she looked at him without recognition. Then she blinked her eyes.

"Lord Rosthorn," she said.

He could hardly believe the evidence of his own eyes.

"The Earl and Countess of Caddick have not taken you back to safety?" he asked her. "Lord Alleyne Bedwyn has not?"

"There were no conveyances to be had when we would have left," she explained to him. "And Alleyne was delayed in Antwerp. He returned only today. He had to ride toward the front on embassy business."

"What are you doing *here?*" he asked her.

"Is it not obvious?" She smiled wanly. "There is so much to do, Lord Rosthorn. I must not stand here conversing with you."

At that moment he realized that she was indeed a woman through and through—a woman with a tender heart and the strength and courage to go with it. He had known almost from the start of their acquaintance that she was no simpering miss, but now he had incontrovertible proof. Today, at this moment, she looked more beautiful than she had on any previous occasion.

He released her elbow.

"Go, then," he said. "Go back to work."

He worked there too for a number of hours—he lost track of just how many. He unloaded the wounded and helped sort them into groups—those who needed some ministration but not the services of a surgeon, those who were in need of amputation, those whose needs were reduced to a drink of water and a comforting hand to help them die. He found himself offering that drink of water and that comforting hand over and over again. At the same time he tried to fulfill his primary function in being where he was. He tried to find billets for all the wounded men who could not simply walk away on their own two legs.

Finally, at some time during the evening, one of John Waldane's friends came to relieve him, and Gervase set both hands on his hips and stretched his back and rolled his shoulder muscles. It was strange how quickly one's eyes and ears could become accustomed to such sights and sounds and one's nose to such smells. It had not even occurred to him after the first few moments to feel squeamish.

Lady Morgan Bedwyn, looking dirtier and more disheveled than ever, was kneeling beside a grizzled sergeant in rifle green, tying an arm sling in a firm knot behind his neck while saying something that made the man laugh gruffly.

Gervase approached her and waited until she had finished and got to her feet.

*"Chérie,"* he said, "it is time that you rested. Allow me to escort you home to the Rue de Bellevue."

But she shook her head. "I cannot go back there until I have heard some definite news," she said. "That sergeant"—she indicated the man she had just tended—"told me that Lord Uxbridge led a massive cavalry charge this afternoon, and they swept aside all in their path and set the French to rout. But they kept going for too long, beyond enemy lines, and got cut down in their turn. He does not know what the casualties were."

For a moment her face threatened to crumple, but she pulled herself together and smiled instead.

"None of them has come back here yet," she said. "I suppose that is good news. No one knows if the battle is won or lost. But it will be dark soon. They cannot fight after dark, can they?"

"You need some rest," he told her firmly. "You will be no good to anyone if you push yourself too far."

"Mrs. Clark has opened her house to the wounded," she said. "We have been meaning to go there for the past hour, but there always seems one more thing to do. The house is ready, though. I have agreed to take the night shift. I would not be able to sleep anyway." She tipped her head from side to side as she spoke, and half closed her eyes.

Gervase set his hands on her shoulders and turned her to face away from him. He massaged her shoulders and neck muscles with his thumbs and fingers until she sighed and dropped her head forward.

"Alleyne has not come back yet," she said. "He told me he would be back before nightfall. That is now. He will surely be here soon."

"Let me take you to Mrs. Clark's," he suggested. "Someone can direct your brother there. If there are not many wounded there yet or if there is plenty of help, perhaps you can snatch a short rest. Or a cup of tea at the very least."

"That sounds like heaven," she admitted.

"Or a wash," he said.

She looked down at herself ruefully. "This is one of my smartest dresses," she said. "Or was. I doubt I will be able to wear it again—or want to."

He offered her his arm and she took it. It was difficult now to remember how she had looked to him the first time he set eyes on her—breathtakingly lovely but haughty and aristocratic too. She had looked to him rather like a spoiled child. It was shameful to remember that he had sought an acquaintance with her only because she was Bewcastle's sister—as if she could not possibly have any identity of her own.

"I am glad I am still in Brussels," she said. "I am glad I have seen what I have seen today. Most of all I am glad that I have been able in some way to make myself useful. But how pointless it all is. If we lose this battle, what will have been the point of it all? If we win, what will have been the point for all the French dead and wounded? I cannot make any distinction, can you? The French and the English and Germans and Belgians and Dutch—they are all foolish, brave men. Though perhaps not so very foolish. It is not they, after all, who have decided to fight this battle today. It is their leaders. I am sorry. I have harped on this theme before in your company. I must let it go and simply face the reality of what has happened and is happening."

He set a hand over hers on his arm.

"I will, if I may," he said, "take word of your whereabouts to the Countess of Caddick."

"Oh, yes, please," she said. "It is remiss of me not to have thought of that for myself."

The Caddicks, he thought uncharitably, deserved to be strung up by their thumbs. Had they made no effort all day to discover where she was? And why had they not insisted days ago that she leave Brussels even if they were unwilling to go themselves?

"It will be my pleasure, *chérie,*" he told her.

"Your mother is French," she said. "Do you ever find that your sympathies lie with her countrymen, Lord Rosthorn?"

"I do," he said, "though I do not often say so aloud to an Englishman or an Englishwoman. But my father was English, you see. I have loyalties to both countries, which is perhaps why I have never felt any great inclination to become a military officer myself."

She looked gravely up at him, but she did not ask any more questions. She stopped outside the house that must be Mrs. Clark's and turned to thank him for escorting her. The doors of the house, he noticed, were wide open, the building full of light. She would stay up all night doing what she could to make the wounded comfortable, ensuring that those who had survived the battlefield would not now die of fever or neglect.

He took both her hands in his, bowed over them, and raised them one at a time to his lips.

"Go on in, then, *chérie,*" he said. "I will call in the morning to make sure that you are resting."

"Thank you," she said. "What will you be doing tonight, Lord Rosthorn?"

"Returning to the gates," he said. "Perhaps even riding a little way into the forest. It *is* getting dark. The guns have stopped, as you may have noticed. The battle will have been won or lost. Or perhaps it is in a stalemate and will resume on the morrow."

"If you happen to see Alleyne," she asked him, "will you direct him here, Lord Rosthorn? And if you have word of—of anyone else, will you let us know here?"

He was not sure if she meant Captain Lord Gordon specifically or all the Guards of her acquaintance generally. But she might have been moping over them all day at Caddick's house on the Rue de Bellevue. Instead she had spent the day out on the streets tending the wounded, keeping her own feelings under control and deeply hidden. But the feelings, the raw pain of worry, were there, he knew.

"I will, *chérie,*" he said, and watched her until she was inside the house before turning away in the direction of the Rue de Bellevue. He found the countess so distraught over the lack of news of her son that it seemed to Gervase she had not even noticed that her charge had not returned home since morning.

"She is with Mrs. Clark, is she, Lord Rosthorn?" she said after he had given his message. "A good sort of woman though the major might have done better for himself. I daresay she and Lady Morgan have been holding each other's hand all day and comforting each other."

Gervase did not explain what the ladies *had* been doing. He took his leave and walked to the stable where his horse was kept and rode out for a few miles to the south of the city even though the heavy dusk had turned almost to darkness.

The news he heard as he went was progressively more encouraging. The battle had been won, it would seem, though no one appeared quite certain. The Prussians had come late to reinforce the hard-pressed British and Allied forces, and the French had been routed. The Allies were going after them and were prepared to chase them all the way to Paris if necessary.

Gervase might have ridden farther for more definite news, but as he made his slow way past cart upon cart of the wounded, he spotted a bier being carried by two soldiers—a wounded officer occupied it, he guessed. He could see the Guards uniform of the stricken man even in the darkness and rode closer.

"Who?" he asked.

"Captain Lord Gordon, sir," one of the men said. "Wounded in the cavalry charge this afternoon but only recently found."

"Badly wounded?" Gervase asked.

But the captain was conscious and could answer for himself.

"A damned broken leg," he said. "It is you, is it, Rosthorn? If I could have pulled my foot free of the stirrup I would have taken no harm, and I would have slashed my way through a few more of the Frogs. But my horse fell on me and I had to play dead until the action was all over."

He set one hand over his eyes.

"The battle *is* over, then?" Gervase asked.

"By Jove, yes," Gordon said. "We broke the back of their attack, and after that it was just a matter of time." He swore suddenly and viciously at the bearers of his bier, one of whom had just stumbled over a stone.

"Bastards! Oafs!" he said in conclusion. "No one seems to understand the extent of my pain. Would you be a good fellow, Rosthorn, and ride on ahead to warn my mother that I am coming and to make sure my father summons the best physician in Brussels?"

"What do you know of the fate of the rest of the Life Guards?" Gervase asked. But he had to wait awhile for his answer as Gordon ground his teeth against a spasm of pain.

"Too many of us died," he said. "The Life Guards will never be quite the same. But we saved Europe and England from Bonaparte."

"Major Clark?" Gervase asked.

"Oh, he lives," Captain Gordon assured him. "He came to talk to me when they were loading me up. He is pushing on to Paris with the rest of the army. Lucky bastard."

"I'll ride back to Brussels, then," Gervase assured him.

He went first to the Rue de Bellevue to assure the Earl and Countess of Caddick that their son was alive though hurt. But he did not wait for Gordon to arrive or offer to go in search of a physician. He rode over to Mrs. Clark's house instead.

A maid answered his knock on the door. He could see even before he stepped inside that every available space was being used for the wounded. There were three pallets in the small hallway alone.

Lady Morgan herself came hurrying out of an inner room less than a minute after the maid had disappeared. She was looking drawn and tired, but she had washed her face and brushed her hair and still bore herself with proud, upright carriage.

"The battle is over and was a victory for the Allies," he told her without preamble. "Major Clark is safe, and Captain Gordon is being carried back home, alive but with a broken leg. My guess is that he will live and make a full recovery."

He watched her eyes grow huge and her teeth clamp onto her lower lip. Then she hurried toward him, stepping around one pallet as she came, held out her hands to him, and stood on tiptoe to kiss his cheek.

"Thank you for bringing the news," she said, squeezing his hands. "Thank you, Lord Rosthorn. You are very kind. And Alleyne?"

"I did not see him or hear anything of him," he said regretfully. "But he will surely be back tomorrow or, more probably, later tonight."

"Yes," she said. "I suppose so."

One of the men in the hall coughed and groaned and called out. Lady Morgan pulled her hands free and bent over his pallet without further ado.

Mrs. Clark, he could see, was hurrying down the

stairs, her eyes on him, one hand pressed to her throat.

"Your husband is safe, ma'am, and the battle is won," Gervase told her.

## CHAPTER VII

THERE WAS NOWHERE FOR MORGAN TO SLEEP AT Mrs. Clark's when she was relieved of her night duty early the next morning, though she would have stayed close if she could. However, she was also eager to hurry back to the house on the Rue de Bellevue. Captain Lord Gordon would be there. Perhaps he would have more news of the battle and of the other officers she knew. At the same time, she dreaded meeting him again. Would he try to hold her to the promises he thought she had made at the Richmond ball? Or would he be embarrassed by the memories and be as ready to forget as she?

The Earl of Caddick and Rosamond were at breakfast. The latter got to her feet when she saw Morgan, hugged her tightly, and burst into tears.

"The battle was won," she said when she could, "but we do not know yet who lived and who died. Ambrose lives. Mama has been up all night with him and is even now in his bedchamber."

"His leg?" Morgan asked, genuinely concerned for him. There had been so many amputations . . .

"It is broken in two places," the earl told her. "It got caught beneath his horse when he fell. But they were clean breaks and the leg did not have to be sawn off. It has been set, and the physician believes he will make a full recovery and not even have a permanent limp."

Morgan sighed aloud with relief and Rosamond hugged her again and shed a few more tears.

"I am dreadfully sorry that I prevented everyone's leaving for safety a few days ago," she said. "You must have been in a panic, Morgan. But all has turned out for the best, after all, has it not? There is no more threat to Brussels, and we have Ambrose here with us instead of in a field hospital somewhere with hundreds of others. I cannot even bear the thought of it, can you?"

Morgan shook her head.

"We are going to take him home to England," Rosamond told her. "Mama wants to have him tended by our own physician in London. Papa has procured two carriages and we are to leave early in the morning. Is not that delightful news?"

Morgan nodded.

"You look tired, Lady Morgan," the earl observed. "The worry, I daresay. But all has ended well."

Rosamond, her own news exhausted, took a step back and appeared to notice her friend's less than pristine appearance for the first time.

"There is *blood* on your dress," she said. "Whatever have you done to hurt yourself, Morgan? Do come and sit down. I thought you stayed at Mrs. Clark's last night."

"I did." Morgan sank down onto the chair a servant pulled out hastily from the table. "I tended the wounded there. There are so many, Rosamond—hundreds upon hundreds. I daresay there are a thousand more still on the battlefield or on the road back to Brussels. There are twenty at Mrs. Clark's alone. There were twenty-one, but one died in the night. I have been relieved for a few hours, but I must go back before noon. There is so much to do and so few hands."

Rosamond sat on the chair beside hers and gazed at her in wide-eyed fascination.

"Tending the wounded?" she said. "How splendidly brave of you. I'll come with you when you return even though just the sight of the blood on your dress makes me feel faint. I have almost completely recovered from my migraine."

"You will not go anywhere, miss," her father said firmly. "The battle may be over, but the streets will be filled with all sorts of ruffians today. You will remain indoors where your mama and I can keep an eye on you. I have no doubt Lady Caddick will require the same of you, Lady Morgan. I would have expected Mrs. Clark to behave more responsibly."

Lady Caddick herself arrived on the scene at that moment. She looked haggard, but as her eyes fell upon Morgan, they lit up with happiness.

"Wonderful news, my dear Lady Morgan!" she exclaimed. "I daresay you have heard that the French have been soundly beaten. Gordon has become a great hero. He is dreadfully wounded, the poor boy, but he is suffering bravely—and gladly too. His wounds are no more than badges of honor, he tells me. Can you imagine such nobility of mind?"

"I am very relieved that he is safe, ma'am," Morgan assured her.

"We will be taking my boy back to England tomorrow," Lady Caddick said. "You will be delighted to return to the bosom of your family, Lady Morgan."

"Did Alleyne call here last evening?" Morgan asked.

"Lord Alleyne Bedwyn?" the countess said. "I do not believe so. Did he, Caddick?"

The earl grunted, a sound Morgan interpreted as a negative. "Like you," he told his wife, "Lady Morgan has been up all night. I would suggest toast and tea for both of you and retirement to your beds. Rosamond will sit with Gordon."

"He has just taken another dose of laudanum," the countess explained, seating herself at the table, "and will sleep for a while, I daresay. He will certainly wish to see you when he awakes, Lady Morgan. He spoke of you several times during the night. I must warn you, though, that you may find the sight of him too much for your tender sensibilities. He has numerous other wounds besides his broken leg."

Morgan's heart sank—he had spoken of her. He would wish to see her. But at least he was safe. What about Alleyne? And there were twenty men at Mrs. Clark's who all needed almost constant tending. Many of their lives hung in the balance. More than anything else at that moment, though, she needed to sleep. She was silently thankful that Lord Gordon had taken laudanum and was in no condition to receive a visitor. Later she would have to see him—and later too she would deal with the prospect of going back home and abandoning all the misery here.

She ate a slice of toast and drank a cup of tea, more

because she felt she ought than because she was hungry. Rosamond took her arm then and led her up to her room. She kissed Morgan's cheek before leaving.

"I am so very proud of you," she said, "for tending the wounded. Oh, Morgan, I do so *hope* we will be sisters."

Morgan smiled wanly as she went into her room and closed the door behind her. Her maid helped her off with her dress and she sank onto her bed and closed her eyes. But just before she drifted off to sleep, she remembered something.

She had kissed the Earl of Rosthorn on the cheek last evening. Not because they had been flirting or dallying. Not because he had challenged her or because she had felt challenged. But because he had shown compassion for her and for Mrs. Clark. Because he had been at the Namur Gates for hours earlier in the day, trying to make sure that all the wounded had somewhere to go to recover and be comfortable.

Because she had felt his kindness.

Because he had somehow been transformed in her eyes from a potentially dangerous rake whose flirtations it had been a challenge to resist to a friend.

Was that a fanciful thought?

She fell asleep before she could answer her own question.

GERVASE CALLED AT Mrs. Clark's after an early breakfast with the intention of escorting Lady Morgan Bedwyn back to the Caddick house on the Rue de Bellevue. He had, however, missed her by ten minutes.

He spent the rest of the morning doing his best to help organize the huge influx of wounded from the battlefield south of Waterloo. The number of casualties was truly staggering, yet he realized he was seeing only those who had been removed from the battle site. There must be thousands more still out there.

He called at Lord Caddick's house at noon and sent in his card.

"It was good of you to come, Rosthorn," the earl said, coming into the hall in person to shake hands with his visitor, "especially when all must be chaos out in the streets and it is safer to remain indoors. My son is doing as well as can be expected, you will be pleased to know. His leg has been set and his other wounds treated. We have hopes that he will make a full recovery as soon as we have him home in England."

"You are leaving soon, sir?" Gervase asked. The very best thing for Lady Morgan Bedwyn was to be taken out of such an insalubrious environment. Yet he realized that he would miss her—strange thought.

"We will make an early start in the morning," the earl told him.

But at that moment Lady Morgan herself came hurrying into the hall. She was looking somewhat pale, but her hair had been freshly brushed and coiled, and she wore a clean dress.

"Lord Rosthorn," she asked as he bowed to her, "have you heard anything of my brother?"

To his shame he had scarcely given a thought this morning to Lord Alleyne Bedwyn, who could, he supposed, look after himself.

"I am afraid not," he said.

Some of the light went out of her eyes.

"I daresay," she said, "he was so busy with yesterday's emergencies that he forgot he was supposed to be coming to take me away from here. He would have known after the victory that I am safe here in Brussels, anyway, and that there is now no great hurry to leave."

"I would not say that, Lady Morgan," Caddick told her. "Lady Caddick is afraid that if our own physician does not see Gordon's leg within the week and ascertain that it has been properly set and splinted, he will limp for the rest of his life after all."

Gervase kept his eyes on Lady Morgan and saw her frown slightly.

"Permit me," he said, "to find Sir Charles Stuart and ask news of Lord Alleyne from him. I will bring word back here to you as soon as possible in order to relieve your anxiety."

"How very kind of you," she said. "But would you please bring that word to Mrs. Clark's? I must return there immediately. I slept longer than I intended."

*"Return?"* Caddick sounded genuinely shocked. "To Mrs. Clark's, Lady Morgan? When she has twenty wounded men occupying her house? That is not a proper environment for a lady."

"Or for anyone else, my lord," she agreed. "But those men are suffering as Lord Gordon is suffering, except that they are without the ministrations of a fond mother and sister and father. Yesterday they fought as fiercely and as bravely as Lord Gordon did. *Someone* must tend them."

"But not Lady Morgan Bedwyn," he said. "It is unfitting. Besides, we will be leaving early tomorrow, and you will need to rest today."

"I have rested this morning, my lord," she assured him briskly. "I will do what I can today at Mrs. Clark's and then return tonight in order to be ready to travel tomorrow."

"But the streets are unsafe," the earl protested.

"They are not, sir," Gervase assured him. "But if it will relieve your mind, I will undertake to escort Lady Morgan and her maid to Mrs. Clark's myself and bring them back here this evening."

She looked gratefully at him and left quickly to fetch her bonnet while Caddick blustered with indecision, muttering about his wife's being still asleep in her chamber.

Five minutes later they were out on the street, the two of them, her maid a decent distance behind them.

"You have seen Lord Gordon?" he asked her.

She shook her head. "He was sleeping when I arrived home," she explained. "He had a restless morning but was sleeping again when I awoke. I will see him this evening."

He wondered how much she cared for the boy. Her feelings during the Richmond ball had been confused and in tumult. Perhaps knowing him wounded had aroused her affections for him. She looked up at him with that characteristic direct glance of hers and appeared to guess his thoughts.

"Captain Lord Gordon is just one of thousands of wounded," she said. "He has a loving family, a houseful of servants, and a quiet, luxurious home to contribute to his comfort. I am needed more elsewhere."

"You do not pine for a sight of him?" he asked with a smile.

She frowned. "He was talking about me last night," she said, "and wanting to see me. He *is* wounded, though not half as desperately as most of the men at Mrs. Clark's, I daresay, and so I must not say anything to upset him unduly if I can avoid it. But I must, of course, see him." She sighed. "I suppose I should have made my sentiments clear long ago. But I was staying with his parents and his sister."

"Tomorrow," he said, patting her hand, "you will be starting your journey home. You will be back with your family and will be able to tell young Gordon to go to the devil if you wish."

"And what will you do when you leave here?" she asked him. "Are you still banished?"

He laughed softly. "My father is dead, *chérie,*" he said, "and my mother has begged me to return home. Perhaps I will oblige her before the summer is over."

"Do you have only your mother?" she asked him.

"I have a married brother," he told her, "who is vicar of the church at home in Kent. And two sisters, both married and living away from home. And a second cousin, my father's former ward, who still lives at Windrush Grange with my mother."

"I am pleased for you," she said. "Family is very important. I do not know what I would do without mine. I love them all very dearly."

"Including the Duke of Bewcastle?" he asked. "It is

said that he is a humorless tyrant."

She visibly bristled. "Both those words are unkind," she said, "and do not capture the essence of Wulfric at all. He does not know how to laugh, it is true. But he has had the weight of many responsibilities on his shoulders since he succeeded to the title at the age of seventeen—younger than I am now. He takes his duties very seriously and rules those in his care or employ with firm discipline."

"Including you, *chérie?*" he asked.

"Oh, we Bedwyns are made of stern stuff," she said. "We are not awed by Wulfric, though we all respect him. And love him."

It was hard to imagine anyone loving Bewcastle—though he himself had once admired him and aspired to be one of his small inner circle of friends.

They had reached Mrs. Clark's house by that time, and it was immediately apparent from the open doors and general bustling air that new wounded were being moved in.

Gervase took one of Lady Morgan's hands in both of his and raised it to his lips.

"I will bring you word of Lord Alleyne within the hour," he told her. "Do not wear yourself quite to a thread, *chérie*."

She turned away and ran lightly up the steps.

When, he wondered, looking after her, had she become in his eyes a person in her own right and not just the sister of the Duke of Bewcastle? Yesterday? And that person was someone he liked and even admired. Even the age difference between them no longer seemed so huge. She was a woman of principle and compassion—compassion without sentimentality.

He felt more ashamed than ever of his earlier dealings with her. And yet without those he would not even have met her and got to know her, would he?

THE ONLY WORD Gervase was able to bring at the end of the hour was that Lord Alleyne Bedwyn had not reported back to Sir Charles Stuart yesterday—a serious omission, given the fact that he was to have brought an immediate reply to the important letter he had undertaken to deliver.

Neither had he reported back this morning.

The rest of the embassy staff appeared half annoyed, half concerned—but not concerned enough, it seemed, to have initiated any active inquiries. Gervase announced his decision to take a ride down through the forest as far as Waterloo to see what he could discover of the whereabouts of the missing man.

"Is it possible," he asked before he left, "that Lord Alleyne Bedwyn rode off with the troops last evening in the direction of Paris?"

But he received only blank stares and questions instead of answers. Why would an embassy official do such a thing? For what purpose? On whose authority? He was not, after all, attached to any embassy in Paris.

Lady Morgan was a great deal more than half concerned when Gervase reported back to her at Mrs. Clark's house.

"He has *still* not returned?" she asked. "Wherever can he be?"

He could see fear in her widened eyes. Her already-pale face lost even more color.

"All was confusion south of Brussels yesterday," he said, taking her by the elbow and stepping outside the house with her, "and doubtless still is today. Something important has delayed him, you may be sure."

"But he is not a free agent as you are—or as I am," she said, frowning. "He had business to attend to, and no doubt he was expected to hurry back here for further orders. Alleyne would not neglect his duty."

He did not tell her about the reply Bedwyn had been expected to bring back.

"I am going to take a ride out there," he said. "I'll see what I can discover and come right back to you. All will be well with him. He is not, after all, a military man and was not engaged in the battle."

But he *had* ridden close to the fighting. He had had a message for Wellington, and Wellington was notorious for being always in the very thick of battle. Gervase could see from the look in Lady Morgan's eyes that she knew this too and had drawn no comfort at all from his words. He drew her against him without forethought, wrapping his arms about her as if he could protect her from all the world's ills.

"I'll find him," he said. "I'll find him and bring him to you."

She tipped back her head and gazed into his eyes without speaking, and he lowered his head and set his lips to her forehead, regardless of the presence of a number of pedestrians who were out on the street. He cupped her face in both hands and smiled at her.

"Courage, *chérie,*" he said.

But it was a rash promise he had made—if indeed he *had* promised. The horror of the scenes he saw as he rode south through the forest where less than two weeks before he had entertained dozens of guests to a moonlit picnic was too vast for words, or even for thoughts. The road was clogged with traffic, most of it heading north—and much of it bearing yet more wounded. The abandoned bodies of the dead were strewn everywhere, no burial detail having yet come this far north. Many of the bodies had been stripped naked by fellow soldiers looking for uniforms less threadbare than their own or by local people intent upon finding some loot to compensate them for all they had lost in yesterday's hell.

Even as Gervase stopped for perhaps the dozenth time to ask about Lord Alleyne Bedwyn, one woman was kneeling beside one of the naked bodies a short distance away in the forest and looking up to call for help.

"He is *alive!*" she cried. "And he is my *husband.* Please help me, somebody."

Even as Gervase hesitated a sergeant with a bandage around his head and over one eye detached himself from a group trudging along the road and called good-naturedly to her.

"Coming, missus," he said. "How bad hurt is he?"

Gervase did not wait to watch the development of this one small happily-ever-after—*if* the woman's husband survived, that was. But the incident served to remind him that he was not by any means the only one out on this road or on the battlefield itself today searching for a missing person. There were dozens—perhaps hundreds—of others, many of them women, searching desperately among the dead and wounded for the familiar figure of a loved one.

He rode all the way to Waterloo and beyond—onto the surprisingly small area where such a ferocious battle had been fought the day before. There was still the acrid smell of smoke on the air, mingled with the harsher stenches of blood and death. People were hurrying about here through churned mud and trampled crops with a great sense of urgency—burial details were already hard at their grizzly work.

Gervase wandered about, both on horseback and on foot, asking continually—in vain—if anyone knew and had seen Lord Alleyne Bedwyn. He looked down into the faces of a thousand dead, it seemed, but none was the one he looked for and dreaded seeing. In the end, with the advent of another day's dusk not far off, he had to give up his search and return to Brussels.

Perhaps, he thought hopefully, he had somehow missed Bedwyn on the road and he had been back in Brussels for several hours. Or perhaps he had been in the city since yesterday. Perhaps he had spent the night with a woman, forgetting both the message he was to have delivered to Sir Charles and his promise to find his sister and take her out of Brussels to safety. Perhaps . . .

And perhaps Lord Alleyne Bedwyn was dead somewhere between Brussels and the far edge of that battlefield. If that were so, he would never be found now, especially if his body had been stripped. It was possible that he had already been buried in some mass grave.

He would just have to hope that there was some other explanation, Gervase decided.

Lady Morgan had not yet returned to the Rue de Bellevue, he discovered when he called there. Neither had Lord Alleyne Bedwyn been there. Gervase left, assuring a somewhat agitated and annoyed earl that he would escort her home within the next hour.

WITH TWENTY-FOUR WOUNDED men in the house, a number of them amputees who were suffering the raging fever that so often followed surgical procedures, Morgan had had scarcely a moment for thought all afternoon and evening. When she *did* have a moment, she found it amazing that she was actually doing this—and doing it without flinching.

She was a Bedwyn, it was true, and the Bedwyns prided themselves upon being tough and intrepid. But even so, she was only eighteen years old. This time last year—this time *six months* ago—she had been at Lindsey Hall in Hampshire, carefully sheltered from all harm and from all that was ungenteel, under the close chaperonage of Miss Cowper, her governess and companion for the last several years. It was only in February that Miss Cowper had moved away to live with a newly widowed sister, taking with her a generous pension from Wulfric.

Morgan wondered what Wulfric would have to say when he knew how she had spent yesterday and today—and last night. Not one of the men at Mrs. Clark's was even an officer. There were two sergeants and three corporals among them. All the rest were privates, men whose coarse accents proclaimed their lowly origins.

It simply did not matter, she had discovered. They all needed her. She felt as far removed from the schoolroom and her aristocratic world as it was possible to be.

Mrs. Hodgins touched her on the shoulder as she held a cool cloth to the cheeks of a man who was delirious with fever.

"I'll do that," she said. "You take a break for a few minutes, my love. You have not stopped for hours. That gentleman is here who brought the news about Major Clark last night. He wants to speak with you."

"The Earl of Rosthorn?"

Morgan stood up and gingerly stretched her back. It was only at that moment that she remembered what errand he had undertaken earlier in the afternoon. And it was only then that she realized Alleyne still had not come. She hurried into the crowded hall, pulled her shawl from a hook there, and joined Lord Rosthorn, who was waiting outside on the steps.

She drew a deep breath of fresh air, realizing as she did so how very *unfresh* the air was indoors. At the same moment she became aware of her untidy, blood-streaked appearance. But it did not matter. None of it mattered. She turned an anxious face to his.

"Alleyne?" she asked.

He shook his head slightly. "I have been unable to find him," he told her, "even though I rode all the way to Waterloo and beyond—out to where the fighting was yesterday, in fact. But you cannot imagine all the confusion out there, all the people and conveyances milling about and crowding the roads. It would have been a miracle if I *had* found him."

She looked closely at him in the darkness.

"Lord Rosthorn," she said, "you know better than to talk to me in that tone of voice."

"*What* tone?" he asked.

"That deliberately hearty and cheerful one," she replied. "As if I were a child."

He looked steadily and gravely back at her for a few moments.

*"Chérie,"* he said softly at last, "what would you have me say?"

"Simply that you could not find him," she said.

"I could not."

She closed her eyes and drew a slow breath. Her knees were feeling as if they had turned to the consistency of jelly. She fought panic and hysteria.

*Where was Alleyne?*

"He was delayed in Antwerp when you expected him to come and take you home a few days ago," Lord Rosthorn said, taking her firmly by the elbow and drawing her down to sit beside him on the doorstep. "You told me so. I suppose you worried about him then, did you not?"

"Yes," she admitted.

"But he came," he said. "Doubtless it will happen again. Who knows what could delay a man yesterday? And today. Tomorrow he will come and be surprised that you worried so much today."

Her hand, she realized suddenly, was firmly in his clasp. His fingers were laced with hers.

"Do you believe that?" she asked him.

"I believe it is a possibility," he said.

Alleyne could not be dead, she thought. He simply could not. There could not be a world without Alleyne in it—or without any of her brothers or her sister, for that matter. It was a thought she had had over and over again as a girl, whenever her worries over Aidan had threatened to overwhelm her. And she had always been right. There had always been a new letter from him to prove that he still lived. And then one glorious day last year he had ridden up the driveway to Lindsey Hall without any warning and she had flown down from the schoolroom—without either Wulfric's permission or Miss Cowper's—and hurtled into his arms.

Alleyne would come tomorrow. There would be some simple explanation for this absence and this silence.

She would *kill* him when she saw him.

*"Chérie."* Lord Rosthorn had one arm pressed firmly against her shoulder. His head was bent close to hers—she could feel the warmth of his breath on her cheek. Her hand was still firmly in his clasp. *"Chérie?"*

It was hard to remember a time when she had been offended with his calling her by that French endearment. Now it wrapped more warmly about her than her shawl, and she closed her eyes and gave in to the temptation to tip her head to one side to nestle on his shoulder. She had always prided herself on her strength to stand alone. She had four older brothers to fight her battles for her. She had never called upon them to do so.

She had *four* older brothers . . .

*"Chérie."* The voice was soft and husky against her ear and yet seemed to come from far away. "You have been dozing on my shoulder for all of five minutes. It is time I took you home."

She lifted her head, embarrassed. She could not really have fallen asleep, could she? When she was worried out of her mind over Alleyne?

"Home," she said wistfully. "But I cannot leave here. There is so much to do."

"Someone else will do it," he told her. "Besides, I promised Caddick that I would bring you home without delay."

Captain Lord Gordon was at the Earl of Caddick's. She would have to see him when she went back there—unless by some miracle he was asleep again. Life could be *so* wearying!

"I'll step inside and tell Mrs. Clark that I will return early in the morning," she said.

"But you will be departing early in the morning for England, *chérie,*" he reminded her.

"Before Alleyne has come?" She raised her eyebrows with unconscious arrogance. "Before I have discovered what has happened to him? I think not, Lord Rosthorn."

"Ah, no," he said as he got to his feet and reached down one hand to help her to hers. "You would not leave here under such circumstances even if the battle still raged and had reached the city gates, would you? In you go, then, so that I may escort you home before midnight. I'll bring you back here myself in the morning, and then I will go in search of your brother again."

She was standing on the step above him. She set her hands on his shoulders and gazed into his eyes. When had he come to seem so strong and dependable to her? So much like a trustworthy comrade?

"I am sorry in my heart," she said, "that I misjudged you on first acquaintance and thought you nothing more than a trivial-minded rake. You *did* flirt outrageously with me, Lord Rosthorn, and it was *enormously* extravagant of you to organize that picnic in the Forest of Soignés just for my amusement. But I know now that you were merely bored and finding a way to divert yourself. Now, in the last few days, when life has become deadly serious, you have shown yourself to be the kindest, most dependable man in my world."

"Ah, *mais non, mon enfant,*" he said.

He kissed her. Very lightly on the lips, his own warm and soft and slightly parted. Very similarly to the way he had kissed her in the Forest of Soignés, except that it felt entirely different. It felt less lascivious, less naughty, less thrilling. And yet she felt it down to her toes and through to the depths of her heart. It felt . . . right. Yes . . . it felt right. She wanted to twine her arms about his neck and lean into him and lose herself in his dependable strength.

But it was a luxury and a weakness she would not allow herself—not now and not ever! Not even with the man she would finally love for the rest of her life, whoever he turned out to be. She would never allow her own strength, her own will, her own uniqueness, to be submerged beneath those of any man—or woman.

She looked gravely into Lord Rosthorn's lazy, heavy-lidded eyes and then turned and hurried into the house to find Mrs. Clark.

He was her dear, dear friend, she thought, that was all. It was strange after their earlier foolish, flirtatious, even dangerous relationship. But it was true nonetheless. He felt like her dearest friend in the whole world.

## CHAPTER VIII

MORGAN HAD VERY LITTLE SLEEP THAT NIGHT. How could she? She was exhausted after long hours of work and the emotional drain of being among the wounded. She was so worried about Alleyne that her stomach could not seem to stop churning. And she had endured an upsetting hour with the Caddicks after Lord Rosthorn escorted her home.

They were still planning to leave in the morning. All their bags and trunks were packed and piled in the hallway. Rosamond came running to hug Morgan and apologize for not joining her at Mrs. Clark's. Her papa had expressly forbidden it, she explained, and her mama had needed her assistance in the sickroom.

It took two women and a houseful of servants to look after one wounded man? Morgan had thought in some amazement, though she had made no comment aloud.

"You are to come and see Ambrose now," Rosamond said, taking her by the hand. "Mama is with him. He has been asking about you all day." She smiled warmly at her friend.

The earl was in his son's room too. Captain Lord

Gordon was lying in the middle of a large canopied bed, his broken leg elevated on cushions beneath the blankets. His head was propped up on a pile of white, down-filled pillows. He was wearing a snowy white nightshirt. A fire crackled in the hearth despite the warmth of the June night. Heavy curtains had been drawn across the windows. At first glance Morgan could not help making the comparison with the less than ideal conditions under which the poor wounded men she had been tending for two days were suffering. Yet even they were more fortunate than hundreds, maybe thousands, of others.

But it was only a momentary thought. Lord Gordon had been undeniably hurt while fighting in the thick of a ferocious battle. He might just as easily have been killed. There were ugly purple bruises down one side of his face, and one hand, resting outside the bedcovers, was heavily bandaged. His cheeks were slightly flushed with fever, his eyes bright.

He looked every inch the romantic hero warrior, and Morgan's heart went out to him. She gazed at him with sympathy and his eyes brightened as he turned his head on the pillow.

"I am alive, Lady Morgan," he said. "I have survived a cavalry charge that put fear and admiration into all who beheld it. I have returned with a victory to lay at the feet of all those most dear to me." He did not take his eyes off her as he spoke, and she knew that his words were intended just for her. He had come back *to her*. *She* was the one at whose feet he laid his victory.

She smiled at him at the same time as her heart sank into her slippers. The Richmond ball seemed such a long time in the past. She felt that she had lived a whole lifetime since then. Yet, despite all he had gone through, he was speaking now exactly as he had spoken then.

"Lord Uxbridge led the cavalry charge just when it seemed that the French infantry would overwhelm ours and break through the center and win the battle," he explained. "We showed them a thing or two, Lady Morgan—the infantry of both sides, that is. I daresay we cut down hundreds, even thousands, of the Frogs. I wish you could have seen us. It was no pretty parade such as the one you watched on the Allée Verte last week. This was a desperate life-and-death charge against enemy guns and enemy bayonets. There were horses and comrades falling all about us. But we galloped onward undaunted. I daresay this will be remembered as the battle the cavalry won."

Morgan was feeling almost dizzy with exhaustion.

"I believe the courage of the men on both sides will long be remembered," she said. She had heard something of it from the men at Mrs. Clark's. Several of those men—especially the veterans—spoke with as much respect for the French as for their own soldiers, both infantry and cavalry.

"Men evil enough to fight under the banners of tyranny can hardly be described as brave," Lady Caddick said, sounding faintly shocked. "But we must allow Gordon to get some rest now. It has been a long, painful day for him. I sent my own maid up to pack your things, Lady Morgan, since you had your maid with you. You will find that all has been made ready for your departure in the morning."

"Oh, please, ma'am," Morgan said, turning to her and the earl, "may we wait just a little longer? Alleyne seems to have disappeared. He rode to the front yesterday to take a message from Sir Charles to the Duke of Wellington. He told me he would be back before nightfall, but he has not yet returned. Lord Rosthorn rode out to Waterloo this afternoon to seek word of him, but there was none. I am very worried. Lord Rosthorn has promised to search again tomorrow morning."

"Oh, poor Morgan!" Rosamond said, hurrying to her friend's side and setting a comforting arm about her waist. "Whatever can have happened? *Of course* we will wait, will we not, Mama?"

"Lord Alleyne Bedwyn has no doubt been delayed by important business," Lady Caddick said. "In the meantime he knows that you are in excellent hands with me, Lady Morgan, and that I will make the right decisions for your safety and well-being. We will leave after an early breakfast as planned. There must be no delay in Gordon's seeing a good English physician."

"I cannot think of leaving without word of my brother." Morgan looked at the earl with troubled eyes.

"There are many other sisters and mothers and wives who have heard no word from their menfolk since yesterday," the earl said in the gruff, pompous voice he tended to use when speaking to women. "Your anxieties must be less than theirs, Lady Morgan. Bedwyn was not in the fight, after all, was he? You must cultivate a stiff upper lip, my dear. You will hear from him soon after you return to London with us, I daresay."

"I believe," Lord Gordon said, "I need another dose of laudanum, Mama."

Morgan retired to bed after that without resuming the argument. Rosamond accompanied her to her room, her arm still about Morgan's waist.

"Lord Alleyne will be safe," she assured her. "I feel it in my bones. But, oh, my poor Morgan, I *know* how you must be feeling. I know how I felt all day yesterday before we heard news of Ambrose. But *he* came home safely. Your brother will too."

Morgan fell, exhausted, into bed soon after that, but then she found that she simply could not sleep. She arose soon after dawn, washed in cold water, and dressed without summoning her maid—she had to search among packed boxes to find the plainest of her clean dresses, ignoring the smart travel clothes that had been laid out for her.

She had made her decision during the night. Actually it had not been difficult.

The earl and countess and Rosamond were already at breakfast when she went down.

"Ah, there you are, Lady Morgan," the countess said, smiling graciously at her. "Do eat without delay. We will be leaving within the hour. Gordon had a reasonably restful night, you will be happy to know."

Morgan did not sit down. She clung with both hands to the back of a chair. "I cannot leave, ma'am," she said, "until I have heard that Alleyne is safe. I beg you to wait one more day. He surely will come back sometime today, and then I will be able to take good news of him home to my family."

"Wait one more day? When every hour I worry that Gordon's leg has been inexpertly set?" Lady Caddick was all amazement. "My dear Lady Morgan, you are being unreasonable—even selfish—to ask such a thing. No, we will not delay by even so much as an hour. Lord Alleyne Bedwyn is well able to look after himself, you may be assured."

"Oh, Mama." Rosamond was looking at Morgan, all concern. "Surely one day will not make a great deal of difference. What if it were *my* brother who was still unaccounted for?"

"Gordon was fighting in the battle, Rosamond," her father reminded her. "There is all the difference in the world between his situation and Bedwyn's."

"I am not leaving," Morgan announced firmly.

The earl bullied. The countess bullied and cajoled. She reminded Lady Morgan that she was there under *her* care, a responsibility conferred upon her by the Duke of Bewcastle himself, who would be justifiably angry with his sister if he knew that she was behaving so badly. She *commanded* Lady Morgan to accompany them on their journey. She *begged* her. She shed copious tears and called her a stubborn, undutiful, horrid girl. She knew—she had always known—that the Bedwyns were a wild, unruly lot, but she had mistakenly thought Lady Morgan a sweet, biddable girl, different from the others. Now she realized how wrong she had been. The duke would be understandably furious with his sister if she refused to obey the direct command of the person he had entrusted with her care and safety. He would likely banish her to Lindsey Hall or one of his remoter estates—was there not one in Wales?—and never allow her into society again.

But Morgan was indeed a Bedwyn.

Throughout the tirade she clung to the chair and retreated behind the facade of cold hauteur at which all her siblings excelled. She remained obstinate and adamant. She would *not* leave Brussels until she had heard from Alleyne. It soon became obvious to her that the Caddicks intended to leave this morning anyway, whether she accompanied them or not. But if they had intended to call her bluff, they were to be sadly disappointed. She would stay with Mrs. Clark or one of the other officers' wives, she told them. Any one of them would gladly offer her a temporary home. And staying would enable her to continue helping with the care of the wounded.

"I have never known such a wicked, obstinate, *disobedient* girl, Caddick," Lady Caddick said, waving a handkerchief before her face. "I am about to swoon."

As Lady Caddick suited action to words, Morgan made her escape and summoned her maid to her room. They were going to have to make some arrangements to have their things moved to Mrs. Clark's for the time being, she explained to the girl. But there was a further blow in store for her. Her maid burst into loud sobs when she knew that they were to stay and that moreover they were to go back to that horrid house with all those men and their bandages and their smell. She could not stand it. She would go out of her mind, she would. She had been hired to dress my lady, not to run and fetch for gutter scum. She waxed quite eloquent in her own defense. She demanded to go home.

Morgan gave the girl money for her passage to England and her journey to London as well as the month's salary owed her plus one month extra and dismissed her from her service. Strictly speaking, the maid was in *Wulfric's* service and was paid by him, but Morgan considered she was doing the girl a kindness in making it unnecessary for her to have to apply to Wulfric himself for her money and explain to him why she had abandoned her mistress alone in Brussels.

By the time Morgan went back downstairs, intent upon walking to Mrs. Clark's and seeing if a manservant could be spared to carry over her boxes, there were two carriages and a baggage coach outside the door and Captain Lord Gordon had just been carried down and set in one of the former. For the moment he was alone except for a few coachmen out on the pavement and his batman, whom he waved away when he saw her.

"Lady Morgan!" he called.

She hurried eagerly toward the open carriage door. Why had she not thought of applying to him earlier? His mother would do anything he asked.

His bruises looked blacker in the daylight, his complexion paler except for the flush of a slight fever high in his cheeks. His splinted and heavily bandaged leg was stretched out along the seat. His eyes were clouded with pain. She felt a rush of genuine sympathy for him and set her hand in his outstretched one.

"Captain," she said, "did you know—"

But he started speaking almost simultaneously.

"What is this I hear?" he asked her, his very handsome brows drawn together in a frown. "You choose not to come with us, Lady Morgan? I beg you to reconsider. It is unthinkable for a young lady of your social standing to remain unchaperoned in a foreign city—or any city, for that matter."

"I do not know what has happened to my brother," she told him. "He went to—"

"But you *do* know what has happened to *me,* Lady Morgan," he said. "Am I not at least as important to you as your brother? Are you not concerned that I may limp for the rest of my life if my leg is not properly attended to within the next few days?"

She stared at him, frozen into silence. *This* was the man who had begged for the honor of fighting for *her?* Who had begged her to mourn him for the rest of her life if he should die in battle? But he was in pain. She could see that in his eyes. It must have caused him terrible agony to be carried down from his bed and settled in the less roomy carriage.

"If you care at all for me, Lord Gordon," she said earnestly, "persuade your mama and papa to remain here for one more day. Please? Surely I will have heard from Alleyne before its end. There is no more danger in remaining here, is there? And your broken bones have been competently set by a reputable physician. Surely another day's rest here in the house will do you infinitely more good than a long carriage journey. *Please* persuade them. I am sick with worry."

He looked back at her as earnestly as she gazed at

him, and for a moment she expected that he would agree to do as she asked. She smiled at him. Her hand, she noticed, was still in his.

"I am disappointed," he said. "I thought I was of more importance to you than a brother. *You* are more important to *me* than my sister. If I thought it would do any good for you to stay, I would speak up for it in a moment. I would even lead the search, in this carriage, if necessary. But men do not need ladies hanging about them when they are engaged in official business, Lady Morgan. Lord Alleyne Bedwyn will be embarrassed when he knows what a fuss you have made about his absence. In the meantime Mama is upset, Rosamond is in tears, my father is angry, and I am disappointed. I had looked forward to the distraction of your company during the journey, which will doubtless be painful for me. I had looked forward to perhaps addressing myself to the Duke of Bewcastle upon our return. Are you determined to remain stubborn? Mama says it is a Bedwyn trait."

Morgan withdrew her hand from his.

"All I ask is one day," she said. *"One day."*

Even then she hoped that he would look beyond his own pain to see hers and redeem himself somewhat in her eyes. But all he did was look beyond her shoulder.

"Ah, is that you, Rosthorn?" he asked. "I must thank you for riding ahead of me to Brussels the day before yesterday and setting my mother's mind at ease. Anxiety is a dreadful thing for women of tender sensibilities, and one really ought to do all in one's power to alleviate it. I am doing as well as can be expected, you will be pleased to know, but of course I wish to consult an English physician as soon as possible."

Morgan turned to look at the earl.

"You are leaving now, this morning?" he asked. "And you too, Lady Morgan?" His eyes swept over her simple muslin day dress.

"I am staying," she told him, "until I have heard something from Alleyne. I am going to stay with Mrs. Clark or one of the other regimental wives if they will have me."

"And how will you then return to England?" he asked her.

"I will find someone to travel with." She lifted her chin. "Or Alleyne will find someone for me."

"And your maid?" He looked about the pavement, which held no other female but her.

Morgan felt herself flush.

"She does not with to remain with me," she said, "and so I am sending her home."

He raised his eyebrows.

"Talk reason to her, if you will, Rosthorn," Lord Gordon said wearily. "Tell her that it is quite impossible for her to remain here without my mother to chaperon her. It is *unthinkable*. Tell her that her anxieties are foolish. Tell her she has no choice but to come with us."

The Earl of Rosthorn looked at her with inscrutable eyes. She lifted her chin again. If he tried to order her to leave with the Caddicks, she was going to be very angry indeed and everyone on the street was going to know it.

"Why is Lady Caddick leaving Brussels when Lady

Morgan cannot?" he asked Lord Gordon without taking his eyes off Morgan.

*Cannot.* Ah, he did understand, then.

"My mother is anxious to get me to an English physician," Lord Gordon explained, his voice clearly irritated now. "Lady Morgan is in her care. It is outrageous of her to set her will against my mother's and put her in such an awkward position. I daresay Bewcastle will have a thing or two to say on the matter if she remains stubborn. He is the one who appointed my mother chaperon."

It amazed Morgan that she had ever felt even mildly attracted to him.

Lady Caddick herself stepped out of the house at that moment with Lord Caddick and Rosamond.

"Ah, there you are, Lady Morgan," she said, a martial gleam in her eye. "I simply must *insist* that you accompany us whether you are dressed for travel or not. I will not take no for an answer. The Duke of Bewcastle will be informed of how much trouble you have been to me. Ah, good morning, Rosthorn. You will be gratified to see that Gordon is brave enough to travel though he is still in considerable pain."

"Ma'am?" He bowed in acknowledgment of her greeting. "I have come to escort Lady Morgan to Mrs. Clark's house. Her belongings are still here? I will have someone come to remove them within the hour. I wish you a safe journey."

His French accent was quite pronounced. He spoke with pleasant charm—and a thread of steel Morgan had not heard in his voice before.

"See here, Rosthorn—" the Earl of Caddick began.

"Lord Alleyne Bedwyn, when he rode out of Brussels the day before yesterday," Lord Rosthorn said, interrupting him, "instructed Lady Morgan to await his return, after which he promised to take her home to England himself. She remains by his authority. I will escort her in person to Mrs. Clark's. She will be quite safe there. I will personally undertake to see that no harm comes to her."

"Lord Rosthorn," Lady Caddick said faintly, "you are a single gentleman in no way related to Lady Morgan. It would be most improper and irresponsible for me to leave her in your care."

"Then you must remain, ma'am, so that she may be in yours," he retorted.

Morgan turned and strode away along the pavement. She would not stay one moment longer to wrangle or, worse, to hear herself being wrangled over. Life had suddenly become very tiresome indeed. She was almost blind with anxiety over Alleyne, yet the people she had thought cared for her treated her as if she were a stubborn, willful, disobedient girl for wanting to find him. And the man who less than a week ago had declared such extravagant love for her expected her to put him before all other loves—even her love for her own family.

She would have given anything in the world at that moment to have seen Wulfric striding toward her—or Aidan or Rannulf. Or Alleyne.

Alleyne was dead. He must be.

*He could not be dead.*

Running feet sounded behind her, and Rosamond dashed around her and caught her up in a tight hug.

"I am so sorry about this, Morgan," she said, tears swimming in her eyes. "I am so very sorry. I *wish* I could stay with you but I cannot."

Then she was hurrying away again, back to the carriages, and Lord Rosthorn had come up beside Morgan and offered his arm without a word.

No, she was not quite alone, she thought, pulling herself together again. She still had this friend. And Mrs. Clark would welcome her. The wounded men needed her. And even besides all those facts she was Lady Morgan Bedwyn. She lifted her chin and unconsciously lengthened her stride as she took the earl's arm.

Alleyne had always predicted that she would out-Bedwyn the Bedwyns one day. It seemed that he had been right all along. She was eighteen years old and striding along the street of a foreign city on the arm of a gentleman she scarcely knew, having just defied the will of the chaperon to whose care Wulfric had entrusted her and having just dismissed her maid.

But Alleyne was still here too. Today he would come, and tomorrow he would take her home himself.

*He could not be dead.*

HE HAD DONE SOME MAD things in his time, Gervase thought, things that had got him into any number of nasty scrapes. This was no scrape. This was downright trouble. What the devil had he done?

He had aided and abetted a young lady in defying and walking away from her appointed chaperon, that was what. Not just for an hour or a morning. Not even for a day. The Caddicks were leaving for England. Lady Morgan Bedwyn was staying in Brussels. And he had defended her decision to remain without them. He had promised to look after her himself.

*I will personally undertake to see that no harm comes to her.*

What he had personally undertaken, unless he was very fortunate indeed, was a leg shackle. What he had just accomplished, unless he could find some way of wriggling out of the situation, was the fulfillment of all his dreams of avenging himself upon Bewcastle. Once the Caddicks had arrived home and spread the word in the drawing rooms and clubs of London, Lady Morgan Bedwyn would either be totally ruined *or* she would be forced into marriage with him—either of which outcomes would be a vicious slap in the face for her brother.

He no longer wanted to avenge himself upon Bewcastle this way. Not through her. He *liked* her. He respected and admired her.

"Was I the one in the wrong?" she asked, her hand light on his arm, her eyes looking straight ahead, a martial gleam in them. "*Was* I?"

He guessed that it was a rhetorical question, but he answered it anyway.

"You were not wrong," he told her. "The Caddicks are anxious to ensure the full recovery of their son, of course, and are understandably eager to take him home to England. But they also undertook a duty when they agreed to bring you with them to Brussels. They undertook to treat you with as much care and consideration as they would show their own family. They failed in that duty today."

"Thank you," she said. "It is what I thought too."

"Once we have reached Mrs. Clark's," he told her, "I will make arrangements to have your belongings fetched. Then I will call on Sir Charles Stuart again and, if necessary, ride out to Waterloo once more."

Perhaps, he thought, he would find Bedwyn today. Perhaps he was injured and lying in a field hospital somewhere. Or perhaps the man would simply ride into Brussels from wherever he had been for the past two days, some reasonable explanation on his lips. Perhaps after all he could set out for England with his sister later today, or at the very least take over responsibility for her.

If that were to happen, Gervase decided, he himself would not delay in riding off into the proverbial sunset. But if it *were* to happen, it would be a miracle indeed.

Lord Alleyne Bedwyn was almost certainly dead.

"Thank you," she said. "Is he dead, do you suppose, Lord Rosthorn?"

"You must not give up hope yet, *chérie,*" he said, setting a hand over hers on his arm. "I will do my very best to find him."

"He is the most sunny-natured of us all," she said. "The most charismatic, the most restless. He has so much vitality to share with the world, so much living yet to do. He only recently decided to try the life of a diplomat instead of taking the seat in Parliament that Wulfric would have secured for him. This is his first posting—is not that ironic? He cannot be dead, Lord Rosthorn. I would feel it *here* if he were." She touched the fingers of her free hand to her heart.

He wondered how many hundreds or thousands of women were telling themselves the same thing today.

"If he were dead, he would have been found, would he not?" she asked.

He merely squeezed her hand. How could he tell her that untold hundreds of the unattended dead, especially the better dressed ones, would have been stripped naked even before the night following the battle was over? Only in the unlikely event that such a man was identified quickly by someone who knew him could an anonymous burial in a mass grave be avoided.

"Try not to think such thoughts if you possibly can," he said. "Not yet."

They passed four of his acquaintances—and hers—before they finally reached Mrs. Clark's. He nodded affably at each of them. He doubted she even noticed them. But he wondered how long it would be before one or more of them discovered that the Earl and Countess of Caddick had left for England this morning. Then there would be scandal in Brussels as well as in England.

He had exposed Lady Morgan Bedwyn deliberately to gossip and speculation at his picnic in the Forest of Soignés less than two weeks ago. Now, when he had no such intention, he was about to expose her to a great deal more. Not that this was all his fault, of course. She would have stayed anyway. She would have come striding over to Mrs. Clark's with or without him.

On the whole, despite the danger to himself, he would prefer that she came *with* him.

Mrs. Clark met them on her doorstep, hugged Lady Morgan when she heard her story, and was soon assuring her that she was very welcome indeed to stay, provided she did not object to sharing a very small room with her hostess.

NONE OF SIR CHARLES STUART'S embassy staff had heard anything of or from Lord Alleyne Bedwyn. It was clear to Gervase that the annoyance they had shown yesterday had by now turned to alarm. There was no logical explanation for his failure to return except that he had somehow been wounded or killed in the action south of Waterloo. Efforts were even then being made to discover whether the letter he had carried to the Duke of Wellington had been delivered. Gervase announced his intention of riding out to the battle site again. He would check with Sir Charles's staff when he returned, he promised, and pass on any information he might pick up.

He found nothing, of course. The road south was still crowded with men and conveyances moving in the opposite direction from the one he took, though it was not quite as clogged as it had been the day before. The Forest of Soignés was still strewn with debris. The battlefield looked more than ever like a wilderness from hell. But there was nothing to be learned of Bedwyn's fate even though Gervase spoke to many people and checked at villages and farmhouses along the way. He searched among the wounded wherever they were gathered.

Lord Alleyne Bedwyn seemed to have vanished from the face of the earth—probably literally.

It was with a heavy heart that he rode back to Brussels. What hope could he still hold out for her? Would it be irresponsible even to try?

But Lady Morgan Bedwyn, he had discovered, despite her extreme youth, had character. It was not up to him either to give her hope or to withhold it. All he could offer her were the facts.

Neither Sir Charles's embassy staff nor he had been able to discover any trace of her brother's whereabouts. And yet there was a small piece of news. The letter Lord Alleyne Bedwyn had carried to the Duke of Wellington had indeed been delivered into his hands.

## CHAPTER IX

IT WAS STRANGE HOW THE HEART CLUNG TO HOPE even when there was no reasonable basis for it, Morgan found. And how life went on.

She was strolling in the Parc de Bruxelles with the Earl of Rosthorn. They were watching the swans glide gracefully across the lake, leaving a gently rippling series of V's behind them on the blue water. It was a lovely area in the heart of the city and a beautiful summer's day. She could feel some of the tension of hours of tending the wounded seep from her bones in the warmth of the sun.

They had not talked about Alleyne. Not really. When one of the ladies had called her to the door at Mrs. Clark's and she had seen who her visitor was, she had seen too the answers to all her questions in his eyes.

"Nothing?" was all she had asked.

He had shaken his head gravely. "Nothing."

It was perhaps absurd that they had said no more on the subject. But what more was there to say? He had suggested that she take a break for an hour or so and walk to the park with him. Mrs. Clark, who had just risen from her bed after snatching a few hours of sleep, had agreed that Morgan needed some fresh air and relaxation and excused her from her duties. It was a measure of their preoccupation, perhaps, that neither she nor Morgan had thought about the desirability of a maid's accompanying her so that the proprieties would be observed. But then, there was no maid to spare.

Besides, the whole idea of strict propriety and etiquette seemed irrelevant under present conditions.

Alleyne was dead, Morgan supposed. But her mind could not grasp that harsh reality. Not yet.

"I wish Wulfric were here," she said suddenly, breaking a lengthy silence.

"Do you, *chérie?*" He looked down at her in that way he had of making her feel that she had his undivided and sympathetic attention.

She thought then that perhaps her words might seem insulting.

"You have been wonderfully kind," she said. "But I cannot expect you to keep on giving your time to me and my concerns."

"I can think of nothing and no one to whom I would prefer to give it," he said, his voice low and very French.

Just a week or two ago she would have interpreted both his words and his tone as provocatively flirtatious. She would, perhaps, have answered him in kind. Now she was prepared to take his words at their face value, as the expression of the strange, unexpected friendship that seemed to have blossomed between them.

"Wulfric would know what to do," she said. "He would know what to decide." He would know when reality could no longer be avoided.

*He would know when to pronounce Alleyne dead.*

"If it is your wish," Lord Rosthorn said, "I will take you to him, *chérie*."

"He is in *England,*" she said, looking up at him, startled.

"I will take you there if you wish."

She stared mutely at him, the lake, the swans, the beauty of the park forgotten. Had it really come to this, then? Was she going to have to go home to tell Wulf—and Aidan and Rannulf and Freyja? Was that to be *her* task, her role? She tried to imagine herself saying the appalling words.

*Alleyne is dead.*

"I will wait a few days longer," she said. "Perhaps he will come even now. Perhaps there is an explanation. Perhaps . . ." She could not think of any more possibilities with which to complete the thought.

"Let us sit down for a few minutes," he suggested, pointing to a seat beneath the shade of a tree.

She slid her hand free of his arm as she sat. She rested her hands in her lap, palm up, and looked down at them.

"You are feeling betrayed, *chérie?*" the earl asked her.

"By Lady Caddick?" She clasped her hands. "I have not thought of her all day. I will miss Rosamond."

"I meant by your young officer," he said gently. "Captain Lord Gordon."

"He is not *my* officer," she said, pressing her hands more tightly together. "He never was."

"But *he* thought he was," he pointed out, "and you expected perhaps that you could rely upon his love. Do not be too harsh on him. He was quite badly wounded two days ago, and he was in obvious pain this morning."

"I have seen a great deal of wounds and pain in the last two days, Lord Rosthorn," she said. "And I have seen a great deal of nobility. I have seen a man die without uttering a sound even though he must have been suffering agonies—merely because, he told me, he did not want to distress the other men. I have seen desperately wounded men direct us to others more in need of our attentions than they. I have heard men apologize to us for being so much trouble. I heard a man tell Mrs. James to go and rest because she was almost asleep on her feet even though his dressing needed changing and he must have been very uncomfortable. I have heard men praise their comrades and other regiments and battalions than their own. I have heard no one praise himself."

Except Captain Lord Gordon.

"He is very young, *chérie,*" Lord Rosthorn said.

"Two of the men at Mrs. Clark's," she said, "are fourteen and fifteen years of age. There are no two men braver though one of them may yet die from his wounds."

"You are determined to be hard on young Gordon, then?" he asked her, patting one of her hands.

Without thinking she turned her hand and curled her fingers about his.

"He had a fanciful notion about fighting the French for me," she said. "He pictured himself as something akin to a medieval knight fighting for his lady's honor, I believe. And yet this morning, when he could have fought for me in a much more practical way, he could think only of his own comfort on the journey home. I am glad I was never silly enough to fall in love with him."

"I believe, *chérie,*" he said, "you would find it impossible to be silly. But I am glad there is no lingering regret for a young man who was never worthy of you. He is merely a peacock, a popinjay, a featherbrain."

She laughed despite herself.

He moved their clasped hands from her lap to rest on his thigh. It did not occur to her to be shocked even though she felt the smooth, tautly stretched fabric of his riding breeches and the hard-muscled warmth of his flesh beneath. She let her shoulder sway against his arm and felt comforted.

"He never loved me," she said. "It is a common failing of men. They see someone they consider beautiful and desirable and eligible, and they imagine that they love her. In fact, though, they love themselves reflected in her eyes. They have no interest in discovering *who* she is."

"Ah, *chérie,*" he asked her softly, "is that true only of men? Do not many women do the same thing?"

She drew breath to deny it. But she had always tried to be honest with herself. Was it true? *Did* women do that too—project their love of themselves onto a handsome man in whose eyes they could admire their own image? Had *she* ever done it? Had she not at first been delighted with Captain Lord Gordon's attentions? Had she not accepted Rosamond's friendship and courted the invitation to come here to Brussels because he admired her and she approved of his good taste? If it was true—and she was honest enough to admit that it was at least *partly* so—it was lowering in the extreme.

"I suppose we do," she admitted. "When we admire a man we are far more interested, at least at first, in our own feelings, in what he says and does to make us feel good about ourselves. But love is so much more. It is knowledge—knowing and being known."

"And who *is* Lady Morgan Bedwyn?" he asked her.

She smiled ruefully and looked up into his face. It was very close to her own. His lazy eyes smiled back at her and she remembered suddenly that he had kissed her on the lips again last night after she had woken up with her head on his shoulder. But she repressed the memory. She did not want to think of him in sexual terms—not now when she needed him as a friend. And when she liked him as a person.

"There is no question more certain to tongue-tie me," she said. "How can I explain who I am, Lord Rosthorn? Sometimes I do not even know the answer myself. I knew that I was strong-minded—my old governess would have used the word *headstrong*—and stubborn, but I would not have thought I could defy a chaperon to whom Wulfric had entrusted me and dare to remain in a foreign city alone, without even a maid. I knew I was not missish or squeamish, but I did not know I could tend horribly wounded men without flinching or watch a man die without breaking all to pieces. I did not want a come-out Season because I objected strongly to becoming a commodity on the great marriage mart. And yet I did enjoy my presentation and some of the social events surrounding it. I did not think of myself as a romantic, but I was enchanted by the sight of officers in scarlet uniforms and would have begged and pleaded with Wulfric to be allowed to come here if begging and pleading ever had any effect upon him. I have always been opposed to war, and yet at least half my reason for wanting to come here—no, more than half—was a fascination with the historic battle that was brewing right upon England's doorstep. I would have thought myself immune to the blatant flirtations of a practiced rake, and yet not only did I not stop yours when I met you, I also encouraged and responded to them. I would have thought it impossible to develop a friendship with such a man. And yet now, at this moment, it seems to me that you are the dearest friend I have ever known. I really do not know myself at all, you see. How can I tell you, then, who I am?" She laughed.

He chuckled too. "You are very young," he said.

"You must not be hard on yourself. You have scarcely begun the voyage into discovery that is adulthood. But I doubt any of us ever know ourselves completely. How dull life would be if we did. There would be no room for growth. We would never take ourselves by surprise."

"All I do know for certain," she told him, "is that I am not just a lady. I am a woman—and a person too."

"I have never doubted it, *chérie,*" he said.

And here she was, doing exactly what she had just deplored in others. She was so wrapped up in herself that she was virtually ignoring the man next to her. She looked up at him again.

"And who are *you,* Lord Rosthorn?" she asked.

He chuckled again. He really was very handsome when he smiled, she thought—and even when he did not, for that matter. But there were laughter lines at the corners of his eyes and about his mouth when he laughed, suggesting that he was normally a good-humored man. He would age well, she thought, even when the lines became etched into his face.

"You would not want to know me, *chérie,*" he said. "I have lived the life of a wastrel."

"Both before and after your banishment to the Continent?" she asked him. "Did you learn nothing from the events that caused that catastrophe, then?"

"Apparently not."

He looked down into her face, his eyes lazy and laughing. Their lips were only inches apart. And yet she did not feel in any danger from him. She felt perfectly relaxed with him. Despite his reputation and the undeniable fact that his father had banished him from England nine years ago, she could not believe that he was a wastrel.

"But even if I knew all the sordid details of your life," she said, "they would still not tell me *who* you are. You have not answered my question."

"Perhaps there is nothing to tell," he said. "Perhaps I am a man without any depth of character at all."

"I very much doubt that," she said, "though I might have believed it a week or so ago. Why have you taken me under your wing, Lord Rosthorn?"

"Like a mother bird?" He chuckled again. "Perhaps because you are the most beautiful woman I have ever seen, *chérie,* and I admire beauty."

She had lost him. He had retreated behind the facade of mocking amusement he had displayed during their first few meetings, including the picnic in the Forest of Soignés.

But why *had* he befriended her? There was no real reason why he should have, was there? She could only conclude that it was kindness itself. There—she did know *something* about him after all.

But did he think of her as a friend or only as a responsibility? She was not the latter. She must be the former, then. She was his friend as surely as he was hers.

"A wastrel," she said, smiling at him. "What a bouncer, Lord Rosthorn." She withdrew her hand and patted the back of his. "I must go back. I am to sleep this evening and take the night shift."

He stood immediately and drew her arm through his.

"I will come and see you each day if I may," he said

as they walked, "and bring any news there is. If at any time you decide that you wish to return to England, I will make arrangements. If you need me for any other reason, you know where to find me, or at least where to leave a message for me."

"The Rue de Brabant," she said. "Where is it?"

"I'll take you past there on our way to Mrs. Clark's," he said. "It is not much out of our way. I'll show you the house."

"Thank you," she said. "I will not be leaving, though, until I have heard something definite about Alleyne."

It jolted her somewhat to realize that she had not thought of him for the past hour. No, that was not quite accurate. Always, beneath every thought, every emotion, ran her leaden anxiety over Alleyne. But for an hour she had spoken of other things and enjoyed someone else's company and drawn some peace from the outdoors and the natural surroundings of the park.

She had the Earl of Rosthorn to thank for that.

But what would happen, she wondered, if she *never* heard anything definite? When would she admit to herself . . .

But whenever that time might be, it was not yet. She fell into step beside the Earl of Rosthorn.

FOR THE NEXT FOUR DAYS Morgan tended the wounded with as much energy and devotion as before. They lost one more to death and battled to keep several more alive as the fever raged in them. But gradually most of the men began to recover, some of them quite rapidly.

By the end of the fourth day there were only seventeen still at Mrs. Clark's.

It felt like suspended time to Morgan. She knew the days could not go on forever just like this. Soon most or all of the men would be gone—either back to their regiments or shipped off home to England. And she knew that most of the other women, Mrs. Clark included, were only waiting for word from their husbands before following them to Paris.

Soon, Morgan knew, she was going to have to face up to reality. There could be no reasonable explanation for Alleyne's long absence—only the obvious one. Wulfric had a right to know that he was missing. Sir Charles Stuart would surely inform him of that fact soon if she did not. But she was not ready yet. Whenever her mind touched upon the subject, she turned it firmly away.

True to his promise, the Earl of Rosthorn came each afternoon to take her walking. Often he ran errands for Mrs. Clark first or helped lift a patient too heavy for them. Once he wrote letters for a couple of the men who had friends or neighbors literate enough to read the letter to their family.

All the wives were a little in love with him, Morgan thought fondly. They all believed that she was fully in love with him. She was not. At the moment she could not even think of him in terms of love and courtship—or dalliance. But she did not know quite what she would have done without him. She would have managed alone, she supposed. Indeed, she undoubtedly would. But she was very grateful for his presence.

Sometimes they hardly spoke at all as they walked.

She was often too tired to get her thoughts straight, and she believed that he sensed this and merely strolled with her so that she could breathe in fresh air and feel the warmth of the sun on her face without having to feel obliged to make conversation. Sometimes they chattered on a variety of topics. He was well read, she discovered, and knew a great deal about art and music. He had visited some of the most famous galleries on the Continent and had seen some of the most famous sights. He shared his impressions with her with an eloquence that convinced her of his intelligence and the quality of his education.

Perhaps, she thought sometimes, she *was* a little in love with him. But such feelings were unimportant. Romance was the furthest thing from her needs during those days.

And then on the evening of the fourth day there was news at last.

Morgan was bandaging the stump of an arm when Mrs. Clark came to relieve her.

"You have a visitor," she told Morgan. "I have put him in the kitchen."

There was nowhere else to put a visitor. But he could not be Lord Rosthorn. He would have come to announce himself or he would have sent word and waited outside. Some instinct stopped Morgan from asking who it was. Mrs. Clark had bent very quickly over the wounded man being bandaged.

He was an aide of Sir Charles Stuart's. He introduced himself with a deferential bow. Morgan had met him before, but she did not remember his name. She did not catch it this time either. She could feel the blood drain out of her head and curled her hands into fists at her sides, imposing control over herself.

"Sir Charles has sent me, my lady," he said after clearing his throat. "He is busy at this very moment penning a letter to the Duke of Bewcastle."

Morgan lifted her chin and looked very directly at him.

"A letter was delivered into the hands of Sir Charles an hour or so ago," the aide explained. "It was mud-caked and tattered and several days old. But it was recognizable, my lady, as the letter his grace, the Duke of Wellington, dictated to an aide, who then gave it into the care of Lord Alleyne Bedwyn."

Morgan continued to stare at him. He cleared his throat again.

"The letter was discovered earlier today," the aide told her, "in the Forest of Soignés north of Waterloo."

The letter. Not its bearer. He did not say so. He did not need to.

"Sir Charles authorized me to inform you, my lady," he said, "that with the deepest regret he must now abandon hope that Lord Alleyne Bedwyn still lives. He sends his warmest sympathies and asks what he may do for you. May he arrange for your return to England, perhaps?"

Morgan stared at him but did not really hear him.

"Thank you," she said. "And please thank Sir Charles for informing me. I wish to be alone now, please."

"My lady—" he began.

But from pure instinct Morgan leveled upon him the

Bedwyn look of amazed hauteur.

"Now," she said. "Please."

She was alone then, staring at a row of onions hanging from the ceiling and listening to the kettle humming on the hearth. She did not know how much time passed before she heard the rustling of skirts behind her and two warm hands grasped her by the shoulders.

"My poor dear," Mrs. Clark said. "Sit down and I'll make you a cup of tea."

"The letter has been found." The sound came out as a whisper. Morgan cleared her throat. "But not Alleyne."

"Yes, dear," Mrs. Clark said, squeezing her shoulders almost painfully. "Have a cup of tea. It will help dispel the shock."

But Morgan was shaking her head. She felt something like panic building inside her. She could not sit down and sip tea. She would surely explode. She must . . .

"I am going out," she said. "I need to walk. I need to think."

"It is evening," Mrs. Clark said. "I cannot spare anyone to go with you. Come and sit—"

But Morgan broke from her grasp.

"I am going out," she said. "I do not need a chaperon or maid. I need to be alone."

"My dear Lady Morgan—"

"I am so sorry to abandon you in the middle of my shift, but . . . I must go outside." They were in the hall already and Morgan snatched her shawl off a hook and wound it about her head and shoulders. "I will be quite safe. And I will be back soon. I need to *breathe!*"

She was out of the house then, hurrying down the steps and along the street, not knowing where she was going, not even caring. She dipped her head down and walked fast—as if she could outstrip the knowledge that she had still not admitted into her deeply guarded spirit.

She had known for days.

There had been no real hope almost from the start.

For days she had thought she was preparing herself. But there was no preparing oneself for the moment when it came.

Alleyne was . . .

She was panting when she eventually stopped walking, as if she had been running for miles. She did not even know where she was. But when she looked about her in the growing dusk, she realized that she was outside the house on the Rue de Brabant that the Earl of Rosthorn had pointed out to her four days ago. There was light behind an upstairs window.

Had she intended to come here? she wondered, dazed. Or was it pure coincidence?

It did not matter.

She stepped up to the door, lifted the brass knocker, hesitated for only a moment, and then let it rattle back against the door.

# CHAPTER X

WHEN HE HEARD THE KNOCK ON THE OUTER door, Gervase drew back the curtain in his sitting room and peered downward. His landlady and her daughter were out for the evening. So was his valet, this being his regular half day off work. There were servants in the house, but they were probably gathered in the kitchen area at the back. There was no one on duty in the hall since no visitors were expected.

Her head was covered with a shawl, but he recognized her instantly. Good Lord! Whatever was Lady Morgan Bedwyn doing on his doorstep at this time of the day? It was well into the evening and almost dark—the candles were already burning. His first thought as he dropped the book he had been reading onto the nearest chair and shot from the room and down the stairs was of propriety. If anyone were to see her . . . But even before he reached the bottom of the stairs he remembered telling her to come here to him if she was ever in need. This, obviously, was no social call.

A manservant was shuffling into the hall from the nether regions of the house.

"I'll get it," Gervase said to him in French. "It is a friend of mine."

Fortunately, the servant did not wait to see who the friend might be. He nodded, turned, and shuffled back in the direction from which he had come.

Gervase opened the door, took one look at Lady Morgan's face, shadowed by darkness though it was, and dismissed any thought he might have had of stepping outside with her and marching her away from the house. Instead he grasped her by the upper arm and drew her inside before closing the door.

"Come upstairs where we can be private," he said. "Then you can tell me how I may serve you."

She was pale and obviously distraught. She said nothing as he hurried her up the stairs and into his sitting room and shut the door. Actually, he thought, it did not take much intelligence to guess what must have happened.

"The letter Alleyne was bringing back from the Duke of Wellington to Sir Charles Stuart has been found," she said, lowering her shawl to her shoulders. "It was lying abandoned in the forest between Waterloo and here." Her voice was hollow and expressionless. She gazed at him with eyes like huge pools of night in her face.

"Ah, yes, *chérie,*" he said. He took both her hands in his. They were like ice blocks.

She half smiled. "He is dead, is he not?"

Was she still trying, then, to cling to some shred of hope? But it was time to face the grim reality. It was why she had come to him, he realized. Someone from the embassy must have brought her the information, but he was the one to whom she had instinctively turned for the final interpretation of the facts. He wondered when exactly they had become such precious friends.

"Yes, *chérie,*" he said, "you must accept that he is dead."

She stared at him though her eyes were focused on something a million miles beyond him. Her shawl slipped slowly and unregarded from her shoulders and settled in a soft heap on the carpet at her feet. He released her hands and set his arms around her, one about her waist, the other about her shoulders. He drew her against him, and she turned her head to rest one cheek against his neckcloth.

"He is dead." She shivered.

"I'm afraid so."

She wept almost silently. He would hardly have known she wept at all if he had not felt the tremors of her body and the warmth of her tears as they soaked through the layers of cloth at his neck. He held her close and closer. He did not know quite how it had come about, this friendship that was deeper than any other he had known with either man or woman. It was the circumstances, he supposed—the far from ordinary circumstances that had drawn them into a far from ordinary relationship. Certainly it was not something that had developed from the early days of their acquaintance.

He continued to hold her long after she stopped weeping. She made no move to pull away. If she still needed the illusion of comfort, he would offer it for as long as she needed it. But finally she tipped back her head and gazed into his eyes in the shifting candlelight. Her tears had dried, though her face was heavy and puffy with grief.

It was the most stupid thing in the world to do. He could not explain it either at the time or afterward. It certainly seemed to be about the most inappropriate thing he could possibly have done—except that he was not afterward convinced that the action was not mutual.

He lowered his head and set his mouth to hers.

It was not like either of the two kisses they had shared before. This one was a hot and urgent embrace during which her mouth opened wide beneath his and his tongue plunged inside. Their arms closed about each other and clung like iron bands. It was a deeply, mindlessly, inexplicably passionate kiss. Life making its fierce protest, perhaps, in the face of death? But he had no real excuse, as he admitted to himself later.

And no excuse whatsoever for what followed.

He lifted his mouth a few inches from hers and looked into her dazed, passion-clouded eyes.

*"Chérie,"* he murmured.

"No." Her voice was throaty with need. "Ah, no." And she closed her eyes and pressed her parted lips to his again and kept one arm about his waist while the fingers of her other hand tangled in his hair.

He felt her grief, her agony, her need. And he felt his own need to comfort her, to give whatever it was she craved. But it was an emotional response that did not touch upon his intellect at all. He was not thinking. This was not an occasion for thought or cool reason. She needed him. And so he folded her to him, kissing her more deeply, more passionately even than before.

When she plucked frantically at the buttons of his coat and then his waistcoat, he helped her so that she could burrow closer, so that he could hold her more warmly to his heart. Her hands and arms went beneath his outer garments, one to clasp him about the waist, the other to press upward along his spine, only the fabric of his shirt between it and his bare flesh. He cupped her buttocks with his hands and half lifted her against him. If he could have taken her right inside himself, taken her pain for his own and so relieved her of it, he would have done so.

He kissed her lips, her chin, her neck, her throat. She rubbed herself against him, her breasts against his chest, her abdomen against his erection.

"Please." Her voice was throaty, her lips moving against his. "Please. Ah, please."

*"Chérie."*

He drew her backward a couple of steps and sat down on the sofa, drawing her with him. But instead of turning sideways and sitting on his lap, she knelt astride him, and the frenzy of their passion continued unabated. He raised her skirts to give her greater freedom of movement, and then reached under them to stroke her inner thighs and to find the hot, moist core of her.

She clutched his head with both hands, held it to her bosom, and alternately moaned and gasped. She moved against his hand.

He unbuttoned the flap of his breeches, drew her into position over his erection, grasped her by the hips, and eased her downward. But she would not let him be gentle. She pressed down hard and cried out as he became fully embedded in her.

Something in his mind registered the fact that of course it would have known anyway—that she was a virgin—but if instinct alone would have caused him to be gentle, to take her slowly, instinct would have counted for naught. She swept him along with the frenzy of her own passion, and they finished the deed with a fierce, pounding, gasping urge to reach some central core of oneness and peace and forgetfulness together.

Incredibly—it would have seemed incredible if he had been thinking—she tensed a moment before he plunged one more time and released into her, and she cried out again. But with the abandon of sexual climax this time instead of pain and shock.

They clung damply together for a minute or two while the world resumed its regular spinning course.

His first rational thought seemed to come from nowhere at all. But it spoke with clear, malevolent distinctness.

*Now,* it said, he had avenged himself on Bewcastle right enough.

HE WAS SITTING ACROSS one corner of the sofa, and she was curled up on his lap, her skirts decently about her legs again. His arms were about her while his head was back against the headrest. Amazingly, she thought she had been dozing. She did not believe he had. She thought he was awake though he was not saying anything.

What had happened between them had been something she needed, and she was not sorry. But she *was* sorry if it had changed the nature of their friendship. And how could it not have done? She had come to him—because he was her dearest friend in the world. Now, if only for this one occasion, he had been her lover. No, things could never be quite the same between them.

"You must not blame yourself," she told him without moving; for she would wager he *was* blaming himself. "That was not in any way your fault."

One of his hands was against her hair, she realized. His fingers lightly massaged her scalp, proving that he was indeed awake.

"Perhaps, *chérie,*" he said, "we should not think of tonight's event in terms of blame. That implies that something was wrong about it. It was not wrong, merely premature. I will talk to the Duke of Bewcastle when I take you home."

She sat upright then and turned to stare at him in dismay. She might have known he would react in just this stupid way. He was a gentleman, after all.

"About *marrying* me?" she asked him. "You most certainly will not."

He smiled lazily at her without lifting his head. "I will ask, *chérie,*" he said. "You may, of course, choose to say no, though I would not advise it."

"Of course I will say no!" she retorted. She blinked her eyes furiously then when they misted with tears—she almost *never* cried. "Don't spoil things, Lord Rosthorn. You have been my dearest friend during these dreadful days. Even tonight you have been my friend—you comforted me in the way I needed comforting. Don't spoil things by believing now that you must offer me marriage."

"But perhaps I wish to, *chérie,*" he said. "Perhaps I love you."

"You do *not,*" she told him. "You feel sympathy for me because of . . . because of Alleyne. And you like me, I believe, and respect me, as I like and respect you. There is a certain love in those feelings, but it is not the love of two people who are ready to commit their lives to each other."

*"Chérie,"* he said, "I have been inside your body. I have had your virginity."

*. . . inside your body.* She could feel her cheeks grow hot.

"That is exactly my point," she told him. "If we had merely sat down on the sofa here after I had come and told you my news, you would not now be telling me that you were going to speak to Wulf. Would you?"

He continued to smile at her but did not reply.

"You cannot say it, you see," she said. "You cannot lie. I will not marry you, Lord Rosthorn, simply because I have been intimate with you."

"*Chérie.*" He reached up one hand to cup her cheek. "We will not quarrel over this. Not tonight of all nights. I am sorry about Lord Alleyne Bedwyn. More sorry than I can say."

The wretched tears sprang to her eyes again.

"I thought," she said, "that if I denied the truth long enough, I would be better prepared when I *did* have to admit it. I expected that my emotions would have been cushioned against the worst of the pain. But they were not. And then tonight when I came here, I thought . . . I suppose I thought . . . But the pain has not gone away. I do not believe it has really even started yet."

"No, I suppose it has not." He drew her head down

with both hands and kissed her softly on the lips again. "And I thought to comfort you. But there *is* no comfort, *chérie*. Pain like yours is something that has to be lived through. You need to be with your family. You must go home to England."

She felt a great surge of longing for Wulfric—and for Freyja and her other brothers. Her *remaining* brothers.

"Yes," she said.

"I will take you," he said. "We will leave tomorrow."

"But I cannot ask such a thing of you." She frowned at him.

"You did not ask," he said. "We will leave early. I'll escort you back to Mrs. Clark's now and you can pack your belongings."

He set her on her feet and was bending to retrieve her shawl.

She could not go back to England alone, she thought. Independent as she liked to think herself, there were certain things that even she would not attempt without an escort. Traveling from one country to another was one of them. She had completely forgotten Sir Charles Stuart's offer to make arrangements to send her home.

"Thank you," she said, wrapping her shawl about her and shivering despite the warm evening air now that his arms were no longer about her.

He held her arm close to his side as he walked her home. She ought not to need such support, she thought, but she was grateful for it. Her mind had opened fully to reality—and pain. Alleyne was dead. Tomorrow she was going home. She was going to have to break the news to Wulfric.

And tonight she had been intimate with the Earl of Rosthorn. It was no wonder her legs felt distinctly unsteady.

There was altogether too much to think about, too much to feel. She did not speak as they walked. Neither did he. She did not notice any of the people they passed on the streets. She did not even notice when twice Lord Rosthorn said good evening to acquaintances.

"Mrs. Clark will doubtless be waiting for you," he told her as they approached the house. "Go in now, *chérie,* and rest if you can. It is going to be a long journey."

"Yes. Thank you."

He led her up the steps. But even as he lifted his hand to knock on the door, it opened from the inside and Mrs. Clark appeared, her face all anxious concern and relief.

"Oh, thank heaven!" she said fervently. "I have been almost out of my mind with worry. I am so glad you found her, my lord."

"I will be escorting Lady Morgan home to England tomorrow, ma'am," he said. "I will be back as early as possible in the morning. I will have to see about hiring a maid to accompany her first, though."

"That will be the best solution even if not quite ideal," Mrs. Clark said, "since I cannot go with her myself. Come, my dear." She set an arm about Morgan's shoulders. "Come to the kitchen and I'll make you that cup of tea I promised earlier."

Morgan gave in to the temptation to be coddled, at

least for a short while. Her mind, her emotions, had overwhelmed her.

It was a long and tedious journey home, though Morgan would not afterward have been able to say if it lasted for a day or a week. As much as she could, she kept herself cocooned deep inside her frozen grief so that she would not have to deal with the rawness of it alone—or in an inappropriate manner again, as she had done with the Earl of Rosthorn in his rooms. She felt deeply mortified that she had forced him into such an indiscretion and had left him feeling guilty and obliged to offer her marriage.

She had a new maid, a girl who spoke almost no English and knew very little about the duties of her position. But she had been hired, of course, only so that at least some of the proprieties might be observed. Ilse was to return to Brussels as soon as she had accompanied Morgan to London. The Earl of Rosthorn had explained that.

Morgan scarcely saw him between Brussels and Ostend. He rode beside the hired carriage while she sat silently inside with Ilse. But all that changed during the sea crossing to Harwich in England. Ilse was horribly seasick and could not leave the cabin she shared with her mistress. Morgan, on the other hand, could not bear to stay belowdecks. She needed to pace the ship's deck or stand at its rail or sit somewhere up in the open, where she could feel the salt air on her face and breathe in its freshness and gaze into eternity.

She did not care a fig about the proprieties.

She felt weighted down by the lonely burden of being the only one of her family to know the terrible truth. She tried to rehearse in her mind exactly what she would say, but even in her imagination there were no words. She still could hardly believe the truth of it herself. There was no body, no tangible proof that Alleyne was no more. If she closed her eyes she could see his handsome, laughing face and hear his light, teasing voice just as if he were right there with her. Sometimes she opened her eyes suddenly, as if to catch him there looking at her and laughing at the splendid joke he had played on her.

The Earl of Rosthorn was her constant and her only companion on the ship's deck even though there were other people on board with whom they were both acquainted. Morgan could not face being sociable but donned her haughtiest, most forbidding countenance and stood or sat apart from them. He always stayed at her side. Usually they were silent. Occasionally they talked on topics she could not afterward remember. Once, at the ship's rail when the wind was more like a gale and almost everyone else had gone belowdecks, he wrapped her cloak more warmly about her shoulders and kept his arm comfortingly about her. They stood thus for an hour or more.

Even through the self-imposed numbness of her heart she was very aware that she now knew him in a different way than before. But it was an incident to which he made no reference, and it was one with which her mind could not cope at present. She was simply grateful that they had somehow found it possible to revert to the friendship they had shared since the night of the Richmond ball.

If it occurred to Morgan at all that being up on deck thus without her maid was improper, that that fact and her closeness to the Earl of Rosthorn, her escort, might well be instigating gossip among their fellow passengers, and that word might quickly spread once they were all ashore, she would have dismissed the thoughts with contempt. She was no one's concern but her own—and Wulfric's, and *he* would understand once she had explained.

More than anything else in this world she wanted to be home—at Lindsey Hall, at Bedwyn House in London, *anywhere* where her sister and brothers were. Anywhere where Wulfric was. Wulfric would take the burden from her shoulders. He would know what to do. And yet going home was also what she dreaded more than anything else in this life. How would she face them? What would she *say?*

They disembarked at Harwich on a windy, wet afternoon that felt more like autumn than the height of summer. They would stay at the Harbour Inn close to the quay, the Earl of Rosthorn told her, pointing toward it, and continue on their way to London in the morning.

"I'll have you settled in a room there in no time at all," he promised. "Then I will see about hiring a carriage for tomorrow while you try to rest. One more day and you will be home."

She held on to the brim of her bonnet against the wind and looked at him with a frown.

"How selfish I have been," she said, "thinking only of myself through the whole journey. You have come to England for the first time in nine years."

"I have indeed, *chérie,*" he said with a smile. "And so far I have survived the shock."

For the first time it struck her that this journey, this arrival, must be almost as great an ordeal for him as for her. He had to meet people he had not seen in nine years. Somehow he had to pick up the reins of a life he had been forced to abandon when he was a very young man. Had she forced him to come before he was quite ready? She looked at him with deep remorse. She could have been speaking to him about these things during those silent hours on the ship. Instead, she had been self-absorbed. She would make *him* the topic of their conversation at dinner, she resolved.

"I hope," she said, "it will be a happy return for you."

Lord Rosthorn took her gloved hand on his arm and smiled at her.

Ilse, somewhat recovered from her indisposition now that they were on solid ground, trailed along behind them as they made their way toward the inn, their faces bent to the wind and the rain. It was a great relief to step inside the building at last and see a fire roaring in the large hearth of the reception hall. Morgan moved closer to it, shaking raindrops from her cloak, while the Earl of Rosthorn approached the desk.

How different were her feelings now from those she had experienced the last time she had been in Harwich, not even two months ago. Surely then she must have been ten years younger than she felt now. If only she could go back, make everything turn out differently. But how? Have a tantrum there at the Namur Gates and insist that Alleyne stop what he was doing and take her back to England then and there?

She held her hands out to the warmth of the fire and turned her head to watch Lord Rosthorn make arrangements for their night's stay—and found herself gazing at a tall, elegantly cloaked gentleman who was striding across the reception hall in the direction of the outer doors.

*Wulfric!*

For a moment she was so overwhelmed by shock and disbelief that she could neither move nor cry out.

He had not seen her. But he *had* seen the Earl of Rosthorn. He stopped abruptly, his face a mask of narrow-eyed coldness, his nostrils flaring.

But Morgan did not really notice. She had found both her feet and her voice.

"Wulf!" she cried, and then she hurtled toward him, panic clawing at her back and at her heels. *"Wulf!"*

Wulfric was not the sort of man into whose arms one would normally think of dashing. But at that moment he represented for her all that was solid and safe and dear. She hurled herself into his arms and felt all the reassurance of his presence as they closed about her.

It was a moment that was soon over. He took her firmly by the upper arms, set her away from him, and glanced briefly down at her before looking over her head at the Earl of Rosthorn. His expression would have made icicles shiver.

"Doubtless someone," he said so softly that he was

clearly at his most dangerous, "is about to offer an explanation."

He had clearly heard a thing or two, a part of her mind told her. The Countess of Caddick had doubtless been busy talking. But it was not that thought that was uppermost in Morgan's mind. She did not even think to wonder what he was doing here in Harwich. Panic was clenching her stomach, threatening to make her retch.

"Wulf," she said, her voice shaking so badly that the words blurted out of her in jerky spurts. She pawed ineffectually at the capes of his cloak and forgot all about dignity and partially rehearsed speeches. "Wulf, Alleyne is dead." Then all she could hear was the clacking of her own teeth.

His cold silver eyes changed. Something—some light—went out behind them, leaving them flat and opaque. His hands felt like iron bands about her arms. Then he nodded his head once, twice, and again and again, slowly, almost imperceptibly.

"Ah," he said in a voice so distant that Morgan scarcely heard him.

It was a truly terrifying moment—Wulfric at a loss for either words or actions. She had never seen its like before. He was suddenly a human who might at any moment show a vulnerability she had never suspected him capable of. She did not *want* him to be a human being. She wanted him to be her eldest brother, Wulfric, the invincible Duke of Bewcastle. She did not want to be eighteen years old and a woman at that moment. She wanted to be a child again in the safe orbit of his immutable power.

But the moment of near vulnerability passed. His eyes focused on Lord Rosthorn again and he was Wulfric once more. His hands dropped away from Morgan's arms. She opened her mouth to make the necessary introductions, but Wulfric spoke first.

"Well, *Rosthorn,*" he said, with a slight emphasis on the name.

"Bewcastle?" the earl said in return. "My sincerest condolences. I was in the process of escorting Lady Morgan and her maid home to London. Perhaps we can find some room where we may be more private? You have asked for an explanation."

Morgan darted him a glance. He sounded different, his words more clipped and precise, his French accent almost undetectable. He was looking back at Wulfric with hard eyes and hard-set jaw. Wulfric really *had* heard something, and Lord Rosthorn knew it. And so she was going to be caught between the pride and infernal sense of honor of two gentlemen.

*Just moments after she had told Wulf that Alleyne was dead.*

"I believe we may dispense with the need for explanations," Wulfric said. "After the visit Lady Caddick paid me yesterday, I was on my way to Brussels in person to find Lady Morgan and bring her home. Now it would appear that it is unnecessary for me to proceed on my original errand, though perhaps I will need to go to make arrangements to have my brother's body brought home." Morgan watched his hand close about the handle of his quizzing glass, his knuckles very white. "Either way your escort is no longer needed,

Rosthorn. I will see to Lady Morgan Bedwyn's protection from this moment on. Good day to you."

Morgan looked at him in astonishment. He was not even going to listen to an explanation? He was not going to thank Lord Rosthorn for escorting her home? Or tell him exactly what Lady Caddick had accused him of? And was it her imagination, or did these two men *know* each other?

She turned her head to look at Lord Rosthorn. His expression was still tight, granite-jawed, hard-eyed. She scarcely recognized him. But he looked back at her and made her a deep, formal bow.

"Good-bye, *chérie,*" he said.

"You are *leaving,* then?" she asked him. Just like that?

But he had already turned away from them and was moving with long strides toward the outer door. She could not let him simply go like that, she thought. But before she could take one step after him Wulfric took one of her upper arms in his grasp again and she turned her wide-eyed attention back to him.

He had not thought it necessary to find a private room when Lord Rosthorn had suggested it. But he must have given some indication to the staff on duty in the reception hall. Within moments they were being ushered with much bowing and scraping into a private parlor, and the door was closing behind them.

Her legs felt weak beneath her then as she realized anew the enormity of the moment. Her dearest friend was gone, so swiftly and unexpectedly that she had not even had a chance to say good-bye to him. But she was home. Wulf was here and she had already unburdened herself of her terrible secret knowledge.

He was looking at her with his pale silver eyes. His hand, in a familiar gesture, had already possessed itself of the handle of his quizzing glass.

"You will tell me now, Morgan, if you will," he said, "how Alleyne lost his life."

She looked steadily back at him, ignoring the ringing in her ears, the coldness in her head, and the weakness in her knees.

"He died at the Battle of Waterloo," she told him.

## CHAPTER XI

THE RAIN WAS STILL FALLING IN A STEADY DRIZZLE and the wind was still blowing in chilly gusts. Gervase nonetheless rode his hired horse at a pace close to a gallop, heedless of either danger or discomfort.

He had been dismissed out of hand. Bewcastle, who had clearly heard enough from Lady Caddick to send him on his way to Brussels in person, had first demanded an explanation and then refused to listen to one. He had dismissed his old enemy just as if he were nothing and nobody.

Gervase seethed with a hatred that had flared to new life as soon as he set eyes upon Bewcastle. It was a hatred he had not yet paused to consider. It blinded him, pulsed in his mind, clouded his judgment. But of one thing he was satisfied —for all his cold control, Bewcastle was clearly rattled. And he would be more so, Gervase vowed. They were not finished with each other yet.

Oh, no, not by a long way.

He pulled his horse over to the side of the road to allow a mail coach to pass from the opposite direction, spraying up water and mud as it did so. He moved forward again at a more cautious, mindful pace.

He would be paying the Duke of Bewcastle a visit in London soon. But not *too* soon. Even through his hatred he recognized the need for some decency. The Bedwyn family must be allowed a short while to mourn.

*She* needed time. Foolishly, he tried not to put a face or a name to the one person who might soften his resolve at the same time as she gave him the opening he needed to cause lasting mischief.

In the meantime gossip from Brussels and from the ship was bound to spread to London, and with the Caddicks to fan the flames Gervase did not doubt that it would be vicious and unrelenting enough to erupt into a full-blown public scandal.

He would not go to London immediately, he decided. It was high time he went home to Windrush Grange in Kent. It was time somehow to pick up his life where he had left it off nine years ago. He wondered if it would be possible, though. He was neither the man he had been then or the man he had been growing into.

He rode onward, very aware that he was in England again, very aware too that it was not a soft welcome that was being extended to him. The landscape was gray and dreary, the clouds heavy and low. Raindrops dripped from the brim of his hat and somehow found their way down the back of his neck. The road ahead glistened with mud and gleamed with puddles denoting mild depressions or deep potholes—there was no knowing which unless one were incautious enough to step into one of them. Perhaps, he thought, it would have been wiser to remain in Harwich, to have taken passage on the first ship back to the Continent.

But he had business here in England. It was time.

He continued to ride onward.

And despite himself he thought of Lady Morgan Bedwyn—exquisite in her youthful loveliness at the Cameron ball, haughty and intelligent and alluring at the picnic in the Forest of Soignés, disheveled and beautiful and unflinching at the Namur Gates as she bent over a human bundle of bloody rags, huge-eyed with grief in his rooms on the Rue de Brabant, fierce with passion as she reached for comfort. A fascinating woman of many facets.

"Damnation!" He reined in his horse when he realized that he had urged it to a gallop again. "Damnation!"

How could he use her . . .

But he already had, of course.

*He already had.*

FOR TEN DAYS MORGAN seemed to live in a fog of unreality. She explained everything to Wulfric, much of it spilling out of her in a great rush in that private parlor at the Harbour Inn, more of it drawn from her by his careful questioning both then and during the seemingly interminable journey home to London the next day. She told him all she knew about Alleyne's disappearance and about the reappearance of the letter, which seemed to be incontrovertible proof that he had been killed. She told him about the Caddicks and their determination to return home and their consequent refusal to remain in Brussels with her. She told him about Mrs. Clark's giving her a temporary home and of all the work they and the other regimental wives had performed tending the wounded.

The story Lady Caddick had told when she called at Bedwyn House, all righteous indignation, had been somewhat different from her own, Morgan gathered. She had made no mention of Alleyne's being missing or of Morgan's tending the wounded. In Lady Caddick's version Morgan had been simply a headstrong, wayward, disobedient girl who had refused to be torn away from the pleasures of the city and the ineligible beaux who danced attendance upon her there, most notably the Earl of Rosthorn.

"And you believed," Morgan asked haughtily, turning her head to look out of the carriage window, "that I stayed for the sake of frivolity, Wulf? Do you know me so little?"

"It would seem so," he agreed. "I did not expect that you would be so bold as to dismiss a chaperon like yesterday's outworn bonnet. However, neither did I expect that your chaperon would discard you. I had a word with Lady Caddick on the subject before she took her leave."

Morgan would love to have been an invisible witness to that particular set-down, which she did not doubt had left the countess feeling half an inch tall.

She tried several times to tell him about the kindness the Earl of Rosthorn had shown her, but each time he listened without comment and then spoke about something quite unrelated to what she had just told him. Wulf would not be able to understand, of course, that there had been nothing ordinary about the past couple of weeks, that the usual rules of propriety had seemed supremely irrelevant to her. But there was, undeniably, the great guilt of what had occurred between them during that final evening in Brussels. It was hard to believe that either of them could have allowed it to happen.

"Do you have a previous acquaintance with the Earl of Rosthorn?" she asked Wulfric at one point of their journey.

"Enough to know that he is no suitable escort for you," he said. "I trust this inn we are approaching is the one appointed for our next change of horses. I will need an explanation of why we are half an hour late."

Nine years ago Wulfric would have been twenty-four. Doubtless he had known the earl. Doubtless too he knew of the scandal that had sent the younger man into long exile. It was on the tip of her tongue to ask him for an account of those sordid events, but she held her peace. The Earl of Rosthorn had never volunteered the information himself. She would not now try to worm it out of Wulfric, who was clearly hostile to him.

She missed him. Their parting had been far too sudden and abrupt. He had left a certain void in her life. She wondered if he would come, as he had said he would, to make a formal offer for her hand to Wulfric. She sincerely hoped not. But when he did not come at all, when he did not even call to see how she did or to pay his official condolences, she was undeniably disappointed, even hurt.

She tried not to think about him. He owed her nothing, after all—despite what his sense of honor might say to the contrary. Indeed, matters were quite the other way around. It was *she* who was in *his* debt.

Freyja and Joshua were still in London, Parliament being still in session. It was not just Joshua's political obligations that had kept them here, though. Freyja had sponsored Morgan's presentation and come-out, but at the same time she had sponsored Lady Chastity Moore, Joshua's cousin and ward, who was living with them at their London home. Chastity had recently become happily betrothed to Viscount Meecham. But even apart from their other obligations they would probably have delayed their return to Penhallow in Cornwall for Freyja to consult a reputable physician. She was in the early months of pregnancy.

Aidan came from Oxfordshire with Eve and their adopted children, Davy and Becky, and Rannulf and Judith came from Leicestershire even though William, their son, was only a little over two months old. They all came in immediate response to the letters Wulfric wrote them and sent by special messenger.

It should have been enormously comforting to

Morgan to be surrounded by her family. And in many ways it was. But Wulfric, apart from providing the bare facts, was more than usually reticent and spent most of his time in the library. It fell to Morgan's lot, then, to answer the myriad questions they all asked.

It was a dreadful thing to witness the grief of her strong-minded siblings. Freyja bore up the best, on the outside, at least, remaining determinedly brisk and cheerful even though her face looked chiseled out of marble and Joshua hovered over her almost every moment, lines of worry etching his normally good-humored face. Rannulf—bluff, hearty Ralf—became almost totally withdrawn and spent much of his time in the nursery holding his new son even when the baby slept. Aidan—the tough, dour ex-cavalry officer—wept as he held Morgan in a viselike grip, embarrassing himself with painful, gulping sobs that he tried in vain to swallow.

There was a terrible, yawning emptiness in their family circle where Alleyne had been.

Perhaps the very worst aspect of the whole tragedy was that there was no body—none to weep over and sit vigil beside. None to bury and visit with flowers and gradually softening memories as the years passed. No body—just emptiness.

Wulfric arranged a memorial service to be held on the eleventh day after Morgan's return at St. George's in Hanover Square. It was an event that was very well attended. Morgan sat beside Wulfric in the front pew and would have held his hand if he had offered it. But he was colder, more unapproachable, than ever, as if he had frozen himself deep within a massive, all-encompassing iceberg. Perhaps only a sister would understand that he did indeed *feel* grief. But that understanding was little consolation to her. Aidan had Eve, Rannulf had Judith, and Freyja had Joshua. She had no one. She sat through the service with her hands in her lap and her eyes on her hands.

The Earl of Rosthorn had not come. She could no longer hope otherwise when the service was over and most of the congregation lingered outside the church to allow the Bedwyn family to drive away first. He was nowhere in sight even though she looked around deliberately for him. Nor did he come to Bedwyn House with almost everyone else for tea.

Perhaps he was not in London, she thought. Perhaps he had gone back to Belgium or somewhere else on the Continent—Paris maybe. Perhaps he had gone into the country to his own estate. But she was hurt by his absence. Even apart from that evening in Brussels, she had really thought they were friends. He had not even written. He could not write personally to her, of course—it would not have been at all the thing. But he might have written a letter of condolence to the whole family, might he not?

Other people came back to the house that she would rather not have seen. The Earl and Countess of Caddick came with Rosamond. Even Captain Lord Gordon was there, looking dashingly romantic in full dress uniform, with one boot missing to accommodate his splinted leg. He moved about on crutches, his batman hovering at his elbow, and won for himself the admiring regard of many of those in attendance—a hero and survivor of the Battle of Waterloo.

Rosamond hugged Morgan and was reluctant to let her go.

"I do not care what they say, Morgan," she said. "I always tell anyone who will listen how splendidly brave you were. I am so dreadfully sorry about Lord Alleyne." She was too choked with tears to say more.

Her mother suffered from no such impediment.

"I am delighted to see you safely at home again, Lady Morgan," she said, a sharp edge to her voice. "It is a good thing for you that you returned bearing such sad news or I daresay Bewcastle would have shown his displeasure over your selfish disobedience to me in a manner you would not have enjoyed. At first he was inclined to blame *me* for leaving without you, if you can imagine such a thing. I daresay he has realized his error since then, though. Indeed, I do not know how he could avoid doing so."

Morgan merely lifted her eyebrows, regarded her former chaperon with silent disdain, and moved on to another group.

She would have preferred to avoid Captain Lord Gordon altogether, but he deliberately put himself in her way and asked for a private word with her. She sat with him in one corner of the drawing room, a little removed from everyone else. She would, she supposed, forgive him. But it would take an effort of will to speak the words. She would do so only because really he was of no importance to her whatsoever.

His facial bruises had faded. He looked, she thought,

quite as handsome as ever. It was hard to believe, though, that once, not so very long ago, she had been slightly infatuated with him.

"Lady Morgan," he said, "I do hope you will forgive me."

"They were difficult days, Captain," she said. "I daresay none of us behaved as well as we ought or as we would have done in more normal circumstances. It is best forgotten."

"You are most generous." He was visibly relieved. "I was about to ride into my first battle, you see, and was neither thinking nor speaking rationally."

*About to ride into battle?* She frowned.

"For what do you beg forgiveness, Lord Gordon?" she asked him.

He flushed and did not quite meet her eyes when he spoke.

"I thought that perhaps I had raised expectations where I intended none," he said. "I thought that perhaps I had aroused hope when I did not mean to suggest anything of a permanent nature."

He was not, she realized, talking of their final encounter outside the house on the Rue de Bellevue but of what had happened between them at the Duchess of Richmond's ball.

"You thought perhaps, Lord Gordon," she said, her voice very soft, "that I was under the impression we were betrothed?"

"I-I . . ." He looked sheepish.

"I was not under any such impression," she told him. "Had you asked me outright on that occasion, I would have said no. Any petition for my hand must, of course, be made formally and correctly. I would *never,* Lord Gordon, so forget myself as to engage in a clandestine betrothal with a man who had not first addressed himself to the Duke of Bewcastle. But even if you *had* proceeded thus, and even if he *had* given his approval, I would most certainly have refused you."

His flush deepened. "I am perfectly eligible, Lady Morgan," he said stiffly. "I will be Caddick one day."

"I do not care if you were in expectation of becoming the Prince of Wales one day," Morgan said, lifting her chin and looking along her nose at him as if he were some particularly nasty specimen of humanity. "You are not a gentleman I would deem worthy of *my* hand, Captain Gordon. I am thankful that it is not your behavior on the morning you left Brussels for which you came to beg my forgiveness. In a moment of weakness I might have granted it." She stood.

"Mama is quite right about you," he said sharply. "So is everyone else."

"Indeed?" She regarded him with one of her frostiest looks.

"You are mighty haughty, my lady," he said, "for someone whose name is being bandied about every club and drawing room in London like that of the veriest trollop. You do not imagine, do you, that you were not seen all over Brussels on the arm of the Earl of Rosthorn and even *embracing* him on a public street or alone on the ship with him all the way to Harwich, his arm about your shoulders, his hand in yours? Even for a Bedwyn your behavior has been too shocking for words." He sounded like a spiteful boy retaliating for an insult.

"And yet," she said, her eyes sweeping disdainfully over him, "you have found enough words with which to wax positively eloquent, Captain. I congratulate you."

She continued to stare coldly at him for a few moments longer. But inside she was shocked indeed. Could it possibly be true? There was *gossip* about her? Because she had remained behind in Brussels to tend the wounded and await word of Alleyne, and the Earl of Rosthorn had been kind enough to watch after her and to escort her about Brussels when she had needed relaxation? Because he had been kind enough to escort her to England when she had needed to come? She had had a maid with her.

When had she been seen embracing him? She could remember only one occasion, outside Mrs. Clark's when she had been weary from overwork and had slept with her head on his shoulder for a few minutes. She had stood on the step above him afterward and leaned forward and kissed him.

There were always pedestrians on that street.

She might have guessed that there would be gossip in London, of course. The Caddicks would have brought plenty with them. And those other things, so supremely unimportant during those days in Brussels, would seem shocking indeed to English people who had not been there to know what it had been like.

And she was not entirely innocent, was she? Not innocent at all, in fact. There was no point in resorting to righteous indignation.

Captain Lord Gordon must have been beside himself with fear that somehow he had trapped himself into a commitment to her during the Duchess of Richmond's ball and that she might be unwilling to release him. He would not enjoy hobbling his way—literally as well as figuratively—through a sordid scandal with her on his arm, this military hero who had almost won the Battle of Waterloo single-handedly. Morgan smiled with arctic contempt at him and turned away without another word.

Was *this* why the Earl of Rosthorn had not come to Bedwyn House during the past ten days or to the memorial service today? she wondered. Had he been driven from London by the gossip? Perhaps even from England? That would be grossly unfair.

But if it *were* so, she could never expect to see him again. It was a horribly depressing thought. Today of all days she longed to see him, to watch that lazy smile light his eyes again, to listen to his attractive French accent, to hear him call her *chérie*. She wanted someone of her very own with her—a dear friend. But how abject that sounded now that the thought had verbalized itself in her mind. She did not need him. She did not need anyone. She straightened her shoulders and joined another group of visitors.

Finally everyone had left. Aunt and Uncle Rochester had gone home. So had Freyja and Joshua, Chastity and Lord Meecham with them. Aidan and Eve, Rannulf and Judith had all gone up to the nursery to see their children. Morgan felt horribly lonely despite all her resolves—and despite the fact that she had refused an invitation from Joshua to go back with them for the evening and from both Eve and Judith to go to the nursery with them. She would go to the library, she decided, and sit with Wulfric. She would not disturb him. She did not expect him to talk to her or entertain her in any way. She just wanted to curl up on one of the leather chairs there and feel the reassurance of his company.

She did not knock on the door. She opened it quietly, intending to creep inside without drawing attention to herself.

He was standing before the empty hearth, staring into the fireplace, his back to her. His shoulders were shaking. One of his hands was balled into a fist on the mantelpiece above his head. He was sobbing, choking on the sounds as Aidan had done days before.

Morgan gazed in horror for a few paralyzed moments.

Then she closed the door even more quietly than she had opened it and fled upstairs to her room.

If Wulf was weeping, the end of the world seemed near indeed.

She cast herself facedown across her bed and gathered fistfuls of the bedcover on either side of her head.

Alleyne was dead.

He was gone forever.

For the first time since that evening in Brussels she gave in to a storm of grief.

# CHAPTER XII

THE SUN WAS FINALLY BREAKING THROUGH THE clouds on the afternoon that Gervase arrived home. The gravel of the driveway that wound its way in leisurely meanderings through the woods and over the rolling hills of the park surrounding Windrush Grange was wet but not soggy. Water dripped from the leaves overhead and clung in sparkling drops to the grass. There was a richly verdant smell in the air.

He was powerfully reminded of how he had always loved Windrush, how thankful he had always been that he was the elder son, that he would be the one to inherit while his brother, Pierre, was the one destined for the church. This lengthy approach to the house had always lifted his spirits.

But it was nine years since he had last ridden along it. His father had been alive in those days. Both his sisters had still been at home. He had been a carefree young man, eager to enjoy the pleasures of town and the companionship of his peers, but eager too to learn all that he needed to know as his father's heir. He had been a basically happy, blameless young man whose life was progressing smoothly along a path that had been mapped out for him since childhood.

And then disaster had struck in a series of nightmarish events over which he had seemed to have no control whatsoever.

He felt as if he were riding back into someone else's life.

There was a large flower garden to one side of the gabled, red-brick house, complete with a trellised arch, cobbled pathways, and wrought-iron seat beneath an old weeping willow. There were three women there, he could see as he rode closer, two of them bent over the flowers, long baskets over their arms to hold the blooms, the third holding an infant on one hip as she watched. There was a man on the seat.

One of the women straightened up at the sound of his horse's hooves and held the floppy brim of her straw hat. And then she cried out, hastily set her basket down, and came running toward him, one hand holding up the hem of her dress. She was petite, still youthfully slender, still dark-haired. Her face was alight with welcome.

Gervase dismounted, tossed the reins over his horse's neck, and strode toward her, his arms outstretched.

"Gervase!" she cried. "Gervase, *mon fils.*"

*"Maman!"* He caught her up in his arms, spun once about with her, and set her on her feet again.

"You are home." She stood back and raised one slightly trembling hand to his cheek while her eyes devoured his face. "Ah, my beloved boy, and you are more handsome than ever."

"Whereas you have stayed the same age, *Maman,*" he said with a grin. "You are a mere girl."

It was not quite true, of course. There were streaks of gray in her hair and there were lines in her face. But she had aged well in nine years. She was still lovely.

The man had come hurrying up behind her. He had been still a boy when Gervase saw him last. He was a bespectacled, soberly clad gentleman now, tall and lean and balding.

"Pierre?"

For a moment it seemed that the brothers would hug each other. But both hesitated and the moment passed. Gervase held out his right hand, and Pierre clasped it.

"Gervase," he said. "It is fitting that you have come home. I am glad. Allow me, if I may, to present my wife. This is Rosthorn, Emma, my dear."

She curtsied to him, a brown-haired, unremarkable young woman. Gervase took her hand and bowed over it.

"Mrs. Ashford," he said. "My pleasure, ma'am. And this is your son?"

The child gazed at him with fine gray eyes. There was a halo of blond curls about his chubby face.

"This is Jonathan, my lord," she said.

"Jonathan." His nephew. He had one other and three nieces, offspring of his sisters. Life had gone on in nine years as if he had never been.

"And here is Henrietta come to greet you, Gervase," his mother said.

She was his second cousin and had lived with them since the death of her parents had made her his father's ward. She at least looked much as she always had—small and solid, dark-haired, square-faced, by no means ugly but not pretty either. She had never married. She must be seven or eight and twenty by now.

"Henrietta." He smiled and bowed to her.

"Gervase." She curtsied without smiling.

It was not a poor welcome, he thought as his mother

took his arm and drew him in the direction of the house and a groom led his horse to the stables. There was no sign of hostility or resentment in any of them. But there was a guardedness, a certain awkwardness, as if they were all strangers—as indeed they were.

He had been robbed of his family, he thought, among other things. Would the closeness that had always characterized their relations with one another ever return? Could it be retrieved? He felt the absence of his father keenly. His father had been his hero.

And then his father had rejected him. Utterly. He had preferred to listen to the lies and fabrications of others rather than to the protestations of innocence of the son he had always claimed to love.

That had been a terrible betrayal.

Worse than Marianne's.

Worse than Bewcastle's.

It had been devastating.

DURING THE COMING DAYS there were the servants to meet and the steward to consult with—almost all strangers to him. There was the home farm to be inspected and the park to be explored—all familiar yet somehow irrevocably different. There were tenants to call upon and neighbors to receive since word of his return home spread quickly in the countryside and people came to pay their respects. If they had ever known the reason for his hasty departure to the Continent years ago and his lengthy stay there, nothing was said of it now. Indeed, one or two seemed to assume that he had gone in order to live for a time with his mother's relatives. Almost all these people were familiar to him, and yet all felt like strangers.

Gervase felt uncomfortable and uneasy in his own home. Whenever he had thought of coming, he supposed he had thought of returning to everything and everyone exactly as he had left them. He had thought of returning to himself as he had been.

But everything had changed, himself most of all.

He resented it. He deeply resented it. But after a few days he realized that he could not simply return to the Continent and continue with the life of wandering dissipation that he had lived for the past number of years. Because he had come home, he could not go back. He was a man caught in limbo, belonging nowhere and to no one.

Not that he had any tangible reason to complain. His mother in particular doted on him.

He asked her one morning at breakfast about his absent neighbors. Several families were away in London for the Season. Indeed, Gervase had only just escaped coming home to an empty house. His mother and Henrietta had been planning to leave for London themselves within a few days, to do some shopping and to attend the theater and perhaps a few select *ton* entertainments.

His mother prattled on with stories about the neighbors, filling him in on much that he had missed in his years away. There had been very few changes of any significance, he gathered—very few losses of families, very few new ones.

"And the Marquess of Paysley?" he asked her. "Has

he been much to Winchholme Park lately, *Maman?*"

He hoped the man was not there now. There would be all the dilemma of deciding whether he ought to be called upon. But Winchholme was one of the smaller of the marquess's properties. He never had been in residence there a great deal.

"Ah, but the marquess you remember died some time ago, Gervase," his mother told him, leaning slightly sideways so that the butler could pour her a second cup of coffee. "Did I not tell you so in one of my letters, *mon fils?*" She darted him a quick smile but then concentrated upon stirring sugar into her drink.

"No," he said. She knew she had not, of course. It was not something she would have mentioned.

"The new marquess does not own Winchholme," she said. "It was unentailed, if you will remember. The old marquess left it to his daughter in his will."

Gervase looked sharply at her. The marquess had had only the one daughter.

"To Marianne?" he said. "And does she live there?"

"Yes, she does," his mother said. "You should perhaps see her and talk with her. It would be very distressing for you to be avoiding each other for the rest of your lives when you live a mere four miles apart, would it not? All that happened was a long time ago."

He stared mutely at her. Yes, a long time ago indeed—all of which time he had spent in exile. Did she seriously expect that he could forgive and forget and simply let bygones be bygones? He had known Marianne since childhood. His sisters and Henrietta had played with her. So had he on occasion. And then she had betrayed him so horribly.

"Henrietta and she are still friends," his mother continued when it became obvious that he would not reply. "You cannot ignore her existence entirely."

"Who is her husband?" Gervase asked.

"But she never married," his mother said. "Beautiful as she is, she has never found the man who will please her. Promise me you will call upon her."

"No!" he exclaimed more sharply than he intended. "No, I will not do that, *Maman*. I cannot think kindly of her."

Indeed, it hurt that his mother accepted her as a neighbor with such complacency and had not discouraged the friendship between Henrietta and Marianne. It hurt that Henrietta had not spurned her erstwhile friend. Had it mattered to no one that he had been cut off from his life almost as effectively as if someone had put a bullet through his heart? Had they imagined that he was *enjoying* himself on the Continent?

But even within the confines of his own head his complaints were beginning to sound annoyingly self-pitying. He got to his feet, kissed his mother's hand, and excused himself to go about his day's business.

The old life was gone, never to be retrieved. His years of wandering and debauchery were over. It was time he carved a new life for himself. And that new life, of course, was to involve a journey to London in the near future. He was just not sure exactly when he would go.

He had been home for a week when Horace Blake came to call on him. Blake was one of the neighbors who had been absent in London—he had arrived home just the day before. He was a few years older than Gervase, but they had nevertheless shared an easy camaraderie in the past. They shook hands amiably now and settled in the library, one on each side of the fireplace, each with a drink in his hand.

"Well, Rosthorn," Blake said with a grin after they had exchanged pleasantries and some idle chitchat, "you are still the devil you always were, I hear."

Gervase raised his eyebrows. He never had been much of a devil.

"You are the talk of town," Blake said. "There are even wagers in the betting books in all the clubs on whether you will offer for the chit or not—and on whether Bewcastle will accept even if you *do* offer. There was some sort of altercation with him, was there not, before you went away?"

Ah. It *had* happened, then, had it? They had not escaped the gossiping tongues of the *ton.*

"One might say so," he said. "I assume you refer to Lady Morgan Bedwyn, Blake? I had the honor of escorting her home from Brussels since she needed to return in a hurry with the news of her brother's death."

"Ah, yes," his friend said. "Lord Alleyne Bedwyn. Tragic that, poor devil. There is to be a grand memorial service at St. George's on Hanover Square in a few days' time. It is a good thing Lady Morgan has the excuse of mourning to keep her at home until it is over. Did you really dance with her alone in the middle of a forest one night, Rosthorn? And whisk her away with you when the Caddicks would have brought her home to England? And kiss her in the middle of a street in Brussels? And stand on the ship's deck alone with her, your arm about her shoulders? And then abandon her as soon as you set foot on English soil? The girl will be fortunate if Bewcastle does not lock her up for the next decade or two on a diet of bread and water."

He appeared to find the idea amusing as he laughed down into his glass and swirled the contents before tossing them back in one swallow.

It was every bit as sensational as Gervase had guessed it might be—perhaps more so. Dancing alone with her in the middle of a forest indeed! Kissing her in the middle of a street! Whisking her away . . .

He wondered how much she was suffering from the scandal. His guess was that she would snap her fingers in its face and lift that chin of hers and those arrogant eyebrows and invite it to do its worst. But of course she had Bewcastle to deal with now, and that gentleman would not be amused.

He changed the subject, and the visit continued for another half an hour before he rode down the driveway to the gates of the park with his guest. He rode back, alone with his own thoughts.

It was time, he realized.

He left his horse with a groom at the stables and hurried back to the house. He took the stairs two at a time and found his mother alone in her private sitting room, as he had hoped. She set aside her embroidery and smiled warmly at him.

*"Maman,"* he said. "I believe you should resurrect your plan to spend a week or so shopping and social-

izing in London. It will take a day or so for Pickford House to be made ready, but I can send word immediately. How soon can you and Henrietta be ready to leave? Two days after tomorrow?"

She jumped to her feet, her hands clasped to her bosom, her eyes shining.

"And you will be coming too, *mon fils?*" she asked him. "I was never more happy in my life. I will be seen going about London on the arm of the most handsome gentleman there."

GERVASE CALLED AT Bedwyn House the day after the memorial service for Lord Alleyne Bedwyn. He rapped the brass knocker against the door, handed his card to the butler, asking specifically for the Duke of Bewcastle, and waited in the hall.

The house was quiet. During the five minutes he waited—or was kept waiting—there was no sign of anyone except one liveried footman who stood silently on guard. And then the butler returned, nodded regally, and invited Lord Rosthorn to follow him. He led the way to a downstairs book room, impressively male, its four walls lined with filled bookshelves from floor to ceiling, its large oak, leather-topped desk dominating the far end, plush leather chairs and sofa arranged about the high marble fireplace.

Bewcastle was seated behind the desk. He did not rise as Gervase advanced across the room, but he did watch him every step of the way with his hooded silver eyes. The room had been arranged deliberately thus, Gervase thought—so that servants or family members called to account for some misdeed or petitioners and lowly supplicants or unwelcome guests would be made to feel all their lack of power as they approached the august presence of the man who had an abundance of it.

Gervase fell, he supposed, into the category of unwelcome guest. There was a strong temptation to lower his eyes to the Persian carpet beneath his feet as he approached, but he fixed his eyes upon his erstwhile friend instead and kept them there. He would be damned before he would feel cowed even before he had uttered a word.

"Bewcastle?" He nodded genially and spoke briskly when he was close.

"Rosthorn." The duke's hand closed about the handle of the quizzing glass hanging from a black silk ribbon about his neck. "You are doubtless about to explain the purpose of this visit."

He did not invite his visitor to be seated. It was a very deliberate ruse to make him feel like an unequal as well as an unwelcome guest, of course. Gervase acknowledged his understanding of that fact with slightly pursed lips and a half-smile.

"You have been preoccupied with a family bereavement for the past two weeks," he said. "Even so, I doubt it has escaped your notice that Lady Morgan Bedwyn has become the focus of a great deal of unsavory gossip."

"There are few things pertinent to my family that escape my notice," Bewcastle said. "If you came here to inform me of the current topics of conversation now doing the rounds of London drawing rooms, you may be spared the trouble and I will bid you a good morning."

Gervase chuckled and set two hands flat on the desk. He had once envied the cool, seemingly effortless manner with which Bewcastle wielded power and assumed the ascendancy over everyone in his path. He had wanted to be like the duke himself, had even tried to imitate him. He had been a rather silly puppy in those days. They had never been particularly close friends. He had always been the junior hanger-on, the very young man who had not yet discovered either his own strengths and weaknesses or his own identity. He was no longer to be intimidated by someone who was, when all was said and done, but a man.

"The gossip concerns your sister and *me,*" he said. "I spent some time in her company in Brussels, first because we moved in the same social circles, and then because she had been abandoned by both her chaperon and her maid and needed the protection of someone who could ensure her safety."

"Ensure her safety," Bewcastle repeated very softly. "You?"

"I escorted her home to England because she needed to come and because there was no one else to bring her," Gervase said. "Yes, for a few weeks I was in her company far too frequently to avoid the gossiping tongues of those who thrive upon such seeming indiscretions."

"Am I to thank you for the care you offered Lady Morgan Bedwyn and the gossip to which you exposed her—quite deliberately, if I am not much mistaken?"

Bewcastle asked, raising haughty eyebrows. "You may wait a long time for such thanks, Rosthorn. Sir Charles Stuart would, without a doubt, have taken care of Lady Morgan if you had not—and in a far more seemly manner."

Strangely, Gervase had not thought of that possibility at the time. But it was surely true. Lady Morgan was the sister of one of Sir Charles's staff, after all. She was also the sister of a duke. He smiled somewhat ruefully.

"The past is, of course, unchangeable," he said. "All of it. I have come to offer for Lady Morgan Bedwyn, to make a marriage agreement with you, to beg leave to pay my addresses to the lady herself."

Nine years ago he had wondered if Bewcastle's austere, handsome frame housed a heart or if the arteries and veins that fed it ran with ice water instead of blood. He wondered the same thing now as he felt himself the object of a cold, expressionless stare. The ducal quizzing glass was raised halfway to the ducal eye.

"Lady Morgan Bedwyn," he said with quiet distinctness, breaking a rather lengthy silence, "will not be sacrificed upon the altar of gossip, Rosthorn. Neither will she, *under any circumstances whatsoever,* be sacrificed to you."

Gervase straightened up, his lips tightening.

"Perhaps," he said, "the lady will have different thoughts on the subject."

"The lady," Bewcastle said, "will not be consulted. Good day to you, Rosthorn."

Gervase did not move. How it must irk Bewcastle even to have felt obliged to grant this interview. How it must gall him to know his sister the object of unsavory gossip, her name linked with Rosthorn's. For a few moments Gervase savored his own satisfaction and toyed with the slight temptation to deliver the coup de grâce.

*I have lain with her. Did she think to mention that, Bewcastle? No? Ah, then, perhaps you would wish to reconsider your decision?*

But that was one length he was not prepared to go. She did not deserve that. That was something no other human being would ever know through him.

"You do not care about the slurs on her reputation?" he asked. "You do not care that she is being offered a chance to silence the gossip? Or that the offer is an eligible one even for a lady as socially elevated as Lady Morgan Bedwyn? Or that she might wish to consider it?"

"Lady Morgan Bedwyn is under my guardianship," Bewcastle said, his quizzing glass now to his eye and sweeping over his visitor. "And will be for the next two and a half years. I bid you a good morning yet again, Rosthorn."

"I was given the distinct impression during my acquaintance with her that she has a mind of her own," Gervase said. "I would like to hear her opinion on my offer of marriage. She may very well reject it. Indeed, she told me she would when I informed her that I would speak with you on our return to England. But I would like to see her offered the chance to decide for herself."

"Until Lady Morgan reaches the age of majority," Bewcastle said, reaching out one hand to the bell rope and pulling on it, "it is my responsibility to decide which of the offers for her hand—and there have already been several—I deem in her best interests to consider. This one I deem *not* among that number. Fleming." He had looked beyond Gervase's shoulder. "The Earl of Rosthorn is leaving. Show him out."

Gervase nodded and half smiled at the duke before turning and striding from the room, past the butler, who stood to one side of the door. There was still no sign of anyone else in the hall, except the same footman. He wondered if Lady Morgan would be informed that he had called and made an offer for her. He rather expected not.

He pulled his hat down on his head as he stepped outside and eased on his gloves as his newly employed tiger brought up his new curricle from the spot he had found for it against the grassy curb of the park in the center of the square.

Now he must consider his next move.

There did not have to be a next move, of course. Bewcastle had been annoyed and must find some way of dealing with the scandal that was still raging through the drawing rooms of London. He had refused an offer of marriage for his sister. So had she—she had been quite firm about it when Gervase had mentioned it in Brussels.

But it was not finished, Gervase thought as he swung himself up into the high seat of the curricle and gathered the ribbons into his hands.

Not with Bewcastle.

And not with Lady Morgan Bedwyn herself, either.

# CHAPTER XIII

JUDITH AND RANNULF WERE PLANNING TO RETURN home to Leicestershire and invited Morgan to go with them. The prospect was attractive to her for several reasons. She would see her grandmother, with whom they lived. She would get to spend more time with baby William, whom she adored. And she would get away from all the entertainments of the Season, most of which she could no longer attend anyway since she was in mourning. Not that she *wanted* to attend any more. Her first Season had been considerably less dreary than she had expected, it was true, but she was very ready to put it behind her.

One fact, and one fact alone, made her decide, though, to stick it out to the bitter end, to remain in London until Wulfric was ready to return to Lindsey Hall for the summer. That fact was the discovery that Captain Lord Gordon had spoken the truth—there was indeed a great deal of vicious gossip about her and the Earl of Rosthorn. General opinion even seemed to have it that she was in utter disgrace and ought to withdraw from society to hide her shame since the man who had disgraced her had not offered to redeem her by rushing her to the altar.

Morgan had discovered the nasty truth during tea at Freyja and Joshua's the day after the memorial service. She had asked the question and her family members—Wulfric had been absent—had admitted that it was true. They had kept it from her only because she had been upset over Alleyne and had not needed additional provocation.

The truth had acted like the proverbial red flag to the proverbial bull.

She would neither leave London nor avoid society simply because everyone expected her to do just that. And her family, of course—with the usual exception of Wulfric, who did not even know about it—applauded her decision.

And so she went riding in Hyde Park with them all the next morning. Lady Chastity Moore and Viscount Meecham were of the party too. It was a lovely day and Morgan needed the exercise after the unaccustomed inactivity of the past two weeks. But more than that, Rotten Row was the fashionable place to go for a morning ride and was therefore the perfect place in which to show her defiant face. It was also somewhere even mourners could go.

Morgan gazed proudly about her as they rode onto the Row, looking everyone they passed in the eye and inclining her head in courteous acknowledgment of those with whom she had an acquaintance. Nobody, she was interested to see, gave her the cut direct. But then, of course, she *was* Lady Morgan Bedwyn and she *was* riding in the midst of a group of eminently respectable persons. Fellow riders could always pretend they were greeting the others and had not even noticed her.

It was not good enough.

"Who wants to race me to the other end of the Row?" she asked.

"You snatched the words right out of my mouth, Morg," Freyja said.

"I suppose," Joshua said with an exaggerated sigh, "if I were to forbid you to do any such thing because of your condition, sweetheart, you would then feel obliged to race to the far end *and* back again? Yes, I thought so."

Freyja had directed her haughtiest stare at him—and she had the distinct advantage of the prominent Bedwyn nose to look along as she did so.

They were off then, the two of them, without further ado. Morgan bent low over her horse's neck and felt all the exhilaration of speed and potential danger. Not that Rotten Row posed much of the latter, of course. It was kept in immaculate condition. The Bedwyns, who were all neck-or-nothing riders, were accustomed to far worse in their frequent cross-country dashes. But it felt *so* good to be outdoors again.

They galloped along the Row, almost neck and neck the whole way until Freyja surged into the lead as they approached the Hyde Park Corner gates and won by a head. They were both laughing as they reined in their horses.

A small group of gentlemen was riding into the park through the gates a short distance away, and Morgan glanced toward them, lifting her chin as she did so in order to force them to acknowledge her or openly cut her. But then her eyes focused and held on one of them. He was gazing back at her, a lazy smile in his eyes, and looked so dearly familiar that she quite forgot for the moment that she was out of charity with him.

He detached himself from the group and walked his horse toward her.

"Lady Morgan." He swept off his hat and inclined his head to her.

"Lord Rosthorn." She was breathless from her ride, she told herself.

Freyja was suddenly all bristling attention.

"Freyja." Morgan glanced at her, bright-eyed. "May I have the pleasure of presenting the Earl of Rosthorn to you? My sister, the Marchioness of Hallmere, my lord."

The earl bowed again, and Freyja inclined her head with stiff hauteur.

"I did not know you were in town," Morgan said.

"Ah, but I am," he said. "I came up from Windrush the day before yesterday."

The day of the memorial service. That explained why he had not attended it, then—and why he had not called upon her during the past two weeks. But he *had* been here since the day before yesterday. She felt sorry then that she had smiled at him with such enthusiasm a few moments ago.

"I trust all is well at your home and with your family," she said with a more becoming dignity.

"Indeed it is." His eyes smiled at her as if they shared a private joke, and she was reminded of their first meeting, when she had concluded that he could be nothing more than a rake and a rogue.

By that time the rest of her group had come up with them and Morgan made the introductions. The men all pokered up, of course, as she would have expected—*this,* after all was the man who had caused all the infamous gossip in which she was involved. Eve was warm and gracious—also as expected. Judith and Chastity were polite. Lord Rosthorn was charming.

His companions were by now well on their way along the Row, and Morgan's own group had nowhere to go but back the way they had come. The earl fell into place beside Morgan as they moved off, her family forming a powerful ring of chaperonage around them. It was only then that Morgan became aware that this encounter was arousing considerable interest among the other riders, who would doubtless bask in the glory of being able to report on it throughout London drawing rooms for the rest of the day.

There was a chance for some almost-private conversation.

*"Chérie,"* the earl said, his voice low, "have you missed me?"

"*Missed* you?" More than she had admitted even to herself. Seeing him again was almost overwhelming her with awareness, with *knowledge*. He looked handsome and attractive and virile. He looked like a dearly familiar friend. And he *felt* like a long-lost lover. The air between them seemed fairly to bristle with her awareness. "I have been too busy with other concerns to have spared you more than a passing thought, Lord Rosthorn."

"Ah." He set one hand briefly over his heart. "You wound me. *I* have missed *you*."

She darted him a haughty, suspicious glance. He was flirting with her again, teasing her, just as if everything that had happened since that infamous picnic in the

Forest of Soignés had never been.

"Have you?" she asked him, her voice cool, even bored. "You came to London the day before yesterday, Lord Rosthorn? I daresay I was out when you called at Bedwyn House yesterday, then."

"I suppose you were, *chérie,*" he said. "Certainly I did not see you there even though I waited in the hall for all of five minutes before your brother admitted me to the library."

She forgot about her hauteur and gazed at him in open amazement.

"You called on *Wulfric* yesterday?" Just as he had said in Brussels that he would? To *offer* for her?

"I did," he told her. "But, alas, he had that solemn butler of his toss me out on my ear—or he would have done if I had not scurried off in fright before the man had the chance to roll up his sleeves. Bewcastle would not even permit me to address myself to you, *chérie.*"

"Would he not?" Her nostrils flared. She completely forgot that she did not *want* him to address himself to her. "And did he explain why? It is because he blames you for all this stupid gossip about us, I suppose?"

"Perhaps." He smiled at her. "And perhaps it is that my reputation was somewhat unsavory even before I embroiled you in scandal."

"What nonsense this all is," she said, looking about her and realizing again that they were in a very public place—and that they had ridden almost the whole length of Rotten Row. "All of it."

"Your loss of reputation is of concern to me, *chérie,*" he said. "I would restore it if I could."

"It is nonsense," she said again. "None of these people know how very much you were my friend in Brussels."

"And more than that too, *ma petite,*" he said, lowering his voice.

"It would be best," she said, "if we forgot about that, Lord Rosthorn."

"Ah," he said. "You ask the impossible, then, do you?"

It was a relief to see that they had reached the end of the Row. Their few minutes of relative privacy were over. Rannulf was looking pointedly at the earl and Aidan had moved closer to Morgan's other side. Lord Rosthorn's companions were waiting a short distance away.

He addressed himself to Freyja.

"Lady Hallmere," he said, "perhaps you would agree with my mother that often the best defense against scandal and gossip is offense. She would be delighted to entertain you to tea tomorrow afternoon with Lady Morgan and Lady Chastity—and perhaps with Lady Aidan and Lady Rannulf as well? I believe you have an acquaintance with my mother, ma'am?"

Freyja looked appraisingly at him. "I have," she said. "And much as I scorn gossip, I would have to agree with her on this occasion. Morgan is only eighteen years old and has only recently been presented, as I am sure you are well aware, Lord Rosthorn. We will come to Pickford House to tea tomorrow."

"And I will come too," Eve said. "Please thank the Countess of Rosthorn for her kind invitation, my lord."

"Rannulf and I are returning to Leicestershire tomorrow," Judith said. "Please convey my regrets to your mama, Lord Rosthorn."

Morgan held her peace.

"I will bid you all a good morning and be on my way, then," Lord Rosthorn said, nodding genially to the whole group. "Lady Morgan?" He touched his whip to the brim of his hat and rejoined his friends without a backward glance.

Why had Wulfric rejected his suit out of hand? Morgan wondered. He was, after all, the Earl of Rosthorn. He was not a nobody. And there *was* this silly scandal surrounding the two of them.

"Are we to prance about here on the spot gazing after the Earl of Rosthorn for the rest of the morning?" Freyja asked.

"He called on Wulfric yesterday," Morgan said, still gazing after him. "He offered for me, but Wulf refused him."

The Bedwyns all had something to say about *that,* of course.

"He has just gone up in my estimation, then," Rannulf said.

"Rosthorn or Wulfric?" Joshua asked.

"And Wulf did not even *tell* you, Morg? How very like him," Freyja said scornfully.

Eve smiled. "He is very charming."

"I adore his French accent," Chastity added.

"He is," Judith said, darting a mischievous smile at Rannulf, "really rather gorgeous, is he not?"

"He is too old for Morgan," Rannulf said firmly. "You

do not fancy him, do you, Morg?"

"You do not understand," she said. "*No one* understands. He was—he *is* my friend." Yet she could not stop remembering the fierce, impassioned way she had reached for comfort in his rooms that one night and the equally fierce way in which he had offered it. It had not been romance or tenderness or love—or even friendship. But it had been *something,* and she could not simply shrug it off. It was only when her courses had begun a week ago that she had suddenly realized that she might have conceived a child during that encounter. *Then* her life would have been forever changed.

She felt absurdly close to tears.

"Come and ride back down the Row with me, Morgan," Aidan suggested, "and tell me more about your time in Brussels. Tell me why Rosthorn is your friend."

"Will you *listen?*" she asked him sharply. Nobody ever listened, especially when one was only eighteen.

But she had done Aidan an injustice. He had always been stern, even dour, in manner. He rarely smiled even now that he had found Eve and was happily married to her. Morgan had not seen a great deal of him while she was growing up because he had always been off somewhere with his regiment fighting the French. But she had always adored him perhaps most of all her brothers. Whenever he *had* been at home, he had always made a point of spending time with her, doing with her things that she enjoyed doing, like painting outdoors without the intrusive presence of her governess hovering over her every brushstroke. And he had always listened to her as if she were a real person rather than just a nuisance of a younger sister.

"I will listen," he said gravely now. "Come. Let's ride."

GERVASE RETURNED HOME for breakfast instead of going to White's Club as he had originally planned. His mother and Henrietta were already at the table. He kissed his mother's cheek and squeezed his cousin's shoulder before taking his place and allowing the butler to fill a plate for him.

"You will be entertaining a few ladies to tea tomorrow, *Maman,*" he said after a few pleasantries had been exchanged.

"Will I, *mon fils?*" she asked him. "And am I to know in advance who they are?"

"The Marchioness of Hallmere," he told her, "with her sister, Lady Morgan Bedwyn, her sister-in-law, Lady Aidan Bedwyn, and Hallmere's cousin, Lady Chastity Moore."

"Ah," she said, "a formidable group of ladies, Gervase. And one of them the lady with whom your name is being coupled in a less than flattering way, I believe?"

"You have heard the gossip, then, have you?" he asked her, cutting into his sausage. "It is unfortunate. I had the honor of offering the lady some protection when she remained in Brussels after the return home of her chaperon. She stayed to nurse the wounded and to seek word of her brother after he rode to the front during the Battle of Waterloo to deliver an urgent letter to the Duke of Wellington but did not return. I had the honor of escorting her and her maid back to England after she received word that Lord Alleyne Bedwyn was certainly dead."

"And yet," she said, "the gossip is vicious. No one would tell *me* that, of course, but Henrietta was entertained to a full recounting of the sordid details at Mrs. Ertman's concert last evening, were you not, *ma chère?*"

"I would not believe that you acted dishonorably, Gervase," his cousin said. "I defended you as well as I could without knowing the facts."

"Thank you." He smiled at her. "It is my idea to squash the gossip by showing that you are on friendly terms with Lady Morgan Bedwyn and her family, *Maman*. Perhaps you could invite a few other ladies to tea too."

"Like all the patronesses of Almack's?" she suggested dryly. "Gervase, why have you not made an offer for the girl? It would seem the honorable thing to do since you have damaged her name, however inadvertently."

"I *have* offered," he told her. "Bewcastle rejected my suit and would not even permit me to address Lady Morgan."

"Would he not?" She gazed long and hard at him, the toast on her plate forgotten. "And did it give you pleasure, Gervase, so to confront him? Did it give him pleasure to refuse you? Has nothing changed, nothing been solved?"

He had been trying to untangle his own motives since yesterday. He had not expected to meet Lady Morgan again so soon, but he *had* meant to see her. And having done so, he had thought of a way of perhaps dampening the force of the scandal. It *was* wise for his mother to be seen to receive her and her sister. But at the same time it would incense Bewcastle, who would be faced with the dilemma of either allowing the visit or openly snubbing a lady of his mother's standing in society.

He had felt a rush of tenderness for Lady Morgan in the park. He had also felt a distinct physical awareness of her that went beyond mere attraction. He had possessed that body. He had been inside her. He *knew* her. All the feelings had been unwelcome. He would like to have used her mindlessly to get back at Bewcastle. But she was a *person,* and apart from any other feelings he might have for her, he liked her. He even admired her.

"I offered," he said, "because I had compromised the lady. Bewcastle refused for reasons he did not share with me."

His mother continued to look steadily at him.

"And do you care for this lady, Gervase?" she asked him. "Do your feelings for her go beyond simple honor? Have you conceived an affection for her?"

"An affection, yes," he admitted. "But you must not make a grand romance out of it, *Maman*. She is very young and I am very jaded. We shared a friendship in Brussels, forced upon us by circumstances. It is not something that can be transplanted to England now that she is back with her family and I am with mine. My only wish is to restore her reputation."

But his mother had clasped her hands to her bosom and was beaming at him.

"You do not know what you say, Gervase," she said. "How foolish men are! You care for Lady Morgan Bedwyn, whom I have never seen in my life. But I will. Tomorrow I will entertain her here and give my opinion on whether she is worthy of my son. I would have chosen anyone but a Bedwyn for you if given the choice, but love cannot always be chosen rationally. My prayers are going to be answered, and I am going to see the last of my children and the eldest happily married."

Gervase looked with mute appeal at his cousin. She was smiling at him.

"I will not embarrass you with gushing enthusiasm, Gervase," she said, "but I would have you know that nothing would make me happier than to see *you* happy at last."

CHASTITY AND LORD MEECHAM rode off to have breakfast with his sister. Freyja and Joshua rode back to Bedwyn House with the others. Wulfric joined them at the breakfast table before they started eating.

"We met the Earl of Rosthorn in the park," Freyja announced—it had never been her way to beat around any bushes, "and he issued an invitation from the Countess of Rosthorn for us ladies to take tea with her at Pickford House tomorrow afternoon. I will take Eve and Morgan up in our carriage, Wulf, so that you will not need to order one around."

"That is remarkably kind of you, Freyja," he said, spreading his napkin across his lap. "Joshua and Aidan have doubtless given permission for you and Eve to accept this kind invitation. I am not aware that I have given mine for Morgan to accompany you."

"As if I would need Joshua's permission to do whatever I please!" Freyja retorted, glaring at Joshua as if it were he who had just expressed such a gothic notion. "And why ever would you think of withholding yours from Morgan, Wulfric?"

"I assume," he said, indicating to his butler by the slight lifting of one eyebrow that his coffee cup was to be filled, "that your question is rhetorical, Freyja? The Earl of Rosthorn is not a suitable acquaintance for anyone in this family. His reputation is not that of a gentleman of good *ton,* and the way in which he has carelessly embroiled Morgan in unnecessary scandal has proved the point. I would rather you sent a refusal to the countess."

"It seems to me, Wulf," Rannulf said as Morgan was drawing breath to speak, "that it would be in Morgan's best interests to be seen to be on amiable terms with Lady Rosthorn. If the countess is known to have received her, then the gossip will surely die for lack of further fuel. Something far more interesting is bound to take its place soon."

"I would have to agree," Joshua said. "And it ought to be remembered that Freyja is still Morgan's sponsor during this first Season of hers. If Freyja sees fit to accept this invitation and accompany Morgan to Pickford House, then it must be unexceptionable."

Wulfric was eating his way through a large plate of food just as if they were talking about nothing of any greater significance than the weather.

"I resent the fact," Morgan said, setting down her knife and fork with a clatter—she had eaten nothing anyway, "that everyone is talking about me as if I were not here to talk for myself. If you have any definite or personal objection to the Earl of Rosthorn, Wulf, then speak out. If you do not, you can only object to the fact that instead of abandoning me as the Caddicks did when they left Brussels, he escorted me to Mrs. Clark's and arranged for my belongings to be brought over. And that then he gave of his own time and energies to try to discover what had happened to Alleyne. And that he escorted me whenever I needed to get air and exercise after nursing the wounded—so that I would not have to go about alone. And that after I had heard from Sir Charles Stuart about the discovery of the letter that Alleyne had been carrying, Lord Rosthorn hired a maid for me and brought me home in person, though I do not believe he had planned to return to England so soon. *This* is why you call him no gentleman, Wulf? *This* is why you turned him away yesterday and would not even allow him to pay his addresses to me?"

"Bravo, Morg," Rannulf said.

Judith had covered her hand on the table with her own. She patted it comfortingly.

"Ah," Wulfric said, looking up briefly from his food, "he worked that into the conversation this morning, then, did he?"

"He did," Morgan told him. "I would have said no, Wulf. Did you realize that? I would not force anyone to marry me simply because he believed himself honor-bound to offer. And I would not marry any man I did not love with my whole heart. But I resent the fact that you did not even give me the chance to choose my own future. I deeply resent it."

He looked at her for a few silent moments, both eyebrows raised.

"Perhaps you have forgotten, Morgan," he said then, raising his coffee cup to his lips with a despicably steady hand, "that you are eighteen years old, that until you reach your majority I am the one to make major decisions concerning your future."

"How could I possibly forget!" she retorted, slapping her napkin onto the table and giving up all pretense of preparing to eat. "Am I forbidden to go to tea tomorrow, then? Am I to be locked into my room with bread and water?"

He set down his knife and fork and looked coldly at her.

"I have always considered tantrums tedious," he told her. "But as Joshua has just pointed out, you are under the sponsorship of Freyja during your first Season. If Freyja considers this a suitable connection, then I will say no more."

"I do think that is a wise decision, Wulfric," Eve said, drawing his surprised eyes her way. "Of course you are concerned that Morgan not become the dupe of an unprincipled man, but most important at present is somehow to dispel this foolish scandal that has developed."

"Quite so," he said.

"Besides," she said, "Morgan is as sensible as the best

of us and is to be trusted to behave in a manner befitting her family and station."

"Which is not saying a great deal, Eve, if you really think about it, is it?" Rannulf said with a grin.

"We are planning to take the children out sightseeing today," Aidan said. "Becky wants to see the pagoda in Kew Gardens. Davy wants to see the lions at the Tower. Any suggestions on how we might please both?"

The conversation moved into other channels and Morgan, darting a grateful glance at Aidan, who winked back at her, finally picked up her knife and fork and tackled her breakfast.

## CHAPTER XIV

HE MUST TAKE HIS RIGHTFUL PLACE IN THE HOUSE of Lords next year, Gervase decided. All of his peers were there and were inclined to treat him with distant civility at best—as someone, perhaps, who did not take his responsibilities seriously. Those gentlemen with whom he did consort tended to be those leftover companions from his youth who were still idle but were now bored and jaded too—and they thought him the devil of a fine fellow for his escapades on the Continent and the manner of his return to England. He had described himself as jaded to his mother the morning he met Lady Morgan in Hyde Park. He was also bored and had been idle for nine long years. Nevertheless, he felt years older in experience than those companions, who no longer felt quite like friends.

It was time, he supposed, that he settled down and earned the respect of his peers. He deeply resented the fact that it had to be earned, that he had been robbed of both his good name and nine years of his life, but he would only rob himself of more time if he allowed himself to wallow in bitterness.

Bewcastle was his Achilles' heel, though. He could not seem to talk himself out of his deep desire to harm the man.

His mother had invited a few ladies of her acquaintance to take tea at Pickford House on the afternoon his own invited guests were expected there. At first he had not intended putting in an appearance himself. It was his mother who pointed out the desirability of his doing so.

"It is important that you be seen together," she said, "on the best of polite terms with each other and under the benevolent eye of your *maman*."

And so he strolled into the drawing room while the tea was in progress. The room seemed to be full of fashionably dressed ladies—it really was quite daunting to walk in upon them as the only male. His mother sat on a small sofa close to the fireplace, Lady Morgan beside her, looking astonishingly youthful and lovely in black. Gervase bowed to both of them, kissed his mother's hand, asked Lady Morgan how she did, and turned away to make himself agreeable to the other guests.

Although there was no noticeable pause in any of the conversations, Gervase guessed that every eye had watched his approach to Lady Morgan Bedwyn and every ear had strained to catch every word they exchanged. An account of this afternoon's visit would doubtless enliven conversations at dinner tables and in theaters and ballrooms and drawing rooms this evening.

Would the scandal now be at an end?

Or would everyone be waiting for a betrothal announcement to be made before either party to the scandal could be accepted back fully into the fold?

Over the course of the next half hour Gervase was careful to exchange a brief word with everyone present. He discovered that he liked the Marchioness of Hallmere for all her air of hauteur and her strange though handsome looks—she was small with masses of barely tamed fair hair, darker eyebrows, and the prominent nose that characterized all her brothers too. She spoke in a forthright manner on a number of topics and did not disguise the fact that she was sizing him up on her sister's account. Lady Aidan Bedwyn was gracious and amiable and pretty—and surprised him by smiling warmly at the maid who came to remove the tea tray and thanking her. Lady Chastity Moore was a sensible, pretty young lady.

The Bedwyns were the last to take their leave.

"We have been invited, Gervase—you and I and Henrietta—to a ball being given by the Marquess and Marchioness of Hallmere three days hence," his mother told him. "Is that not delightful?"

Gervase looked in some surprise at the marchioness. He had not expected that after this afternoon's display for the sake of silencing gossip any of the Bedwyns would encourage further encounters between himself and Lady Morgan.

"The ball is in honor of Chastity's engagement to Viscount Meecham," the marchioness explained. "Both were quite willing that we cancel it so soon after my brother's death, but Hallmere and I decided that that would be unfair. And so the ball goes on."

"We will be delighted to attend, ma'am," Gervase told her, darting a glance at Lady Morgan, who was playing the part of haughty grand lady, as she had been doing all afternoon. He half smiled at her.

"Of course," the marchioness added, looking very directly at him—it must be a family trait, that look, he decided, "none of the members of my family will be able to dance as we are in mourning."

She rose to leave, and her sister and sister-in-law and Lady Chastity followed suit. His mother, he noticed, linked an arm through one of the marchioness's, and Henrietta moved between Lady Aidan and Lady Chastity. Gervase, considerably amused at such an unsubtle maneuver, offered his arm to Lady Morgan.

His mother, he concluded, must approve of her.

There was a space of perhaps two minutes when they were virtually alone together, his mother having stopped with the other ladies at the top of the stairs to point out some feature of a portrait hanging there.

"It will not distress you, *chérie,*" he asked her, "if I attend the ball to be given by your sister and brother-in-law?"

"No, why should it?" Her eyes sparked up at him, and he knew that there must have been some spirited family discussion over him.

"What did the Duke of Bewcastle have to say about

your coming here today?" he asked her.

"I am here, am I not?" she said.

"And what does he say about my attending the ball?" he asked.

"As far as I am aware," she said, "he does not know of it. Why should he? It is not his ball."

"But perhaps," he said, "I will not go after all. I will not even be able to waltz with you, *chérie*."

"Why," she asked him, turning her head to give him one of her very direct looks, "would Wulfric be so adamantly opposed to allowing you to pay your addresses to me, Lord Rosthorn? You *are* an earl, and by the standards of the society in which we live you did do the decent, honorable thing by going to him to offer for me. Why does he hate you so much?"

*"Chérie,"* he said, "must he *hate* the man who caused his sister to be the subject of gossip? May he not just simply disapprove of me? Were you so disappointed, then? Would you have said yes?"

"You know I would not," she said with a look of disdain.

He smiled at her. "Then Bewcastle did us both a favor," he said. "He saved you from embarrassment and me from heartbreak. With the question still officially unasked and still officially unanswered, I may still hope."

"How absurd you are," she said, frowning. "I preferred you when you were my dear friend."

They were outside on the pavement by that time, and the other ladies had caught up with them. Gervase handed Lady Morgan into the Marquess of Hallmere's waiting carriage and turned to do the like for the others.

*"Mon fils,"* his mother said, linking her arm through his as the carriage rocked on its springs and rolled into motion, "she is a perfect delight. I would relinquish my title with the greatest pleasure to Lady Morgan Bedwyn."

"I assure you, *Maman,*" he said, patting her hand and winking at Henrietta, "that you will not be called upon to make any such sacrifice. Bewcastle has refused my suit, if you will remember."

But *she* had not. Not yet. And he was to see her again before the eyes of the whole *ton*. At a ball, no less.

He gazed after the departing carriage with narrowed eyes. Had he just told her he would be unable to waltz with her because she was in mourning?

They would see about that.

MORGAN HAD BEEN OUT riding each morning. She had attended church with her family. She had toured some of the galleries with Aidan and Eve and had gone to Gunter's with them when they took the children there for ices one afternoon. And she had, of course, taken tea at Pickford House, where she had been surprised to discover other guests apart from her own family group.

Nowhere had she been given the cut direct. If the ladies at the tea had seemed somewhat distant, they had also been polite. And they had not had a great deal of opportunity to snub her anyway since the Countess of Rosthorn had kept her by her side all afternoon. Morgan had found her charming—she had the same slight French accent as her son.

A ball was a different matter entirely, of course. She would discover there whether the scandal had affected her standing in the beau monde. Not that she really cared. If the *ton* was tired of her, then she was mortally weary of them—or so she told herself. She could not wait for the Season to be over so that she could return home to the sanity of Lindsey Hall.

Except, she admitted to herself in unguarded moments, that it was also going to seem flat and dull after all that had happened since she left there in the spring.

She dressed carefully for the ball. She could not wear any of her loveliest gowns, of course—but most of those were white anyway, and she despised them. And she would not be allowed to dance—but dancing with all the callow youth with which London ballrooms tended to abound had never held any great appeal for her. She watched her new maid dress her hair in a high topknot, from which curls and ringlets cascaded, some to trail along her neck and over her temples, and decided that she liked the girl's work.

She would not be able to dance. She thought wistfully of waltzing beneath the swaying lamps and the stars in the Forest of Soignés and felt guilty that she could want to waltz again when Alleyne was so recently gone. He had been at that picnic. He had scolded her roundly for allowing the Earl of Rosthorn to pay her such particular attention.

She still could not believe that she would never see him again.

Eve and Aidan rode in the ducal town carriage with

their backs to the horses while Morgan sat beside Wulfric on the other seat. She wondered as the other three conversed if Wulf knew that Lord Rosthorn had been invited tonight.

She was, she had been realizing with the greatest reluctance over the past few days, ever so slightly in love with him. No, perhaps even that was self-deception. She had been attracted to him from the start. And then, when she had found an intelligent, compassionate man behind the rakish facade, she had come to like and respect him. And finally, when she had turned to him in the passion of her grief over Alleyne, they had shared the deepest intimacy of all. It was not that alone that had made her fall in love with him, but it had certainly made her realize that she had been deceiving herself by thinking of him only as a friend. He was a great deal more than a friend.

The carriage rolled to a halt behind a line of others drawing up to the entrance doors to Joshua's mansion on Berkeley Square.

"Freyja and our aunt Rochester will no doubt have arranged for several young gentlemen to make your acquaintance this evening, Morgan," Wulfric said. "Our consequence is, of course, too great for a little gossip to have made you entirely ineligible. You may not dance, but you may walk or converse with such partners."

"Provided none of them is the Earl of Rosthorn, I suppose," she said.

He turned his head and looked at her with raised eyebrows.

"He *has* been invited," she told him, "with the

countess and Miss Clifton, his cousin."

"Ah," he said softly. "It is interesting that no one saw fit to inform me of this fact until now."

"Why should anyone?" she asked him. "This is Freyja and Joshua's ball."

"Quite so," he said, his voice softer still.

The Earl of Rosthorn had not answered her question, she realized, but had skirted around it and changed the subject. She had asked him why Wulfric hated him.

"It is as well, Wulf," Aidan said, "for Rosthorn and Morgan to be seen together at an event of this nature so that the last shreds of scandal may be dispelled."

A footman was opening the carriage door and setting down the steps. Wulfric handed Morgan down onto the red carpet that had been rolled out over the steps and across the pavement. She avoided looking into his keen silver eyes. She lifted her chin and smiled as he led her inside and along the receiving line and into the ballroom, where he deposited her in the safekeeping of their aunt Rochester, who was looking even more formidable than usual dressed in black satin, with a monstrous black turban and plumes. Even the long handle of her jeweled lorgnette was black.

Morgan settled in for what she fully expected to be a tedious evening. And indeed it did not start well. Her aunt presented her with two partners in a row who were just the sort of gangly, pimply, stammering youths she had anticipated meeting during her first Season—gentlemen of her own age or no more than a year or two older, with whom she was expected to be comfortable and whom she was expected to consider seriously as marriage partners.

It was quite enough to make her want to scream, especially as she could not even make the time pass quickly by dancing but was forced to sit on a sofa with each of them in turn, making labored conversation about such inconsequential matters that she twice forgot what she was talking about in the middle of a sentence. Yet politeness compelled her to smile and fan her face and look for all the world as if she had never been so well entertained in her life.

It was the middle of the second set when the Earl of Rosthorn arrived with his mother and cousin. He was looking very splendid indeed, Morgan saw, in gray and silver and black. But she could not even allow herself the luxury of feasting her eyes on him. She was very aware of the buzz of heightened interest in the ballroom. It had been bad enough when she arrived, but now the two partners in crime of recent scandal were there together. Freyja's ball was bound to be declared a resounding success tomorrow.

The earl disappeared from the room while his mother and cousin joined a group within it. But at the end of the set he reappeared and brought his mother across the ballroom to greet Aunt Rochester.

"Oh, it is you, is it, Lisette?" Aunt Rochester said, raising her lorgnette to her eye while Lord Rosthorn bowed. "I have not seen you this Season. I supposed you had stayed at Windrush. However do you keep yourself looking so young?"

"You are kind," Lady Rosthorn said. "But you must not look too, too closely, *mon amie,* especially in the daylight. May I take this seat beside you? Henrietta is with friends. Lady Morgan, *mon enfant,* even in black you outshine every other lady at the ball. Do let me kiss your cheek." Having done so, she turned back to Lady Rochester. "May I have the pleasure of presenting my son, the Earl of Rosthorn?"

Aunt Rochester regarded him through her lorgnette, and her hair plumes nodded forward perhaps an inch.

"You are the scamp who hired a maid for my niece without thinking to ask her if she suffered from seasickness, are you?" she asked. "And then stood on deck with my niece yourself while the girl heaved out her stomach below?"

"Alas, ma'am," he said, "I am guilty. But what was I to do? Remain belowdecks myself and pretend to be suffering from seasickness too? Leave Lady Morgan in Brussels in the care of a lady who was about to be summoned to join her husband in Paris? Lady Morgan needed to be returned to the bosom of her family."

"Lord Rosthorn was extraordinarily kind to me, Aunt," Morgan said, aware again that though no one seemed to be paying their little group any particular attention, in reality everyone was drinking in every detail. It was a skill at which members of the *ton* were particularly adept—being able to do two things at once. It was how the gossip mill was constantly fed.

"Ma'am." The earl bowed to her aunt. "With your permission I will ask Lady Morgan to stroll about the ballroom with me."

Wulfric was not in the room, Morgan noticed in one hasty glance about. She held her breath as she nonchalantly plied her fan to cool her cheeks. Aunt Rochester was a far more formidable chaperon than Lady Caddick had been.

"Very well, young man," she said after scrutinizing him closely through her lorgnette again—a pure affectation, of course, as was Wulfric's quizzing glass. Their naked eyes missed very little. "I will be watching."

"Lady Morgan?" The earl bowed to her. His expression was sober and polite, but she knew him quite well enough to recognize the laughter lurking in his eyes.

"Thank you, Lord Rosthorn." She snapped her fan closed and took his arm, careful to keep her own expression cool, slightly bored, slightly haughty.

"You are having a wonderful time, *chérie?*" he asked.

"I am ready to expire of boredom," she told him. "Amuse me."

"Alas," he said, "I fear I must break your heart instead. This next set is to be a waltz."

"Oh." She sighed. "Too cruel."

After the excruciating boredom and inactivity of the last hour or so, her feet itched to dance.

"We will stroll like a couple of gouty octogenarians," he said, "and tell each other what a scandalous dance the waltz is."

She smiled at him. "I like the Countess of Rosthorn," she told him. "She is charming and amiable."

"And she likes *you, chérie*." He bent his head a little closer to hers. "Now that I have come home, she is eager to see me settle down with a wife and set up my nursery."

"Indeed?" Morgan felt her cheeks flush. Was he

flirting with her again—and quite outrageously?

"Yes, indeed," he told her. "Mothers can be remarkably uncomfortable persons to be around, I am discovering. She believes that thirty is altogether too advanced an age for a man with a title and a fortune to remain a bachelor."

"Indeed?" He was thirty. Twelve years older than she. It should have seemed like too wide an age gap.

"And she does not believe that eighteen is too young for the bride of such a man," he said.

"Lord Rosthorn," she said, "your conversation is bordering on the improper."

"Is it, *chérie?*" He dipped his head a little closer yet. "Just because your brother has said no? Even though we have been dear friends? And lovers?"

His accent was suddenly very French indeed.

"You would be better employed," she said sharply, "paying your addresses where they are more welcome, Lord Rosthorn. And to a lady you can love."

"Ah, but my mother believes," he said, "that I love *you*. So does Henrietta. I begin to believe that perhaps they are right, *chérie*."

Morgan could feel her heart beating against her ribs. She could hear her pulse throbbing in her ears. She could see that the ballroom floor had filled with dancers and that the music was about to begin. Chastity was going to waltz with Lord Meecham. They were smiling warmly into each other's eyes, oblivious to all around them. Morgan was so glad Chastity had found love this spring. She had had a difficult, lonely girlhood.

"This is not the time or place for such talk, Lord Rosthorn," she said. "How I *wish* I could dance." The music had begun.

"You can," he said, stopping close to the doors. "If you wish, *chérie,* we will waltz."

"No," she said. "You know I cannot."

"Not here in public," he agreed. "But in private?"

She looked at him with raised eyebrows and plied her fan again as the dancers twirled past.

"There is an anteroom beside the refreshment room," he said, "that is not in use. We could waltz together in there without anyone being any the wiser. If our absence is noted, it will be assumed that I have taken you for a glass of lemonade."

"But Aunt Rochester will miss me," she said.

She was horribly tempted, though. Not just because she longed to waltz and not just because he was the Earl of Rosthorn and she had just realized that perhaps he was falling in love with her as she was falling for him. She was also bored. She was feeling hemmed in by propriety and strict chaperonage again after the freedom and sense of purpose and responsibility she had known in Brussels. It seemed to her that the last weeks of heavy grief had been endless. And it would be just for a very short while. No one would ever know.

She could *waltz* again. Right now. With the Earl of Rosthorn.

"Come, *chérie,*" he said, his head moving closer to hers again, his eyes smiling lazily. "Come and waltz with me."

She took his arm again, and he whisked her out

through the doors before she could persuade herself to observe a more strict decorum.

IT WAS A SQUARE ROOM, not very large, with a sofa and a few chairs arranged around the perimeter. Gervase had discovered it earlier and guessed that it had been set aside for those guests who would wish to rest in quiet for a short while. He had extinguished the candles and shut the door. It had been a fortunate find. A private room would serve better than the balcony, his original choice.

He lit the candles on the mantelpiece now and turned to Lady Morgan. Behind her he had left the door slightly ajar. What he should do, he thought as she smiled at him, was take her back to the ballroom right now at this very moment before someone opened that door and it was too late. He liked her too much for this. She had done nothing to deserve this.

"Listen," he said instead, holding out his arms to her. "It is not a fast melody. We can contrive to dance it in here, I believe, without bumping into furniture and bouncing off walls."

She came closer, laughing softly as she did so, and he set his right hand behind her waist and took her right hand in his. She set her other hand on his shoulder. The intimacy of the waltz position felt at least twice as intimate in this private setting. He could smell violets. He was reminded of the last time they had been alone in a room together.

They danced in silence, lights and music and voices and laughter mingling beyond the slightly open door, dim candlelight and intimacy within. She tilted back her head and smiled at him again. He smiled back. Perhaps no one would come. Perhaps after all he would be released from the consequences of this terrible thing he was doing.

After a few minutes he drew her closer. He turned her hand to rest palm-inward over his heart, his own hand spread over the back of it. He felt her other hand slide inward along his shoulder and come to rest behind his neck. She turned her face and, with a soft sigh, rested her cheek against the intricate folds of his neckcloth and danced on with him, their bodies touching.

She was all slender, warm femininity. She felt familiar—and dear.

*"Chérie,"* he murmured against her ear a few minutes after that, and she drew back her head and raised her face to his. Her eyes were dreamy and heavy-lidded from the music and the candlelight and the shared warmth of their bodies.

"Yes," she whispered, her lips parting.

He lowered his head and kissed her, dancing her to a halt as he did so and wrapping one arm more completely about her waist while cupping the back of her head with the other. Her arms came tightly about him and her body arched into his. Her lips parted beneath his and heat and urgency engulfed them both. He pressed his tongue deep inside her mouth, and her arms strained him closer as she made a low sound of encouragement. One of his hands found a breast and closed about it.

It was the moment at which he felt sudden panic. *No!* He was losing himself in passion while in the process of betraying her. She had done *nothing* to deserve this of him. He simply could not do it. He must get her out of this room undetected and hurry her back to the ballroom before someone made the discovery that they were neither there nor in the refreshment room. He was desperate suddenly to save her—and himself.

He loosened his hold on her and lifted his head.

*Too late.*

The door was now more than half open and a number of guests were either openly peering inside or were moving slowly past, too well bred, perhaps, to be seen standing and staring.

The Duke of Bewcastle, one hand on the door, had already stepped inside the room and was shutting it firmly behind his back.

## CHAPTER XV

MORGAN'S FIRST FEELING WAS GUILT. SHE WAS wearing black and had curtailed her social activities out of respect for Alleyne's memory and yet she had given in to the temptation to waltz. Her second feeling was intense embarrassment. Wulfric and half the polite world had seen her in a deep embrace with the Earl of Rosthorn. Her third feeling was elation. He *must* have feelings to match her own. Her fourth feeling was anger. How dare Wulfric walk in on them like this as if they were naughty, wayward children. Actually, all four feelings washed over her almost simultaneously.

"Do you never knock on doors, Wulf?" she asked, glaring haughtily at him.

He had his quizzing glass to his eye and was regarding through it the earl's arm, which he had placed protectively about her waist. He did not remove it. Wulfric ignored her question.

"I have already petitioned you once for Lady Morgan's hand, Bewcastle," Lord Rosthorn said. "I shall present myself at Bedwyn House tomorrow morning to repeat my offer. I think you will agree that this is neither the time nor the place to discuss the matter further."

His voice was cold, his tone clipped. There was almost no trace of his French accent. Wulfric's face was a mask of icy control.

"I must congratulate you, Rosthorn," he said. "You have outmaneuvered me—for the moment."

"Oh, but this is ridiculous!" Morgan cried, breaking away from the earl's hold. "We were just waltzing together in here and then kissing—by mutual consent, I will add."

Wulfric turned his eyes on her. And if that were not disconcerting enough, his quizzing glass was still held to one of them. Had she really said they were *just* waltzing and kissing?

*Just?*

But before Wulfric could say whatever he had been about to say, the door opened again to admit Freyja. She looked from one to the other of them with raised eyebrows.

"I expected to find a duel in progress at the very least," she said, "with Morgan in a swooning heap in one corner. Our ball, it seems, is fated to be talked about tomorrow and for many tomorrows to come. But what can one expect of an entertainment hosted by Josh and me? Lord Rosthorn, were you really seen to be *kissing* my sister in here? That is shocking indeed, and I have to muster a great deal of fortitude to keep myself from collapsing in a fit of the vapors. Wulf, you are looking as if you had swallowed a whole iceberg. Morgan, you look like Lady Macbeth. I would remind you all that this ball is in honor of Lady Chastity Moore and Lord Meecham and I *will not* have it become a circus show."

"I have just been informing his grace, ma'am," Lord Rosthorn said with a bow, "that I mean to make a formal call at Bedwyn House tomorrow morning with the purpose of offering for the hand of Lady Morgan Bedwyn."

"Both Wulf and Morgan will doubtless have something to say on the matter when you do call," Freyja said. "But that is for tomorrow, not this evening."

"It is all nonsense," Morgan said.

"Of course it is," Freyja agreed, striding across the room to link arms with her sister. "But deadly serious at the same time. The *ton* will be ready to plunge you into the deepest disgrace after this, and unfortunately, the *ton* is a monster that even we Bedwyns must appease on occasion. It is time to put a bold face on this newest sensation. We will go into the ballroom together, Morg, and take a turn or two about the room, just as if nothing untoward had happened. It is a shame you do not have the Bedwyn nose. It is a distinct advantage in situations like this. But you *can* smile. Do it."

It had always been difficult not to be swept along by Freyja when she was at her most formidable. On this occasion Morgan did not even try. She left the room without even a glance at either of the two men, and smiled.

She was half aware that Wulfric came out after them and fell into step behind them.

MORGAN SAW THE EARL of Rosthorn arrive by curricle the following morning and stride purposefully up to the front door and through it after knocking and waiting a few moments. She was sitting on the window seat in her bedchamber, her knees drawn up before her, her arms wrapped about them. She had deliberately withdrawn here so that she could be alone to compose herself for what was coming.

She *needed* to compose herself. Her mind and her emotions were in turmoil. They had all wanted a piece of her, either last night or this morning. All had had an opinion or some advice to offer, or both.

Aunt Rochester, clearly incensed, had found a private moment last night in which to inform her niece that she was a discredit to the name of Bedwyn. The Bedwyns, her aunt informed her, had always had a reputation for wildness and unconventionality, but never for vulgarity. Now Morgan might repent her own foray into the distinctly vulgar at leisure, married to a rake who was far too old for her, and would doubtless neglect her and flaunt his harem of light-skirts before her. She would be fortunate indeed if any of the highest sticklers were willing to receive her within the next fifty years or so.

Freyja had given her opinion during that ghastly stroll about the ballroom, when Morgan had thought her lips might well split from so much smiling.

"Alleyne always did say you would out-Bedwyn all of us one of these days," she said. "Actually I did far worse with Josh last year than waltz in an anteroom with him and kiss him with the door open for all to see. Though there has been a great deal more than just this in your case, of course. You have been spectacularly indiscreet during the past month or so, have you not? And tonight takes the cake. Alleyne was right. A piece of advice, though, Morg. The man is devastatingly attractive—I'll admit that. But be a Bedwyn to the end. Don't accept his marriage proposal tomorrow unless you are quite, quite sure that he is the one and only man with whom you could contemplate spending the rest of your life."

"Lord Rosthorn is a charming man and a handsome one too." That was Chastity, also last evening. "And he was kind to you in Belgium. I cannot blame you for wanting to waltz with him tonight, Morgan. I know I could not have borne it if I had been forbidden to waltz with Leonard. Do you love him? I think you must if you allowed him to kiss you. How I long to see you as happy as I am."

"When I married Aidan last year against the advice of everyone who loved me, I did so for all the wrong reasons." That was Eve after they had returned home from the ball. "It was extremely fortunate that we very soon fell deeply in love with each other. We might just as easily have been miserable for the rest of our lives. Do be sure, Morgan, that if you marry Lord Rosthorn, it is not because of this renewed scandal but because you know you can find happiness with no man but him."

"Forget about the scandal, Morgan." It was Aidan's turn. "If you do not want Rosthorn, tell him so and send him on his way. Come with Eve and the children and me for the summer and then go to Lindsey Hall for the winter. By next spring you will be remembered simply as one of those headstrong, wild Bedwyns." He had regarded her closely then from his keen dark eyes. "On the other hand, if you want him, then tell him *that* and we will all forgive him for tonight's indiscretion and welcome him into the family for your sake."

Wulfric had waited for the morning—until after Morgan had spent a restless, almost sleepless night. He had summoned her to the library before she went down to breakfast. She had walked the whole length of the room with his eyes resting on her from his seat behind the desk. And of course she could not make it easy on herself—she had stared right back at him.

"Be seated," he had invited her, and she had perched on the edge of a gilt chair while he sat back and rested his elbows on the arms of his own chair and steepled his fingers.

"Nothing is irrevocable at the moment, Morgan," he told her, "although this time I do feel obliged to discuss marriage terms with the Earl of Rosthorn and then grant his request to pay his addresses to you in person. Your admitted acquiescence in what happened last evening dictates that I go through such distasteful motions. However, my consequence is great and therefore so is yours. I would urge you to say a very firm and definite no. If you do so, no further word will be spoken of this matter between you and me. I will escort you back to Lindsey Hall within the week or you can go to Oxfordshire with Aidan before that."

There were to be no major recriminations, then, no blistering scold? She twisted her hands in her lap, almost disappointed. It was easier to deal with Wulf when she could defy him over some issue.

"I will reply to Lord Rosthorn as I see fit," she told him. All through the night she had wondered if he loved her. She was almost certain that she loved him.

"You have been duped, Morgan," Wulfric said after gazing at her in brooding silence for an unnerving length of time. "Rosthorn does not love you. Rather, he hates *me*."

"What nonsense!" she retorted crossly. "It is *you* who hate *him* merely for doing what you would have applauded in Sir Charles Stuart. You are being quite unreasonable."

The silver eyes gazed back into her own.

"I asked you before," she said, "and you did not answer. I have asked him and he evaded my question. Why do you hate him? It has nothing to do with me really, does it? You knew each other before—before his exile."

Lengthy silences never seemed to disconcert Wulfric. Morgan refused to let the one that followed disconcert her either. She looked steadily back into her brother's eyes and waited.

"He ravished a lady," he said, "and robbed her. Rosthorn—his father—expelled him from England and told him never to return."

*"What?"* Morgan reached out one hand and grasped the edge of the desk as if to stop herself from falling.

"He was discovered in her bedchamber and in her bed during the course of a ball," Wulfric said. "It was not entirely unlike what happened last evening, and probably the motive was similar."

Morgan's mouth was dry. She tried to lick her lips with a dry tongue.

"How do you know the lady was unwilling?" she asked him. "*I* was not last evening."

"She was *not* willing," Wulfric said. "Her betrothal to another man was to have been announced that evening. She was too ashamed to continue with that plan though he would still have had her. She refused the offer Rosthorn's son made her the next day. She retired from society and never married despite position, wealth, and beauty, all of which she possessed in abundance. Her life was ruined."

"I will not believe it," she said, getting to her feet. "We all know how stories become distorted and exaggerated in the telling. How do you know that what you have told me is true?"

"I was the man to whom she was to be betrothed," Wulfric said softly. "I was one of the three men—her father and Rosthorn were the others—who burst in upon them in her bedchamber. Too late, as it turned out."

She stared at him, transfixed. *Wulfric* had once been almost betrothed? And had been so horribly hurt? By the present Earl of Rosthorn? It was too dizzying to be digested all at once.

"Perhaps you misunderstood the evidence of your eyes," she said.

"Hardly."

"It happened nine years ago," she said.

"Yes."

They stared at each other, her eyes stormy, his silver and ice cold.

"Such a man," he said after a lengthy silence, "ought not to be allowed within one mile of my sister. But he has maneuvered his way very cleverly into your affections and into such a public position that I am forced to allow him to address himself to you. Since I will not forbid him to make you an offer, I cannot forbid you to accept him. And if I tried, I am well aware that you might then feel obliged to defy me and ruin yourself permanently by eloping with Rosthorn. But what I can do is trust you to make the right decision about your own lifelong happiness."

After continuing to stare at him for long moments, she had left the library without another word.

And so she sat on the window seat, knowing that Lord Rosthorn had arrived, that even now he was in the library with Wulfric discussing a marriage contract. She did not know how long such matters took. But some time within the next half hour, or the next hour at the longest, there was going to be a knock on her door and she was going to have to force her legs to carry her back down to the library. She was going to have to face him.

The man who had ravished the woman Wulf had loved. They had been caught in bed together. The woman's words and subsequent actions would seem to confirm that she had not given herself willingly.

The man who had flirted with her, Morgan, quite outrageously and extravagantly before the Battle of Waterloo.

The man who had supported her and given her his protection and companionship and friendship in the days following the battle.

The man with whom she had made love after learning that there was no more hope of Alleyne's having survived.

The man who had brought her home to the comfort of her family.

The man she had been growing to love, the man she had believed was growing to love her.

Did what had happened nine years ago nullify all her instincts about him, all her feelings for him? He had *ravished* a woman. She could not believe it of him. But how could she not? Wulfric had *been* there and he was not the sort of man who would deliberately twist evidence.

Morgan had never been so confused in her life.

The summons came after forty minutes, when her

maid scratched on her door. Morgan jumped with alarm and then got to her feet and brushed her hands over the skirt of her black dress. She squared her shoulders and lifted her chin.

The Earl of Rosthorn was going to have some explaining to do.

THE DUKE OF BEWCASTLE had kept Gervase waiting in a visitors' reception room for all of twenty minutes before having him admitted to the library. There had followed a brief, cold meeting in which business had been discussed as if there were no personal element involved in the terms. Bewcastle had made no bones of the fact that he had advised Lady Morgan Bedwyn against accepting the offer. But finally he had risen and left the room, leaving Gervase to stare into the unlit coals of the fireplace.

All night he had been feeling cold satisfaction.

And all night too he had been trying to ignore a heavy feeling of guilt. In his obsession with getting revenge on Bewcastle he had allowed himself to become almost as bad as they had all supposed him to be nine years ago. *Almost* as bad? Worse. Marianne had brought about her own ruin. Lady Morgan had not.

He turned and clasped his hands behind his back when the door opened again and Lady Morgan stepped past a footman and came into the room.

She looked composed, he thought, though her face was devoid of all color. Her shoulders were back and her chin lifted. He frowned when he recalled that embrace they had shared last night. He had not intended that. It had not been part of the plan. He had intended that they be caught waltzing together in a private anteroom. It would have been quite enough to fan the flames of a dying scandal.

The embrace had happened of itself.

"Well, *chérie,*" he said. "Here we are."

She came toward him and stood a mere two feet away, her eyes lifted steadily to his. Had he expected timidity? Blushes?

"If you are about to drop to one knee and make a picturesque scene of this," she told him, "you may as well not bother, Lord Rosthorn. I want to know what happened nine years ago."

Ah. Had Bewcastle told her, then—his version at least? It was altogether likely. What surer way was there to persuade her to reject his suit?

"There was an indiscretion with a lady, *chérie,*" he said. "I would tell you that it is nothing to worry your pretty little head over if I thought I could get away with it." He smiled at her.

But she was not to be amused by that old joke.

"Answer me one question first," she said. "Did you ravish her?"

Yes, of course, Bewcastle had been busy. Gervase turned back toward the fireplace.

"You want the simple answer?" he asked her. "I will give it, then. It is no. No, I did not."

"I suppose," she said, her voice trembling slightly, "I want more than the simple answer, Lord Rosthorn. If it was not ravishment, what was it, then? You were caught with the lady in hopelessly compromising circumstances. She accused you of forcing her. She refused your marriage offer. She retired permanently from society. I do know the facts of what happened, you see. I want you to explain to me how you could *not* have been guilty."

He sighed and clasped his hands at his back. She now knew the worst, which was just as well. He did not really wish to marry her, did he? And it certainly would not be in her best interests to marry him. He had achieved what he had set out to do . . . and truth to tell, the victory was hollow. Revenge was a foolish, immature motive for any action. It never solved anything but merely deepened hatreds. Bewcastle had been a victim too. He sometimes forgot that.

He was aware though he did not turn that Lady Morgan had crossed the room away from him until she stood behind the desk, gazing out the window.

"I had known the lady for a long time," he told her. "She was occasionally a neighbor of ours and a friend of my sisters and cousin. I suppose I was even a little infatuated with her after we grew up—she was rather lovely. But I never seriously considered wooing her. I was too young. Besides, I was a friend of Bewcastle's—at least, I moved on the outer perimeter of his set, hoping to be admitted to the inner circle one day—and he began to pay court to her himself when Marianne made her come-out."

"I never knew until today," she said, "that Wulf had ever even considered marriage. I suppose he must have loved her."

"Her father was a marquess," Gervase said. "It

would, of course, have been a splendid match for his daughter. He promoted it aggressively. Their betrothal was to be announced during a grand ball he hosted in the middle of the Season."

"None of us ever knew about it," she said.

When he half turned his head, he could see that she had sat down on the chair Bewcastle had vacated a short while ago.

"There was one problem, though," Gervase said. "She did not wish to wed *him*. But he was a powerful man and so was her father. The marquess had overridden all her objections and threatened all sorts of dire consequences if she did not behave as she ought when Bewcastle paid her court, and if she did not accept when he offered her marriage."

"How do you know this?" Her eyes met his across the room, wide with what might be anger.

"She told me," he said. "She danced with me that evening and then, in the middle of the set, she drew me away from the ballroom, telling me that she must talk with me. She took me up to her private sitting room and poured out her heart to me. She was quite distraught. She told me her betrothal was to be announced after supper and then her marriage to the duke would be inescapable. She told me she would rather die. She begged me to help her."

"What did you say?" Her nostrils flared and she set both hands flat on the desk.

"What *could* I say?" He shrugged. "I am not even sure I remember my exact response. I advised her to go immediately to both her father and Bewcastle, I suppose, to tell them quite firmly that she would not go through with the marriage. I do recall offering to go and have a word with Bewcastle myself even though I was hardly a close enough friend of his to presume to do this. The next thing I remember is waking up with a start when the door to her bedchamber crashed open and Bewcastle came thundering in, followed closely by her father and mine."

"Her *bedchamber?*"

"I was lying on the bed," he said, "in a thoroughly, shockingly disordered state of dishabille. So was Marianne. The bedcovers were tossed about as if a violent orgy had just been in progress over and under them. Marianne was weeping hysterically. I believe I was blinking like a bewildered moon calf."

He had turned back to the fireplace and could not tell if she believed him or not. It was a pretty incredible tale, admittedly. That was why no one had believed him at the time—not that he had defended himself immediately. He had been paralyzed by shock and by his infernal code of gentlemanly honor. A gentleman just did not openly contradict a lady.

"Was it something that had happened by mutual consent?" he asked of the fireplace with a low laugh. "Or was it ravishment? I believe that at the time Marianne was too hysterical to give any coherent answer to the bellowed demands of her father, and I was not saying. I was too aware of the shocked, horrified stare of my father and the cold scrutiny of Bewcastle."

"Which *was* it?" Lady Morgan asked sharply.

"I am firmly of the opinion," he said, "that it was neither. I had not had a great deal to drink, but even if I had I would not have completely forgotten such an event, would I? Besides, if I had imbibed that much I daresay I would have been incapacitated even if I had felt amorously inclined. I suppose I was drugged."

"By Marianne?"

He shrugged. "One does not accuse a lady of such a thing," he said. "Or of lying when she finally got around to claiming that I had taken her by force. But if she did drug me, it was a spectacularly effective plan. There was, of course, no announcement that night or anytime after that night."

He raised one arm to rest on the mantelpiece above his head. A strange marriage proposal, this. But then he supposed that he had been half expecting it. It was something of a relief to have it out in the open between them.

"All this would explain very well," she said, getting to her feet and coming around the desk toward him again, "why Wulfric would hate you, Lord Rosthorn. But he says that *you* hate *him?* Did he believe you had done it out of hatred for him rather than love for her?"

He laughed softly and turned to look at her. Poor girl—she had been only a child when it had all happened. She ought not to have been dragged into it at this late date. Would he ever forgive himself? He doubted it.

"It really was like an atrocious melodrama, that scene," he said. "Bewcastle left the room while the Marquess of Paysley was still blustering at his daughter and threatening to kill me, and while my father was assuring him that I would pay him a formal visit in the morning to make my own marriage offer. I left the room on Bewcastle's heels, intent upon explaining the situation to him without calling Marianne a liar to her face, but he hurried downstairs ahead of me and Henrietta delayed me at the bottom. She was pale-faced and very nearly distraught and wanted to know what had happened. By the time I caught up with Bewcastle again he was in the hall, about to leave the house. He was surrounded by a number of our mutual friends, and of course there were numerous servants present and perhaps a few other guests too. I was beside myself with bewilderment and anger and mortification. I struck a pose and nobly invited Bewcastle to call me out if he wanted satisfaction."

"You fought a duel?" Her eyes widened again.

"He looked at me," Gervase said with another chuckle, "as only Bewcastle can, as if I were a little lower on the chain of life than the worm. He had his quizzing glass to his eye. He told me that he made it a rule to duel only with gentlemen. He added that he would take a horse whip to my hide if he saw me anytime soon after that night. And then he left and everyone else stayed—and stared accusingly at me."

She gazed mutely at him for several moments.

"And then your father banished you," she said. "Did you refuse to offer marriage to Marianne, then?"

"I was not given the chance," he said. "Neither was she given the chance to refuse me. My father came to me the next morning while I was still in my dressing room. He had an open letter in his hand and a look of thunder on his brow like nothing I had ever seen there before—even the previous night. It was from Paysley, demanding the return of the brooch I had taken from Marianne's bedchamber the night before. It was a priceless heirloom, it seemed, rarely taken out of the family safe, but given her to wear for what had been expected to be the occasion of her betrothal announcement."

"No." She frowned. "This of all else is ridiculous. You would have done no such thing."

"Thank you, *chérie*." He smiled at her. "But I *had* seen it. It was on the floor when I was about to leave the bedchamber. Bewcastle almost stepped on it. He stooped and picked it up and set it on a table—and then I followed him out. I told my father so the next morning and persuaded him to let me go to Bewcastle so that he might confirm my innocence. He was not at Bedwyn House. I found him at White's, surrounded by basically the same group of mutual friends as the night before. I blurted out my request for all to hear, and he raised his glass to his eye again and asked if anyone knew the impudent puppy standing in the doorway. After that he ignored me and I slunk away—I was a *very* young and foolish man in those days, *chérie*. My father wrote to him, but he sent back only a very curt reply claiming that he knew nothing of any brooch. And so, you see, my disgrace was compounded. I stood accused and condemned as a ravisher of innocence and as a dastardly thief. My father did what he felt he had to do."

She stared at him for a very long time.

"I believe you," she said at last. "I believe Wulfric too. He saw and heard what seemed incontrovertible proof of your guilt, though it *does* seem spiteful of him to have refused to give you the alibi you needed over the matter of the brooch. I suppose he thought to punish you for what you had done to him. But I believe you were innocent."

"Thank you, *chérie*."

She did not resist when he possessed himself of one of her hands and raised it to his lips. She was the only one ever to have believed him. He felt strangely close to tears. She was also the very one he had betrayed.

"And so," he said, "we return to the reason for my visit here this morning."

"I would rather you did not ask the question," she said.

"Would you, *chérie?*" he asked her. "You do not wish to marry me?"

"We ought not to consider marriage when the offer has been forced upon you and the answer upon me," she said. "We ought not to let society dictate to us what we do with all the rest of our lives. It is absurd."

"But perhaps," he said, "society and I agree on this one issue."

"It has all been too hasty," she said with a frown. "Too much has happened within the past couple of months. You have been my friend, even though on one occasion we both allowed more to happen between us than we ought to have allowed. I feel an affection for you, Lord Rosthorn, and it seems to me that perhaps you return the feeling. But I want more of marriage."

"Love?" He smiled ruefully at her.

"I want to go home to Lindsey Hall for the summer," she said without pursuing the topic further. "I believe you want to return to Windrush to resume the life of which you were robbed nine years ago. We should both do what we wish, unencumbered by a commitment we may regret."

He was to be set free? Where was the elation he ought to be feeling?

"And next spring?" he said. "We will meet again?"

"Perhaps," she said. "Perhaps not. The future must be allowed to unfold in its own way. I thank you for coming, Lord Rosthorn, but I beg you not to ask your question. I could not bear to say no, you see, when I like you so well, but I would be compelled to do so nonetheless."

*"Chérie."* He still had her hand in his. He raised it to his lips again and held it there. He tightened his hold on it as he closed his eyes. "You break my heart."

And the foolish thing was that he felt as if he spoke the truth.

There was a light tap on the library door before either of them could say more, and it opened to reveal Lady Aidan Bedwyn, looking both apologetic and embarrassed.

"I do apologize," she said. "Wulfric was determined to come back in here since you have been alone together for longer than he thinks appropriate. I persuaded him to allow me to come instead. I shall sit in the farthest corner with a book and become both deaf and blind. Please ignore my presence."

Lady Morgan had withdrawn her hand.

"There is no need, Eve," she said. "Lord Rosthorn is leaving."

Lady Aidan looked at him inquiringly. "He will not come to the drawing room for refreshments?" she asked.

He bowed. "No, ma'am, I thank you," he said. "I must leave."

"Oh," she said, "I am so sorry."

"You need not be," Lady Morgan assured her. "We part on amicable terms, Eve. Lord Rosthorn and I are friends."

There was nothing to do then but bow to the two of them again and take his leave. As he drove his curricle out of the square a few minutes later, a free man again, Gervase doubted he had felt more wretched in years.

# CHAPTER XVI

NOBODY SO MUCH AS MENTIONED THE NAME OF THE Earl of Rosthorn. It was as if he had never called, as if he had never been expected to come with an offer of marriage.

Everyone was determinedly cheerful. Eve and Aidan were planning to return home within a few days. They wanted Morgan to accompany them.

"We may go to the Lake District for a few weeks," Eve added. "We were going to go last year if you will recall, Morgan, but we went to Cornwall instead when it seemed that Joshua was in need of our support. This year we will try again. We would love to have you accompany us, would we not, Aidan?"

"The children would be delighted too, Morgan," he told her.

Freyja and Joshua came during the afternoon. Somehow they must have learned that there was no betrothal.

"We are going home the very moment the parliamentary session is over," Freyja said. "No physician here has had any success in persuading me that I suffer from morning sickness or any of the other delights that would surely accompany my condition if I were a properly genteel lady. Besides, we both long for Penhallow—and there will be Chastity's wedding to organize. Come with us, Morg? You can do more of that painting you longed to do there last year."

"Do agree, Morgan," Joshua added with a grin. "Perhaps you will have a restraining influence on my wife, who will otherwise be climbing cliffs and rowing fishing boats and otherwise sending me into a daily fit of mortal anxiety. It must be remembered that we are both in a delicate way these days."

Wulfric announced his intention of returning to Lindsey Hall as soon as the session was over.

"Now that you are out, Morgan," he said, "you will be able to make and receive calls and relieve me of some of my social burdens—unless you decide to go to the Lake District or Cornwall for the summer instead, of course."

None of which social burdens had ever seemed to bother him before, Morgan thought.

"It would seem," she said, "that I have so many choices I will find myself paralyzed by indecision."

But all the plans for involving her in busy activity were future ones, she noticed. There was absolutely no mention of morning rides in Hyde Park or shopping expeditions on Oxford Street or Bond Street or visits to the library or any of a number of other activities that would have been quite unexceptionable even in her mourning state.

She was, of course, in absolute disgrace. Not only had she behaved badly in Brussels and with a vulgar disregard for her name and rank—to quote Aunt Rochester—here in London, but now she had also refused to make amends in the only socially acceptable manner. She had refused to marry the Earl of Rosthorn.

Why had she done so?

It was a question that nagged at her for the whole of the rest of the day. She believed that she loved him. After hearing his account of what had happened nine years ago and realizing the terrible injustice under which he had been living for nine years, she had been even more sure of her feelings.

Why had she refused, then?

Had she expected him to be more persuasive, to assure her much more forcefully of his love for her? But she did not play games like that.

Perhaps she had been right, she thought, after excusing herself early from an evening with her family in the drawing room. She allowed her maid to prepare her for bed and then sat in the window seat in her bedchamber, as she had during the morning, her arms wrapped about her raised legs.

Perhaps she had been right to do what she had done.

There had been altogether too much turmoil in her life this spring. How could she make a rational decision about something as momentous as marriage? And perhaps she did not really love him. Perhaps it was only friendship and gratitude after all—and sympathy.

She could hardly remember that encounter in his rooms in Brussels. It had been wild and passionate and shocking—and intensely satisfying at the time. And even now her insides performed strange somersaults at the memory that she had been with him in that way. But had that been love? It really had not been, had it? She had needed comfort and he had given it—because they were friends and perhaps a little dearer to each other than friends.

But now she had *refused* him. She might never see him again. And even if she did, next year or the year after, they would perhaps merely nod politely and distantly to each other, like strangers.

She could not bear it.

*Why* had she refused him?

She dropped her forehead to her knees, closed her eyes, and practiced what she had discovered years ago invariably stilled her mind and calmed her emotions. She listened to her own breath, concentrated upon it as if there were nothing else to do or be thought of. And perhaps there was not. She had made her decision, and now her life would move onward into the unknown. The past was over and done with, the future had not yet come, and this moment was poised like a blessed gift between the two. It was, in fact, the only reality.

But sometimes the trouble with suspended thought

was that its cushioning effect on the mind was removed, and truth could seep in to replace it and to make itself heard as soon as she lost her concentration upon her breath.

She had stopped him from asking his question because she had not finished asking her own. Yet she had been afraid to ask the other questions. So afraid, in fact, that she had not even admitted to herself until now that there were more to ask.

She lifted her head and gazed out into the darkness beyond her window.

Perhaps, she thought, because she knew the answers but could ignore them as long as they were never expressed in words.

But since when had she been afraid to face truth? Since Brussels, when she had denied to herself for a whole week the reality of Alleyne's death?

When had she been afraid to ask questions, even when she knew that the answers would crush her? Since this morning?

Since when had she become a coward, cowering here in her room, preparing to go home to Lindsey Hall or to go off to the Lake District or Cornwall, pretending that it was good sense and a growing maturity that had held her back from committing herself to a betrothal this morning?

Love was a hollow thing—and essentially a nonexistent thing—when the object of it was not what one had thought him, when he never had been.

It was a long time before Morgan climbed into bed and lay there, staring at the canopy over her head, knowing that tonight would be as basically sleepless as last night had been. What she really felt like doing, she thought, aware of the silence all around and realizing that everyone else must have gone to bed too, was giving vent to a very noisy tantrum.

But, alas, she was no longer a child.

MORGAN LOOKED ASSESSINGLY at Eve during breakfast the following morning. Eve might seem meek and mild, but Morgan knew the story of how last year she had defied Wulf and Aunt Rochester and Aidan by secretly ordering the color of her presentation gown changed to black so that she could honor the memory of her brother, recently killed in battle, instead of wearing a color, as Wulf had decreed. And then she had defied Wulf again by insisting upon returning home to deal with a family crisis when he had ordered her to stay for an important dinner at Carlton House. Interestingly enough, Wulf now held Eve in the deepest respect even though she was the daughter of a Welsh coal miner. That said something about the quality of her backbone.

Nevertheless, Morgan rejected the idea of asking for her company. This was something she really must do alone.

And so, less than an hour later, when Wulfric had left for the House of Lords and everyone else was busy about various daily concerns, Morgan stepped out of the front door, her maid a few paces behind her, and set out to walk the distance to Pickford House. If she met anyone she knew on her way, she decided, she would incline her head regally and bid whoever it was a good morning and let them behave as they would.

She did not care if she met a dozen people and they all gave her the cut direct.

But the very people she did happen to meet, of course, were Lady Caddick and Rosamond, on their way somewhere on foot. Lady Caddick's bosom swelled and she sniffed the air, turning to address her daughter just when Morgan was drawing abreast of them.

"I smell rotten fish, Rosamond," she said. "It is deplorable how even in a fashionable area of London one cannot avoid all the worst smells."

"Good morning, ma'am," Morgan said. "Good morning, Rosamond."

Her friend darted her one agonized look and would have stopped, Morgan believed, but her mother caught her by the sleeve and dragged her onward.

Morgan would have been amused by the whole episode if she had not remembered the nature of her errand. She hurried onward and knocked on the door of Pickford House before she could lose her courage.

The Countess of Rosthorn was from home, she was informed. But Miss Clifton would surely be happy to receive her. Morgan followed the butler upstairs while her maid disappeared into the nether regions of the house, and was shown into a sitting room that was smaller than the drawing room where she had been entertained to tea a few days before. Henrietta Clifton rose to her feet as she was announced, a look of surprise on her face.

"Lady Morgan," she said, "do come in and have a

seat. I am sorry that Aunt Lisette is not here to receive you. She will be sorry too."

Miss Clifton was in her late twenties, Morgan judged. She was plain and slightly overweight. But she had pleasing manners and Morgan liked her.

"I am the last person you must have expected to see today," she said, seating herself.

"We were surprised and a little disappointed when Gervase came home yesterday and told us that you had refused his marriage offer," Miss Clifton said. "I really thought the two of you would suit, and I very much wish for his happiness. But I daresay you had a good reason."

"You did not turn against him nine years ago, then?" Morgan asked her.

Miss Clifton flushed. "Ah, you know about that, do you?" she said. "No, none of us blamed Gervase except my uncle. None of us expected him to react as he did. I have been dreadfully unhappy about it ever since. May I offer you refreshments?"

"Actually," Morgan said, "I came to speak with Lord Rosthorn. I will wait for him to return home if I may."

"With Gervase?" Miss Clifton looked surprised again, as well she might.

"There is something I forgot to say yesterday," Morgan said. "Please do not tell me now that you do not expect him home until tonight."

"He is not even from home," Miss Clifton said, getting to her feet. "Do you wish to speak with him alone?"

"Yes, please," Morgan said.

"I will go and fetch him, then," the other woman told her, and left the room before Morgan could change her mind. It was too late for that now anyway.

He came less than a minute later. He came striding into the room while an unseen servant closed the door behind him. Both his hands were outstretched to hers. There was a frown on his face.

"What has happened?" he asked her. "What is the matter? Has someone made your life quite intolerable? Bewcastle?"

"Nothing is the matter." She got to her feet and moved around her chair so that it stood between them. He dropped his arms to his sides. "Lord Rosthorn, why did you ask me to dance at Viscount Cameron's ball?"

His eyes searched hers for a few moments.

"You were by far the loveliest lady there, *chérie,*" he told her. "I saw you and knew I had to seek an introduction to you."

"Try again," she told him, holding his eyes with her own. "And try honesty this time. You danced with no one else that evening. I am eighteen years old. I was wearing the white gown of a girl who has just made her come-out. I must have looked the veriest infant to you, a rake of long experience. Did you know my identity before you asked to be presented to me?"

A faint half-smile played about his lips and eyes.

"I did," he said.

"And you were not repulsed," she asked him, "to know that I was the sister of the Duke of Bewcastle?"

"I was not," he said. "I waltzed with you, did I not?"

"*Why* did you do so?" she asked him.

Even now there was a part of her that hoped she might be wrong. But she knew she was not. She just needed to hear him say it.

"It would have been best, *chérie,*" he said softly, his head to one side, "if you had not come here today. It would be best even now if you would accept the easy explanation. But you will not do so, will you? You will never take the easy path through life, I suspect. I waltzed with you, *ma petite,* because you were the sister of the Duke of Bewcastle."

With one hand she clung tightly to the back of the chair. She lifted her chin.

"And the picnic in the Forest of Soignés?" she asked him.

"Because you were Bewcastle's sister," he said.

"You meant to ruin me there?" she asked him.

"Ah, no," he said. "I meant merely to single you out for marked attention and perhaps even a little indiscretion so that the gathered *ton* would gossip about us and word would get back to London and to the ears of Bewcastle."

It felt almost as if she had not guessed the truth, as if it were assaulting her now for the first time. She felt almost numb with hurt. She remembered allowing him to flirt with her there and flirting right back at him, feeling in control of the situation and in control of him. She remembered the kiss she had allowed.

She had not understood the game at all. She had come nowhere close to winning it.

She had been no more than a puppet on a string.

Even then she was tempted to leave it at that. But he

continued to look at her from his place in the middle of the room, and he continued to smile that half-smile she had seen so often in Brussels—and thought teasing and attractive.

Now she knew it was a smile of contempt for her youth and her ignorance and her lineage.

"The Richmond ball?" she said, plowing onward. "You waited until all the officers had gone and then came to comfort me. Or was it to lay the grounds for more open scandal?"

"Ah, *chérie,*" he said, "you needed comforting."

"And then I needed escorting to and from Mrs. Clark's," she said, her eyes flashing at him. "And then I needed someone to find Alleyne for me. And someone to champion my cause when the Caddicks would not stay in Brussels. You fought so firmly and righteously for me then, Lord Rosthorn. And then I needed escorting about Brussels when I was not on duty with the wounded. All the time scandal was growing about us, and all the time you were my *friend*. My oh-so-dear friend. The funny thing is that I thought myself so mature for my age. I was impatient of others of my own age or even older who were less bold, less in control of their own destinies. I was your *dupe*. Wulfric used that word yesterday before you came to Bedwyn House and I would not listen to him." She was clinging with both hands now.

"How can I defend myself?" he asked her. "I have been horribly guilty where you are concerned. But not *always* guilty. Not after Waterloo."

She came around the chair toward him when she realized that he might believe she was cowering there.

"And that night," she said to him, her hands balling into fists at her sides, "when I came to your rooms, distraught and in shock over what I had discovered about Alleyne—"

"Ah, *non, ma chère,*" he said, raising both hands palm-out as if to ward off an attack.

"I thought," she said, "that I initiated what happened there. I still believe I did, but only because you had tricked and manipulated me so that I liked and trusted you more than anyone else in this world. How you must have *exulted.*"

*"Non, ma petite."*

She raised her right hand and whipped it across his face with a ringing slap.

"Oh, yes!" she cried. "Do not deny it. Yes, yes, yes, *oui, oui, oui*. In either language, it is useless to lie to me."

"As you say," he said, dropping his arms to his sides while the marks of her fingers showed scarlet against his left cheek.

"You have *used* me," she said. "You have preyed upon me and hated me and pretended to care for me. You are the worst kind of villain."

"Yes," he agreed. "Perhaps I am."

Her hand was hot and stinging, but she had the satisfaction of knowing that his face probably felt far worse.

"The meeting in Hyde Park," she said, "and the tea here with your mother were all part of a clever plan, I suppose, to embarrass Wulfric further and force him to allow you to pay me your addresses. And the ball—how did you happen to know that there was an unused anteroom close to the ballroom? How did it come about that the door was left carelessly ajar after we had gone inside? And why were we overcome with passion while we waltzed and so were found conveniently locked in each other's arms? You *planned* it that way."

He continued to look steadily at her. "I planned it," he admitted.

She lifted her left hand and slapped it across his other cheek. And then she gazed at him as he winced but made no move to defend himself, her nostrils flared, her lip curled with disdain.

"And yesterday was the coup de grâce," she said. "You told me your story and won my sympathy—there is no tale better designed to arouse pity than one that tells of wrongs committed and injustices endured. And I suppose I turned your schemes into perfection itself when I refused to allow you to offer for me. I set you free. You had wreaked havoc with my life and Wulfric's and all my family's and I let you go to enjoy the memory of all your triumphs."

"Right, *chérie,*" he said softly when she waited for his comment.

"*Wrong,* Lord Rosthorn." She glared at him and pointed at the floor. "Down on your knees. I have changed my mind. Ask your question. And know, if you refuse, that I will spare no effort to let it be known all over London, all over England, that you are a man without all honor and decency. I still have *some* influence. I have powerful relatives."

His head tipped to one side again, and the half-smile returned to his eyes.

"You wish me to propose marriage to you?" he asked her. "After all this? So that you may have the satisfaction of refusing me? It would be monstrous of me to deny you that, I suppose. Very well, then."

He went down on one knee before her and lifted his eyes to hers, taking both her hands in his own as he did so. The amusement had gone from his face. He looked at her with what just yesterday she might have interpreted as tenderness.

"Lady Morgan Bedwyn," he said, "will you do me the great honor of accepting my hand in marriage?"

She mustered all the considerable haughtiness of which she was capable and gazed down at him, not even trying to mask the contempt she felt. She kept him waiting. She savored the moment.

"Thank you, Lord Rosthorn," she said at last. "I will."

He stared back at her, an arrested look in his eyes.

"Have I missed something?" he asked her.

"I doubt you are deaf," she said, "and so I suppose you have missed nothing at all. You may rise now."

He got slowly to his feet. His eyes were smiling at her again.

"You will punish me, *chérie,*" he asked her, "by marrying me and never letting me forget what a villain I am?"

"Wrong again, Lord Rosthorn," she told him. "I have accepted your marriage offer. I have no intention in this world of marrying you."

The laughter deepened in his eyes.

"Ah," he said, "now all is perfectly clear."

"You thought to go free," she said, throwing back her head and gazing very directly into his eyes, "your revenge nicely wreaked on all of us. And I was to creep off to the country in disgrace. Not so, Lord Rosthorn. You must have forgotten that I am a Bedwyn. I am not finished with you yet. And I will not slink away and hang my head merely because I was too stupid and too naive to spot a rogue. You are my betrothed. You will shower me with attentions and tender devotion until I decide to set myself free."

"Ah, *chérie,*" he said, clasping his hands behind his back and leaning a little closer to her, "you are magnificent when you are in a fury. I will court you until you change your mind about leaving me."

"Wrong once more," she told him. "*I* will court *you,* Lord Rosthorn. I will make you fall in love with me, and then I will break your heart."

"You have already done the former, *ma petite,*" he said, "and will surely do the latter if you will show no mercy on me."

"Or perhaps," she said, "I will make you hate me and then marry you after all. You will never know my feelings or my intentions. But you will dance attendance upon me for as long as *I* choose to make you do so. And if you refuse, if *you* end our betrothal, then I will see to it that you are hounded out of this country again—and for the rest of your life this time."

His eyes smiled.

Her bosom heaved.

The door opened.

"Lady Morgan, *ma chère!*" the Countess of Rosthorn cried as she swept into the room. "Henrietta told me that you were in here with Gervase and no maid to make all proper. Has something happened to upset you? I scolded my son soundly after the Hallmere ball, you may be sure. I was not in any way pleased with him."

*"Maman,"* he said, drawing Morgan's arm through his and smiling down at her in a way that might have turned her weak at the knees just a day or so before, "Morgan has just made me the happiest of men."

"Indeed, ma'am, it is true," Morgan said, smiling dazzlingly. "Gervase has just asked me to marry him, and I have said yes."

She looked up at him, and right there, with his mother watching and exclaiming rapturously in French and clasping her hands to her bosom, he lowered his head and kissed her on the lips.

Not to be outdone, Morgan kissed him right back.

## CHAPTER XVII

GERVASE WONDERED IF MORGAN HAD REALIZED when she insisted upon a betrothal between them that the Season was all but over. Perhaps she had imagined their appearing together at numerous entertainments, herself haughty and triumphant, him dancing smiling attendance upon her, before she spurned him publicly and so wreaked her revenge on him.

That she would also thereby embroil herself in even

more scandal would not deter her, he knew.

But of course the Season *was* almost at an end. The announcement was made in the morning papers, and there were teas and dinners hosted by both their families. They rode in the park together a couple of mornings, and he took her up in his curricle one afternoon to drive in Hyde Park at the fashionable hour. But there was nothing much else. Many families had already left for the country.

His mother and Henrietta were delighted at the unexpected turn of events, his mother quite exuberantly so. Morgan's family seemed pleased too and was certainly polite. Bewcastle was arctically courteous.

Morgan was radiant, even much of the time when they were alone—though even then, of course, they were almost always on view. Had he not known differently, he might almost have imagined that she was wildly in love with him. Though he was not quite convinced that she was not—or that he was not in love with her. But her radiance, he was aware, was like a bright, hard shield beyond which he could not penetrate and no one else was aware of.

He wondered what the summer would bring. She had made it very clear to everyone who asked that they had no immediate plans to marry. They wished to enjoy their betrothal for a while, she explained. It was he who supplied a way in which they might do that more fully. He and his mother and Henrietta had been invited to dine at Bedwyn House, and Lady Aidan Bedwyn had just made reference to plans for a journey to the Lake District she and her husband were making.

"Morgan was thinking of coming with us," she said. "Are you still considering it, Morgan?" She darted a curious glance at Gervase.

"But no," he said. "I absolutely could not bear such a long separation from my betrothed, and I am confident that Morgan agrees with me." She was sitting beside him. He turned his head and smiled into her eyes. "You will not be going to the Lake District, will you, *chérie?* You will come to Windrush instead?"

"But of course she will," his mother cried from farther along the table, as if it had all been settled long ago. "I have my heart set upon introducing my future daughter-in-law to our friends and neighbors. I have already written to my daughters with the happy announcement. I am quite sure they will want to come to Windrush to meet her and to see Gervase again. I will plan some grand betrothal celebration—a garden party or a ball, or perhaps both."

"Perhaps, *Maman,*" Gervase suggested, "Morgan's family would care to join us too and help us celebrate."

"But that is a delightful idea, *mon fils,*" she said, clasping her hands to her bosom and beaming at everyone about the table. "In another minute I would have thought of it for myself. Lady Aidan? Lady Hallmere? Bewcastle? Do agree to join us in the country."

Gervase turned his head and smiled at Morgan again while touching his fingertips to her hand on the table.

"This will please you, *chérie?*" he asked her, his voice low. "That we spend the summer together at your future home, so that you may make the acquaintance of all my family and your future friends and neighbors?"

"It will please me of all things." Her eyes glowed.

He was, he realized, enjoying himself enormously. He was very glad she had decided to fight him. He was horribly guilty where she was concerned. Although not all her accusations against him were true, he *had* used her quite deliberately and abominably. He had sunk into a deep gloom after she sent him away from Bedwyn House when he had gone there to offer for her. Even though he was free and even though it had seemed to him that she did not suspect the truth about him, he had felt wretched about the deceit and about all the scandal he had drawn her into.

But she was fighting back in a totally unexpected and intriguing manner. She would use him until she was ready to discard him, she had promised. She would make him fall in love with her and then break his heart. Or she would make him hate her and then force him to marry her anyway.

He could not help but be amused. At the same time, he thanked providence for giving him a chance somehow to make amends. He was not quite sure how he would do that. Perhaps it would involve nothing more than allowing her to do exactly what she had threatened to do. But he was not going to be abject about it, he had decided. He was not going to allow her to punish him simply because he deserved punishment.

She would not enjoy that.

He would play her at her own game. If she won fair and square, then he would have to accept graciously that he had lost. But he was not going to *let* her win. She would surely spit in his eye if he tried any such thing.

He would play her love game to win, then.

He had not yet asked himself what winning would mean exactly.

They had postponed their journey to the Lake District last year in order to go to Penhallow in Cornwall after Freyja became betrothed, Lady Aidan explained with a laugh. They must do the same this year for Morgan, then. Did not Aidan agree with her? Lord Aidan did, it seemed. And since she did not know when she would leave Cornwall again once she returned there, as she was in a delicate way, Lady Hallmere thought it would be a shame not to see Morgan's future home while they had a chance. Hallmere agreed that a week or so in Kent would be perfectly agreeable.

Bewcastle declined the invitation—with courteous thanks to Gervase's mother.

And so it was all settled. The summer was to be spent at Windrush.

"I suppose," Morgan said to him the following morning when they were riding on Rotten Row, a little ahead of Lord and Lady Aidan, "you think to embarrass me by inviting both your family members and mine to Windrush and by planning lavish betrothal celebrations there. I am not easily embarrassed, Gervase."

"I know it, *chérie,*" he said. "But it is I who am to be embarrassed, is it not? It is my family and my servants and tenants and neighbors who will be witness to my deep infatuation for you and who will then pity and scorn me when you spurn me."

"That is exactly correct," she said.

"Unless," he said, smiling and drawing his horse a little closer to hers so that his knee almost touched hers, "I can persuade *you* to have pity on me instead, my charmer."

"It is not going to happen," she said, smiling dazzlingly and actually reaching out quite outrageously and touching her gloved hand briefly to his thigh.

"I will take you shopping later this morning," he told her. "I must buy you jewels, *chérie*. I would be a sorry excuse for a fiancé if I did not buy you a betrothal gift, would I not?"

"I am not interested in jewels," she told him. "What would I do with them after we have parted? I would despise the very look of them."

"What, then?" he asked her. "I may not buy you clothes yet. It would be deemed scandalous."

"Paints and painting supplies," she said after a moment's consideration. "I did not bring my own with me to London, and I am pining to paint again. I will paint at Windrush. You may buy me easel and paints and brushes and canvases and paper and charcoal and anything else I think of in the next hour or so."

"*Do* you paint?" he asked her. "Are you good at it?"

"That is a foolish question," she told him. "How am I to know if I am good or not? And what does it matter anyway? I paint because I love to do it, because I *must* do it. I paint so that I may get inside reality, get behind surfaces, search out the heart of meaning. I am not a dabbler, a lady who paints picturesque canvases in picturesque surroundings so that I may encourage some lovelorn swain to swoon over me."

"Ah." He chuckled. "Then I will exercise great fortitude, *chérie,* and endeavor not to swoon over you. Paints and painting supplies it will be—all of the very best quality and in copious amounts so that the world will know how I love you."

She smiled into his eyes, her own shining all the way back to their inner depths—or so it seemed.

"Thank you, Gervase," she said. "Oh, *thank* you. How I *adore* you."

For a moment he gazed at her, arrested. She was beautiful and vibrant, and all the beauty and vibrancy were focused upon him. It seemed almost impossible to believe that she did not mean every word.

And then she laughed.

WULFRIC WAS RETURNING to Lindsey Hall on the same day as Morgan left for Windrush with Aidan and Eve, Freyja and Joshua. He had said very little about the betrothal even though after she had told him about it on his return from the House of Lords the day it happened he had raised his quizzing glass all the way to his eye and regarded her silently through it for what had seemed like five minutes though in reality it had probably been less than one.

He had a private word with her before she went out to the waiting carriages, though.

"Nothing is irrevocable," he said, "until the nuptial service is over. I urge you, Morgan, to consider whether this is something you are doing merely because I advised you not to."

"How foolish you are, Wulf," she told him crossly. "I

am marrying Gervase because I *wish* to do so. And you are wrong about him, you know. He did not ravish Marianne. She entrapped him because she did not want to marry *you*."

She wished then that she had not put it quite like that, but it was too late to change the wording. He gazed back at her with hard, bleak eyes.

"I thought you less credulous," he said. "I forget sometimes just how young you are."

"And it was *cruel* of you," she said, "to pretend that you had not seen the brooch and set it on a table yourself as you were leaving Marianne's room with Gervase."

He nodded slowly. "You are besotted indeed," he said. "One can only hope that he has changed in the course of nine years, though so far the evidence would suggest otherwise. I would have you know this, though, Morgan, before I let you go. Your happiness is more important to me than being right is. Consider your own happiness without any reference to me."

She had always loved Wulfric. She could not remember either of her parents. Wulfric had been a father figure to her all her life, and she had always felt wonderfully safe and secure under his rule and guidance. She had never doubted that he had her best interests at heart. At the same time, she had never really thought of him as loving her—or her sister or any of her brothers either. She had always seen him as a man incapable of any warm emotion—including anger.

It struck her now with some shock that perhaps he did care after all—not just for her safety and consequence and reputation, but for *her*. And she almost blurted out a reassurance, an explanation of the nature of her betrothal, a promise that soon it would be at an end and he would finally be able to forget all about Gervase Ashford, Earl of Rosthorn. But if she said anything, he would probably forbid her to go to Windrush and to open herself yet again to scandal—a worse scandal than before.

She stepped forward impulsively and hugged him.

"I am going to be happy," she told him. "And I am going to make you happy for me. You will see."

"Yes, well," he said, his tone cool—and perhaps embarrassed? "You are keeping Eve and Aidan waiting, Morgan."

By late in the afternoon they were approaching Windrush Grange in Kent, and Morgan was looking beyond the windows with great interest. The park was large. The carriage moved along a winding, wooded driveway for a full mile or two before the house came into sight. It was a romantic-looking mansion with its red brick and gables. It was surrounded by smooth lawns and colorful flower gardens.

"It is quite magnificent, Morgan," Eve said from the opposite seat on the carriage. "How very exciting this must be for you."

"It is," Morgan agreed.

It was a week since she last saw Gervase. It was a time during which her outrage and resentment against him had grown. If there had not been that week or so in Brussels after the Battle of Waterloo, she had thought over and over again, perhaps she would not now hate him so much. Before and after that, after all, he had not made much pretense of doing anything more than flirting with her. But there had been that week when he had become more dear to her than anyone else in her life had ever been, and she felt horribly betrayed.

But it was a week too that had felt dreadfully flat. She had missed him, his ironic smile and his banter and attractive French accent. She hated him even more for the fact that at some time over the past few months she had slipped into love with him and was having a hard time adjusting her emotions to the reality of his character and the nature of their relationship.

The double doors at the head of the horseshoe steps stood open, she could see as the carriage passed a flower arbor and turned onto the wide, cobbled terrace before the house. Two liveried footmen were descending the steps, one on each side, a black-clad servant who must be the butler stood at attention outside the doors, and a whole host of people, it seemed, including Gervase and the countess, were emerging from the doors and hurrying down the steps behind the footmen.

So this, Morgan thought with mingled elation and nervousness, was what she had set in motion. She drew a deep, steadying breath and smiled.

It was all very dizzying. Gervase handed her out of the carriage and then reached out his hand to help Eve alight. The other carriages—the one bringing Freyja and Joshua, and the one bringing Becky and Davy and their nurse—drew in behind and disgorged their occupants. Morgan found herself being enfolded in the countess's embrace and then being introduced to the Reverend Pierre Ashford and his wife, Emma, to Lord and Lady Vardon—Lady Vardon was Gervase's sister, Cecile—and to Sir Harold Spalding and his wife, the other sister, Monique. The gentlemen all bowed and Emma curtsied. The sisters, with the Gallic enthusiasm of their mother, both hugged Morgan and exclaimed over her beauty.

Gervase meanwhile had taken charge of greeting Morgan's relatives and presenting them to his own.

Children—hordes of them, it seemed—were dashing exuberantly about with no sign of any nurse to curtail their glee except Nanny Johnson.

There was a great deal of noise and laughter. Servants were unloading the baggage coaches, which were last in line. Summer sunshine beamed down on the scene of happy confusion. Gervase caught Morgan by one hand—and then the other too.

"The week has been endless, *ma chère,*" he said, raising her right hand to his lips. "Welcome to Windrush." He raised her left hand to his lips. "Welcome home."

While his sisters exclaimed with delight and several other unidentified persons murmured with satisfaction, he leaned forward and kissed her on the lips.

"Every day has seemed like a week in itself, Gervase," she said, squeezing his hands tightly. "I am so happy to be here at last."

It pleased her, she thought as he offered his arm and they led the way up the stone steps and into the house, that he was still shamelessly flirting with her. If he had turned grim and apologetic and abject since she had forced this betrothal on him, she might have forgiven him and let him go, but she surely would have despised him—more than she already did, that was.

And every day really *had* seemed like a week, she admitted to herself.

THE WEEK REALLY HAD seemed endless. Gervase had tried to busy himself with estate business and had spent a considerable amount of time with his steward—and his father's before him—either in the office or outside touring the home farm. But his father, as of course he had always known, had been a superb manager who had always had his finger on the pulse of estate business. And the steward had obviously admired him greatly. His name came up constantly—his lordship did this, his lordship believed that, his lordship would never allow the other—until it was as much as Gervase could do not to bellow at the man that *he* was his lordship now.

But he could not compete with his father. He knew so little. It would take him a great deal of time to learn. In the meantime he depended upon his steward.

He had quarreled with Henrietta, and to a lesser degree with his mother. When he had inquired casually of his cousin where she had been one afternoon and she had informed him that she had been visiting Marianne, he had asked her rather sharply if she considered it loyal to him to have continued that particular friendship. And when she had reminded him that what happened between him and Marianne had been nine years ago, he had lost his temper and assured her that he was *very* well aware of how long ago it had been. He had been living in exile all those years. She had ended up fleeing to her room in tears, and his mother had suggested gently that it was perhaps time he put the past behind him.

The thing was, he could not forgive his father.

He could not forgive Marianne.

He could not forgive Bewcastle.

And now he was finding it hard to forgive Henrietta.

He was in bad shape, he realized. He was consumed by a bitterness he thought he had put behind him until fairly recently—until he had set eyes upon Lady Morgan Bedwyn at the Cameron ball in Brussels, in fact.

And so he was glad of the distraction of so many houseguests. And he was genuinely glad to see Morgan again. Perhaps she would torment him—undoubtedly she would, in fact. But at least she would stimulate his mind and his senses. She would make him laugh.

He made a grand production of presenting her with her betrothal gifts the evening of her arrival. Everyone watched her unwrap one parcel after another and exclaim in delight over the contents, which she had chosen in London, but which he had had wrapped and transported to Windrush. When she had finished, she came to him, wrapped both arms about his neck, and kissed his cheek.

If her family was shocked by such indiscreet behavior, they gave no sign. His own family was charmed. He was considerably amused. He hoped she would let him watch her paint.

The following day was as warm and sunny as the day of her arrival. He suggested a picnic at the lake during the afternoon, and they all went out there in a noisy group, the children too. Pierre and Emma had come over from the vicarage with Jonathan. There was a vigorous game of hide-and-seek to begin with and then Joshua—all the Bedwyns had asked to be called by their given names—and Harold took out the boats and gave rides to everyone while Emma and Eve splashed around in the water with some of the children. They all feasted on the tea carried out by some of the servants, and then most of the adults settled to laziness on the blankets beneath the shade of a large oak tree, while the children devised games of their own.

"Come walking with me, *chérie?*" Gervase suggested to Morgan.

She took his arm and he led her along a grassy, tree-lined avenue perpendicular to the lake.

"What is that in the distance?" she asked him, pointing.

"A summerhouse," he told her. "It is a quiet refuge on a rainy day with a lovely view in all directions. Perhaps down the years you will enjoy sitting there with a book."

"In order to escape all the children in the nursery, I suppose," she said.

"Or the constant demands of an amorous husband," he suggested.

"But would the amorous husband not suspect where I had gone?" she asked him.

"I believe, *chérie,*" he said, "he would pursue you there and convince you that what you had wanted to escape was visitors who might have arrived to disturb our privacy."

"Delightful," she said. "Are there any other such retreats in the park? It would be too unsporting if I could not at least keep you guessing as to which one I had chosen on a particular day."

"There is the grotto," he said. "It is at the end of the wilderness walk, but not obvious to anyone who does not know it is there. I will take you there one day. You may wish to paint there."

"Ah, but you would not wish me to do that," she told him as they strolled onward between the straight lines of trees, which shielded them from the full glare of the sun. "I get *very* absorbed in my painting."

"But I have all the patience in the world," he told her. "I will sit and wait, and when you have finished I will help you relax before carrying your things back to the house for you."

"Indeed?" she said.

"We will make love there," he told her, "and in the summerhouse here and in the more secluded areas bordering the lake."

"I thought the boats looked interesting," she said.

"And in the boats too," he agreed. "Both of them. We will decide which is the more comfortable and which rocks more pleasantly."

She turned her head at the same time as he did and their eyes met. They both laughed.

"Have you forgiven me yet, *chérie?*" he asked her.

But she would only laugh again and then look about her with a great sigh of what sounded like contentment.

"How beautiful this all is," she said. "I love summertime."

They had reached the summerhouse by then. He had not intended that they stop there but that they turn back to rejoin the others. There was no reason they should, though. They were officially betrothed. Both his family and hers were consequently indulgent about their being alone together for lengthy periods of time. He opened the door and stood aside for her to precede him inside.

It was hot in there, though not as bad as it might have been as it sat within the shade of two tall trees. It was a round structure with a stone wall to waist height, glass windows above, and a painted wooden dome over their heads. A wide leather seat circled the wall with a round oak table in the center.

She did not sit down immediately. She looked back along the avenue they had just walked and then turned to look at the narrower, flower-bordered avenue to the house and at the thin line of trees with part of the wilderness walk beyond and at the river flowing toward the lake on the fourth side.

"So much beauty," she said, and sat down.

"So much indeed, *chérie*." He smiled down at her before taking a seat beside her. She had left off her mourning. He had noticed that yesterday when she arrived. She was wearing a pretty pale blue muslin dress with a flower-trimmed straw bonnet.

"How does it feel," she asked him, "to have all your family about you again?"

"Strange," he said. "Monique and Cecile were just girls the last time I saw them. Now they are married ladies with children. Pierre was little more than a boy. And I have two nephews and three nieces."

"Do you feel bitter," she asked him, "that you have missed so much of their lives?"

He considered his answer. But there was no point in denying it, was there?

"Yes," he said. "I feel almost as if I had come back from the dead, expecting that everyone must have spent the intervening years mourning me only to discover that they had continued with their lives and proved to me that I was not indispensable to them after all. It is a foolish objection. Why do we always assume we are so important to other people? None of us is irreplaceable even to those closest to us."

"There is one member of your family missing," she said. "How do you feel about your father, Gervase?"

He gazed down the avenue toward the house.

"He was the model husband and father," he said, "and the model landowner too, it seems. I admired him greatly. We were very close. I always believed I was his favorite even though he was dearly fond of all of us. I was never rebellious as other sons were and never wild despite the fact that I liked to cut a figure in London and cultivated the friendship of men of influence, like Bewcastle."

"His rejection of you must have been devastating," she said.

"One might say so." He glanced at her and chuckled, though quite without mirth. "None of us had ever done anything to disappoint him before then. We were a singularly dull lot, *chérie*. And thus, I suppose, he reacted to what he thought I had done with all the implacable fury of a man who had never had to deal with anything like it before."

"Do you still hate him?" she asked.

"Ah," he said softly. "It is too late for that. He is dead."

"Where is he buried?" she asked. "In the village churchyard?"

"Yes," he said.

"Have you been there?" she asked him.

He shook his head. The vicarage was beside the church and the churchyard, and he had been there several times. He had been to church too. But he had averted his face from the churchyard each time.

"We will go together." She rested her hand on his.

"Will we?" He chuckled again.

"And what about Marianne?" she asked him. "What has happened to her? Do you know?"

"She lives not five miles away," he said. "You must ask Henrietta if you want to know more about her. They have remained friends."

"Ah," she said, "that must rankle too."

"Why should it?" he asked her. "Nine years is a long time and they are neighbors. They were always friends."

"Gervase," she said, "all this has been dreadfully hurtful to you. More than I realized."

Her hand was still on his. He set his free hand over it.

"But I will not be seen as a victim, *chérie,*" he said. "I

made a life for myself on the Continent. I saw places I would not otherwise have seen and met interesting people and experienced things I would not have done if my life had continued along its dull, blameless course. I met *you*."

"And that is something you will yet regret," she told him. "But I think it is the only way you can make your life bearable again, is it not? To believe that everything that happens in life can serve a positive purpose, that no time is wasted unless we refuse to learn the lesson that is there in that apparently wasted time. You can be a better person than you were."

"Or a worse."

They sat for a long while before walking back to the house together, in a silence that was surprisingly companionable, their hands joined, their shoulders almost touching. If he relaxed, he could almost imagine that they were back in Brussels during that week when time had seemed suspended and all his energies, all his emotions, had been centered upon her and her courage and energy and impending grief.

She would make him fall in love with her, she had promised. Was that what she was doing now? If so, she was succeeding.

Or was this all genuine?

There was no way of knowing.

# CHAPTER XVIII

MORGAN WAS THE YOUNGEST OF A FAMILY OF SIX. Life had been boisterous while they were growing up. She could particularly remember wild, vigorous, often dangerous games with the neighboring Butlers, sons of the Earl of Redfield. But the trouble was that they had all grown up long before she did. The last few years had been relatively lonely ones. And until recently she had been technically in the schoolroom. She had had very little experience of being one among other adults. Even through the spring she had been merely a young girl making her come-out.

She loved being at Windrush. She was surrounded by her own family and Gervase's. And she was very much one of them, the focus of all attention. They called upon neighbors, and neighbors called upon them, and she was no longer the very young Lady Morgan Bedwyn, but the affianced bride of the Earl of Rosthorn. Everyone was excited at the prospect of the garden fete and evening ball the countess was busily planning in honor of the betrothal. The mansion and the park were spacious and beautiful surroundings for a summer of social activities in which she could finally play a full part.

Sometimes she forgot that it was all a charade, that she had been driven into this false position by outrage and the burning desire to exact revenge.

She really had not realized how badly Gervase had been damaged by an ancient injustice. When he had spoken of it in vague terms in Brussels, she had assumed that now that he was no longer exiled, he could return to England, take up his duties as Earl of Rosthorn, and live happily ever after. But it had been very unimaginative of her to think thus. In a very real sense his youth had been taken from him. He was a man who had wandered aimlessly for nine years, building an impressive and doubtless a well-deserved reputation as a rake, but nevertheless robbed of the life that ought to have been his in the country that was his own.

He was full of hatred and bitterness, much of which he was denying.

She still strongly resented what he had done to her. She could never forgive him for that. She could never trust him again. But it was basically against her nature to hate. And since she was here at Windrush for a while, she might as well try to do some good.

Becky wanted to play with Jonathan on a chilly, blustery day when everyone else was content to remain indoors. Morgan offered to take the child to the vicarage, and of course Gervase came along too. Pierre was out on a sick call, but Emma was at home and was delighted to have another child to amuse her son, since she was busy in the kitchen with her housekeeper making jam.

"We will not disturb you," Morgan assured her. "We will go for a walk and come back for Becky later, if we may."

The walk turned into several calls on villagers, all of whom worked for Gervase in some capacity.

"I need to get to know my people, *chérie,*" he explained to her. "I still feel like a stranger among strangers. Worse, I feel like an impostor. When people ask me for some favor, it is on the tip of my tongue to refer them to my steward, as if I do not have the authority to grant or refuse requests myself. And when I *do* agree to something, like reroofing the schoolhouse, which leaks like the proverbial sieve every time it rains, I feel instant guilt and wonder if my steward will scold me when he learns of it."

He chuckled, but she guessed he was confiding real truths to her. She could not imagine Wulfric's steward daring to voice an opinion even if ordered to have every field on the home farm sown to salt. But Wulf had been carefully trained for his position from the age of twelve and had been Duke of Bewcastle since he was seventeen.

"They like you," she said. "Your people like you, Gervase."

It was true too. He talked with them and laughed with them and listened to them. They responded to his charm, which seemed very genuine in his dealings with them.

"I believe, *chérie,*" he said, "it is because they perceive that they can wrap me about their little fingers. They set eyes upon me and biblical quotations leap to their brains. Ask, and it shall be given."

"What you need to do," she told him, "is to discover how profitable Windrush is. You need to study the books and talk with your steward. Generosity is a fine thing, but if you give what you cannot afford to give, then ultimately everyone will suffer and you will be in ruin."

"Yes, ma'am." He looked down at her, laughter in his eyes.

"I suppose," she said, "you are already doing that."

"I am," he said. "I am also realizing how irresponsible it was of me to stay away for a full year after I succeeded to the title and inherited all this. But then if I had not, *chérie,* I would not have met you."

"We both would have been better off if you had not," she said tartly.

He laughed softly.

They had been strolling back along the main village street, a full hour or more after leaving the vicarage. The clouds were still low overhead and the wind still blustering, but at least it was at their backs.

"I want to see the churchyard," she said when they drew abreast of it.

"It is chilly," he said. "Let us go and wangle a cup of tea out of Emma. Maybe Pierre is back home."

"I want to see the churchyard," she said again, turning to face him. He was looking rather grim, the laughter all gone from his eyes. "You cannot avoid it for the rest of your life, Gervase. If you try, you will find that it looms larger and larger each time you come to the village."

"And who filled your head with such foolish wisdom?" he asked her, flicking her chin with one gloved finger.

"Show me the graves of your ancestors," she said.

It seemed appropriate that it was a gray and blustery

day. But at least, she thought, there *was* a grave for his father. Wulfric intended to erect a stone memorial for Alleyne in the churchyard at home, but they would all be painfully aware that his remains were buried in some unknown grave in Belgium.

He did not waste time, as she had expected he would, making a show of giving her a guided tour of the churchyard. He led her straight toward the marble headstone whose shining whiteness proclaimed it a recent addition. There were flowers on the ground before it—Cecile and Monique had come here together yesterday.

*Here lie the earthly remains of George Thomas Ashford, Sixth Earl of Rosthorn . . .*

There followed a reminder to the living of his virtues and the fact that he had been beloved by all who knew him.

They stood silently side by side, the wind at their backs.

"Did you hear from him at all after you left England?" Morgan asked.

"No," he said.

"Did you write to him?"

"Every week for six months," he said. "Often more than once a week. Begging, groveling, indignant, reasonable, furious, self-righteous, self-pitying, accusing letters—they ran the gamut of human emotions. And no, he never answered any of them. My mother wrote occasionally, though her letters often took a year or more to find me. So did Pierre and my sisters, though only for the first two or three years."

"He must have suffered," she said.

"My father?" He looked inquiringly at her. "*He* suffered?"

"You told me that you were a close family," she said, "that he loved you. He must have believed the worst of you to have acted as he did. He must have been convinced beyond a reasonable doubt. He acted harshly and probably hastily. But having done so, he must have felt bound by his decision. I daresay he wished there were a way out."

"There *was* a way out," he told her. "He could have *believed* me. He could have *trusted* me."

"He is the unfortunate one," she said. "It is too late for him to admit that perhaps he made a mistake. It is too late for him to discover or to admit that perhaps love is more powerful and more enduring than all the negative emotions with which we punish ourselves as well as the person against whom they are directed. If he had time before he died to know that he was dying and to look back on his life, I feel almost certain that he would have given anything in the world to have you there so that he could forgive you."

"So that *he* could forgive *me,*" he said softly.

"And perhaps he wanted your forgiveness too," she said. "Hatred and love—they can be such overpowering emotions, and very often it is hard to distinguish the one from the other. If he had not loved you deeply, would he have been so harsh on you—and on himself?"

He touched one hand to the headstone and patted it lightly and then over and over again, not so lightly.

"What are you suggesting?" he asked her. "That I forgive him? Does it matter? If I shout curses into the wind or whisper forgiveness into the ground, will he hear me? He is gone."

"But you are not," she said. "If you shout curses, poison will lodge in your heart. If you forgive, you will be cleansed."

He turned his head to look at her and laughed.

"How old are you, *chérie?*" he asked her. "Eighteen or eighty?"

"I have spent a great deal of time alone," she said. "I may not have done a great deal of living, but there are things I understand about life."

She was a Bedwyn through and through—she was bold and unconventional and not easily cowed by other people or by life itself. But she was different from the others too. She had always known it. There was a solitary, mystical side to her nature that she very rarely revealed to other people.

He was still patting the stone. He had looked away from her again.

"It is something I should do, then," he said, laughing again. "It is strange, is it not, that all these years I have convinced myself that it is another man whom I hate most in this life—a man who meant nothing to me and so was safe to hate. But it is my father . . . My father . . . Can you even *imagine* what it would be like if Bewcastle did to you what my father did to me? It was like a living death—to be so misjudged, so utterly rejected, so completely cut off . . . If I ever have children of my own . . . If . . ."

He turned then and strode abruptly away until he was standing some distance off, one hand propped against the ancient stone wall of the church, his head bowed. His shoulders were shaking.

Morgan did not go after him.

He came back after perhaps five minutes. He did not look at her but at the grave and the headstone.

"I daresay he did suffer," he said. "Even if he never had doubts, he would have suffered. But how could he not have had doubts? I suppose he got caught in a trap of his own making, and pride—or the conviction that he must have done the right thing—kept him snared in it for the rest of his life. Rest in peace . . . Papa."

There were unshed tears in his eyes when he turned to Morgan and tried to smile.

"Are you satisfied, *chérie?*" he asked her, mockery in his voice.

She stepped against him and wrapped her arms about his waist. His arms came tightly about her, and he lowered his head and kissed her.

What was it about death, she wondered, that impelled the living into a passionate embrace of life and one another? She moved her hands to spread over his back and opened her mouth to the hot invasion of his tongue. She leaned into him, feeling the hard masculinity of his body, the moist intimacy of his kiss.

But what she felt was not passion—not at least the blind, urgent sexual need that she felt was driving him. It was more a tenderness—a deep, knee-weakening, heart-stopping tenderness. She remained fully aware of everything, including the fact that this particular corner of the churchyard was out of sight from the street behind two ancient yew trees.

She was aware of who he was and what he had done to her, and what *she* intended to do to *him* in retaliation. But for the moment none of that mattered. This was different, as outside the normal course of life and events as her visit to his rooms in Brussels had been after she discovered the truth about Alleyne.

He lifted his head after a couple of minutes and smiled down at her with heavy-lidded eyes.

"If this is your way of making me fall even more deeply in love with you, *chérie,*" he said, "it is a devilishly clever plan. But I have time. There is a week to go before the ball. A week in which to make *you* fall in love with *me*. As well as the rest of the summer after that."

She stepped back from him and brushed at the skirt of her dress beneath her pelisse.

"This wind has chilled me to the bone," she said. "It is time to go back to the vicarage."

He chuckled softly.

THERE WERE TWO DAYS OF showers after that and a continuation of the chilly, blustery weather. They occupied themselves mostly indoors, playing billiards and cards and charades and on one afternoon a lengthy, noisy game of hide-and-seek with the children in which no part of the house was out of bounds. They read and they conversed.

Gervase managed to spend some of the time with his steward, though he did not neglect his guests. Inevitably the question of the schoolhouse roof came up again. The repairs should be done now, before winter came on again, Gervase had decided. His steward was very deferential and very tactful, but nevertheless the gist of his opinion was that such major capital expenses had always been cautiously undertaken by his lordship's father with at least a year's careful consideration before any decision was made.

Gervase looked squarely at him.

"*I* am Rosthorn now," he said. "My understanding of this year's profits balanced against expenses and the risk that the summer crops may not be as abundant as they promise to be is that I will not be beggared if the repairs are done. And from my own observations of the roof as it is now, I would conclude that the job has been needed for far longer than one cautionary year. You will make the arrangements if you please."

"Yes, my lord," the man agreed with what appeared to be considerable respect. "I will see to it without delay."

Perhaps after all, Gervase thought, he would be able to settle to this new life and lay the ghost of his father.

Summer returned after the two days were over, with clear blue skies and sunshine and heat. They were all able to resume outdoor activities—morning rides, afternoon walks or visits, even an evening swim, during which he discovered that all the Bedwyns swam like fish and enjoyed themselves with noisy enthusiasm. But then so did his sisters and brothers-in-law.

But on one afternoon when an excursion to a nearby castle had been suggested and organized by Cecile and Monique, Morgan announced her intention of remaining at Windrush.

"I need some quiet time," she told everyone at breakfast. "I need to be alone. I need to paint. Gervase gave me all those lovely supplies as a betrothal gift, and I have had no chance to use them."

There was a chorus of protest and suggestions of where they might go instead if Morgan did not fancy the castle, but Aidan spoke up in his sister's defense.

"Morgan is different from the rest of us mortals," he said, "who need company and activity every moment of every day. She always did need time and space for herself before becoming sociable again."

"Where will you paint, Morgan? At the lake?" Cecile asked.

"Perhaps at the summerhouse," she replied. "I have not decided yet."

The excursion would proceed without her, then, it was decided. Gervase waited until they had all left the breakfast parlor and he could have a private moment with her.

"You would like the grotto, I believe, *chérie,*" he said. "I will show you how to get there. But it is some distance away and you will need someone to carry your easel and other supplies. May I be your servant?"

"I can manage," she told him.

"And may I sit there with you," he asked, "if I promise not to speak or otherwise disturb you?"

"Oh, very well," she said after considering for a few moments. She smiled beguilingly at him and set one hand on his arm. "How could I not want my betrothed with me, after all? Is it a *very* picturesque spot? I shall endeavor to look my most picturesque self too and perhaps make a swooning swain of you after all."

He grinned at her. This was how he liked her best, fighting him, keeping him guessing. And she certainly knew how to do that. For a while after that afternoon when they had visited the churchyard, her manner had softened toward him and he had wondered if she had forgiven him and was prepared to accept his courtship. But she had not so easily capitulated. Last evening while they swam, she had frolicked merrily with him, sputtering and shrieking when he swam beneath her and bobbed up right in front of her, jumping on him from behind when he was not looking and dragging him downward all the way to the bottom of the lake. She had let him kiss her on the way up and smiled dazzlingly when they broke the surface together. But afterward she had walked back to the house with one arm linked through Joshua's and one through Aidan's, chattering merrily all the way, as if he did not even exist.

He no longer wondered if he was in love with her.

He knew.

He was.

They set out after waving everyone else off on their expedition. The park suddenly seemed very quiet and peaceful. Gervase carried the easel, some canvases, and a sketch pad, Morgan her paints and brushes and charcoal. She looked very fetching indeed in a wide-brimmed straw hat he had not seen before and a loose painting smock—also a part of his gift—worn over her sprigged muslin dress.

The wilderness walk had been wrongly named as it

was in fact always carefully cultivated and tended. It wound among the trees and rolling hills to the east of the house, sometimes dim and secluded and fragrant with the smells of greenery and rhododendrons, sometimes coming out unexpectedly into the open to afford a pleasing prospect over the park and surrounding countryside. There were follies and rustic benches for the convenience of the casual stroller, but he continued on past them all. The walk ended at one such folly, a small temple with a stone seat inside. But hidden from view and reached by a short scramble among the trees and up over the hill was the grotto, always his favorite part of the park, his private haven as a boy.

The stone grotto had been built into the wooded bank and made a splendid cave for youthful pirates or highwaymen or spies. But its surroundings were what made the area special. The river flowed a few yards from the bank. A weeping willow hung over the water beside the grotto and a stone cherub balanced a stone jug on its head with one chubby stone arm and held it tilted so that its contents arced endlessly out into the river. Large mossy stones and lavish clumps of low-growing wildflowers surrounded cherub and tree. The bank before the grotto was level and grassy.

He had not been here since his return. He was glad to see that it was still carefully tended here.

"Oh, how lovely!" Morgan exclaimed.

He smiled at her as he put down his burdens and set up her easel. He had known she would appreciate it.

She closed her eyes and inhaled deeply.

"Ah, but there is more here besides just visual

beauty," she said, opening her eyes. "Listen to the sound of the water, Gervase. But it is not just the sound either. It is sight and sound and smell and—ah, something that strikes one *here*." She touched one hand to her heart. "Do you feel it?"

"It is the place I always liked to come to when my spirits needed restoring," he told her.

"Yes." She turned her head to smile at him beneath the broad-brimmed straw hat. "To restore your spirits. There are some places particularly suited to that, are there not? Places where one feels closer to . . . to *what?* To peace? To ultimate meaning? To God?"

"This is the first time I have been back here," he told her. "But, *chérie,* you needed to be alone. You needed to paint. You must do so. I am going to sit here with my back against the grotto wall and consider the state of my soul. I may even put myself to sleep doing it, though I will try not to snore. You must ignore me."

"Very well," she said. "I had a governess whom I loved dearly—I still miss her—but whenever I painted she would insist upon constantly looking over my shoulder and instructing me on how I ought to be doing it. She drove me close to insanity. Poor Miss Cowper."

He settled himself on the grass, his back against the wall, and drew his hat lower over his brow. In addition, he looked away from her, toward the stone cherub, so that she would not feel self-conscious. She was not a mere dabbler, she had told him, and he believed her. He was beginning to realize that there were enormous depths to the character of his betrothed, young as she was.

She did not immediately paint, he noticed. She set out everything in readiness and then she sat on the grass close to the river and clasped her arms about her knees. As soon as he realized she had become unaware of his presence he watched her. Anyone coming upon them at that moment might have supposed she was idle, seduced away from her intended painting by the heat of the day. He knew differently. He knew that she was not merely looking for a pretty subject for her painting but was waiting for her surroundings to speak to her artistic soul.

*Morgan is different from the rest of us mortals, who need company and activity every moment of every day.*

It was what Aidan had said about her at breakfast.

*. . . the rest of us mortals, who need company and activity every moment of every day.*

That described him exactly, Gervase thought, or the person he had made himself into during the past nine years anyway. Once he had understood the enormity of his predicament, he had been afraid to stay in one place too long, afraid to be alone, afraid to stay away from places where there were crowds, afraid not to flirt with every pretty woman he saw and to sleep with as many of them as could be persuaded to fill his nights with as much activity as he filled his days.

What exactly had he been afraid of? Himself? The silence?

It was silent now. Oh, it was not without sound, as she had just pointed out. If he concentrated, he could hear that the silence was loud with the sounds of nature. But it was a silence in which his soul could rest.

His soul had not rested for years and years.

He had busily buried it deep, deep so that he would not recognize the emptiness of his existence.

She got to her feet then and arranged a canvas on the easel, whose direction she adjusted. She prepared her brushes and paints and palette and proceeded to paint with as much absorption as she had displayed while sitting. He guessed that she truly had forgotten his presence and was very careful not to move in any way that would distract her.

A picturesque setting with a picturesque female artist and a swooning, lovelorn swain.

Ah, yes, indeed.

Would she punish him to the bitter end? She was strong-minded enough to do it.

How the devil could he talk her out of it?

## CHAPTER XIX

SHE WAS INSIDE THE WATER OF THE RIVER. SHE KNEW that water was a thing in itself with properties of its own that made it different from anything else. But it was not independent of everything else. It needed the sun and the sky to renew itself. It gave itself to the grass and the willow tree that leaned over it. It was colorless in and of itself. Yet it picked up color from its surroundings—gray and brown from the stony, gravelly bed, blue from the sky, green from the willow tree, sparkle from the sunlight. And later today, tonight, tomorrow, next week, next winter, it would look quite different.

There was no river, no grass, no willow tree—nothing at least in any permanent form to be understood by the mind or captured with paint on canvas. That was the marvelous challenge of painting—to catch a joy as it flies, as the poet William Blake had phrased it. She wondered if Gervase had read his poetry. She must ask him.

It was the challenge of life too, was it not? People could never be fully understood. They were ever changing, different people at different times and under different circumstances and influences. And always growing, always creating themselves anew.

How impossible it was to know another human being.

How impossible to know even oneself.

Finally her painting was done, and Morgan stood back and looked at it, almost as if she were seeing it for the first time. Miss Cowper would be horrified, she thought. This was no smooth, picturesque rendition of the river and the willow tree.

She remembered suddenly that Gervase was with her and turned her head to see that he was still sitting with his back to the stone wall outside the grotto, his hat tipped forward over his eyes, one leg stretched out before him on the grass, the other bent at the knee, his booted foot braced against the ground. He looked relaxed and contented. He was looking at her through squinted eyes.

"How long have we been here?" she asked him.

"One hour? Two?" He shrugged. "It does not matter, *chérie*. Did I snore very loudly?"

"I thought it was a hoarse cricket." She smiled at him. "I do not believe you have been sleeping at all."

"I have been enjoying my role as lovelorn swain," he told her, "though no one has been paying me any attention. May I see the painting?"

"I am not sure it is fit for human eyes," she said, looking dubiously at it again. "But yes, if you wish."

He got to his feet and crossed the distance between them. He set an arm casually about her shoulders as he turned to look at her canvas. He said nothing for a long while.

"If it were Miss Cowper looking," she said, "she would be asking why I had not included the cherub and the flowers since they would add color and decorative interest to the canvas. She would tell me that a painting with only water and a willow tree is far too uninteresting."

"Miss Cowper must have been an idiot," he said.

She bit her lip, half delighted, half guilty for allowing ridicule to be poured upon her former governess.

"Why do I have the feeling," he asked her, "that I am under the water and inside the very roots of the tree?"

Oh! No one—not even Aidan—had ever understood. Her siblings were all tolerant of her need to paint and proud of her strange, eccentric style, but none of them understood. Miss Cowper had despaired of ever teaching her correct technique and correct observational skills.

"It is the brushstrokes," she said. "I have not smoothed them out."

"And everything blends into everything else," he

said, "if *blends* is the right word. There is sunlight in the water and willow branches in the sky and water in the tree roots. Everything is connected."

"And I am there too, painting it from the inside," she said, "and you, observing it. All, all connected."

She felt a little foolish then, for she had spoken with the breathless enthusiasm of a girl. But he continued to stand and gaze at the painting, his eyes slightly squinted, his hand still draped about her shoulders.

*"Chérie,"* he asked her, "may I keep this painting?"

"You really want it?" she asked him.

"I will hang it in my bedchamber," he told her, "so that I may see it every day. After you have broken my heart and left me, I will remember that we are always and ever connected."

She turned away from him then and busied herself with cleaning her brushes and palette and removing her smock, now slightly smeared with paint. She moved a short distance away and sat down on the level grass, drawing up her knees so that she could wrap her arms about them. The sun was bright and warm on her arms. She could smell flowers and water and greenery. She could hear birds singing and insects whirring. A white-winged butterfly fluttered past on its way to raid the flowers.

Gervase came to join her. He sprawled out on one side, tossed his hat to the grass behind him, and propped himself on one elbow. He plucked a blade of grass and tickled the side of her face with it. She batted it away with one hand and turned her head to laugh at him.

"You are going to have permanent wrinkles at the corners of your eyes soon," she told him, "if you keep on smiling with them all the time the way you do."

"Better that than a permanent frown line between my brows, *chérie,*" he said.

It was usually a mocking smile, she thought. But perhaps he was right. Bitter and unhappy as he had been—and still was in some ways—he had somehow learned to laugh at the world and himself rather than frowning in embittered hatred.

She had been staring at him, she realized when he dropped the blade of grass and lifted his hand to cup her cheek. He ran his thumb across her lips.

She ought to have got to her feet then and there and picked up her things to return to the house. But she did not want to leave. Not yet. Besides, she had promised to torment him, had she not?

His hand slipped behind her neck and drew her head toward his. Their lips met in a warm, sun-bright kiss.

"Mmm," he said, rubbing his nose across hers.

"Mmm," she sighed simultaneously.

Their lips met again, parted this time, teasing, searching lightly. He licked her lips with his tongue. She did the same to him. His tongue slid into her mouth and curled up to stroke the sensitive roof. She felt raw desire tighten her breasts and stab downward to her womb.

He came up off his elbow then, tossed her straw hat away, and gathered her into his arms. She was aware of summertime and sunshine and nature—and of the man she wanted more than anything else in life, it seemed.

Foolish, foolish woman.

She was lying flat on the grass then, not quite sure how she had got there, reaching up her arms to draw him down with her. And passion flared. He kissed every part of her face, including her eyes, her ears, her earlobes. He kissed her throat and her bosom above the low square neckline of her dress. And while her fingers tangled in his hair and she lifted herself to rub against him, he lowered the neckline so that her breasts were exposed. He caressed them with his hands, rubbed his thumbs lightly over her nipples until she was all raw need, and then suckled her until she moaned with mingled pleasure and pain.

*"Mon amour,"* he murmured, returning his mouth to hers. *"Je t'adore. Je t'aime."*

"Gervase," she whispered back to him. "Gervase."

When he raised himself to slide both hands up beneath the skirt of her dress, it did not occur to her to stop him. This had happened before between them, but so urgently and so hastily that she had longed ever since to have it happen again so that she could savor the process. With him. With Gervase. She would not think of all that had happened since then to make it undesirable. She would not think.

His hands stripped her of undergarments and stockings and shoes and himself of coat and waistcoat and shirt. And then he lifted her skirt, and one hand caressed its way up her inner thighs while he propped himself on the other elbow again and looked down at her with half-closed eyes. He was beautiful—broad-shouldered, his well-muscled chest lightly dusted with hair. She could smell his soap, his body heat, his masculinity.

He kissed her again softly, almost lazily, as his hand found the core of her and teased its way through folds to stroke her, to enter her with one finger and then two. She could feel her own wetness. She could hear it, and understood that the wetness was her body's response to him, her invitation to him. She slid one bare foot up along the soft, warm grass, bending her knee and dropping it outward as she did so. His fingers pressed deeper, and she heard herself moan as her inner muscles clenched about them.

*"Chérie,"* he murmured. *"Mon amour."* And he withdrew his hand to undo the buttons at the waist of his pantaloons and came over her to lie on top of her, his legs coming between hers.

She braced her feet against the supple leather of his boot tops and lifted her hips when his hands slid beneath her. She felt him, hard at her entrance, and tilted herself as he came into her with one firm stroke.

There was no pain, she discovered, only a lovely stretching and sense of being deeply occupied. She would have held on to that moment forever if she could, she thought, suddenly very aware again of sunshine and birdsong and the sound of water splashing into the river from the fountain. But need, an ache of longing, a demand for some completion, drove them beyond the moment.

He withdrew to the brink of her and then entered again—and repeated the motion over and over again until she could hear the smooth, liquid rhythm of their coupling. It was very different from last time. It lacked the frenzy and the sense of urgency. This was slow and thorough and engaged all the senses. And she was very aware of it as a shared experience. She was not just a woman engaged in a carnal act with a man. He was not just a man taking his pleasure from a willing woman's body.

She was very aware that he was Gervase, that she had loved him almost from the first moment. He was aware—he was surely aware—that she was Morgan. He lifted his head while he worked in her and while she answered his rhythm with her own and watched her for a while, his eyes heavy-lidded with passion. He murmured to her in French.

They were a man and a woman making love.

But physical love was not something that could be observed for very long from inside the mind. It was an experience of sensation, of shared need and pain and excitement and pleasure. Morgan discovered that when, after a few minutes, the raw ache she had felt earlier spread to every part of her until it seemed that she could bear it no longer. She broke her own rhythm and strained up against him, reaching for something she could not even identify.

But instead of stopping as well, his hands came beneath her again, and he held her firmly while he thrust harder and deeper into her. And then, just as she cried out, convinced that she really could not bear it one moment longer, the ache, the need, burst into something quite different, something so unexpected that she could only cling to him and fall into a new place, one she had never entered before.

He moved in her again, once, twice, three times, and then he held deep in her and sighed, and she felt heat at her core.

He came down heavily on top of her after that, relaxed and panting and smelling enticingly of soap and sweat.

"Ah, *mon amour,*" he murmured once more against her ear.

She must have fallen asleep, she realized some time later. He had moved to her side, one of his arms beneath her head. Her skirt was covering her legs again, and his shirt was draped loosely over both of them to shield them from the burning rays of the sun. Her straw hat was shading her face.

She turned her head to look at him. He was gazing back.

"That was not well done of me, *chérie,*" he said.

"Of *you?*" She raised her eyebrows. "I thought it was mutual."

"Ah, and so it was, then." He moved his head forward and kissed the tip of her nose. "We will set a wedding date. Perhaps for the early autumn? I am not sure I can wait much longer than that."

She smiled slowly at him.

*"Mon amour. Je t'adore, Je t'aime,"* she said softly, quoting him. "*I am not sure I can wait much longer than that.* You disappoint me, Gervase. Have I so easily succeeded?"

She sat up, tied the wide ribbons of her hat beneath her chin, and pulled on her discarded undergarments and stockings and shoes. She was relieved to see that her hands were not shaking.

When she got to her feet, she could see that he was lying on his back, his shirt still over his torso, though his arms were bare, his hands clasped beneath his head. He was smiling lazily at her.

"Behold me abject and defeated, utterly annihilated," he said. "But admit one thing, *chérie*. You enjoyed every moment."

She raised her eyebrows haughtily. "But of course I enjoyed it," she told him. "Did you not enjoy every moment with every one of the women you knew on the Continent?"

He chuckled.

*"Mon amour,"* he said, *"je t'adore."*

She picked up all her painting supplies except the easel and newly painted canvas and with her chin elevated scrambled up the bank and down the other side onto the path of the wilderness walk.

She had won that battle, she thought, by the skin of her teeth. But the war was not over yet. She had come here to Windrush intending to tease and torment him before showing her disdain for him by ending their betrothal and thus embarrassing him before all his family and friends and neighbors. But she certainly had not intended *that* to happen.

Her legs felt slightly unsteady. Her breasts felt tender and she was sore inside—rather pleasantly so, perhaps, though she would rather not have had the feeling at all.

But she certainly could not accuse him of seducing or ravishing her, could she?

She was rather surprised—and perhaps a little disappointed—when he did not come along behind her. When she looked back to the trees across open lawns after reaching the house, he was nowhere in sight.

He was probably sleeping outside the grotto.

Enjoying the slumber of the smugly just.

It was a good thing he was not within reach. She would have been tempted to slap his head right off his shoulders.

GERVASE HAD LEFT ALL THE planning for the fete and ball to his mother and sisters and cousin. All his laborers, all the villagers, and all the lower classes for miles around had been invited to the fete, which was to take place in the park of Windrush and was to include cricket and races and other competitions and lavish amounts of food and drink. The ball that was to take place the same evening was for neighbors and tenants of a higher class. Everyone had accepted the invitation, his mother assured them all at breakfast the morning after the visit to the grotto. There would be quite enough people to fill the ballroom though it would not, of course, rival a London squeeze.

Gervase made the mistake of asking to see the guest list, and his mother sent a servant to fetch it from her private sitting room right then. He sat at the head of the table running his eye down the list while Cecile came and looked at it over his shoulder.

"I was out with the children when *Maman* and Monique and Lady Aidan wrote the invitations," she explained.

Gervase was less concerned with who was on the list

than with who was *not* on it. He had not mentioned to his mother that she was not to be invited under any circumstances, but of course it had been unnecessary to do so. The name was not there, he saw with considerable relief.

"Well," Cecile said, altogether too loudly, "I see you have not invited Marianne Bonner, *Maman*. And a good thing too. It is a wonder to me that she has the gall to make her home so close to Windrush."

Gervase set the list facedown on the table while his own family members looked uncomfortable and the Bedwyns looked politely mystified.

"I thought she should be invited, Gervase," Henrietta said. "It is time the past was forgotten about. Besides, no one in this part of the world knows what happened. But they will surely notice and start guessing when it is seen that Marianne is the only one of our neighbors for miles around who has not come."

"You surely cannot be serious, Henrietta," Monique said.

"Well, I am," their cousin said, her voice shaking slightly.

"I think this conversation will terminate right here," Gervase said firmly, "after I have explained to Morgan's relatives that the lady in question offended me years ago before I left England and has not been forgiven."

"I always consider other people's family skeletons a dead bore," Freyja said. "When are we to begin the ride you promised us today, Gervase? Josh says I must on no account jump any hedges, so I suppose you are going to have to choose a route that provides a few challenging fences instead."

"I believe, sweetheart," Joshua said as Gervase shot her a grateful glance, "I said hedges *and* fences, but you must be fair. My exact words—you will correct me if I am wrong—were that I supposed if I forbade you to jump any hedges *or* fences you would deliberately seek out both."

"I'll be a little more plainspoken, Free," Aidan said. "If you so much as cast a longing glance at a hedge or fence—*or* gate—between now and sundown I will personally wring your neck."

Virtually everyone at the table laughed—Freyja included—and the uncomfortable moment passed.

But it was not over.

"I suppose," Morgan said to him later, when they were riding across country side by side, "you plan to live here for the rest of your life not five miles from Marianne without once seeing her."

"I do," he said quite decisively. "It may not be something a Bedwyn would do, *chérie,* but it is very definitely something an Ashford intends doing."

"But Henrietta is right," she said. "Word will soon spread that there is a quarrel between the two of you, and the whole thing will never die."

"If she does not like the gossip," he said, "then she may move away from here."

Harold Spalding, his brother-in-law, rode up on her other side then and engaged her in conversation, and Gervase moved between Becky and Davy, the two children, both of whom had joined the ride. He set himself to amusing them for a while before moving up beside Freyja and making himself agreeable to her.

"I always did despise the notion of crawling over the countryside on a horse's back," she told him with a sigh, "and I have never yet been tossed from the saddle. But life becomes tedious when one is in expectation of a happy event, Gervase. And is that not a ridiculous euphemism? Life becomes tedious when one is *expecting a baby*. Tedious and infinitely exciting," she added with a laugh.

He was reminded of what had kept him awake half the night—that he might well have impregnated Morgan yesterday afternoon. Not that he would particularly mind having to rush into marriage with her and having a child in the nursery in nine months' time. But *she* might mind. It was impossible to know for sure. She certainly had him guessing.

He was not even sure that a pregnancy *would* force her to marry him. It might simply make her stubborn. The very idea was enough to cause him to break out in a cold sweat.

He found himself beside her again before they rode back into the park, a good three hours after they had left it. And she had not forgotten.

"Gervase," she said, "do you not think you ought to call upon Marianne? Confront her? Ask her why she did what she did?"

"No!" He looked very directly across at her. "You had your way with the churchyard. You will not have your way this time."

"But you are glad you went there," she said. "You

made your peace with your father. You do not have to hate him any longer."

"There is no peace to be made with Marianne, *chérie,*" he told her. "And that is my final word."

She opened her mouth to say more but thought better of it. She merely nodded instead. But she was silent for only a minute or so.

"It is not *my* final word, though," she said. "My brother suffered from that incident too."

He did not comment.

IT WAS NOT IN MORGAN'S nature to let sleeping dogs lie, especially when people she loved were involved—or a *person* she loved. She loved Wulfric.

And something had been niggling at the edges of her mind for a while. It had become persistent since that scene at breakfast.

One table of cards was set up in the drawing room during the evening. Conversation among everyone else was lively. Henrietta sat at the pianoforte half a room away from everyone else, playing quietly. Morgan joined her there and stood behind the bench looking at the music until she had finished playing that particular piece.

"Henrietta," she said then, keeping her voice low, "you were *there* the night my brother's betrothal to Lady Marianne Bonner was to be announced, were you not?"

Henrietta looked back over her shoulder, instantly wary.

"Yes, of course," she said. "We were neighbors—that

is, the Marquess of Paysley used to spend a part of each year at Winchholme. It was natural enough that he invite all of us to the ball—Uncle George and Gervase and me, that was. Monique and Cecile were still in the schoolroom, and Aunt Lisette had been called back to Windrush because Cecile was indisposed. Aunt Bertha, Uncle's sister, was my chaperon."

"It must have been dreadful for you," Morgan said, perching on the end of the bench. "What happened at that ball, I mean."

"Yes." Henrietta closed the music and clasped her hands loosely in her lap. "It was. Dreadful."

"How did they know where Marianne and Gervase had gone?" Morgan asked, leaning forward slightly to look into the other woman's face. "If it was a large squeeze of a ball, how did they even know the two of them were together? And what made them think that they were in her bedchamber? Why did they go charging in there—apparently without even knocking on the door first? Why all three of them—Wulfric, Gervase's father, and Marianne's?"

Henrietta stared blankly back at her. "I do not know," she said.

"But did you never wonder?" Morgan asked her. "Did you never ask your uncle?"

"No," Henrietta said. "I never did."

"Do you wonder *now?*" Morgan gazed intently at her. Surely she must.

"I suppose I do," Henrietta said, running one hand along the keys though she did not depress any of them. "Someone had seen them go upstairs together, I suppose. Some servant."

"Henrietta." Morgan moved to the edge of the bench. "Do you believe that Gervase did what they said he did? Do you believe he betrayed my brother and then stole a priceless heirloom from Marianne?"

Henrietta's eyes were clouded with something that looked very like grief when she looked up. "No, of course not," she said. *"Of course not."*

"You believe, then," Morgan said, "that it was Marianne who was the betrayer? That she drugged Gervase and got him into her bed and had someone send up Wulfric and the two fathers—all because she did not have the courage to tell Wulfric in person that she would not marry him?"

"*Courage* had nothing to do with it," Henrietta said, "or cowardice either. You did not know the Marquess of Paysley, Morgan. You did not know what a tyrant he was. And you did not know the Duke of Bewcastle and what a tyrant—" She clapped a hand to her mouth when she realized what she had said and flushed scarlet. "I do beg your pardon."

"I *do* know Wulfric and his tyrannical ways," Morgan said. "But he has a sense of fairness for all that, Henrietta. I know he would never force any lady into marrying him against her will. Why should he? He would have to live with her all the rest of his life. You have spoken of these things with Marianne, then, have you? Gervase says she is still your friend."

"We have not spoken much on the topic," Henrietta said. "It is too painful to us both."

"And yet," Morgan said, "knowing what she did and

what the terrible consequences were to your cousin—and perhaps guessing the humiliation my brother must have suffered—you continued your friendship with her?"

"A true friendship runs deep," Henrietta said.

"I do not believe," Morgan said, unable to keep all the scorn she felt entirely from her voice, "I would feel very kindly disposed to a friend who had ruined the character of a relative of mine and doomed him to nine years of exile. I believe she would quickly become my *former* friend."

"You do not understand," Henrietta said.

"No," Morgan agreed, "I do not. But I am sorry, Henrietta. I did not mean to quarrel with you. I just feel a need to understand the past, to know why it was Gervase who was chosen for such suffering. And why my brother had to suffer so much humiliation."

"I do not know," Henrietta said again, and Morgan was surprised to see tears in her eyes.

"I want to see the lady," she said. "I want to talk with her. Will you go there with me, perhaps tomorrow, and introduce me?"

"Is it wise?" Henrietta asked.

"I have no idea," Morgan said. "But I will go there alone if you will not accompany me. Will you?"

Henrietta drew a deep breath and released it on a sigh.

"If I must," she said. "Very well, then. You are going to be living here anyway after you marry Gervase. It is fitting that you call on her sometime. I just hope there will not be any . . . unpleasantness."

"Gracious," Morgan said. "So do I."

She smiled up at Monique and Eve, who were approaching the pianoforte together.

## Chapter XX

THE FOLLOWING DAY WAS DRIZZLY IN THE MORNING, though it opened out to a dry, cloudy, cool afternoon. Freyja and Joshua, Cecile and Lord Vardon took out the boats, and Eve and Aidan, Monique and Sir Harold took the children on a long walk. The countess spent the afternoon, as she had spent the morning, making final plans for the fete and the ball with her cook and housekeeper and butler. Gervase, who had gone out after breakfast with his steward, had not yet returned.

Morgan set off with Henrietta in the carriage for Winchholme, less than five miles away. The roads were wet but not impassable. The sun was even trying to break through the clouds as they approached the picturesque old manor, its gardens laden with roses, whose sweet, heavy perfumes Morgan could smell even before the carriage rolled to a halt. She and Henrietta had scarcely spoken to each other, each wrapped in thought.

Lady Marianne Bonner met them herself at the door. While she greeted Henrietta by clasping her hands and kissing her on the cheek, Morgan gazed curiously at her. Even though she had passed the first bloom of youth, she was a remarkable beauty, from her shining golden curls all the way down a shapely, perfectly proportioned body to her small slippered feet. When she turned her eyes on her guest, Morgan could see that they were very blue.

*This,* Morgan thought, was the woman Wulfric had almost married. This was the woman he had loved. He *must* have loved her. Like all the Bedwyns, he believed strongly in love within marriage. He could have had no other reason to marry her—he had not needed her father's influence or her fortune, and he had had three brothers to make the begetting of sons less urgent than it might otherwise have been. This was the woman who might have been her sister-in-law.

Both curtsied as Henrietta made the introductions, and Marianne flushed, looking even more lovely as she did so.

"I am delighted to make your acquaintance, Lady Morgan," she said.

"And I yours, Lady Marianne," Morgan replied.

They were taken into a cozy sitting room on the ground floor that looked out on some of the best of the roses. The French windows were closed against the chill, but Morgan could imagine how fragrant this room must be on a warm summer's day when the doors could be thrown back.

Mrs. Jasper, Lady Marianne's aunt, was in the room, but she excused herself to rest after being presented to Morgan. She was a very elderly lady whose presence at Winchholme offered at least the appearance of chaperonage to a single lady living alone. It was an arrangement that probably suited both.

The tea tray was brought in and they all conversed

politely on a variety of topics for a while. But as Morgan prepared to introduce the topic that she had come to discuss, Marianne broached it herself. It was suddenly clear to Morgan that she had known about this visit in advance. Henrietta must have sent a note over during the morning.

"I understand," she said, setting down her plate, "that you have been asking Henrietta about what was to have been my betrothal ball, Lady Morgan."

Morgan set down her own cup and saucer and clasped her hands in her lap. Marianne and Henrietta were sitting side by side on the settee. Both were looking at her rather warily, and Marianne's cheeks were considerably flushed.

"I asked," Morgan said, "if Henrietta knew how my brother and her uncle and your father learned that you and Gervase were together in your bedchamber. They would have had no way of suspecting such a shocking thing in the ordinary course of events at a ball. Who told them? Who sent them up there?"

"I have never thought to wonder about it," Marianne told her.

But Morgan was gazing steadily at her. "I am afraid I do not believe you," she said bluntly. "You must have wanted to be caught. You had drugged Gervase and taken him into your bedchamber from your sitting room. You wished it to seem that you had lain with him so that you would not be forced to marry Wulfric—my brother. But how could you be caught if no one knew you were together or where you were to be found? Your plan could succeed only if you had an accomplice."

Marianne stared right back at her, flushed and defiant—and guilty. "You are calling me a liar, Lady Morgan?" she asked.

Henrietta set a hand on her arm and made a sound of distress.

"Wulfric must have loved you," Morgan told her. "I know him. No other motive would have led him toward marriage. He must have been deeply hurt as well as dreadfully humiliated by what he saw in that room—or what he *thought* he saw. Gervase was hurt in a far more terrible way. He is still only very gradually recovering. He is still wounded and in some ways permanently scarred. There is no way you can make restitution for what you did. But at least you can tell the truth."

Marianne opened her mouth to speak, but Henrietta spoke first, looking sharply away from them both as she did so.

"I was the one," she said. "*I* told them—all three of them. I told them Gervase had dragged Marianne upstairs against her will."

She had suspected it since last evening, Morgan realized. She had hoped she was wrong, since betrayal from within his own family would be far worse to Gervase than betrayal by a neighbor and former friend. But *why?*

Marianne passed one hand over her face and turned suddenly pale.

"We planned it together," Henrietta explained. "Marianne's father had bullied and threatened her into accepting first the Duke of Bewcastle's courtship and then his marriage offer. If the betrothal announcement had been publicly made, all would have been lost. She would not have been able to avoid the marriage. She turned to me in her misery and desperation, and together we concocted the plan."

"To frame Gervase for that terrible disgrace?" Morgan asked, aghast. "To make it seem that he had ravished Lady Marianne? Your own *cousin,* Henrietta?"

"I never really belonged," Henrietta said, getting to her feet and taking a few steps away from the settee while fumbling for a handkerchief in the pocket of her dress. "There were Monique and Cecile growing up behind me, all vivacity and frivolous beauty, everyone's favorites. And there was Gervase, always teasing me and always trying to find me partners and beaux during that dreadful Season. I wanted—all I ever wanted was to go *home*. Not to Windrush, but home to my mother and father. But they were dead."

"Ah, Henrietta," Marianne said, clearly distressed for her.

"I am sorry," Henrietta said after blowing her nose and coming back to sit on the settee again. "I recovered from all of that years ago and recognized how unfair I had always been to the family that had nurtured and loved me. I truly love them all now. But we tend to be selfish, self-centered creatures indeed when we are very young. At least I was."

"You must understand," Marianne said, addressing herself to Morgan, "that my only thought was to be rid of the Duke of Bewcastle in such a way that my father could not blame me. The fact that Gervase was my neighbor and friend was a point in favor of the plan. I imagined that I could explain all to him the next day and he would understand and perhaps even explain privately to the duke—they were friends, you see."

"You could not explain to Wulfric *yourself?*" Morgan asked her.

"I—" Marianne closed her eyes and shook her head. "No, I could not. You must understand, Lady Morgan, that I was only eighteen. I am not proud of what I did. In fact, it has haunted me ever since. But I was so very young."

"I am eighteen now," Morgan said softly.

Both women stared at her mutely.

"And the brooch?" Morgan asked. "Was it really stolen?"

Marianne shook her head. "Papa would have made me marry *Gervase,*" she said. "I could not have said no—I had told Papa that he ravished me. And *he* could not say no—offering for me was something that was required of him as a gentleman. I had to think quickly, and I did what was truly reprehensible as well as stupid. I wanted to explain to Gervase afterward, but he was gone. I never, *never* expected the events of that night to have such dire consequences. I almost lost even Henrietta's friendship. She was so very angry with me about the brooch."

"But you did not think of explaining to Gervase's father?" Morgan said. "He never saw his son again. He died believing him to be a ravisher and a thief."

"He had always been so proud and fond of Gervase," Henrietta said. "How could I have known that he would actually punish Gervase—and in such a way? It was horrible. It was like a nightmare from which I could not awaken."

"But you would not do the honorable thing and confess your part in what had happened?" Morgan stared at her. Such cowardice was so far beyond her own nature that it was hard to understand it, far less condone it in someone else.

"Morgan," Henrietta said, "there is nothing, *nothing* you can say that I have not said to myself a thousand times, that Marianne has not said to *herself*. It is not easy to live with the guilt of realizing that what one did, knowing even then that it was wrong, had such catastrophic results for several innocent people. I have given thanks daily for Gervase's homecoming and for the happiness he has found with you. But it does not quite compensate or atone."

"No, it does not," Morgan agreed, understanding suddenly why Henrietta had always been so pleased for them. She looked from one to the other of the coconspirators, trying to imagine what could possibly have driven two young girls to such desperate measures. Just youth and naïveté and defiance of authority—and then fear of the consequences if they confessed? But how had Henrietta been drawn into it? Had it been just spite on her part against a cousin who had pressed dancing partners and even beaux on her when she could not attract them herself?

It was as that final question was passing through her mind that the answer came to her like a blinding light. She was only recently out of the schoolroom. She had lived a sheltered life there, taught only those things considered essential for a lady's education and whatever she could glean from boisterous brothers and a bold sister, all of whom had been careful of what they said in her hearing. But she understood nevertheless.

*Of course!*

Marianne and Henrietta were more than friends. They *loved* each other. Marriage, for either one of them, would have been the ultimate disaster, the horror of horrors to be avoided at all or any cost.

And so they *had* avoided it—at a terrible cost to other people.

She looked from one to the other again and, though not a word was spoken, she could see that they *knew* she knew. Briefly, almost imperceptibly, their hands touched on the settee cushion between them.

She understood. She did not condone. She did not forgive, but she understood. She could not hate them, she discovered. She had put herself mentally into their shoes and imagined taking the walk through life that was their destiny, and she could not hate them or condemn them. She could only despise what they had done.

"If I could go back," Marianne said with a sigh, "I would defy my father and speak plainly with the Duke of Bewcastle. Or so I say now when I am safe from both of them. But going back would mean returning to the body and mind and emotions of a timid, frightened girl who was different but could not explain those differences to anyone in the world except the one who shared her fright. Perhaps even knowing what I know now I would not have found the courage."

"And if I could go back," Henrietta said, "I would speak to Uncle George, explain to him, even though doing so would have meant being torn away from all communication with Marianne. I would not allow that to happen to Gervase if I could go back and do things differently. But I cannot go back—and perhaps I would not find the courage even if I could."

"Find it now," Morgan said.

"My uncle is dead," Henrietta said, "and so is Marianne's father."

"But Gervase is not," Morgan said. "And Wulfric is not."

Marianne blanched. "You expect me to confess to the *Duke of Bewcastle?*" she said.

"I expect nothing," Morgan told her. "Wulfric is a strong man. Whatever he suffered then, he will have recovered from by now. And Gervase's long ordeal is over. He was strong enough to survive it with all his best character traits intact, and he is building his life anew. They will both live out their lives in the manner they see fit regardless of what you do. I expect nothing of you."

She got to her feet.

"I wish to leave now, Henrietta," she said.

Henrietta hesitated. "Take the carriage," she said. "Will you mind going alone? Marianne will send me home in her carriage later. We need to talk."

It was a relief to Morgan to be alone on the journey home. The truth was far more horrible than she had ever imagined. How dreadful it must be to love and yet know that the world would never either condone or accept that love. To have to keep it secret throughout a lifetime.

Yet love it must be. They had been constant to each other for years, had committed terrible deeds for each other, had betrayed a cousin and friend for each other, had wreaked immeasurable hurt on other people, and had shared the guilt ever since.

How could she know what she might be capable of doing under similar circumstances?

If Wulfric had persisted in refusing to allow Gervase to pay his addresses to her, she might have openly defied him, perhaps even have eloped. Or she might at worst have waited three years until she reached the age of majority and did not have to consult Wulf at all.

Marianne and Henrietta had had none of those options.

But Morgan's mind was suddenly diverted.

*Eloped? Waited three years?*

She was not going to marry Gervase at all—by her own choice.

She must end the masquerade soon. Perhaps she would do it at the ball. That would be spectacular—and also unnaturally cruel. Afterward, then. Soon afterward. She would tell him quietly that she was ending it and leave Windrush with Freyja or Aidan. It would be enough. She would leave enough embarrassment behind her—and take enough bleakness away with her.

Did he have any feelings for her at all? Sometimes she thought he did, and of course he *told* her that he loved her. Certainly she believed that he had a physical passion for her. The words he had murmured to her while making love to her outside the grotto had surely not been feigned. But it was not enough anyway. He had become too dear to her in Brussels, and all the time he had been cynically and callously using her. There could be no forgiveness for that—or if there could, then there could be no lasting trust after it.

Morgan closed her eyes as the carriage bounced over the ruts of a road that was still rather muddy. How strange life was, she thought. If Marianne and Henrietta had not behaved desperately and dishonorably on a night long ago when she herself was only nine years old, Gervase would not have crossed the ballroom at the Camerons' ball in Brussels and effected an introduction to her. He would not even have noticed her. She would not have noticed him. He would not have been tempted to make his own descent into dishonor. She would never have loved him.

All connected. Ah, yes, all, all connected.

THE SUNSHINE WAS BACK the following day. They all spent it exploring the wilderness walk in the morning, boating and swimming and even diving later. But the heat and exercise tired most of the children by midafternoon and all of them were sent to the nursery for a sleep or some quiet time. The adults variously dispersed through the house or on a stroll outside. Morgan was sitting on the seat in the flower garden with Emma, who had walked over from the vicarage just a short time ago, while Jonathan toddled around near them.

Gervase watched from the library window, having just caught up with some correspondence that had been awaiting his attention on his desk for two days. It pleased him that his family and the bolder Bedwyns seemed to like one another. It particularly pleased him that Morgan had been so well accepted here and that she seemed genuinely delighted by her surroundings and the people in it.

After the ball he was going to convince her somehow to forgive him. He was going to propose marriage to her in earnest.

He was on the verge of going outside to join the ladies and to play with his nephew, but he noticed suddenly that a carriage was approaching up the driveway. He did not recognize it even when it drew closer. He ought to go outside to greet his visitor in person, perhaps. But something held him back.

Both Morgan and Emma raised a hand in greeting as the carriage drew level with them, but it continued on its way past them and turned onto the terrace below the window at which Gervase was standing. He watched as a lady descended, a maid behind her.

His mouth turned suddenly dry. Morgan had gone out in the carriage with Henrietta yesterday but had not told him where they had gone—he had not asked. But he had guessed.

*It is not my final word,* she had told him just the day before. *My brother suffered from that incident too.*

And now Marianne had come to Windrush. He hoped she had come to call on his mother—or Henrietta, tasteless as such a visit would be when he was in residence.

She climbed the horseshoe steps and disappeared inside the house below him. Morgan was looking up at the window. Briefly their eyes met before he turned away. Was this too a part of her revenge?

Had Marianne come to see *him?*

He would refuse to receive her. It was as simple as that.

And then his butler tapped on the door and opened it to ask him if he was at home to Lady Marianne Bonner.

He opened his mouth to say no. Had she come to beg his forgiveness? He had none to give. Some things were unforgivable.

*Like using and defaming and drawing into scandal a young, innocent girl merely because one had a grudge against her brother.*

*Forgive us our trespasses as we forgive those who trespass against us.*

He had never thought of himself as a particularly religious man. But those words popped into his head anyway.

"Show her in," he said curtly, and waited grimly before the window, his hands clasped at his back.

Marianne had been lovely as a girl—all blond, blue-eyed, slender femininity. She was an even lovelier woman. Her figure had developed alluring curves, and the years had added character to her face and made it somehow more beautiful. He wondered anew, as he had wondered years ago, why she had been so adamantly opposed to marrying Bewcastle, who had been—and still was—one of the greatest matrimonial prizes in all Britain. She had not explained that to him in her sitting room before he fell into a stupor from the drink she had given him.

She curtsied low, and he bowed stiffly.

"Lord Rosthorn," she said, "thank you for seeing me."

She was, he realized with some satisfaction when he heard the tremor in her voice, very nervous.

"I do not imagine, ma'am," he said, "that we have anything of great significance to say to each other."

He did not offer her a seat.

"You are quite right," she said. "I will offer no explanation for my behavior that night. I am sure you have long understood *why* I did it. And I can offer no excuse either. A reluctance to marry the Duke of Bewcastle or anyone else for that matter and a fear of my father were no excuses for what I did to you and then what I allowed to happen to you even though I had not foreseen it. An apology is cheap and perhaps even an insult considering how long I made you suffer. But, Gervase, it is all I have to offer. I wish there were more. I wish I could go back and change the past, but it is the one thing none of us can ever do. I stand condemned and offer no plea in my own defense. There *is* none."

"You *could* go away," he told her, "so that we will not have to inhabit the same neighborhood for the rest of our lives."

She visibly blanched. She even swayed slightly, and he almost hurried toward her to support her or bring her a chair. But she brought herself under control again.

"I could," she agreed. "Is that the punishment that would seem fair to you, Gervase? Perhaps you are right. Perhaps it *would* be fair—an eye for an eye, exile for exile. Very well, then, if it is your wish."

"Not quite an eye for an eye," he said. "I was forced to leave behind all that I held dear when I left here."

"Ah, Gervase," she said, "and so would I be. *Is* it what you wish me to do?"

There were tears in her eyes, but they did not spill over. And she did not lower her head or look away from him. He regarded her steadily, frowning.

*A reluctance to marry the Duke of Bewcastle or anyone else for that matter . . .*

*Ah, Gervase, and so would I be.*

It would seem to her like an equal punishment to be banished from Winchholme as he had been from Windrush? But she had no one here as he had.

*Except friends.*

Or perhaps one particular friend.

Who had been Marianne's accomplice at that ball? There must have *been* an accomplice if her plan was to succeed. He had always realized that but had assumed it was some servant or lackey.

*Henrietta?*

It would explain all, would it not?

But did he want to know for sure? Was he willing to ask the question?

"One thing I have discovered recently from my own experience, Marianne," he said, "is that forgiveness can never be deserved. If it could be, it would not be needed, would it? I too would change some events from the past if I could. But of course I cannot. And bad as the past nine years have been, they have not been totally wasted. I am a different man from the one who left England a few days after that infamous ball, and he is a man with whom I have grown comfortable. I met my future countess while still in exile. I may never have met her otherwise, and I would regret that more than anything else I can imagine."

He wished he had not said that out loud. Morgan was going to leave him. He still could not be confident that she would not. But it was true, nonetheless. If he could go back now and erase the past nine years, if he could start again from the day of that ball and cancel that incident with Marianne, he was not sure he would do it.

"Go free of guilt, then," he said.

She set both hands over her face. They were visibly shaking.

"I have written to the Duke of Bewcastle," she said. "That at least I could do for you. He will know that you were not in any way to blame in the events of that night, that what he thought he saw was all an illusion. It is more important than ever that he know the truth now that you are to marry his sister."

"Ah," he said.

"I will take my leave now," she said. "Thank you again for giving me your time, Gervase."

"Marianne," he said impulsively as she turned to go, "we are neighbors, whether we like it or not and probably will be for the rest of our lives. We might as well be civil about it, I suppose. Will you come to the ball here tomorrow evening?"

It was possible that he might regret this. But he did not believe he would. Civility was the grease that kept society's wheels turning.

"Thank you," she said, flushing. "I am not sure . . . Thank you."

And she was gone.

He stood where he was until he heard the carriage leaving. He gave it time to disappear down the driveway.

But when he turned back to the window, the flower garden was deserted. There was no sign of Morgan.

He needed her desperately.

## CHAPTER XXI

LADY MARIANNE BONNER'S ARRIVAL AT WINDRUSH in person had taken Morgan by surprise. At best she had hoped that the lady would write to Gervase. She felt apprehensive—she had not told him about her visit to Winchholme or what she had learned there. When she had looked up at the library window and had seen him standing there, watching Marianne's arrival, she had imagined that she saw intense pain in his eyes—a fanciful notion, perhaps, when she had been far too distant from him to see his eyes clearly at all.

As soon as Emma took her leave with Jonathan a few minutes later to return to the vicarage, Morgan walked away from the house. She headed for the lake, but she could hear the sound of voices and laughter coming from that direction and so veered off along the grassy avenue that would take her to the summer-house. She sat down inside, leaving the door open to catch some of the afternoon breeze.

It was going to hurt to leave here. She had known no other home but Lindsey Hall in Hampshire, and she had always been essentially happy there even if she *had* spent the past few years chafing at the bit, so to speak, longing to be grown up so that she could achieve some measure of independence. But last year she had been to Grandmaison Park in Leicestershire, home of her maternal grandmother, for Rannulf's wedding to Judith, and later the same year she had gone to Penhallow in Cornwall, Joshua's home, on the occasion of Freyja's betrothal. And it had seemed to her that she would like to have a home of her own, one that was not simply Wulfric's.

She loved Windrush. She loved the house and park, the surrounding countryside, the family here, the neighbors. And it could be hers for the rest of her life. She could be mistress of it all. She was betrothed to the Earl of Rosthorn. But it was not to be. Next year she would have to start considering the advances of some other suitors—and there would be an abundance of them, she knew, despite all the scandal in which she had been embroiled this year, a scandal that would be redoubled when she broke off her engagement. She was, after all, Lady Morgan Bedwyn, sister of the Duke of Bewcastle.

She watched Gervase approach the summerhouse along the avenue that connected with the house. Marianne must have left, then. He was hatless, and his hair was blowing in the breeze, making him look young and carefree and handsome. He walked with long, purposeful strides, having spotted her inside the summer-house. She remembered with what gladness she had hailed his arrival every day when she had been at Mrs. Clark's, with what utter ease she had walked with him and talked with him, as if he were a part of herself rather than a separate entity. On that last evening, when she had been distraught over what she had just heard from the embassy, she had found her way to him without conscious thought and cast herself into his arms for comfort.

It was hard to believe—even though he had *confessed* it to her—that at every moment he had been cynically using her for his own ends. They must have been seen alone together on numerous occasions by numerous acquaintances—all carefully orchestrated by him. Yet she had been unaware of it all. Her whole focus had been upon tending the wounded and worrying about Alleyne—and drawing strength and comfort from the daily support of her dear friend.

And now? Was he merely amused by her determination to break his heart or at least to humiliate him? Was he still determined to marry her because he knew it would infuriate Wulfric? Or in order to prove to her that he could charm and seduce her even when she knew the truth about him?

How could she know the answers to any of her questions? How could she ever trust anything such a man said to her?

She *wished* she had not lain with him out by the grotto. That had been a terrible mistake—as much as anything because her body ached for more.

"Every time I look at you, *ma chère,*" he said when he reached the open door, "you are lovelier than you were the last time. That particular shade of rose pink suits you. Behold your lovelorn swain." He grinned at her and came inside, one hand over his heart.

It was when he spoke like this that he was hardest to know. It was the light, flirtatious manner he had used when she first met him in Brussels. The man behind the facade had been quite unknown to her then. He was just as unknown now. It must be her youth, Morgan decided, and the fact that he had done twelve more years of living than she. She did not know him at all. Every day she felt she knew him less and less.

"What did she say?" she asked without responding with a smile of her own.

He sank onto the leather seat across from her and draped one arm along the back of it. He smiled at her with what she recognized as the old mockery and cynicism.

"I believe you know very well what she said, *chérie,*" he said. "It seems I am to be absolved of all blame in the Duke of Bewcastle's eyes. She has written to him. I suppose you commanded her to do so and to come here to grovel before me."

"I did not command," she said, "or even advise. I merely wished to discover the truth. I suppose I *did* show some scorn when she attempted to use the excuse that she was only eighteen at the time."

"Ah, yes," he said, regarding her with lazy eyes, "*you* would never behave so, would you, *chérie?* You would confront your father and your unwelcome suitor both and speak your mind without ever breaking eye contact with them. But you are made of stern stuff, Lady Morgan Bedwyn. I suppose Marianne's accomplice was Henrietta."

"Did she say so?" she asked him.

"No." He chuckled softly. "And I suppose you are not saying so either. I daresay you suffered untold torments at the hands of your older sister and brothers when you were a child. But I would be willing to wager that you never ever went running to Bewcastle with tales of their perfidy."

"I never needed to," she said. "There were other, more satisfactory ways of dealing with them. They never enjoyed finding salt in their coffee or sugar on their vegetables or their best boots floating in the basin of the fountain or all the buttons missing from a favorite coat."

He laughed again.

"Henrietta was always difficult," he said. "I suppose it was understandable that she hated being here and resented all our efforts to reach out to her. She was twelve years old when her parents died, and she had never met any of us before she came here to live. She was a—a *prickly* girl. If we tried to include her in our activities, she let us know in every way possible how bored she was with both the activity and us. And yet if we left her alone, she sulked and pouted and made us feel guilty for neglecting the orphan in our midst. I tried my best that year of her come-out to see to it that she had partners at balls and invitations from some of my friends to drive in the park or attend the theater.

She was not grateful. I daresay we did not understand her. I daresay *I* did not."

He was looking at her quite keenly from beneath his lazy eyelids, Morgan realized.

"She seems contented enough now," she said. "She loves your mother, I believe. And she has her friendship with Marianne."

She looked very directly back at him, and they exchanged an almost-imperceptible half-smile of understanding. She wondered if he was uncomfortable with what he had realized about his cousin. She was not. Love was a precious enough commodity that it ought not to be denied wherever it was to be found.

"If it was Henrietta," she said, "will you be terribly hurt? Terribly angry? Will you be able to allow her to go on living here?"

"If it *was* Henrietta," he said, "I suppose she had her reasons. And I suppose she has suffered—probably rather badly. It would be hard to live with such guilt, would it not, *chérie?*"

He was still looking at her the same way.

"For a person of conscience," she said, "yes."

"Ah, yes, conscience." He smiled. "Some of us are without that. I have invited Marianne to the ball tomorrow. Does that please you? Are you proud of me?"

"It does please me," she told him. "It was the sensible thing to do."

"You have been diligent, *chérie,*" he said, "in encouraging me to look into the darkest corners of my life and to bring light there. You have spent much of your time here helping me to face the past so that it will not forever burden my present and my future. Why?"

"It is so *stupid,*" she told him, "to load oneself down with burdens from the past when the past is over and done with. How can one enjoy the present or shape the future when one is forever looking back into perpetual gloom?"

"And yet," he said, "you carry such burdens yourself, *chérie*. You will not see that your view of the past as it involves me is perhaps a little distorted. You deny present happiness for yourself and future prospects of a meaningful life together for both of us. You persist in looking backward into perpetual gloom, as you phrased it."

She jumped to her feet, set her hands on the table between them, and leaned toward him across it.

"Oh, yes!" she cried. "That is just the sort of argument I would expect you to use, Gervase. Anything to confuse my mind and manipulate me to your will. What I said is in no way applicable to my situation. And you deceive yourself when you say I deny myself present happiness. I will be happy when I leave you. You flatter yourself when you say that I will look back on perpetual gloom. Whenever I *do* look back, it will be with enormous relief that I discovered the truth about you in time to save myself from a lifetime of misery. But I will not look back often. Why should I? The past few months have been *supremely* insignificant."

"You are adorable, *chérie,* when you are angry," he said.

She rushed around the table, but by the time she

reached him, of course, he was well prepared. He caught her right hand by the wrist when it was still two inches from his face, and the left one when it was six inches away. He held on and laughed softly.

"But what is this, *mon amour?*" he asked her. "You have forgotten that you are supposed to be making me fall hopelessly in love with you?"

She moved her head closer to his. "I would rather flirt with a toad," she said. "I would rather make love to the devil."

*"Non, chérie."* He laughed up at her and hung on to her wrists. "This is too bad of you. One thing I have always admired about you is your honesty. Yet you have just lied twice to me. How would you flirt with a toad? And what would the devil do with his pitchfork while you made love to the devil? Actually, it might be better not to think of that one. There are all sorts of wicked possibilities, are there not?"

"Perhaps," she said softly, moving her head closer still, "I should divert your mind from such naughty thoughts, Gervase." And she kissed him on the lips.

She was on his lap a moment later, her wrists free and their arms about each other. They were engaged in a hot embrace.

His fingers tore at the ribbons of her bonnet and tossed it onto the table. He drew down the bodice of her dress to expose more of her breasts. She fumbled with the buttons of his coat and waistcoat so that she could burrow her arms beneath them and feel the enticing heat of his body through his shirt. They kissed each other with fierce longing and desperate tenderness.

But they were both aware, of course, that they were in the summerhouse and visible to anyone who happened to be approaching. Their embrace remained just barely within the bounds of decorum.

He drew her head down to rest on his shoulder after the kiss ended, both his Hessian boots propped against the table so that she would not slip off his lap.

"When I could not see you in the flower garden after Marianne left," he told her, "I thought that perhaps I would not be able to find you, *chérie*. You cannot know how much I needed you or with what gladness I saw you sitting here."

She desperately wanted to believe him. But yet again she was painfully aware of her youth and his greater experience. She had been so totally, so blithely, unaware of his motives just a short while ago. She would not be so easily caught by her own naïveté again.

"I was glad to see you too," she said. "But I thought that perhaps you would be angry with me."

"Angry?" He tipped back her chin with one finger and gazed down at her. "When you have been the angel of my life?"

Ah, no. That was a little too extravagant, she thought.

"Have I been?" She sighed and burrowed her head against his shoulder again.

"Always, *chérie,*" he said. "My angel of beauty and grace, my angel of mercy and compassion, my angel of love."

She sighed again and feathered light kisses along the underside of his jaw.

"Do you love me, then?" she asked him.

"I love you, *ma chère,*" he said, moving his head and speaking against her lips. "With every fiber of my being I love you."

They kissed softly and warmly and then smiled into each other's eyes.

"And you, *mon amour?*" he asked her. "Do you love me?"

She continued to smile.

"No," she told him. "Actually I do not. Not even one little bit, Gervase. Tell me the rest of it. Will you be heartbroken when I leave?"

His eyes crinkled at the corners, and he looked genuinely, despicably amused.

"Of course, *ma chère,*" he said. "I daresay I will let my hair grow and go into a decline and expire, and you will come and weep over my grave and water the roses my mother will plant there with your tears. Or perhaps you will stand there and laugh in scorn and stamp out every blossom that blooms. *Would* you be so hard-hearted? *Could* you be?"

"Not at all," she said, getting to her feet and brushing the creases from her dress before drawing her bonnet back on. "I would be totally indifferent. Someone would mention to me one day that you had died, and I would think a moment and then remark with a careless shrug that I had known you once. And then I would continue with what I was doing."

He chuckled as he stood up. "You are developing into an accomplished liar," he said. "But always and ever you are adorable. Shall we do the civilized thing and walk back to the house together even though I assume we have quarreled? But we must have a topic of conversation. The weather, perhaps? Ah, I have it. Let us speculate on what weather we may expect for tomorrow's fete. Will it rain or will it shine, do you believe, *chérie?* And whatever will we do if it rains?"

She took his offered arm outside the summerhouse and proceeded along the avenue with him.

"You know very well," she said, "that your mother has alternative plans for a rainy day."

"Ah," he said, "so much for that topic. It is your turn to choose one, *chérie*."

FOR A WHILE DURING THE morning it looked as if the countess's alternate plans would have to be implemented. But by midday, not only had the threatened rain not materialized, but the clouds had moved off completely and the sun shone. The afternoon turned out to be pleasantly warm without being oppressively hot.

Everyone came to the Windrush fete from miles around. There were races, games of skill and strength, including an archery competition, and a cricket match on the lawns. There were boat races on the lake and then rides for the children with Aidan and Sir Harold at the oars. There were pony rides on the wide avenue between the lake and the summerhouse. There were tours of the ballroom—already decorated for the evening—and the portrait gallery for interested adults. And there was food and drink in abundance, to be consumed at small tables covered with crisp white cloths on the terrace or more informally on blankets out on the lawn or down by the lake.

Gervase mingled with his guests, making himself agreeable to even the humblest of them. So did Morgan, though mingling with the lower classes was something she was not accustomed to. She was reminded of the surprise she had felt last year when she went to Penhallow and discovered that Joshua, Marquess of Hallmere, actually treated all his servants and laborers and social inferiors as personal friends. She was reminded too of the long days and nights she had spent at Mrs. Clark's, tending the wounded and understanding that class distinctions were just an accident of birth, that the soldiers who had come out of the slums of London, their English almost unintelligible to her, were as precious as any duke or marquess—or prince.

Morgan found that the women curtsied to her a great deal while the men bobbed their heads and pulled at their forelocks. Children stared, their eyes—and often their mouths—wide. But all of them smiled back when she smiled at them. And when she entered the archery contest, the other contestants—all men—actually cheered, and a large group of spectators, mostly women, gathered around to watch.

"I am horribly out of practice," Morgan said as she bent the bow for her first shot. The target looked alarmingly small and far distant.

She did not distinguish herself though she had once been unbeatable at the sport—at least in the environs of Lindsey Hall. She did not disgrace herself either. Out of nine contestants, she placed third and won loud applause for herself in the process. She was flushed and bright-eyed as she moved away.

The three-legged race was about to begin, with seven pairs of children and one pair of adults—Gervase and Monique. They were cheered by the children and jeered by a few brave adults, who were also laughing good-naturedly.

Morgan laughed too after Joshua gave the signal to start and the adults shot into the lead and then fell with such a spectacularly awkward flailing of limbs and feminine shriek and male bellow that Morgan realized it was all deliberate. They staggered to their feet while the five surviving pairs of children bobbed past, then shot into the lead again, only to go through the same performance when they were within a yard of the finish line. Three pairs of children bobbed to victory and to a great deal of applause and laughter.

An arm came about Morgan's shoulders, and Aidan hugged her briefly to his side.

"Happy?" he asked.

She nodded, smiling at him.

"I cannot get over how you have grown up," he said. "Just yesterday, it seems, you were a girl. Now you are a woman and have fulfilled every promise of beauty you ever showed."

"I hope you are as lavish in your compliments to Eve." She laughed.

He nodded in the direction of Gervase, who was presenting prizes to the winners of the race and small coins to all the losers.

"You have made a good choice," he said. "He is a good man."

"Yes." Morgan gazed at him, hatless and slightly disheveled, his face full of laughter and animation. "He is."

"I was a little worried, I must confess," he said, squeezing her shoulder. "We all were. That was why we agreed to come here—as moral support for you should you need it. I am glad you do not, but I am not sorry we came. You can be happy among these people, Morgan."

"Yes," she agreed. "I can."

"Uh-oh," he said. "I see that Freyja is demonstrating to Davy how to throw the horseshoes. I wonder which of them intends to enter the competition. I had better go and see."

It was later, after Morgan had taken Jonathan over to the ponies so that he could pet one of them and had then coaxed him to take a little ride while she held him, that the countess came upon her and linked an arm through hers.

"You have been so busy that you will have no dancing legs left for tonight, *chérie,*" she said. "Come and sit down on the terrace for a little while. How beautiful you look in primrose yellow. You look as fresh as the springtime."

"You must be very pleased with the success of your fete, ma'am," Morgan said. "Everyone appears to be having a wonderful time."

"And it is all for you, *chérie,*" the countess reminded her. "For you and Gervase, in honor of your betrothal. It is easy to see that everyone loves him, as they always used to do and as I knew they would do again. And everyone simply *adores* you. You must begin to call me

*Maman,* rather than that oh-so-formal *ma'am.* Will you, *ma petite?*"

"Yes, *Maman.*" Morgan smiled at her as they sat at one of the tables and a footman hurried up to bring them tea and cakes.

Her revenge was going to be far more horrible than she had imagined when she first planned it, she realized. Doubtless she would be the one mainly blamed since she would be the one breaking the engagement—*and* she was the stranger. But there would be a great deal of humiliation for Gervase.

She just did not want to do it.

How foolishly impulsive she had been. It ought to have been enough to confront him there at Pickford House, to let him know that she *knew,* to force him to confess all to her. It ought to have been enough to force him down onto his knees to offer for her. There would have been enough triumph in looking scornfully down at him and saying no.

Except that he had fully expected that.

And except that, as she had told him, she had not yet been finished with him.

Was she now?

Would she ever be?

But there was no time to dwell upon her thoughts or her dilemma. There was the countess to converse with, and soon Freyja and Emma joined them as the guests began to drift away homeward.

THE BALLROOM LOOKED and smelled like a particularly luxurious garden, Gervase thought as he stepped inside it to look around and to consult with the orchestra, whose members were already seated on the dais at one end of the room, tuning their instruments. The flowers were all shades of purple and fuchsia and pink with lavish amounts of fern and other greenery.

The floral decorations were mostly Henrietta's handiwork, he knew. She always had had an eye for color and design. Tonight she had outdone herself.

She had come to him this morning, early, even before breakfast, as he was returning from a walk. She had taken him by surprise by confessing her part in what had happened nine years ago. She had even offered to leave Windrush if he so desired, though she had not told him where she would go.

He had not been feeling kindly disposed toward her. But he had allowed himself to react from sheer instinct. He had crossed the room to her, caught her up in a tight hug that had clearly startled her, and told her not to be a goose, that it was time they put the past behind them and got on with their lives. And then he had grinned at her while she mopped at her eyes with a handkerchief.

"Besides," he had said, "*Maman* is determined to move to Cherry Cottage after my marriage. I daresay you will want to go there with her."

"Yes, I will, Gervase," she had said. "Thank you for your generosity."

*After his marriage.*

Cherry Cottage was a small manor on the outskirts of the village that his father had leased to a retired army colonel, now deceased. His widow had moved away.

Henrietta had not offered any explanation of her motive in collaborating with Marianne to ensnare him, and he had not asked. He would not deny that the thought of the two of them as a couple shook him considerably, especially since they had caused him such enormous harm, but when all was said and done, what they were to each other was their business. It was certainly none of his.

His thoughts were distracted when the Bedwyns arrived in a body, both men in black with white linen, Freyja all in black, Eve in lavender. But in truth he had eyes only for Morgan, who looked magnificent in a gown of shimmering silver satin partly covered with a silver netted tunic. Silver chains were woven into her high-piled hair, and a silver locket half nestled into her décolletage. Her gloves and fan were white.

He was wearing the same silver, gray, and white clothes he had worn for the picnic in the Forest of Soignés. He had hesitated over the choice, since neither of them needed any reminder of that night. But it was a gamble he had decided to take. Dealing with the past certainly did not involve denying it. That would solve nothing.

He hoped—he desperately hoped—that they could deal with the past.

He bowed to her and took her hand to raise to his lips. She smiled brightly back at him while her family members looked on as well as his own, who were coming into the ballroom on the heels of the Bedwyns.

"Goodness," Freyja said, "you two look very dashing together."

The outside guests began to arrive very soon after that. Gervase greeted them in a receiving line with his mother and Morgan. Morgan had met them all before, but he was impressed at the way she remembered names and a few details about each. It was very obvious that everyone admired her greatly, not just because she was beautiful and not just because she was the sister of the Duke of Bewcastle, but because she was poised and gracious and charming.

Her revenge, he thought, was going to be colossal indeed.

If he could not talk her out of it, that was.

As his mother had predicted, the ballroom was pleasantly filled after everyone had arrived—including Marianne Bonner with her elderly aunt, Mrs. Jasper—but was by no means a grand squeeze. He opened the dancing with Morgan, performing a merry romp of a country dance with her. They both danced with a series of different partners after that and took supper at different tables. It was all very correct behavior, of course, but even by the strict rules of a London Season he was permitted to dance twice with the same partner. He had instructed the orchestra to play the one and only waltz of the evening after supper.

*"Chérie?"* He bowed over Morgan's hand as she stood talking with a group of their neighbors. "You will waltz with me?"

She set her hand upon his sleeve without a word and allowed him to lead her onto the dance floor.

"You are wearing what you wore in the Forest of Soignés," she said. "I thought then that you chose such pale colors because most of the other gentlemen would be wearing scarlet coats."

"Exactly right, *chérie,*" he said. "Who would want to pale into insignificance at his own entertainment?"

"I am surprised you would wear the same clothes tonight," she said.

"Are you?" he asked, dipping his head a little closer to hers as he drew her into his arms in anticipation of the opening bars of the music. "And are you surprised that I have asked you to waltz with me? The last time was at your sister's ball in London—alone together in an anteroom. The time before was at my picnic—alone together for a few minutes before a hundred or more pairs of eyes. And before that at Viscount Cameron's ball, where we met."

"I hardly need to be reminded," she said. "But I am glad I have been. It will make things easier tomorrow or the day after when Eve and Aidan and Freyja and Joshua leave here and I decide to go with them."

The music began, and he led her slowly into the opening steps of the waltz.

"Will you, *chérie?*" he asked her, his eyes steady on hers. "Leave with them? Leave *me?* Never to see me again?"

"You know I will." She tossed her head back but would not remove her eyes from his.

He pressed his hand more firmly to the back of her waist and swung her into a twirl, lengthening his steps as he did so.

She laughed with delight.

He had even told the orchestra leader what tunes to

play. He could see suddenly from the arrested look in her eyes that she recognized the one playing now. It was the very tune to which they had waltzed that first time.

They danced in silence, not once removing their eyes from each other. He danced her in and out among other couples, slowly, faster, twirling and spinning until he could feel the smile on his own face and see the color rise in her cheeks and the sparkle deepen in her eyes.

It was only after the music was ended that they spoke again.

"You waltz so very well, Gervase," she said, dropping her arms to her sides until the music would begin again. "As you do many other things well. You are an expert at flirtation and more than just flirtation. You swore that you would make *me* fall in love with *you*. That is what this is all about, I suppose. Just as it was that very first time. So that you may manipulate me, turn me from my resolve, defeat me even if you must marry me in the process. I am only a little older chronologically than I was in Brussels at the Cameron ball, but I am years and years older in experience. Sometimes I really hate you."

"Hatred is an improvement on yesterday's indifference, *ma chère,*" he told her. "Has it occurred to you that I try to make you love me because *I* love *you?*"

She shook her head impatiently and lifted her hand to his shoulder again as the music resumed.

"I will be leaving with my brother and sister when they go," she told him again.

The trouble was, he thought, that she very probably meant it. Her pride would not let her change her mind. Neither would her newfound maturity and caution. She had been very badly hurt. And he had very little to offer in self-defense. Some, it was true, but not much.

It was no defense that he loved her with every ounce of his being.

They did not speak again until the set was drawing to its end. There was one set of country dances left, but they could not, of course, dance it together.

*"Chérie,"* he said, "come walking with me after this is all over?"

"Tonight?" She looked up at him with raised eyebrows. "Where? Outside?"

"Outside." He nodded.

"Why? So that you may seduce me?" She gazed haughtily at him. "Are you *mad?*"

"Only desperate, *chérie,*" he said. "I am running out of time, and I can see that you are determined to harden your heart and punish me by deserting me. Let us talk. Give me this one chance to change your mind. On my gentleman's honor I swear not to lay one lascivious finger on you without your permission. Give me this chance."

"On your gentleman's honor?" she said softly, her eyebrows arched scornfully. "But there *is* no chance that I will change my mind."

She frowned, and for one moment he glimpsed something in her eyes that gave him hope despite her words—some doubt, some vulnerability, some hint of misery.

"Give me that chance anyway," he asked her.

The music had stopped and the other couples were leaving the floor. Soon—in a very few moments—they would be conspicuous if they stayed where they were. And he knew that if she did not speak during those few moments it would be too late for him. He would have lost her.

"Very well," she said. "But it is pointless."

He smiled at her and drew her hand through his arm.

## CHAPTER XXII

THIS WAS SO POINTLESS, MORGAN THOUGHT. THE day had been an agony to her for the very reason that it had seemed so successful to everyone else. It had been a glorious celebration of her betrothal to Gervase.

It was a betrothal she must break the day after tomorrow when Freyja and Aidan were to leave Windrush. She must harden her heart against all arguments to the contrary. Yet she had agreed to give him this private time in order that he might try to persuade her to change her mind. And it was the middle of a cool, star-filled night when they had just waltzed together and she was raw with emotion.

She was almost sure she knew where he was taking her too, though she would not ask. She would not say a word until he did, and he seemed content with silence while they walked. She had expected that he would stroll on the lawns with her or perhaps take her down by the lake or maybe to the summerhouse, where they would be out of sight from windows in the house. Though secrecy was not necessary. He had announced that they were going out for a walk, and Aidan, though he had given them both a hard look, had remarked that it was unexceptionable for a betrothed couple to say good night to each other away from the prying eyes of their families.

Why had she changed into a serviceable day dress, which was covered up with a warm cloak, if she expected that this was to be just a very brief conversation in which he would attempt to use his charm to persuade her to stay and she would simply say no?

She was afraid of her own self-deceptions, her own weaknesses.

He had brought a lantern with him—an affectation while they were on open ground lit by moon and stars. But of course it was a great help along parts of the wilderness walk, when the sky was almost hidden above a canopy of tree branches. He held her by the elbow to steady her over the uneven ground. Apart from that, he seemed content not to touch her at all.

By the time they reached the grotto after scrambling up one slope and down another in darkness apart from light afforded by the lantern, Morgan was feeling very angry indeed—not so much against him as against herself. Did she not *know* him by now? Did she not know that he was pitting the power of his charm against the strength of her will?

Or was he? Had he changed since Brussels? But would she be a fool simply to forget what he had done to her there—particularly after Waterloo? It broke her heart to remember that week of tenderness, when he had seemed her dearest friend and had even become her lover. It had all been deception, all of it. She could not simply forget now.

She turned to face him as he extinguished the lantern light—it was no longer needed, since the moon was beaming down upon them and glimmering in a band across the water of the river.

"I suppose," she said, realizing as she did so that she was standing on almost the exact spot where she had lain with him just a few days before, "you think these surroundings romantic enough that I will be seduced away from common sense and rational choice?"

The surroundings *were* romantic too—horribly so. Moonlight was sparkling off the stream of water arcing out of the cherub's vase.

"I was wrong, then, *chérie?*" he asked her with an exaggerated sigh. "It is not going to be that easy?"

It was the sigh that did it. Could he never take anything seriously? Was he so sure of her? Or did he really not care at all?

"It is not going to be *possible,*" she cried, her hands curling into fists at her sides. "Do you not understand that, Gervase? You are handsome and charming and attractive. Of course you are. I would be foolish to deny it. It was those facts that made me fall in love with you in Brussels, even though I knew you were also a flirt and a rake. It was those facts that led me into such an indiscretion at Freyja's ball and that led me into lying with you here a few days ago. But I know too the cynicism, the hatred, the cold calculation, of which you are capable. I know myself to have been your victim—right up to Freyja's ball—perhaps right up to the present moment. How can I believe you when you say you love me, that you really wish to marry me? How can I believe anything you say to me? How can I ever *trust* you again? We might as well go back to the house without further ado and get some sleep. I am going away when my family leaves here. I am going to leave you and forget about you."

He had gone to stand against the stone wall to one side of the grotto entrance. His arms were crossed over his chest.

*"Chérie,"* he said softly, "you agreed to give me one last chance to persuade you not to leave me, not to break my heart."

Even now, she thought, he could be teasing her. How could she *break his heart?* Could he possibly love her that deeply? She was afraid to believe. She was afraid to hope.

She hated being only eighteen. She *hated* it.

"Very well," she said, gazing at him with all the hauteur she could muster. "Talk away. But you will be wasting your breath."

She turned and moved off a little way, stepping among the flowers, and set one hand upon a cold stone wing of the cherub.

"I cannot deny my guilt, *chérie,*" he said. "Although it was your beauty that first drew my attention, it was your identity that led me to seek an acquaintance with you. I meant mischief, and I *caused* mischief. I used you quite coldly and quite callously to annoy your brother."

It still hurt to remember that picnic in the forest and

to know that it had not been a mere outrageous, extravagant act of flirtation on his part but a calculated outpouring of hatred.

"But I liked you," he said, "and began to realize—too late—that you were more than just his sister. I ought not to have involved you in something that concerned just him and me. But I make no excuses here. I am guilty and I am deeply ashamed."

She stretched out one hand and held it for a moment in the stream of water coming from the vase. But it was cold. She drew back her hand and tucked it inside the folds of her cloak, drying it against her skirt as she did so. She tried to think of mundane things—what she would wear on the journey home, whether or not she would take her new painting supplies with her, whether she would go to Leicestershire or Oxfordshire or Cornwall—or whether she would simply go to Lindsey Hall and spend the summer with Wulfric.

"When I saw you at the Duke of Richmond's ball," he said, "I stayed away from you, *chérie,* until I saw you standing alone after the officers had all left. You looked upset and forlorn. You looked in need of comforting. And so I went to comfort you if I could. I went because you were *you,* not because you were his sister. I did not even *think* of that fact."

"It was too late by then," she said, bowing her head and closing her eyes.

"And then," he said, "a few days later I saw you at the Namur Gates long after I assumed you were gone, dirty and disheveled and flushed and beautiful as you leaned over and tended a private soldier who had had half his leg blown away. From that moment on, from then until we landed together at Harwich, you were Morgan Bedwyn to me, and I came to like you and admire and respect you and even to love you, though I do not believe I fully recognized that last sentiment until later. You were not the Duke of Bewcastle's sister in those days, *chérie*. You were yourself—and without my even realizing it, you became the focus of my whole world, the love of my heart. When you came to me in my rooms that evening, I ought not to have allowed our embrace to go so far, but I loved you and could think of no other way to take you into myself, to take away your pain. I did not even realize it was love I felt until later, but it was. I am guilty of what went before, *mon amour,* but not of anything that happened during those days. I was your friend and ultimately your lover."

She trampled wildflowers underfoot as she hurried toward him. Her hands were in tight fists again.

"You lie!" she cried. "You are lying to me. Don't do this, Gervase. Don't *do* it. I can't bear it. And what about Freyja's ball? If you loved me after Waterloo, if you were sorry for the way you had used me, why did you do as you did *there?* I cannot trust anything you say. I cannot trust *you*."

She was crying then in noisy, agonized gasps and fumbled for a handkerchief with shaking hands. She hated watering pots. She had never been one.

He kept his arms crossed over his chest. "I wish I could say I was as innocent then as I was in Brussels after Waterloo," he said. "I cannot, though. I went to London to offer for you, but I will not pretend that it was only my love for you that occupied my mind when I faced Bewcastle in his library at Bedwyn House—I am not sure that even then I recognized that it *was* love I felt. I wanted to see his rage and enjoy it. And then afterward I could think only of ways by which I could force him to allow me to pay my addresses to you. It was only when it was much, much too late that I understood my true reason—not so much that I wanted to hurt him as that I could not bear to lose you. It happened in that small room at your sister's ball, when I had meant simply to waltz with you but found myself kissing you. It was then that I understood and knew in a flash that I must get you out of there before scandal erupted. But even as I raised my head I was aware of Bewcastle standing in the doorway and of other guests strolling past or simply standing, staring. And so it was too late to find an honorable way of wooing and winning you."

Morgan bowed her head and lifted both hands to cover her face.

"And so," he said, "I come to the end of the only defense I can make—a poor one at best. I cannot ask you to forgive me, *chérie*—that would be too easy and too glib. I do not deserve forgiveness. I can only assure you—again too easy and too glib, I am afraid—that I love you with all my heart and would spend my life loving you and being your friend if I could. Only you can decide if you *will* forgive me. Or if you will trust me."

She walked to the bank of the river and a few yards along it, away from the willow and the cherub. The landscape darkened suddenly, and she looked up to see that a small cloud had covered the moon. But even as she gazed upward it moved off and her face was bathed in moonlight.

She had told him that he must forgive his father or forever be burdened by the darkness of his hatred.

She had told him that he must forgive Marianne and Henrietta or forever be bowed down by the terrible hurt they had caused him.

She knew that he must forgive Wulfric—just as she knew that Wulfric must now forgive Marianne.

Hatred, grudges were a deadly poison to the soul.

She must forgive Gervase, then. But was forgiveness enough? *Could* she trust him?

But one could not *always* be without trust. What immeasurable harm one would do to oneself if one viewed every person in one's life with cynical suspicion. And she was, she knew, in danger of becoming such a person. She had been hopelessly naive until very recently. Was she now to allow herself to swing to the opposite extreme? Was she to guard herself against future hurt—and in the process also deny herself present and future happiness?

Those final days in Brussels had been *real*.

He had liked and admired and respected her. He had searched for Alleyne for her sake. He had made love to her because he had wanted to share her pain and bring her comfort. He had been her friend. And her lover.

It had all been real.

When she turned to look back, he was standing exactly where she had left him.

She had sworn to herself that she would not be weak. But was being intractable its own form of weakness?

She walked back toward him, still not sure what she would say. And so she said nothing. She walked right against him until she could set her face in the intricate folds of his neckcloth and feel the warm, solid strength of his body and his thighs against her own.

After a few moments she felt one of his arms come lightly about her while the fingers of his other hand stroked the back of her head through her hair. A few moments after that she felt his cheek come to rest against the top of her head.

"I am sorry, Morgan," he said. "Ah, the inadequacy of words. I am so very, very sorry, *ma chère*."

"If you had not seen me at the Cameron ball and discovered that I was Wulfric's sister," she said without lifting her face, "we would never have met, Gervase. And I would have hated that."

He turned his head and kissed the top of her head.

"I *do* trust you," she said. "I really do."

He kissed her—softly and warmly—and she kissed him back with all the yearning of someone who had steeled herself to reject what she loved and who had discovered that the sacrifice was not necessary after all. And then he hugged her very tightly before letting her go. He stepped away from the grotto wall, took both her hands in his, and went down on one knee on the grass.

"Morgan." He gazed up at her. "I love you for everything you are and will become. I admire you as a woman and as a person. I treasure you as a friend and companion. I love your intelligence and your artistic vision and your insights into life and spirit. I adore you as a lover. I would nurture your freedom for a lifetime if you will have me. And I would offer all that is the essence of my true self in return. Will you honor me by marrying me?"

It was terribly theatrical—and marvelously, soul-shatteringly romantic. He had said nothing about possession, nothing about not being able to live without her, nothing that would bind her except the marriage commitment itself. And love, whose bonds could only ever be freedom if it was real love.

"Yes," she said.

Perhaps she ought to have said more. Perhaps she ought to have said something to match what he had said to her. But her chest and throat were sore with unshed tears, and somehow the one word encompassed everything there was to be said anyway.

Yes, she would be his friend. Yes, she would be his lover. Yes, she would be his wife. Together they would seek companionship and physical union and joy—and together they would nurture and cherish each other's uniqueness and freedom.

He got to his feet, wrapped his arms about her waist, lifted her off the ground, and spun her about, tipping back his head and baying at the moon as he did so. She tipped back her own head and laughed.

It was a cleansing, heart-deep laugh that restored to her the treasure of her youth. Though he stopped it soon enough with a kiss.

"I hope you brought something with you to light the lantern again," she said after a while. "The night is getting cloudy. It is going to be very dark on the wilderness walk."

"That settles it, then," he said. "We will solve the problem by not walking it until daylight, *chérie*."

"It is *cold,*" she protested.

"But not for long," he told her. "Lovemaking is warm business, and I *do* intend to make love to you—probably for most of what remains of the night. But though I had very little hope this morning, you see, I did not quite despair either. And so I prepared for what I hoped would be the ending of our private talk together—*if* I could persuade you into it. I brought some blankets very early this morning, before anyone was up, and put them inside the grotto. They are there now."

She opened her mouth to speak, outraged by his presumption. But he waggled his eyebrows at her and then looked sheepish, and she found herself laughing again and wrapping her arms about his neck.

"This," she said, "is probably not what Aidan had in mind when he permitted me to come out here to say good night to you."

"Now there," he told her, "I would wager you are wrong. He would have had to be stupid not to guess my intent, and I do not believe Lord Aidan Bedwyn is stupid."

It was a startling idea to Morgan. Were betrothed couples really allowed such freedom?

But Gervase was already retrieving a pile of neatly folded blankets from the grotto and spreading one of them on the grass. And then he was waggling his eyebrows at her again and opening his arms to her.

It was a cool, almost chilly night, and they did use the blankets, though only for brief spells while they caught their breath and allowed the world to slow to its regular speed on its axis again, as Gervase put it. For the rest of the night, until dawn grayed the eastern sky and even a little beyond that, they made hot, vigorous, joyful love and would have been warm even floating in Arctic waters on an iceberg—also according to Gervase.

They crept back into the house not long before the servants were up. Morgan heard them just before she fell asleep.

## CHAPTER XXIII

MORGAN WAS THE FIRST ONE DOWNSTAIRS. SHE ought not to have started dressing so early. It was ridiculous really to imagine that dressing was going to take so much longer than usual merely because this was her wedding day. But perhaps she had not imagined any such thing. She had simply not been able to wait any longer. She was so excited and so nervous that she thought she might vomit if she dwelled upon the significance of the occasion.

She ought to have remained in her dressing room. She could remember how last year, when Freyja had wed Joshua, they had all crowded into her dressing room to comment on her appearance, to wish her joy, to hug her before leaving for the church so that they might be decently seated in the pews before she arrived with Wulfric.

But here she was downstairs, alone except for a silent footman who forgot himself for a moment when he first saw her and half smiled at her. The great hall of Lindsey Hall, which had been preserved as a medieval banqueting hall, had always been one of her favorite places in the world. She ran her hands over the smooth old wood of the great table as she walked around it, and gazed at the old banners and coats of arms and weapons hanging on the walls.

The enormity of what was happening hit her like a blow to the stomach. After this morning, Lindsey Hall would no longer be home. It would be Wulfric's home, but not hers. She would never again be Morgan Bedwyn after this morning. She would come here in future only as a guest—as Lady Morgan Ashford, Countess of Rosthorn. She shivered and wondered for a moment if she really *was* going to vomit. It did not help, she supposed, that she was very probably with child. Certainly her courses, which should have come two weeks ago, still showed no sign of coming at all.

Wulfric strolled into the hall from the direction of the minstrel gallery and raised his eyebrows at the sight of her. He even stood still to take a better look and raised his quizzing glass to his eye.

"Breathtaking," he said softly, an unexpected pronouncement coming from him.

She had decided to wear white with lavender embroidery about the hems of her skirt and sleeves and lavender ribbons to trim her bonnet and the high waistline of her dress. Lavender in remembrance of Alleyne, for whom she had shed tears last night after retiring to bed. It made her heart ache to realize how life went on after the death of a dearly loved one much as it would if he had lived. Except that if he had lived she would not have remained in Brussels and today would not be happening this way at all.

"And so I am to cheerfully give away the last one of my family to someone who believes he needs her more than I, am I?" Wulfric asked.

He was in a strange mood. When had Wulf *needed* any of them? And yet it struck Morgan suddenly that he would be all alone here now. Would he be lonely? Was Wulf capable of loneliness?

She hurried across the space between them and wrapped her arms impulsively about him, rather as she had done in Harwich.

"You will crease your finery," he said with his customary cool hauteur as he put her from him—but only after hugging her so tightly that she felt the air whooshing out of her lungs.

She could have cried then. She could have bawled with grief for him, for Alleyne, for the sadness of having to grow up and realize that change was part of the very nature of life, that nothing was permanent and immutable. But before she could do anything so strange or potentially embarrassing, Rannulf appeared in the hall with their grandmother on his arm, looking terribly frail though she had insisted upon coming all the way from Leicestershire for the wedding. Judith was with them, and Eve and Aidan and the children were just behind. Becky came hurtling past them and flung herself at Morgan.

"You look so pretty, Aunt Morgan," she cried. "I am going to have bride clothes just like yours when I grow up."

"Trust Morgan to be first to her own wedding," Freyja said, coming into the hall with Joshua behind everyone else.

"We went to your dressing room but the bird had flown," Joshua said with a grin.

"It is a good thing you did not run all the way to the church, Morg," Rannulf said. "You would probably have been there before Gervase, and we Bedwyns would never have lived down the disgrace."

"You look delightful, Morgan, my dear," their grandmother said. "Come and give me a kiss."

Aunt and Uncle Rochester had appeared too.

"And then we must all leave for the church, except Morgan and Wulfric," Aunt Rochester said in her usual strident tones that somehow commanded attention even from a full gathering of Bedwyns. "It would be just as disgraceful, Rannulf, if we arrived after Rosthorn."

Almost as suddenly as they had all arrived in the hall, they were gone again, though they all invited the wrath of their aunt by hugging Morgan first, Rannulf quite bruisingly. Judith actually had tears in her eyes.

It was real, Morgan thought as she turned and looked at the silent figure of Wulfric, elegant and severe in black with white linen.

This was her wedding day.

TO GERVASE IT SEEMED AS he watched Morgan come toward him on Bewcastle's arm along the nave of the church, beautiful beyond belief in white with touches of lavender, that every moment of the past nine years and more had been worth living through just so that there could now be this moment.

What likelihood was there that it would have happened otherwise? Quite possibly he would have married someone else several years ago. Even if he had not, he might not have noticed Lady Morgan Bedwyn this spring. No, correction—he would surely have noticed her even as he had in Cameron's ballroom. But he might not have approached someone so young, so obviously fresh from the schoolroom. And even if he had, without motive to entice and attract her, he might not have caused *her* to grant *him* more than a fleeting moment of her attention.

It was strange how life worked.

Her eyes were on his, and they were bright with warmth and eagerness and love. By what miracle had she forgiven him? He smiled and, aware as he had been just a minute or two ago of Pierre at his side, of the churchful of family and guests filling every pew, now he saw only her.

His beloved Morgan.

The end of his long and difficult rainbow.

Bewcastle had written to him the very day he had received Marianne's letter. His own had been brief and to the point, but in it he had assured Gervase that he was satisfied with her explanation and recognized that he had completely misinterpreted what he saw nine years before. He had also mentioned the brooch, which he genuinely could not remember picking off the floor and setting down on a table before leaving the room, though he must have done so since Marianne had admitted that it was never stolen.

The rainbow's end was sweet indeed—and dazzling in the rush of joy it brought him as they turned together, he and Morgan, to face the rector.

"Dearly beloved . . ." he began.

And then, almost before Gervase could begin to appreciate exactly what it was that was happening, before he could begin to concentrate, the same voice was declaring that they were man and wife together.

Her smile was dazzling.

His, he felt, was all mingled with tears. They had come so close, the two of them, to not making it through.

They signed the register, walked out of church together, past a sea of smiling faces, and emerged into sunshine and cheers and a rain of flower petals hurled by Bedwyns and his own brothers-in-law and a couple of his nieces. They drove back to Lindsey Hall in an open carriage, gaudy ribbons and old boots trailing and bouncing behind, holding hands tightly, gazing like moonstruck idiots into each other's eyes, and indulging in a long, warm kiss as soon as the village was out of sight behind them.

"Happy?" he asked her.

"Happy." She smiled back at him. "The past month seemed endless."

They had been apart for that long. She had returned to Lindsey Hall two days after the ball to prepare for her wedding and arrange for the banns to be called. He had stayed at Windrush. He had come here only yesterday. He had stayed, with his family, at Alvesley Park a few miles away, at the invitation of the Earl and Countess of Redfield and of Viscount Ravensberg, his son, and Ravensberg's wife.

"Years long," he agreed. "The longest separation we are going to have to endure for the rest of our lives, I swear to you, *chérie*. There were no consequences of our night of sin?" He grinned at her and waggled his eyebrows as he remembered their night of passion outside the grotto.

But she was gazing gravely back at him, her eyes large and beautiful.

"I do believe there were," she said.

*"What?"* He grasped her free hand and squeezed both tightly. "There *were?*"

She smiled softly. Her cheeks were flushed. If she had looked beautiful in his eyes before, there were no words to describe her now.

They were indecorously close to the house. Only a large, circular flower garden with a great fountain at its center stood between their moving carriage and the terrace outside the front doors. And as bad luck would have it, there was someone standing outside the doors—a lone gentleman. Fleetingly Gervase wondered whether he was someone who had not been invited to the wedding or someone who had left the church early and ridden neck-or-nothing back to the house.

But truth to tell, at that moment he would not have cared if every servant and gardener and groom in Bewcastle's employ was lined up on the terrace to greet their arrival. He was a newly married man, and he had just discovered that he was to be a father.

*"Chérie,"* he said, lowering his head to hers. *"Mon amour. Ma femme."*

"I am so happy, Gervase," she said, "that I cannot even find words."

"You do not need to," he assured her, feathering kisses against her lips. "There is sometimes a better way of communicating than with words, *chérie*."

And he proceeded to show her, wrapping his arms about her and kissing her thoroughly while her arms came about his neck.

The lone gentleman on the terrace watched the carriage—obviously a wedding conveyance—circle about the fountain and approach the doors, the bride and groom lost to propriety and to the very world itself in each other's arms.

**Center Point Publishing**
600 Brooks Road • PO Box 1
Thorndike ME 04986-0001 USA

**(207) 568-3717**

**US & Canada:**
**1 800 929-9108**